Journeys to Remember

Ruskin Bond is known for his signature simplistic and witty writing style. He is the author of several bestselling short stories, novellas, collections, essays and children's books; and has contributed a number of poems and articles to various magazines and anthologies. At the age of 23, he won the prestigious John Llewellyn Rhys Prize for his first novel, *The Room on the Roof*. He was also the recipient of the Padma Shri in 1999, Lifetime Achievement Award by the Delhi Government in 2012 and the Padma Bhushan in 2014.

Born in 1934, Ruskin Bond grew up in Jamnagar, Shimla, New Delhi and Dehradun. Apart from three years in the UK, he has spent all his life in India and now lives in Landour, Mussoorie, with his adopted family.

RUSKIN BOND

Journeys to Remember

Published by
Rupa Publications India Pvt. Ltd 2025
7/16, Ansari Road, Daryaganj
New Delhi 110002

Sales centres:
Bengaluru Chennai
Hyderabad Jaipur Kathmandu
Kolkata Mumbai Prayagraj

Copyright © Ruskin Bond 2025

All rights reserved.
This is a work of fiction. Names, characters, places and incidents are either the product of the author's imagination or are used fictitiously and any resemblance to any actual person, living or dead, events or locales is entirely coincidental.

No part of this publication may be reproduced, transmitted, or stored in a retrieval system, in any form or by any means, electronic, mechanical, photocopying, recording or otherwise, without the prior permission of the publisher.

P-ISBN: 978-93-6156-918-0
E-ISBN: 978-93-6156-067-5

First impression 2025

10 9 8 7 6 5 4 3 2 1

The moral right of the author has been asserted.

Printed in India

This book is sold subject to the condition that it shall not, by way of trade or otherwise, be lent, resold, hired out, or otherwise circulated, without the publisher's prior consent, in any form of binding or cover other than that in which it is published.

CONTENTS

Introduction   *vii*

1. On the Road to Delhi   1
2. The Grand Trunk Road   7
3. The Open Road   13
4. Belting around Mumbai   16
5. Jaipur   19
6. Mathura's Hallowed Haunts   23
7. Shahjahanpur   26
8. Rishikesh   29
9. Desert Rhapsody   36
10. The Road to Badrinath   41
11. A Song of Many Rivers   49
12. A Walk through Garhwal   65
13. Our Great Escape   75
14. Street of the Red Well   82
15. Footloose in Agra   86
16. The Great Train Journey   94
17. The India I Carried with Me   101

18. A Long Walk for Bina	111
19. The Last Tonga Ride	134
20. Of Rivers and Pilgrims	148
21. A Wayside Tea Shop	153
22. Flowers on the Ganga	156
23. The Girl on the Train	162
24. The Woman on Platform No. 8	166
25. The Night Train at Deoli	172
26. Running Away	178
27. Time Stops at Shamli	195
28. From the Pool to the Glacier	235
29. Cold Beer at Chutmalpur	258
30. The Kipling Road	264
31. At the End of the Road	272
32. The Road to Anjani Sain	282
33. The Magic of Tungnath	286
34. Away from Home	292
35. Sounds of the Sea	295
36. Delhi Is Not Far (Extract)	298
37. A Night Walk Home	304
38. On Foot with Faith	307

INTRODUCTION

No matter where our destination lies, travel often has a way of bringing us back to ourselves. At home, we tend to become fixed in our ways, going through the motions; but when we step out, we are confronted with the vastness of the world, all the sights and experiences and people it contains. It can make us feel like we have taken a step closer to discovering our place in the universe, where we want to be, and how far we have to go to get there. Even the shortest of journeys can be special and memorable, if we set out with our hearts open.

Journeys to Remember is a collection of my stories that recount such journeys, both real and fictional, that stay in our hearts forever. There are the furtive journeys we take as children, thrilled to venture beyond the bounds placed by adults, recorded in stories such as 'Our Great Escape' and 'The Great Train Journey', made all the more fantastical through excitement and imagination. Then there are the journeys we make in adulthood, depicted in stories like 'Footloose in Agra', when we are old enough that even witnessing the mundanity of everyday life can become a profound experience. Some stories, such as 'The Night Train at Deoli' and 'The Woman on Platform No. 8', are about the people whose presence in our lives is as fleeting as a stop at a train station, but whose memory stays with us even after reaching our destination. Others, such as 'Running Away' and

'A Long Walk for Bina', are about journeys made with friends, constant companions without whom the experience would be incomplete. And as any journey would be incomplete without a homecoming, so too would this collection; 'The India I Carried with Me' and 'A Night Walk Home' are both about returning to where we started from.

My journeys across, from and to India have given me innumerable memories, and brought me closer to myself. I hope the stories herein help you set off on your journey of discovery—and when the time comes, will guide you back home gently.

Ruskin Bond

ON THE ROAD TO DELHI

Road travel can involve delays and mishaps, but it also provides you with the freedom to stop where you like and do as you like. I have never found it boring. The seven-hour drive from Mussoorie to Delhi can become a little tiring towards the end, but as I do not drive myself, I can sit back and enjoy everything that the journey has to offer.

I have been to Delhi five times in the last six months—something of a record for me—and on every occasion I have travelled by road. I like looking at the countryside, the passing scene, the people along the road, and this is something I don't see any more from trains; those thick windows of frosted glass effectively cut me off from the world outside.

On my last trip we had to leave the main highway because of a disturbance near Meerut. Instead we had to drive through about a dozen villages in the prosperous sugarcane belt that dominates this area. It was a wonderful contrast, leaving the main road with its cafés, petrol pumps, factories and management institutes and entering the rural hinterland where very little had changed in a hundred years. Women worked in the fields, old men smoked hookahs in their courtyards, and a few children were playing *guli-danda* instead of cricket! It brought home to me the reality of India—urban life and rural life are still poles apart.

These journeys are seldom without incident. I was sipping a coffee at a wayside restaurant, when a foreign woman walked in, and asked the waiter if they had '*à la carte*'. Roadside stops seldom provide menus, nor do they go in for French, but our waiter wanted to be helpful, so he led the tourist outside and showed her the way to the public toilet. As she did not return to the restaurant, I have no idea if she eventually found *à la carte*.

My driver on a recent trip assured me that he knew Delhi very well and could get me to any destination. I told him I'd been booked into a big hotel near the airport, and gave him the name. 'Not to worry', he told me, and drove confidently towards Palam. There he got confused, and after taking several unfamiliar turnings, drove straight into a large piggery situated behind the airport. We were surrounded by some fifty or sixty pigs and an equal number of children from the mohalla. One boy even asked me if I wanted to purchase a pig. I do like a bit of bacon now and then, but unlike Lord Emsworth I do not have any ambition to breed prize pigs, so I had to decline. After some arguments over right of way, we were allowed to proceed and finally made it to the hotel.

Occasionally I have shared a taxi with another passenger, but after one or two disconcerting experiences I have taken to travelling alone or with a friend.

The last time I shared a taxi with someone, I was pleased to find that my fellow passenger, a large gentleman with a fierce moustache, had bought one of my books, which was lying on the seat between us.

I thought I'd be friendly and so, to break the ice, I remarked 'I see you have one of my books with you,' glancing modestly at the paperback on the seat.

'What do you mean, your book?' he bridled, giving me a dirty look. 'I just bought this book at the news agency!'

'No, no,' I stammered, 'I don't mean it's mine, I mean it's my book—er, that is, I happened to write it!'

'Oh, so now you're claiming to be the author!' He looked at me as though I was a fraud of the worst kind. 'What is your real profession, may I ask?'

'I'm just a typist,' I said, and made no further attempt to make friends.

Indeed, I am very careful about trumpeting my literary or other achievements, as I am frequently misunderstood.

Recently, at a book reading in New Delhi, a little girl asked me how many books I'd written.

'Oh, about sixty or seventy,' I said quite truthfully.

At which another child piped up: 'Why can't you be a little modest about it?'

Sometimes you just can't win.

My author's ego received a salutary beating when on one of my earlier trips, I stopped at a small book-stall and looked around, hoping (like any other author) to spot one of my books. Finally, I found one, under a pile of books by Deepak Chopra, Khushwant Singh, William Dalrymple and other luminaries. I slipped it out from the bottom of the pile and surreptitiously placed it on top.

Unfortunately the bookseller had seen me do this.

He picked up the offending volume and returned it to the bottom of the pile, saying, 'No demand for this book, Sir.'

I wasn't going to tell him I was the author. But just to prove him wrong, I bought the poor neglected thing.

'This is a collector's item,' I told him.

'Ah,' he said, 'At last I meet a collector.'

◆

The number of interesting people I meet on the road is matched only by the number of interesting drivers who have carried me back and forth in their chariots of fire.

The last to do so, the driver of a Qualis, must have had ambitions to be an air pilot. He used the road as a runway and was constantly on the verge of taking off. Pedestrians, cyclists, and drivers of smaller vehicles scattered to left and right, often hurling abuse at my charioteer, who seemed immune to the most colourful invectives. Trucks did not give way but he simply swerved around them, adopting a zigzag approach to the task of getting from Delhi to Dehradun in the shortest possible time.

'There's no hurry,' I told him more than once, but his English was limited and he told me later that he thought I was saying 'Please hurry!'

Well, he hurried and he harried until at a railway-crossing where we were forced to stop, an irate scooterist came abreast and threatened to turn the driver over to the police. A long and heated argument followed, and it appeared that there would soon be a punch-up, when the crossing-gate suddenly opened and the Qualis flew forward, leaving the fuming scooterist far behind.

As I do not drive myself, I am normally the ideal person to have in the front seat; I repose complete confidence in the man behind the wheel. And sitting up front, I see more of the road and the passing scene.

One of Mussoorie's better drivers is Sardar Manmohan Singh who drives his own taxi. He is also a keen wildlife enthusiast. It always amazes me how he is able to drive through the Siwaliks, on a winding hill road, and still be able to keep his eye open for denizens of the surrounding forest.

'See that cheetal!' he will exclaim, or 'What a fine sambhar!' or 'Just look at that elephant!'

All this at high speed. And before I've had time to get more than a fleeting glimpse of one of these creatures, we are well past them.

Manmohan swears that he has seen a tiger crossing the road near the Mohand Pass, and as he is a person of some integrity, I have to believe him. I think the tiger appears especially for Manmohan.

Another wildlife enthusiast is my old friend Vishal Ohri, of State Bank fame. On one occasion he drove me down a forest road between Haridwar and Mohand, and we did indeed see a number of animals, cheetal and wild boar.

Unlike our car drivers, he was in no hurry to reach our destination and would stop every now and then in order to examine the footprints of elephants. He also pointed out large dollops of fresh elephant dung, proof that wild elephants were in the vicinity. I did not think his old Fiat would outrun an angry elephant and urged him to get a move on before nightfall.

Vishal then held forth on the benefits of elephant dung and how it could be used to reinforce mud walls. I assured him that I would try it out on the walls of my study, which were in danger of falling down.

Vishal was well ahead of his time. Only the other day I read in one of our papers that elephant dung could be converted into good quality paper. Perhaps they'll use it to make bank notes. Reserve Bank, please note.

♦

Other good drivers who have taken me here and there include Ganesh Saili, who is even better after a few drinks; Victor Banerjee who is better before drinks; and young Harpreet who is a fan of Kenny G's saxophone playing. On the road to Delhi with Harpreet, I had six hours of listening to Kenny G on tape. On my return, two days later, I had another six hours of Kenny G. Now I go into a frenzy whenever I hear a saxophone.

My publisher has an experienced old driver who also happens to be quite deaf. He blares the car horn vigorously and without respite. When I asked him why he used the horn so much, he replied, 'Well, I can't hear their horns, but I'll make sure they hear mine!' As good a reason as any.

It is sometimes said that women don't make good drivers, but I beg to differ. Mrs Biswas was an excellent driver but a dangerous woman to know. Her husband had been a well-known shikari, and he kept a stuffed panther in the drawing room of his Delhi farmhouse. Mrs Biswas spent the occasional weekend at her summer home in Landour. I'd been to one or two of her parties, attended mostly by menfolk.

One day, while I was loitering on the road, she drove up and asked me if I'd like to accompany her down to Dehradun.

'I'll come with you,' I said, 'provided we can have a nice lunch at Kwality.'

So down the hill we glided, and Mrs Biswas did some shopping, and we lunched at Kwality, and got back into her car and set off again—but in a direction opposite to Mussoorie and Landour.

'Where are we going?' I asked.

'To Delhi, of course. Aren't you coming with me?'

'I didn't know we were going to Delhi. I don't even have my pyjamas with me.'

'Don't worry,' said Mrs B. 'My husband's pyjamas will fit you.'

'He may not want me to wear his pyjamas,' I protested.

'Oh, don't worry. He's in London just now.'

I persuaded Mrs Biswas to stop at the nearest bus stop, bid her farewell, and took the bus back to Mussoorie. She may have been a good driver but I had no intention of ending up stuffed alongside the stuffed panther in the drawing room.

THE GRAND TRUNK ROAD

There is a fantasy journey that I have always wanted to make, but one that I know I never will: the long, long journey along the Grand Trunk Road from Calcutta to Peshawar.

For the Grand Trunk Road is a river. It may not be as sacred as the Ganga, which it greets at Kanpur and Varanasi, but it is just as permanent. It's a river of life, an unending stream of humanity intent on reaching their destination and getting there most of the time.

A long day's journey into night, that's how I would describe the saga of the truck driver, that knight errant, or rather errant knight, of India's Via Appia. Undervalued, underpaid and often disparaged, he drives all day and sometimes all night, carrying the country's goods and produce for hundreds of miles on the GT Road, across state borders, through lawless tracts, at all seasons and in all weathers. We blame him for hogging the middle of the road, but he is usually overloaded and if he veers too much to the left or right, he is quite likely to topple over, burying himself and his crew under bricks or gas cylinders, sugarcane or TV sets. More than the railway man, the truck driver is modern India's lifeline, and yet his life is held cheap. He drinks, he swears, occasionally he picks up HIV, and frequently he is killed or badly injured. But we cannot do without him.

In the old, old days, when Muhammad Tughlaq, sultan of Delhi, streamlined the country's roads, bullock carts and camel caravans were the chief transporters. In 1333, when the Moroccan traveller Ibn Battuta visited India, he was deeply impressed by the sultan's road network. Sher Shah Suri, who ruled from 1540 till 1545, made further improvements, especially to the GT Road. He built caravanserais and inns for travellers, and planted fine trees along the GT Road and other important highways. Horsemen, carts and palanquin bearers jostled for pride of position, much as our motorists do today. Traffic was slow-moving, and the best way to get ahead was to mount a horse and canter from stage to stage, that is, between twelve and fifteen miles a day.

Invading armies had, of course, made use of the road long before the British gained control of northern India. On this same stretch of the highway, the Persian invader Nadir Shah defeated the Mughal Emperor in 1739. In a battle lasting two hours, over 20,000 of the Emperor's soldiers were killed. The next day, Nadir Shah marched to Delhi, to ransack the city and massacre its inhabitants. The treasure harvest of Delhi was fair game for acquisitive kings and warlords.

When the British consolidated their power in India, they found the Road, stretching as it did from Calcutta to Peshawar, a great line of communication. Kipling's 'regiment a-marchin' down the GT Road' was a common enough sight throughout the nineteenth century. During the 1857 uprising, after the British were ousted from Delhi, their army assembled at Ambala and came marching down the GT Road to lay siege to the city of Delhi. A few years later, a junior officer, recalling the march, wrote:

> The stars were bright in the dark deep sky and the fireflies
> flashed from bush to bush... Along the road came the

heavy roll of the guns, mixed with the jangling of bits and the clanking of the scabbards of the cavalry. The infantry marched behind with a deep, dull tread. Camels and bullock carts, with innumerable camp servants, toiled away for miles in the rear, while gigantic elephants, pulling the heavy guns, came lumbering down the road.

Some thirty years after the 1857 uprising came the Afghan Wars, and the GT Road became an all-important route for the British army proceeding towards Peshawar and the Khyber Pass. Those were the days of military manoeuvres all over North India, and my grandfather, a foot-soldier in the mould of Kipling's 'soldiers three', found himself 'route marching', that is, foot-slogging all over northern and central India. Wives and children followed the regiment wherever it was sent, and military camps and cantonments sprang up everywhere. Children were often born in the course of these marches and troop movements: my father at Shahjahanpur (not far from the road), his brothers and sisters at places as far apart as Barrackpore, Campbellpur and Dera Ismail Khan!

The tedium of the march was broken only by the sight of fields of golden corn stretching towards the horizon, with mango groves rising like islands from the flat plain; but for the most part it was monotonous tramping, exemplified in this marching song of Kipling's:

> *Oh, there's them Indian temples to admire when you see,*
> *There's the peacock round the corner*
> *An' the monkey up the tree.*
> *With our best foot first*
> *And the road a-sliding past,*
> *An every bloomin' camping-ground*
> *Exactly like the last.*

Kipling immortalized the Road in *Kim* and *Barrack-Room Ballads* (he had a strong empathy with the common soldier); but for him, few outside of India would have heard of the Grand Trunk Road. But Kipling would not recognize the road today. Cars, buses, tractors, trucks, all thunder down the highway, and even the bullock carts are equipped with heavy tyres. It's a very democratic mix. Nowhere else in the world are you likely to find such a variety of traffic, or so many impediments to vehicular progress—cows, cart-horses, buffaloes, cyclists, stray hens, stray villagers, stray policemen.

'Proceed at your own risk.' You could call this the motto of the road, a motto vividly illustrated by overturned lorries lying in ditches, buses upended against trees or dangling over culverts, fancy cars crushed into concertina shapes, squashed cats and dogs, mangled drivers and passengers. These are common sights, along with the endless panorama of field, factory, village or township.

For the towns and cities grow bigger by the day. They spread octopus-like over the rural landscape, and the traffic spills out in an endless, honking procession of humankind on wheels. 'OK Tata' proclaims the truck in front of you, and it would be wise to keep your distance. What's your choice of vehicle for making progress on the road? Motorcycle, taxi, limousine, or buffalo cart? Mine's a steamroller. No one pushes it around.

◆

I have never travelled the entire length of the road, but I have driven along stretches of it. The most memorable one was with Gurbachan Singh.

As his taxi weaved its way in and out of the Amritsar traffic, and headed for Delhi, Gurbachan Singh took his hand off the horn and gave me a brief triumphant look.

'What do you think of my horn?' he asked.

'Oh, it's a fine horn,' I said, wringing out my ears. 'It couldn't be louder.'

'You can hear it half a mile ahead,' said Gurbachan proudly, as he blasted off at two young men who were sharing a bicycle. They moved out of the way with alacrity.

'It makes a lot of noise in the car, too,' I said, and added hastily, 'not that I object, you know…'

'Doesn't your horn have more than one tone of voice?' asked a fellow traveller with a trace of irritation.

'Two!' claimed Gurbachan. 'Male and female. Just see!' And he produced a high note and then a low note on the horn, both equally ear-shattering. Ahead of us, a tonga ran off the road and on to the cart track.

'This is one terrific horn,' said Gurbachan. 'I have had it made especially for this taxi. No foreign horns for me. They are not loud enough. Indian horns are best.'

'Indian noise is best,' said the fellow traveller.

In an interval of comparative quiet, I found myself reflecting on the nature of sound—the unpleasantness of some sounds, and the sweetness of others, and why certain sounds (like motor horns) can be sweet to some and hideous to others. The sweetest sound of all, I decided, was silence. There are many kinds of silence—the silence of an empty room, the silence of the mountains, the silence of prayer or the enforced silence of loneliness—but the best kind of silence, I concluded, was the silence that comes after the cessation of noise.

'It was made in the Jama Masjid area,' continued Gurbachan, interrupting my thoughts. 'Seventy-five rupees only. Made by hand, to my own specification. There's only one drawback: it must not get wet!'

As his hand settled down on the horn again, I thought of praying for rain, but the sky being clear and blue, I decided that a prayer would be an unreasonable demand on the Creator.

'Ah, but you don't know what it is to have a horn like this one. Try it, sir. Why don't you try it for yourself?'

'Oh, that's all right,' I assured him. 'You have proved its excellence already.'

'No, you must try it. I insist that you try it!' He was like a big boy, suddenly generous, determined on sharing a new toy with a younger brother.

He grabbed my hand and placed it on the horn, and, as I felt it give a little, a thrill of pleasure rushed up my arm. I pressed hard, and a stream of music flowed in and out of the car. Now I could understand the happiness and the supreme self-confidence of Gurbachan and all drivers like him; for, with a horn like his, one felt the power and glory that belongs to the kings of the road.

For the rest of the journey, Gurbachan drove and I blew the horn.

The fellow passenger, no doubt realizing that he was locked into a taxi with two lunatics, was too terrified to say a word.

THE OPEN ROAD

As the years go by, I do not walk as far or as fast as I used to; but speed and distance were never my forte. Like J. Krishnamurti, I believe that the journey is more important than the destination. But, then, I have never really had a destination. The glory that comes from conquering the Himalayan peaks is not for me. My greatest pleasure lies in taking a path—any old path will do—and following it until it leads me to a forest glade or village or stream or windy hilltop.

This sort of tramping (it does not even qualify as trekking) is a compulsive thing with me. You could call it my vice, since it is stronger than the desire for wine, women or song. To get on to the open road fills me with joie de vivre, gives me an exhilaration not found in other, possibly more worthy pursuits.

Only this afternoon I had one of my more enjoyable tramps. I had been cooped up in my room for several days, while outside it rained and hailed and snowed and the wind blew icily from all directions. It seemed ages since I'd taken a long walk. Fed up with it all, I pulled on my overcoat, banged the door shut and set off up the hillside.

I kept to the main road, but because of the heavy snow there were no vehicles on it. Even as I walked, flurries of snow struck my face, and collected on my coat and head. Up at the top of the hill, the deodars were clothed in a mantle of white.

It was fairyland: everything still and silent. The only movement was the circling of an eagle over the trees. I walked for an hour and passed only one person, the milkman on his way back to his village. His cans were crowned with snow. He looked a little tipsy. He asked me the time, but before I could tell him he shook me by the hand and said I was a good fellow because I never complained about the water in the milk. I told him that as long as he used clean water, I'd contain my wrath.

On my way back, I passed a small group. It consisted of a person in some sort of uniform (because of the snow I couldn't really make it out), who was hurling epithets at several small children who were busy throwing snowballs at him. He kept shouting: 'Do you know who I am? Do you know who I am?' The children did not want to know. They were only interested in hitting their target, and succeeded once in every five or six attempts.

I came home exhilarated and immediately sat down beside the stove to write this piece. I found some lines of Stevenson's that seemed appropriate:

> *And this shall be for music when no one else is near,*
> *The fine song for singing, the rare song to hear!*
> *That only I remember, that only you admire,*
> *Of the broad road that stretches, and the roadside fire.*

He speaks directly to me, across the mists of time: R.L. Stevenson, prince of essayists. There is none like him today. We hurry, hurry in a heat of hope—and who has time for roadside fires, except, perhaps, those who must work on the roads in all weathers?

Whenever I walk into the hills, I come across gangs of road workers breaking stones, cutting into the rocky hillsides, building retaining walls. I am not against more roads—especially in the hills, where the people have remained impoverished largely because of the inaccessibility of their villages. Besides, a new road is one more road for me to explore, and in the interests of progress I am prepared to put up with the dust raised by the occasional bus. And if it becomes too dusty, one can always leave the main road. There is no dearth of paths leading off into the valleys.

On one such diversionary walk, I reached a village where I was given a drink of curd and a meal of rice and beans. That is another of the attractions of tramping to nowhere in particular—the finding of somewhere in particular; the striking up of friendships; the discovery of new springs and waterfalls, unusual plants, rare flowers, strange birds. In the hills, a new vista opens up at every bend in the road.

That is what makes me a compulsive walker—new vistas, and the charm of the unexpected.

BELTING AROUND MUMBAI

I have lived to see Bombay become Mumbai, Calcutta become Kolkata, and Madras become Chennai. Times change, names change, and if Bond becomes Bonda I won't object. Place-names may alter but people don't, and in Mumbai I found that people were as friendly and good-natured as ever; perhaps even more than when I was last there twenty-five years ago.

On that occasion, I had travelled on the Doon Express, a slow passenger train that stopped at every small station in at least five states, taking two days and two nights from Dehradun to Bombay. It had been a fairly uneventful journey, except for an incident in the small hours when we stopped at Baroda and a hand slipped through my open window, crept under my pillow, found nothing of value except my spectacles, and decided to take them anyway, leaving me to grope half-blind around Bombay until another pair could be made.

Now I carry three pairs of spectacles: one for reading, one for looking at people, and one for looking far out to sea.

On the Kingfisher flight to Mumbai, I used the second pair, as I like looking at people, especially attractive air hostesses. I found they were looking at me too, but that was because I'd caught my belt (my trouser belt, not my seat-belt) in a fellow-passenger's luggage strap and was proceeding to drag both him and his travel-bag down the aisle. We were diplomatically separated by the aforesaid air hostesses who then guided me to my seat without further mishap.

This reminded me of the occasion many years ago when I auditioned for a role in a Tarzan film.

'Who do you wish to play?' asked the casting director.

'Tarzan, of course,' I said.

He gave me a long hard look. 'Can you swing from one tree to another?' he asked.

'Easily,' I said. 'I can even swing from a chandelier.' And I proceeded to do so, wrecking the hall they sat in, in the process. They begged me to stop.

'Thank you, Mr Bond, you have made your point. But we don't think you have the figure for the part of Tarzan. Would you like to take the part of the missionary who is being cooked to a crisp by a bunch of cannibals? Tarzan will come to your rescue.'

I declined the role with dignity.

And now I was in Mumbai, not to audition for a film, but to inaugurate the Rupa Book Festival. For old time's sake, I arrived at the venue in a horse-drawn carriage. Alighting, my recalcitrant belt-buckle got entangled with the horse's harness and I almost dragged the entire contraption into the Bajaj Exhibition Hall.

However, the evening's entertainment went off without a hitch. Gulzar read from Ghalib, Tom Alter read from Gulzar, Mandira Bedi read from Nandita Puri, and everyone read madly from each other, and I sat quietly in a corner to keep my belt out of further entanglements.

The next day I was taken on a tour of the city by a *Hindustan Times* journalist and a photographer. They asked me to pose on the steps of the Asiatic Society's Library, an imposing colonial edifice. While I stood there being photographed, a group of teenagers walked past and I overheard one of them remark: '*Yeh naya model hain.*'

I took it as a compliment. At least they didn't call me a *purana* model. Perhaps there's still a chance to get that Tarzan role. If not Tarzan, then his grandfather.

The same journalist and photographer took me to a market where you could buy anything from books to bras. They thrust a thousand-rupee note into my willing hands and told me I could buy anything I liked, while they took pictures.

'Can I keep the money?' I asked.

'No, you have to spend it.'

So I bought two ladies handbags and two pairs of ladies slippers.

'For your girlfriends?' asked the journalist.

'No,' I said, 'for their mothers.'

Back at the festival hall, I was presented with a beautiful sky-blue T-shirt by a charming lady who wishes to remain anonymous. I wore it the next morning when I was leaving Mumbai.

At the airport, one of the Kingfisher staff complimented my dress sense; the first time anyone has alone so.

'Your blue shirt matches your eyes,' she said.

After that, I shall definitely fly Kingfisher again.

JAIPUR

As we still had a few days left of our holiday, and a little money, and as neither Kamal nor I was anxious to return to Delhi earlier than was necessary, we decided to sneak off to Jaipur for a day or two. We had both been to Jaipur before, but it is a city that one can visit again and again without ever tiring of its charm.

There is an atmosphere about Jaipur—once the most beautiful city in India, and one of the earliest planned cities in the world, which even to the casual visitor distinguishes it from other towns. This is probably due to the almost entire absence of any European or Western influence on the architecture and planning of the town.

Founded in 1728 by the brilliant astronomer-king Maharaja Jai Singh II, it is quite unlike any other town in India or Asia: no tortuous gloomy streets or squalid overcrowded bazaars. Its six main streets are very wide and straight, one running the whole length of the town, the others crossing it at right angles, dividing the city into rectangular blocks. These are enclosed by a high wall, its parapets loopholed for musketry, into which are set seven entrance gates.

On the northwest side the hills rise sheer beyond the city, bearing on their summit the Nahargarh or Tiger Fort. Not needed now for purposes of war, it houses much of the wealth of this former state's ruler. Guarded not by troops but by men of the robber caste, this wealth lay hoarded for centuries, potential but never used capital, typical of the ways of the East.

In the city itself, narrow streets are found in plenty, for a network of them connects the wide main roads. So narrow are some that the bougainvillea sprawls from the upper storey of one building to its opposite across the way. But, curiously enough, they are nearly all straight, and a passing glimpse from the main street reveals their whole length. Sometimes these lanes are full of little shops, but many of them contain only private houses, where occasionally a half-open door reveals a glimpse of the grass and fountain of a garden or courtyard beyond.

The great attraction of the main streets is their spaciousness and the beautiful facade of the tall buildings that line them, most colour-washed in a dull, pale old-rose tone, some showing the soft amber or grey of the original limestone. In some of them the plain walls are varied with beautiful little *chhattri*s, while here and there the old carved domes of some Jain temple break the flat line of roofs.

The street walls of these houses—which are really only the walls of the outer courtyard, the main building being behind and cut off from the street altogether—can boast of only the smallest windows, for these were meant to conceal, and not reveal, the zenana quarters behind. The quaint figures of elephants and other animals painted on the walls give them the appearance of dolls' houses when seen from the road below, though many of them are three or four storeys in height and from a distance look very imposing.

The streets themselves are a feast of colour and interest. Every mode of progression can be seen here, from ambling bullock carts and *ekka*s, with their quaintly shaped and brightly coloured hoods, to buses and streamlined motor cars. There are strings of camels bearing fodder, and elephants that amble up the road to the Amber Palace, and here and there wanders the ubiquitous Brahmani bull. All along the streets and around the squares throng hundreds of pigeons—sacred birds throughout Rajasthan—being fed by the passers-by or helping themselves to food on the stalls.

All along the ground floor of the buildings, and cut off from them by a small projecting tin roof along which the langurs run up and down in play, are the bazaar shops, little hives of industry doing a brisk trade. Busier still are the wide pavements in front; they are chock-a-block with stalls and with groups of artisans plying their trade in the midst of the passers-by.

We saw great piles of yellow maize and corn, of jowar and bajra, heaped upon the pavement, while to one side people were busy grinding the grain on primitive grindstones, laughing and singing as they ceaselessly wound the handle, three of them often working at one grinder. A little further on, what seemed at a distance to be a rich Herati rug flung down resolved itself into masses of chillies spread for yards along the pavement to dry in the sun. Then came the vegetables and fruit piled high in baskets, the countrywomen who had brought them squatting in the midst, sorting and selling and often nursing their babies at the same time.

Next came a little colony of brass workers sitting at the pavement's edge, engraving patterns on brass trays, plates and vessels, and then inlaying them with sticks of coloured enamel. Unlike them, the dyers generally work within their shops. In one of these we saw a whole family variously employed, from the old grandfather, who was mixing brilliant dyes in great brass cauldrons, to the latest infant, sitting in the middle and watching the others with an open mouth, while the family goat and attendant kid ambled in and out at will. Two of the family, a *pugree*-length of gaudy cloth just freshly dyed between them, walked up and down the pavement, waving it in the air to dry. The street had the appearance of being hung with bunting.

Most amusing of all, we came suddenly on three rows of little boys standing on the pavement with their slates at their feet. To one side stood the enterprising schoolmaster, while in front a small urchin with head craned forward loudly chanted the words of some lesson, which the class, in a medley of hoarse and squeaky voices, repeated after him. The intense concentration of this determined little group seemed in no way upset by the surrounding bustle and confusion.

There are few palaces in India to surpass the grandeur of the famous old palace of Amber. It lies northwest of the city, approached by a narrow pass in the hills that shuts off all view of Jaipur and opens on a little valley almost entirely closed by hills. Above a small lake, built on the barren hillside, stand the still perfect walls of this majestic fortress-palace. Their limestone blocks are mellowed to a soft amber colour, and the marble is now a rich cream.

The palace, now deserted except for its temple to the goddess Kali, is still in perfect condition. Its sun-soaked courtyards are open to the sky, and its empty pillared halls are full of echoes.

MATHURA'S HALLOWED HAUNTS

Mathura, most sacred of cities, stands on the right bank of the Yamuna northwest of Agra. All men speak of Mathura with reverence, and it has been said, 'if a man spend in Banaras all his lifetime, he has earned less merit than if he passes but a single day in the sacred city of Mathura.'

It is difficult to pierce the fog that hides the date of the city's birth; but sacred it has always been as the capital of the kingdom of Braj and the birthplace of Lord Krishna: 'Teacher and Soul of the Universe. Destroyer of the earth's tyrant kings, and the First of the Spirits...'

I went to Mathura at the end of the rains. The fields and the trees were alive with strange, beautiful birds: the long-tailed king crow; innumerable doves in shades of blue and green; kingfishers and bluejays and weaver-birds; and, resting on a telegraph pole, the great white-headed kite, which, some say, was Garuda, Vishnu's famous steed. Resplendent, too, were the green and gold parrots, from among whom Kamadeva, the god of love, chose his steed. Armed with his sugarcane bow with its string made of bees, Kamadeva still rides at night over the plains of Mathura. Many are the journeys he makes on nights approaching the full moon. He knows the ways of men and women, and his bow, like Cupid's, is always ready to assist the ardent lover.

In the tanks and 'jheels' around Mathura I saw a variety of game birds—wild duck, hermits, cranes and snipe—but all life is sacred for many miles around Mathura, and not even the bird trapper is permitted to lay his snares.

Strutting under an old tamarind tree are Krishna's birds, the brilliant peacocks. Centuries ago, they gave the city their name, and today Mathura is still known as the Peacock City. The peacocks seem to know that they are the chosen of Krishna. Spreading out their many-hued fantails, they glance at us drab mortals with an air of disdain.

Near Mathura is Brindavan, in whose forests—they have gone now—the boy Krishna and his brother Balram ran wild, playing on their shepherds' pipes. The neighbours found Krishna very mischievous. He was extremely fond of butter and, going by stealth one day to the house of a neighbour, climbed onto a shelf to get at a large jar of butter. He ate the butter as far as he could reach, and then got into the jar. The owner, on returning, found him there and, putting a cover on the jar to prevent the boy from escaping, went to Krishna's father to make a complaint. But when he arrived at the house, it was not the father who met him but the little butter-thief.

There is another story, which tells us of the day Krishna stole his mother's curds, and finished them while no one was looking. 'O, you wicked one!' exclaimed his mother when she discovered what had happened. 'Come, let me see your mouth.' And when she looked into his mouth, she saw the Universe—the earth, sea and heavens; the sun and the moon, the planets and all the stars...

Brindavan stands on a tongue of land surrounded by the river, which has curved here in a strange fashion. Legend tells us that Balram, who was very strong, once led a dance on the Yamuna's bank, but moved his giant limbs so clumsily that the river laughed aloud and taunted him, saying: 'Enough, my clumsy child! How can you hope to dance as Krishna, who is divine?' Balram was very angry with the river, and taking his great plough he traced a furrow from the brink of the river; but so deep was the furrow that the river fell into it and was led far astray.

When the tyrant king Kamsa heard of the unusual exploits of Krishna and Balram, he planned to have them killed in case they became a danger to his power. He sent a message to the brothers, inviting them to a contest of arms in the royal city of Mathura. Krishna and Balram accepted the challenge.

On the day of the contest, King Kamsa sat on a lofty throne near the arena. As Krishna and Balram entered, a mighty elephant was sent against them. But Krishna, seizing the animal by the tail, swung it around his head and threw it to the ground. Then each of the brothers taking a tusk, they slew Kamsa's mightiest champions. Kamsa ordered his army to kill the boys, but Krishna sprang up the steps of the throne, seized the king by his hair and hurled him into a deep ravine.

Visitors to Mathura are still shown the mound where Kamsa's throne once stood. And still venerated is that part of the riverfront where the two boys rested after dragging the body of Kamsa down to the funeral pyre.

I wandered in the streets of the city past shops gleaming with brasswork or piled high with pedas, Mathura's famous sweets. From the bridge, I could see the riverfront with its innumerable temples. And below, hundreds of majestic tortoises watched the bathers and the boatmen with speculative eyes. Sometimes a boatman seized one of these long-necked creatures and held it up to view. The tortoise would immediately draw its legs into its shell—a vivid illustration of the theory that nothing is annihilated but only disappears, the effect being absorbed in the cause!

SHAHJAHANPUR

It is forty-five years since I last saw Shahjahanpur, a sleepy little town halfway between Delhi and Lucknow. I doubt if it has changed much. It wasn't the sort of place...that changes. Even in 1960, when I stopped there for a few hours, it looked as though time had been standing still since the dramatic events of the 1857 uprising, which I described in my novella *A Flight of Pigeons*.

Forty years after those events, in 1896 to be exact, my father had been born in Shahjahanpur's 'military camp', according to Grandfather's army service records. Grandfather's regiment, the Scottish Rifles, must have been quartered there for a few months before moving on to Bareilly, Aligarh, Gorakhpur, Lucknow and other cantonment towns across the hot and dusty Gangetic plains.

This was one reason for me to stop there, but I was also keen to visit the cantonment church, where he had probably been baptized, and where, during the outbreak of 1857, the European residents had been slaughtered. Among the few survivors were Ruth Labadoor and her mother. Their story came down to me from my father and other sources, and I was keen to follow it up.

The church was still there, of course, but locked up; a memorial to those who had been killed on that fatal day at the end of May stood in the parade ground (I believe it has since been removed); the mango groves and some old bungalows going back to Mutiny days were still evident, and crossing the little Khannant river was the bridge of boats that had played so important a part for those who were escaping from the town—first, the fleeing Europeans; later, the mutineers or their families when the British had retaken the district.

Founded in the seventeenth century, the town had a large Pathan population, and still does. The crowded city area and mohallas are still home to the descendants of Javed Khan, his friends and relatives, and those who had set fire to the cantonment bungalows. In his film of the story *Junoon*, Shyam Benegal provided a rather opulent-looking nawabi setting, but in reality Shahjahanpur's streets were occupied by working or lower-middle-class families, and only the nawab (who lived elsewhere) would have enjoyed much affluence.

The dramatic events of 1857 led to the loss of many innocent lives on both sides of the conflict, Indian and British. In retelling Ruth's story I tried to show how the common humanity of ordinary folk—Hindu, Muslim, or Christian—could sometimes overcome the forces of hate, revenge and retribution.

On a lighter note: The Rose Rum factory stands a little way outside Shahjahanpur. It dates back to pre-Mutiny times. During the uprising it was sacked by rioters. Some quenched their thirst, while others poured barrels of good rum into the Khannant. Grandfather would have been appalled. I don't know if he was much of a drinker, but we did find these verses among his papers. He was, of course, referring to the Solan Brewery near Shimla. Like the Rosa distilleries, it is over 150 years old.

'Where's Solan?' the private was asking;
'Somewhere near Tibet, I should think.'
'There's a brewery there,

And it's brimming with beer,
But we can't get a mouthful to drink!'
So we route-march from Delhi to Solan
In the dust and the maddening sun,
And we're cursing away like Hades
Well knowing there ain't any ladies
To hear every son-of-a-gun!
And when we have climbed up to Solan
Our language continues profane,
For right well we know
We shall soon have to go
Down from Solan to Delhi again!

I'm not sure if Grandfather wrote the poem, but we'll credit it to him anyway—Henry William Bond, with a few profanities edited out by his grandson.

I should add that young Mr Carew, the proprietor of the Rosa distillery, went into hiding and survived the mutiny. If he had not done so, I would not be enjoying Carew's Gin today.

RISHIKESH

'*Ganga Mai ki jai!*' Everyone raised the cry as the Haridwar bus moved out of Meerut. Most of the passengers, including Kamal and I, were going to take *darshan* of Mother Ganga. But while many were bound for Haridwar, we were going to Rishikesh, a more secluded temple town, situated on the banks of the Ganga at the point where the river emerges from the mountains and, hemmed in no longer by rocks and trees, stretches itself across the plains of Uttar Pradesh and Bihar, flowing past great cities like Kanpur, Allahabad, Benares and Patna, and into Bengal.

Just next to us sat a well-built woman with three small children. The eldest, a boy of about six, took a fancy to Kamal, and was soon lolling about on his knees. In front of us, obliterating the view, sat a stout lala and his devoted wife. Lalaji proved to be an impatient and ill-tempered man. He quarrelled with the conductor, the driver and the ticket seller. In order to travel in comfort he had reserved three front seats, but was unwilling to pay toll on the third seat which, he insisted, would only be occupied by his and his wife's feet. They gave in to him eventually. An urchin who inadvertently touched the sleeve of his kurta received a stinging slap. But he became more tolerant as time went on, and once, when engaged in an argument with a passenger at the other end of the bus, favoured me with a smile.

The countryside was monotonous up to Roorkee.

Then the road took us along the Ganga canal, and Kamal sat up and began to look at things. We changed buses at Haridwar, and got into a very old and wheezy contraption, which surprised us by going much faster than the government roadways bus. Probably the driver was trying to make up for time lost in stopping every five minutes to pick up some acquaintance on the road. We stopped for ten minutes at the Sat Narain temple, once famous for the tiger that used to visit it every evening. Rattling through the Motichur forest block, we saw two elephants—tame ones, possibly—and a variety of monkeys.

We left the bus at Rishikesh and went in search of my friend Jhardari, with whom we were to stay. He lived at Muni-ki-Reti, two miles upstream, where the wealthier ashrams were situated. His rooms, adjoining Swami Sivanandas Ashram, were on the right-hand bank of the Ganga.

Jhardhari was away, on a routine trip to Devprayag. As secretary of the Tehri-Garhwal Motor Mazdoor Sangh Workers' Union, he has to travel all over the district to keep in touch with the men who drive the trucks and buses on the dangerous hill roads. The buses are privately owned; the government only nationalizes those services that use first-class roads. The state is very cautious about taking over the responsibility of transporting people to remote hill towns like Tehri and Pipalkoti, where pilgrims on the way to Gangotri or Badrinath must start their journey on foot. The motor roads in the interior are narrow, precipitous and unmetalled. To mention this is not to condemn them. Till a few years ago many of these regions had no roads at all. And Garhwalis are excellent drivers—many have experience of Army trucks—and serious accidents are uncommon.

Jhardhari's roommate made us at home, and prepared hot, strong tea. Garhwalis drink more tea than Englishmen, and seldom take water. We were to become accustomed to drinking tea at almost hourly intervals.

One of the first things we did was to dip ourselves in the river. The water was icy cold, and it was impossible to stay in for more than ten minutes. Shivering, we climbed on to the bathing steps to dry ourselves. Our clothes felt hot against our bodies.

Down at the Rishikesh bathing ghat, hundreds of people would be dipping themselves in the sacred waters; but at Muni-ki-Reti (which is in Tehri-Garhwal district, while the town of Rishikesh is in Dehradun district), there were only a few people by the river—a few pilgrims from Bengal, Andhra and Madras—disciples from Swami Sivananda's Ashram—and a number of boys who work in the area.

Logs were always floating downstream, and boys would get across them, lying flat on their stomachs and paddling the planks through the water. Two of the more daring youths paddled their logs right across the river, to the temples on the opposite bank. They were good swimmers, but had they been parted from their floats, they would have been carried away by the current and quite possibly drowned.

We walked down to Rishikesh in the evening, and saw over a hundred sadhus emerging from an ashram where they were given their evening meal. In their saffron robes, they flooded the dusty road, talking animatedly among themselves. Many of them were young men, probably novices. One was a strapping youth of about twenty, a Hercules gracefully wearing the robe of renunciation.

They looked well fed and contented. Most of them spoke a little English. What had brought them to Rishikesh, I wondered, to live as recluses and ascetics? Personal tragedy, the stress of modern city life or the failure of material pursuits... Or did the career of a religious mendicant hold out profitable prospects?

Later on, I was told that some of the novitiates should really have been in prison. But perhaps the rigours of their monastic existence rid them of early criminal tendencies; and if that was so then surely ashrams were better places for them than jails.

Little shacks lined the river banks and, though few people bathed late in the evening, hundreds were beside the water. Offerings of flowers in little leaf boats went sailing downstream. They were lighted by wicks dipped in oil and went bobbing up and down on the water, sometimes for a considerable distance. Kamal sent an offering downstream and requested Mother Ganga to grant him success as an artist. His boat, though, did not go very far.

Undeterred, Kamal fed little balls of flour to the fish. They were huge, completely tame and came to the bank in shoals to be fed by the bathers. Sometimes, they fought among themselves, and a few of them were a raw pink where they had been savagely bitten.

That night, we slept in the open, on a wide ledge above the riverbed. The lights from the temples and ashrams on the opposite bank reflected gently on the water. There was a human quietness everywhere. The sounds were of the river—the distant roar of the rapids, the nearby lapping of water on the bathing steps.

We bathed again in the river as the sun came up over the mountain known as Manikoot Parbat. There is an unbroken ridge along the top of this mountain, stretching all the way to the snows of Badrinath, some two hundred miles away. Only a few hermits live on the mountain. It belongs to the elephants who sometimes visit the river in herds to bathe and drink.

Jhardhari had returned, looking quite fresh after a one hundred and fifty-mile bus journey; he offered to take us up to Narindernagar, a little town on a hilltop, which, though smaller and less central than Tehri, is the capital of the district. The former Maharaja had preferred it to the less congenial valley town of Tehri on the banks of the Bhagirathi; and Narindernagar became the Maharaja's summer capital.

The buses were all full, and we had to travel up separately, one to each bus—first Kamal, then I, and last of all Jhardhari.

◆

Narindernagar is only ten miles from Rishikesh, but it is also two thousand feet higher, and the bus has to climb a dizzy, winding road on which there can be no two-way traffic. But the buses go faster than their counterparts in the plains. With speedometers conveniently out of order, buses and trucks come downhill at a speed of thirty to thirty-five miles an hour. But, as have said before, Garhwalis are very good drivers. Along the main highways of the Punjab are the wrecks of numerous trucks, some jammed up against trees, others in head-on collisions. But in the hills there is no driving at night, and the drivers prefer smoking bidis to drinking rum or country liquor. Mechanical failure is usually the cause of the few accidents that do occur.

From Narindernagar, we went on for another eight miles, and eventually got down at Agra-khal, a pass in the mountains at a height of about five thousand feet. The motor road, soon becoming *kachcha*, continues to Tehri and Dharasu, and from the latter, pilgrims must proceed on foot to the shrines and temples of Gangotri.

After eating some hot puris, we walked back to Narindernagar, leaving the main road and hiking through a forest of oak and pine. Kamal, who was seeing real mountains for the first time, was very excited and asked me innumerable questions about plants and streams and trees and rocks. He chattered away until Jhardhari said something flattering about his many and varied interests, and this embarrassed Kamal so much that he stopped talking altogether. I enjoyed the shade of the gnarled, untidy oaks and the soft, slippery carpet of pine needles.

But after the forest, there was bare hillside, the sun was scorching hot, and we had soon emptied the water bottle. So, we rejoined the main road and stopped a truck going down to Rishikesh.

It was the first time Kamal and I sat in the back of a truck travelling at speed down a mountain. It was impossible to anchor oneself on the floor. A kindly sadhu, also at the back, placed his blanket on a tyre and invited us to share it with him; but at every hairpin bend the tyre slid violently about the floor and we were pitched off it. Kamal and I clung to each other to avoid being thrown against the sides of the truck; Jhardhari hung on to an iron bar; we were all feeling quite sick. Only the sadhu appeared unperturbed. He retained his seat on the tyre, even when it went skidding from one end of the truck to the other.

When we reached Rishikesh, we went straight to the river. Never had Mother Ganga's waters been so refreshing. The giddiness disappeared. Then, we lay down on the sand, and Kamal, like the sleepy giant Kumbhakarna in the Ramayana, did not come to life until it was time to eat.

We slept well that night. In the morning, we would go to Lachhman Jhula and, passing the suspension bridge, walk a little way up Manikoot Parbat.

As the sun rose, turning the river to gold, we climbed into the boat that took pilgrims across to the temples on the other bank. The oarsmen sat in the prow, straining against the current, and the people in the boat raised the same ageless cry: 'Ganga Mai ki jai!'

Climbing ashore, we passed through groves of mango trees, planted by rich pilgrims for the benefit of the sadhus. Then, leaving behind Lachhman Jhula, we walked along the pilgrim route to Badrinath until we came to a *dharamshala* called Garur Chatti. Here, we drank tea, the inevitable but welcome tea, and set off up the hillside in search of a waterfall Jhardhari had told us about.

It did not take us long to reach the waterfall. Set amidst rocks and ferns, it fell about thirty feet onto a platform of smooth yellow rocks and pebbles. Here, it formed a small pool, about waist deep, into which we leapt without hesitation. The water wasn't as cold as the Ganga, and we could splash about for as long as we liked while the waterfall sprayed down on our heads. The water was very clear and fresh, though it had a slightly bitter taste—evidence, I suppose, of a strong mineral content.

Further down the stream, we found a lot of old bones, which Kamal insisted were the remains of a tiger's kill, as, indeed, they might have been, tigers having been seen on the mountain. But no tiger troubled us; only a band of langurs, swinging from tree to tree, that seemed resentful of our presence and urged us to leave.

This we did at our leisure and, after more tea at Garur Chatti and a visit to a small temple—where the courtyard floor was so hot to our bare feet that we had to skip about in agony—we trudged back to Muni-ki-Reti.

It was our last night sleeping beside the Ganga, and we rested with our chins in our hands, watching the river move silently past us, surging onward, India's lifeblood, inexorable and irresistible.

DESERT RHAPSODY

A fierce sun beat down on the desert sand. Heat waves shimmered across the barren landscape. *Did anything live out there?* I wondered, as I sat in a cane chair on the verandah of the rest house on the outskirts of the city of Jodhpur.

It was September, and there was no likelihood of rain. I had spent a night in this remote rest house, and now there was nothing for me to do until late evening when I would catch a train to Delhi. The previous day had been spent in Ajmer, where the grounds of the old Mayo School had provided ample shade. But there was no shade outside Jodhpur.

The only relief from the glare was provided by a small pond that existed in a declivity to one side of the rest house. And this too had shrivelled in recent weeks, leaving large cracks in the dry mud where the water had receded.

I had taken my breakfast in the verandah, served by a room-boy who had also done the cooking and was now about to tidy up the rooms. Apparently, the rest house had a staff of one.

'Do you do everything by yourself?' I asked.

He assured me that it was no trouble, as hardly anyone came to stay in the rest house. He gave me a good breakfast—parathas and an omelette—and set about making up the bed.

As he lifted up a pillow, a large black scorpion ran out and scurried across the bed sheets, its tail raised as if to strike.

I was horrified. I had spent the night with my head on that pillow, unaware that it had also sheltered a scorpion.

The room-boy was unperturbed. 'Must be more here,' he said, and lifted the mattress. Several fierce-looking scorpions emerged, running for shelter. I had spent the entire night on a bed of scorpions.

I decided to spend the rest of the day on the verandah. No afternoon siesta for me, no matter how drowsy I felt.

The room-boy assured me that the room was now free of scorpions, and asked me if I would be staying another night. I told him that it was vital that I catch the train to Delhi that evening.

'There is another room,' he told me.

'I don't think I'll need it,' I said.

But the pond looked inviting.

Not that I was about to plunge into it. A green scum covered most of the surface. But at least it looked cool.

And presently, its cool waters attracted a group of youths who drove their buffaloes into the shallows, and then followed them, shouting and splashing around. Had I been a boy, I might well have joined them. But at seventy-five, you don't go leaping into strange ponds, mixing with a herd of buffaloes and their high-spirited keepers. No, I just didn't have the figure for it any more.

So I sat and watched.

After half-an-hour the youths and their buffaloes left the pond and meandered away. Buffaloes have to be fed if you want them to provide for you. Nobody keeps buffaloes because they make nice pets.

The pond was still again. A cormorant arrived, wading into the shallows on its long legs, looking for a small fish or two for breakfast. A kingfisher flew across the pond, a sparkle of colour, but it did not dive or descend; the water was still too muddy.

A small islet, consisting of sand and a fringe of rushes, stood out in the middle of the pond. What I took to be a small boulder turned out to be a tortoise. It hadn't moved since I'd first seen it, and it remained motionless for the rest of the morning.

Three mynas were squabbling on the patch of grass in front of the bungalow. One of them was bald, having lost its feathers in some previous gladiatorial contest. Its companions did not care for its unconventional appearance, and like humans who resent the presence of a nonconforming outsider, they went at it with their beaks and talons until it fled from the field.

The room-boy gave me lunch in the little sitting room, beneath an overhead fan. This young all-rounder, whose name was Bhim, had made the lunch himself. His dal, roti and aloo-mattar was better than any hotel meal; but I couldn't do justice to the very sticky dessert (a sort of pastry stuffed with coconut and various nuts) that he served up afterwards, and he was a little put out that I pushed my plate away after a couple of mouthfuls.

'Mawa-ki-kachori,' he informed me. 'Special to Jodhpur.'

'Too sweet for me,' I said. 'But the dal–roti was perfect.'

He was mollified, and went off on his bicycle to carry out a few errands.

I was left with the sun and the sand and the pond below. The tortoise was still meditating on its islet.

I slept. I overslept. And young Bhim was late in returning from the city. As a result, no taxi turned up to take me to the station.

'Never mind,' he said philosophically. 'You can leave tomorrow. Tonight, I make mutton kebabs and hot bean curry. You will like!'

I did not feel so philosophical, and wondered if Bhim had conspired to keep me in the rest house for another night. He couldn't be having many guests in that remote place.

At sunset, he turned up with a glass, a bottle of soda, and a half-bottle of rum.

'Good Army rum,' he said. 'No headache.'

I gave in. Drank the rum, consumed the kebabs and bean curry, and slept peacefully in the second bedroom. Bhim had made the bed in my presence, convincing me that there were no scorpions or centipedes among the bed sheets. We turned the mattress over. All clear.

I woke at seven, to be greeted by Bhim with a cup of tea.

Then, I went to the bathroom and settled down on the toilet seat; at peace with the world—as I usually am when the bowels are moving freely.

And then I looked down and froze.

A large, glistening snake had wound itself around the base of the toilet-seat. It had a frog in its jaws, and only the back legs of the frog were visible. I have no idea what kind of snake it was—I did not stop to study it, but leapt from the seat and dashed into the bedroom, shouting for the room-boy.

Bhim appeared almost instantly.

'What is wrong, Sir? Breakfast almost ready.'

'A snake!' I shouted. 'There's a huge snake in the bathroom!'

'Not to worry, Sir. Only a *dhaman*, not poisonous. He comes through the drainpipe. Kills the rats. Very helpful.'

'Well, he has a frog this time,' I said. 'And I'm leaving right away. Just as soon as I can find my trousers.'

He went into the bathroom and returned with my trousers.

'Snake gone,' he said. 'Nothing to fear.'

I felt better after putting on my trousers. It's amazing what a pair of trousers can do for one's confidence.

'Thanks,' I said. 'And now you can get me a taxi.'

'But the train doesn't leave till evening.'

'I'm taking a bus,' I said. 'A bus leaves for Jaipur every hour.'

Disappointed, Bhim cycled off to arrange for some transport. I waited on the verandah, taking a last look at the pond. It was certainly safer outside than in the house.

The buffaloes were back. So were there young minders. So was the cormorant. And the tortoise was there too. It was all very peaceful—just another tranquil day in the desert.

THE ROAD TO BADRINATH

If you have travelled up the Mandakini Valley, and then cross over into the valley of the Alaknanda, you are immediately struck by the contrast. The Mandakini is gentler, richer in vegetation, almost pastoral in places; the Alaknanda is awesome, precipitous, threatening—and seemingly inhospitable to those who must live, and earn a livelihood, in its confines.

Even as we left Chamoli and began the steady, winding climb to Badrinath, the nature of the terrain underwent a dramatic change. No longer did green fields slope gently down to the riverbed. Here they clung precariously to rocky slopes and ledges that grew steeper and narrower, while the river below, impatient to reach its confluence with the Bhagirathi at Deoprayag, thundered along the narrow gorge.

Badrinath is one of the four dhams, or four most holy places in India. (The other three are Rameshwaram, Dwarka and Jagannath Puri.) For the pilgrim travelling to this holiest of holies, the journey is exciting, possibly even uplifting; but for those who live permanently on these crags and ridges, life is harsh, a struggle from one day to the next. No wonder so many young men from Garhwal find their way into the army. Little grows on these rocky promontories; and what does, is at the mercy of the weather. For most of the year the fields lie fallow. Rivers, unfortunately, run downhill and not uphill.

The harshness of this life, typical of much of Garhwal, was brought home to me at Pipalkoti, where we stopped for the night. Pilgrims stop here by the coachload, for the Garhwal Mandal Vikas Nigam's rest house is fairly capacious, and small hotels and dharamshalas abound. Just off the busy road is a tiny hospital, and here, late in the evening, we came across a woman keeping vigil over the dead body of her husband. The body had been laid out on a bench in the courtyard. A few feet away the road was crowded with pilgrims in festival mood; no one glanced over the low wall to notice this tragic scene.

The woman came from a village near Helong. Earlier that day, finding her consumptive husband in a critical condition she had decided to bring him to the nearest town for treatment. As he was frail and emaciated, she was able to carry him on her back for several miles, until she reached the motor road. Then, at some expense, she engaged a passing taxi and brought him to Pipalkoti. But he was already dead when she reached the small hospital. There was no morgue; so she sat beside the body in the courtyard, waiting for dawn and the arrival of others from the village. A few men arrived next morning and we saw them wending their way down to the cremation ground. We did not see the woman again. Her children were hungry and she had to hurry home to look after them.

Pipalkoti is hot (and peepul trees are conspicuous by their absence), but Joshimath, the winter resort of the Badrinath temple establishment, is about 6,000 feet above sea level and has an equable climate. It is now a fairly large town, and although the surrounding hills are rather bare, it does have one great tree that has survived the ravages of time. This is an ancient mulberry, known as the Kalpa Vriksha (Immortal Wishing Tree), beneath which the great Sankaracharya meditated, a few centuries ago. It is reputedly over 2,000 years old, and is certainly larger than my modest four-roomed flat in Mussoorie. Sixty pilgrims holding hands might just about encircle its trunk.

I have seen some big trees, but this is certainly the oldest and broadest of them. I am glad Sankaracharya meditated beneath it and thus ensured its preservation. Otherwise it might well have gone the way of other great trees and forests that once flourished in this area.

A small boy reminds me that it is a Wishing Tree, so I make my wish. I wish that other trees might prosper like this one.

'Have you made a wish?' I ask the boy.

'I wish that you will give me one rupee,' he says. His wish comes true with immediate effect. Mine lies in the uncertain future. But he has given me a lesson in wishing.

Joshimath has to be a fairly large place, because most of Badrinath arrives here in November, when the shrine is snowbound for six months. Army and PWD structures also dot the landscape. This is no carefree hill resort, but it has all the amenities for making a short stay quite pleasant and interesting. Perched on the steep mountainside above the junction of the Alaknanda and Dhauli Rivers, it is now vastly different from what it was when Frank Smythe visited it fifty years ago and described it as 'an ugly little place...straggling unbeautifully over the hillside. Primitive little shops line the main street, which is roughly paved in places and in others has been deeply channelled by the monsoon rains. The pilgrims spend the night in single-storeyed rest houses, not unlike the hovels provided for the Kentish hop-pickers of former days, some of which are situated in narrow passages running off the main street and are filthy and evil-smelling.'

Those were Joshimath's former days. It is a different place today, with small hotels, modern shops, a cinema; and its growth and comparative modernity date from the early sixties, when the old pilgrim footpath gave way to the motor road that takes the traveller all the way to Badrinath. No longer does the weary, footsore pilgrim sink gratefully down in the shade of the Kalpa Vriksha. He alights from his bus or luxury coach and drinks a cola or a Thums-up at one of the many small restaurants on the roadside.

Contrast this comfortable journey with the pilgrimage fifty years ago. Frank Smythe again: 'So they venture on their pilgrimage... Some borne magnificently by coolies, some toiling along in rags, some almost crawling, preyed on by disease and distorted by dreadful deformities... Europeans who have read and travelled cannot conceive what goes on in the minds of these simple folk, many of them from the agricultural parts of India, wonderment and fear must be the prime ingredients. So the pilgrimage becomes an adventure. Unknown dangers threaten the broad, well-made path, at any moment the gods, who hold the rocks in leash, may unloose their wrath upon the hapless passer-by. To the European it is a walk to Badrinath, to the Hindu pilgrim it is far, far more.'

Above Vishnuprayag, Smythe left the Alaknanda and entered the Bhyundar Valley, a botanist's paradise, which he called the Valley of Flowers. He fell in love with the lush meadows of this high valley, and made it known to the world. It continues to attract the botanist and trekker. Primulas of subtle shades, wild geraniums, saxifrages clinging to the rocks, yellow and red potentillas, snow-white anemones, delphiniums, violets, wild roses, all these and many more flourish there, capturing the mind and heart of the flower lover.

'Impossible to take a step without crushing a flower.' This may not be true any more, for many footsteps have trodden the Bhyundar in recent years. There are other areas in Garhwal where the hills are rich in flora—the Har-ki-doon, Harsil,

Tungnath, and the Khiraun valley where the balsam grows to a height of eight feet—but the Bhyundar has both a variety and a concentration of wild flowers, especially towards the end of the monsoon. It would be no exaggeration to call it one of the most beautiful valleys in the world. The Bhyundar is a digression for lovers of mountain scenery; but the pilgrim keeps his eyes fixed on the ultimate goal—Badrinath, where the gods dwelt and where salvation is to be found.

There are still a few who do it the hard way—mostly those who have taken sanyas and renounced the world. Here is one hardy soul doing penance. He stretches himself out on the ground, draws himself up to a standing position, then flattens himself out again. In this manner he will proceed from Badrinath to Rishikesh, oblivious of the sun and rain, the dust from passing buses, the sharp gravel of the footpath.

Others are not so hardy. One saffron-robed scholar, speaking fair English, asks us for a lift to Badrinath, and we find a space for him. He rewards us with a long and involved commentary on the Vedas, which lasts through the remainder of the journey. His special field of study, he informs us, is the part played by aeronautics in Vedic literature.

'And what,' I ask him, 'is the connection between the two?'

He looks at me pityingly.

'It is what I am trying to find out,' he replies.

The road drops to Pandukeshwar and rises again, and all the time I am scanning the horizon for the forests of the Badrinath region I had read about many years ago in James B. Fraser's *The Himalaya Mountains*! Walnuts grow up to 9,000 feet, deodars and 'bilka' up to 9,500 feet, and 'amesh' and 'kiusu' for up to a similar height—but, apart from strands of long-leaved excelsia pine, I do not see much, certainly no deodars. What has happened to them, I wonder. An endless variety of trees delighted us all the way from Dugalbeta to Mandal, a well-protected area, but here on the high ridges above the Alaknanda, little seems to grow; or, if ever they did, have long since been bespoiled or swept away.

Finally we reach the wind-swept, barren valley that harbours Badrinath—a growing township, thriving, lively, but somewhat dwarfed by the snow-capped peaks that tower above it. As at Joshimath, there is no dearth of hostelries and dharamshalas. Even so, every hotel or rest house is filled to overflowing. It is the height of the pilgrim season, and pilgrims, tourists and mendicants of every description throng the riverfront.

Just as Kedar is the most sacred of the Shiva temples in the Himalayas, so Badrinath is the supreme place of worship for the Vaishnav sects.

According to legend, when Sankaracharya in his *digvijaya* travels visited the Mana Valley, he arrived at the Narada–Kund and found fifty different images lying in its waters. These he rescued, and when he had done so, a voice from Heaven said, 'These are the images for the Kaliyug, establish them here.' Sankaracharya accordingly placed them beneath a mighty tree that grew there and whose shade extended from Badrinath to Nandprayag, a distance of over eighty miles. Close to it was the hermitage of Nar-Narayana (or Arjuna and Krishna), and in course of time temples were built in honour of these and other manifestations of Vishnu. It was here that Vishnu appeared to his followers in person, as the four-armed, crested and adorned with pearls and garlands.' The faithful, it is said, can still see him on the peak of Nilkantha, on the great Kumbha day. It is, in fact, the Nilkantha peak that dominates this crater-like valley where a few hardy thistles and nettles manage to survive. Like cacti in the desert, the pricklier forms of life seem best equipped to live in a hostile environment.

Nilkantha means blue-necked, an allusion to the god Shiva's swallowing of a poison meant to destroy the world. The poison remained in his throat, which was rendered blue thereafter. It is a majestic and awe-inspiring peak, soaring to a height of 21,640 feet. As its summit is only five miles from Badrinath, it is justly held in reverence. From its ice-clad pinnacle three great ridges sweep down, of which the southern one terminates in the Alaknanda valley.

On the evening of our arrival we could not see the peak, as it was hidden in clouds. Badrinath itself was shrouded in mist. But we made our way to the temple, a gaily decorated building about fifty feet high, with a gilded roof. The image of Vishnu, carved in black stone, stands in the centre of the sanctum, opposite the door, in a *dhyana* posture. An endless stream of people passes through the temple to pay homage and emerge the better for their proximity to the divine.

From the temple, flights of steps lead down to the rushing river and to the hot springs that emerge just above it. Another road leads through a long but tidy bazaar where pilgrims may buy mementos of their visit—from sacred amulets to pictures of the gods in vibrant technicolour. Here at last I am free to indulge my passion for cheap rings, with none to laugh at my foible. There are all kinds, from rings designed like a coiled serpent (my favourite) to twisted bands of copper and iron and others containing the pictures of gods, gurus and godmen. They do not cost more that two or three rupees each, and so I am able to fill my pockets. I never wear these rings. I simply hoard them away. My friends are convinced that in a previous existence I was a jackdaw, seizing upon and hiding away any kind of bright and shiny object: so be it...

Even those who have renounced the world appear to be cheerful—like the young woman from Gujarat who had taken *sanyas* and who met me on the steps below the temple. She gave me a dazzling smile and passed me an exercise book. She had taken a vow of silence; but being, I think, of an extrovert nature, she seemed eager to remain in close communication with the rest of humanity, and did so by means of written questions and answers. Hence the exercise book.

Although at Badrinath I missed the sound of birds and the presence of trees, it was good to be part of the happy throng at its colourful little temple, and to see the sacred river close to its source. And early next morning I was rewarded with the liveliest experience of all.

Opening the window of my room, and glancing out, I saw the rising sun touch the snow-clad summit of Nilkantha. At first the snows were pink; then they turned to orange and gold. All sleep vanished as I gazed up in wonder at that magnificent pinnacle in the sky. And had Lord Vishnu appeared just then on the summit I would not have been in the least surprised.

A SONG OF MANY RIVERS

1

When I look down from the heights of Landour to the broad Valley of the Doon far below, I can see the little Suswa River, silver in the setting sun, meandering through fields and forests on its way to its confluence with the Ganga.

The Suswa is a river I knew well as a boy, but it has been many years since I took a dip in its quiet pools or rested in the shade of the tall spreading trees growing on its banks. Now I see it from my windows, far away, dream-like in the mist, and I keep promising myself that I will visit it again, to touch its waters, cool and clear, and feel its rounded pebbles beneath my feet.

It's a little river, flowing down from the ancient Siwaliks and running the length of the valley until, with its sister river the Song, it slips into the Ganga just above the holy city of Haridwar. I could wade across (except during the monsoon when it was in spate) and the water seldom rose above the waist except in sheltered pools, where there were shoals of small fish.

There is a little known and charming legend about the Suswa and its origins, which I have always treasured. It tells us that the Hindu sage Kaspaya once gave a great feast to which all the gods were invited. Now Indra, the god of rain, while on his way to the entertainment, happened to meet 60,000 'balkhils' (pygmies) of the Brahmin caste, who were trying in vain to cross a cow's footprint filled with water—to them, a vast lake!

The god could not restrain his amusement. Peals of thunderous laughter echoed across the hills. The indignant Brahmins, determined to have their revenge, at once set to work creating a second Indra, who should supplant the reigning god. This could only be done by means of penance, fasting and self-denial, in which they persevered until the sweat flowing from their tiny bodies created the 'Suswa' or 'flowing waters' of the little river.

Indra, alarmed at the effect of these religious exercises, sought the help of Brahma, the creator, who, taking on the role of a referee, interceded with the priests. Indra was able to keep his position as the rain god.

I saw no pygmies or fairies near the Suswa, but I did see many spotted deer, cheetal, coming down to the water's edge to drink. They are still plentiful in that area.

2
The Nautch Girl's Curse

At the other end of the Doon, far to the west, the Yamuna comes down from the mountains and forms the boundary between the states of Himachal and Uttaranchal. Today, there's a bridge across the river, but many years ago, when I first went across, it was by means of a small cable car, and a very rickety one at that.

During the monsoon, when the river was in spate, the only way across the swollen river was by means of this swaying trolley, which was suspended by a steel rope to two shaky wooden platforms on either bank. There followed a tedious bus journey, during which some sixty-odd miles were covered in six hours. And then you were at Nahan, a small town a little over 3,000 feet above sea level, set amid hill slopes thick with sal and shisham trees. This charming old town links the subtropical Siwaliks to the first foothills of the Himalayas, a unique situation.

The road from Dagshai and Shimla runs into Nahan from the north. No matter in which direction you look, the view is a fine one. To the south stretches the grand panorama of the plains of Saharanpur and Ambala, fronted by two low ranges of thickly forested hills. In the valley below, the pretty Markanda River winds its way out of the Kadir Valley.

Nahan's main street is curved and narrow, but well-made and paved with good stone. To the left of the town is the former Raja's palace. Nahan was once the capital of the state of Sirmur, now part of Himachal Pradesh. The original palace was built some three or four hundred years ago, but has been added to from time to time, and is now a large collection of buildings mostly in the Venetian style.

I suppose Nahan qualifies as a hill station, although it can be quite hot in summer. But unlike most hill stations, which are less than two hundred years old, Nahan is steeped in legend and history.

The old capital of Sirmur was destroyed by an earthquake some seven to eight hundred years ago. It was situated some twenty-four miles from present day Nahan, on the west bank of the Giri, where the river expands into a lake. The ancient capital was totally destroyed, with all its inhabitants, and apparently no record was left of its then ruling family. Little remained of the ancient city, just a ruined temple and a few broken stone figures.

As to the cause of the tragedy, the traditional story is that a nautch girl happened to visit Sirmur, and performed some wonderful feats. The Raja challenged the girl to walk safely over the Giri on a rope, offering her half his kingdom if she was successful.

The girl accepted the challenge. A rope was stretched across the river. But before starting out, the girl promised that if she fell victim to any treachery on the part of the Raja, a curse would fall upon the city and it would be destroyed by a terrible catastrophe.

While she was on her way to successfully carrying out the feat, some of the Raja's people cut the rope. She fell into the river and was drowned. As predicted, total destruction came to the town.

The founder of the next line of the Sirmur Raja came from the Jaisalmer family in Rajasthan. He was on a pilgrimage to Haridwar with his wife when he heard of the catastrophe that had immolated every member of the state's ancient dynasty. He went at once with his wife into the territory, and established a Jaisalmer Raj. The descent from the first Rajput ruler of Jaisalmer stock, some seven hundred years ago, followed from father to son in an unbroken line. And after much intitial moving about, Nahan was fixed upon as the capital.

The territory was captured by the Gurkhas in 1803, but twelve years later they were expelled by the British after some severe fighting, to which a small English cemetery bears witness. The territory was restored to the Raja, with the exception of the Jaunsar Bawar region.

Six or seven miles north of Nahan lies the mountain of Jaitak, where the Gurkhas made their last desperate stand. The place is worth a visit, not only for seeing the remains of the Gurkha fort, but also for the magnificent view the mountain commands.

From the northernmost of the mountain's twin peaks, the whole south face of the Himalayas may be seen. From west to north you see the rugged prominences of the Jaunsar Bawar, flanked by the Mussoorie range of hills. It is wild mountain scenery, with a few patches of cultivation and little villages nestling on the sides of the hills. Garhwal and Dehradun are to the east, and as you go downhill you can see the broad sweep of the Yamuna as it cuts its way through the western Siwaliks.

3
Gently Flows the Ganga

The Bhagirathi is a beautiful river, gentle and caressing (as compared to the turbulent Alaknanda), and pilgrims and others have responded to it with love and respect. The god Shiva released the waters of Goddess Ganga from his locks, and she sped towards the plains in the tracks of Prince Bhagirath's chariot.

> *He held the river on his head*
> *And kept her wandering, where*
> *Dense as Himalaya's woods were spread*
> *The tangles of his hair.*

Revered by Hindus and loved by all, Goddess Ganga weaves her spell over all who come to her. Some assert that the true Ganga (in its upper reaches) is the Alaknanda. Geographically, this may be so. But tradition carries greater weight in the abode of the Gods, and traditionally the Bhagirathi is the Ganga. Of course, the two rivers meet at Deoprayag, in the foothills, and this marriage of the waters settles the issue.

I put the question to my friend Dr Sudhakar Misra, from whom words of wisdom sometimes flow; and true to form, he answered: 'The Alaknanda is Ganga, but the Bhagirathi is Ganga-ji.'

She issues from the very heart of the Himalayas. Visiting Gangotri in 1820, the writer and traveller Baillie Fraser noted: 'We are now in the centre of the Himalayas, the loftiest and perhaps the most rugged range of mountains in the world.'

Here, at the source of the river, we come to the realization that we are at the very centre and heart of things. One has an almost primaeval sense of belonging to these mountains and to this valley in particular. For me, and for many who have been here, the Bhagirathi is the most beautiful of the four main river valleys of Garhwal.

The Bhagirathi seems to have everything—a gentle disposition, deep glens and forests, the ultravision of an open valley graced with tiers of cultivation leading up by degrees to the peaks and glaciers at its head.

At Tehri, the big dam slows down Prince Bhagirath's chariot. But upstream, from Bhatwari to Harsil, there are extensive pine forests. They fill the ravines and plateaus, before giving way to yew and cypress, oak and chestnut. Above 9,000 feet the deodar (*deodar*, tree of the gods) is the principal tree. It grows to a little distance above Gangotri, and then gives way to the birch, which is found in patches to within half a mile of the glacier.

It was the valuable timber of the deodar that attracted the adventurer Frederick 'Pahari' Wilson to the valley in the 1850s. He leased the forests from the Raja of Tehri, and within a few years he had made a fortune. From his horse and depot at Harsil, he would float the logs downstream to Tehri, where they would be sawn up and despatched to buyers in the cities.

Bridge-building was another of Wilson's ventures. The most famous of these was a 350-feet suspension bridge at Bhaironghat, over 1,200 feet above the young Bhagirathi where it thunders through a deep defile. This rippling contraption was at first a source of terror to travellers, and only a few ventured across it.

To reassure people, Wilson would mount his horse and gallop to and fro across the bridge. It has since collapsed, but local people will tell you that the ghostly hoof beats of Wilson's horse can still be heard on full moon nights. The supports of the old bridge were massive deodar trunks, and they can still be seen to one side of the new road bridge built by engineers of the Northern Railway.

The old forest rest houses at Dharasu, Bhatwari and Harsil were all built by Wilson as staging posts, for the only roads were narrow tracks linking one village to another. Wilson married a local girl, Gulabi, from the village of Mukhba, and the portraits of the Wilsons (early examples of the photographer's art) still hang in these sturdy little bungalows. At any rate, I found their pictures at Bhatwari. Harsil is now out of bounds to civilians, and I believe part of the old house was destroyed in a fire a few years ago. This sturdy building withstood the earthquake that devastated the area in 1991.

Among other things, Wilson introduced the apple into this area, 'Wilson apples'—large, red and juicy—sold to travellers and pilgrims on their way to Gangotri. This fascinating man also acquired an encyclopaedic knowledge of the wildlife of the region, and his articles, which appeared in *Indian Sporting Life* in the 1860s, were later plundered by so-called wildlife writers for their own works.

He acquired properties in Dehradun and Mussoorie, and his wife lived there in some style, giving him three sons. Two died young. The third, Charlie Wilson, went through most of his father's fortune. His grave lies next to my grandfather's grave in the old Dehradun cemetery. Gulabi is buried in Mussoorie, next to her husband. I wrote this haiku for her:

Her beauty brought her fame,
But only the wild rose growing beside her grave
Is there to hear her whispered name—
Gulabi.

I remember old Mrs Wilson, Charlie's widow, when I was a boy in Dehra. She lived next door in what was the last of the Wilson properties. Her nephew, Geoffrey Davis, went to school with me in Shimla, and later joined the Indian Air Force. But luck never went the way of Wilson's descendants, and Geoffrey died when his plane crashed.

Wilson's life is fit subject for a romance; but even if one were never written, his legend would live on, as it has done for over a hundred years. There has never been any attempt to commemorate him, but people in the valley still speak of him in awe and admiration, as though he had lived only yesterday.

Some men leave a trail of legend behind them because they give their spirit to the place where they have lived, and remain forever a part of the rocks and mountain streams.

Gangotri is situated at just a little over 10,300 feet. On the right bank of the river is the Gangotri temple, a small neat building without too much ornamentation, built by Amar Singh Thapa, a Nepali general, early in the nineteenth century. It was renovated by the Maharaja of Jaipur in the 1920s. The rock on which it stands is called Bhagirath Shila and is said to be the place where Prince Bhagirath did penance in order that Ganga be brought down from her abode of eternal snow. Here the rocks are carved and polished by ice and water, so smooth that in places they look like rolls of silk. The fast flowing waters of this mountain torrent look very different from the huge sluggish river that finally empties its waters into the Bay of Bengal fifteen hundred miles away.

The river emerges from beneath a great glacier, thickly studded with enormous loose rocks and earth. The glacier is about a mile in width and extends upwards for many miles. The chasm in the glacier through which the stream rushed forth into the light of day is named Gaumukh, the cow's mouth, and is held in deepest reverence by Hindus. The regions of eternal frost in the vicinity were the scene of many of their most sacred mysteries.

The Ganga enters the world no puny stream, but bursts from its icy womb a river thirty or forty yards in breadth. At Gauri Kund (below the Gangotri temple) it falls over a rock of considerable height and continues tumbling over a succession of small cascades until it enters the Bhaironghati gorge.

A night spent beside the river, within the sound of the fall, is an eerie experience. After some time it begins to sound not like one fall but a hundred, and this sound permeates both one's dreams and waking hours. Rising early to greet the dawn proved rather pointless at Gangotri, for the surrounding peaks did not let the sun in till after 9 a.m. Everyone rushed about to keep warm, exclaiming delightedly at what they call '*gulabi thand*', literally, 'rosy cold'. Guaranteed to turn the cheeks a rosy pink! A charming expression, but I prefer a rosy sunburn, and remained beneath a heavy quilt until the sun came up to throw its golden shafts across the river.

This is mid-October, and after Diwali the shrine and the small township will close for winter, the pandits retreating to the relative warmth of Mukbha. Soon snow will cover everything, and even the hardy purple-plumaged whistling thrushes, lovers of deep shade, will move further down the valley. And down below the forest-line, the Garhwali farmers go about harvesting their terraced fields that form patterns of yellow, green and gold above the deep green of the river.

Yes, the Bhagirathi is a green river. Although deep and swift, it does not lose its serenity. At no place does it look hurried or confused—unlike the turbulent Alaknanda, fretting and frothing as it goes crashing down its boulder-strewn bed. The Alaknanda gives one a feeling of being trapped, because the river itself is trapped. The Bhagirathi is free-flowing, easy. At all times and places it seems to find its true level.

In the old days, only the staunchest of pilgrims visited the shrines at Gangotri and Jamnotri. The roads were rocky and dangerous, winding along in some places, ascending and descending the faces of deep precipices and ravines, at times leading along banks of loose earth where landslides had swept the original path away.

There are still no large towns above Uttarkashi, and this absence of large centres of population may be reason why the forests are better preserved than those in the Alaknanda valley, or further downstream. Uttarkashi, though a large and growing town, is as yet uncrowded. The seediness of towns like Rishikesh and parts of Dehradun is not yet evident here. One can take a leisurely walk through its long (and well-supplied) bazaar, without being jostled by crowds or knocked over by three-wheelers. Here, too, the river is always with you, and you must live in harmony with its sound as it goes rushing and humming along its shingly bed.

Uttarkashi is not without its own religious and historical importance, although all traces of its ancient town of Barahat appear to have vanished. There are four important temples here, and on the occasion of Makar Sankranti, early in January a week-long fair is held when thousands from the surrounding areas throng the roads to the town. To the beating of drums and blowing of trumpets, the gods and goddesses are brought to the fair in gaily decorated palanquins. The surrounding villages wear a deserted look that day as everyone flocks to the temples and bathing ghats and to the entertainments of the fair itself.

We have to move far downstream to reach another large centre of population, the town of Tehri, and this is a very different place from Uttarkashi. Tehri has all the characteristics of a small town in the plains—crowds, noise, traffic congestion, dust and refuse, scruffy dhabas—with this difference that here it is all ephemeral, for Tehri is destined to be submerged by the water of the Bhagirathi when the Tehri dam is finally completed.

The rulers of Garhwal were often changing their capitals, and when, after the Gurkha War (of 1811–15), the former capital of Srinagar became part of British Garhwal, Raja Sudershan Shah established his new capital at Tehri. It is said that when he reached this spot, his horse refused to go any further. This was enough for the king, it seems; or so the story goes.

Perhaps Prince Bhagirath's chariot will come to a halt here too, when the dam is built. The two hundred and forty-six metre high earthen dam, with forty-two square miles of reservoir capacity, will submerge the town and about thirty villages.

But as we leave the town and cross the narrow bridge over the river, a mighty blast from above sends rocks hurtling down the defile, just to remind us that work is indeed in progress.

Unlike the Raja's horse, I have no wish to be stopped in my tracks at Tehri. There are livelier places upstream. And as for Ganga herself, that deceptively gentle river, I wonder if she will take kindly to our efforts to contain her.

4
Falling for Mandakini

A great river at its confluence with another great river is, for me, a special moment in time. And so it was with the Mandakini at Rudraprayag, where its waters joined the waters of the Alaknanda, the one having come from the glacial snows above Kedarnath, the other from the Himalayan heights beyond Badrinath. Both sacred rivers, destined to become the holy Ganga further downstream.

I fell in love with the Mandakini at first sight. Or was it the valley that I fell in love with? I am not sure, and it doesn't really matter. The valley is the river.

While the Alaknanda Valley, especially in its higher reaches, is a deep and narrow gorge where precipitous outcrops of rock hang threateningly over the traveller, the Mandakini Valley is broader, gentler, the terraced fields wider, the banks of the river a green sward in many places. Somehow, one does not feel that one is at the mercy of the Mandakini whereas one is always at the mercy of the Alaknanda with its sudden floods.

Rudraprayag is hot. It is probably a pleasant spot in winter, but at the end of June, it is decidedly hot. Perhaps its chief claim to fame is that it gave its name to the dreaded man-eating leopard of Rudraprayag, who in the course of seven years (1918–25) accounted for more than three hundred victims. It was finally shot by Jim Corbett, who recounted the saga of his long hunt for the killer in his fine book, *The Man-eating Leopard of Rudraprayag*.

The place at which the leopard was shot was the village of Gulabrai, two miles south of Rudraprayag. Under a large mango tree stands a memorial raised to Jim Corbett by officers and men of the Border Roads Organisation. It is a touching gesture to one who loved Garhwal and India. Unfortunately, several buffaloes are tethered close by, and one has to wade through slush and buffalo dung to get to the memorial stone. A board tacked on to the mango tree attracts the attention of motorists who might pass without noticing the memorial, which is off to one side.

The killer leopard was noted for its direct method of attack on humans; and, in spite of being poisoned, trapped in a cave, and shot at innumerable times, it did not lose its contempt for man. Two English sportsmen covering both ends to the old suspension bridge over the Alaknanda fired several times at the man-eater but to little effect.

It was not long before the leopard acquired a reputation among the hill folk for being an evil spirit. A sadhu was suspected of turning into the leopard by night, and was only saved from being lynched by the ingenuity of Philip Mason, then deputy commissioner of Garhwal. Mason kept the sadhu in custody until the leopard made his next attack, thus proving the man innocent. Years later, when Mason turned novelist and (using the pen name Philip Woodruffe) wrote *The Wild Sweet Witch*, he had as one of the characters a beautiful young woman who apparently turns into a man-eating leopard by night.

Corbett's host at Gulabrai was one of the few who survived an encounter with the leopard. It left him with a hole in his throat. Apart from being a superb story teller, Corbett displayed great compassion for people from all walks of life and is still a legend in Garhwal and Kumaon among people who have never read his books.

In June, one does not linger long in the steamy heat of Rudraprayag. But as one travels up the river, making a gradual ascent of the Mandakini Valley, there is a cool breeze coming down from the snows, and the smell of rain is in the air.

The thriving little township of Agastmuni spreads itself along the wide river banks. Further upstream, near a little place called Chandrapuri, we cannot resist breaking our journey to sprawl on the tender green grass that slopes gently down to the swift flowing river. A small rest house is in the making. Around it, banana fronds sway and poplar leaves dance in the breeze.

This is no sluggish river of the plains, but a fast moving current, tumbling over rocks, turning and twisting in its efforts to discover the easiest way for its frothy snow-fed waters to escape the mountains. Escape is the word! For the constant complaint of many a Garliwali is that, while his hills abound in rivers, the water runs down and away, and little, if any, reaches the fields and villages above it. Cultivation must depend on the rain and not on the river.

The road climbs gradually, still keeping to the river. Just outside Guptakashi, my attention is drawn to a clump of huge trees sheltering a small but ancient temple. We stop here and enter the shade of the trees.

The temple is deserted. It is a temple dedicated to Shiva, and in the courtyard are several river-rounded stone *lingam*s on which leaves and blossoms have fallen. No one seems to come here, which is strange, since it is on the pilgrim route. Two boys from a neighbouring field leave their yoked bullock to come and talk to me, but they cannot tell me much about the temple except to confirm that it is seldom visited. 'The buses do not stop here.' That seems explanation enough. For where the buses go, the pilgrims go; and where the pilgrims go, other pilgrims will follow. Thus far and no further.

The trees seem to be magnolias. But I have never seen magnolia trees grow to such huge proportions. Perhaps they are something else. Never mind; let them remain a mystery.

Guptakashi in the evening is all a bustle. A coachload of pilgrims (headed for Kedarnath) has just arrived, and the tea shops near the bus stand are doing brisk business. Then the 'local' bus from Ukhimath, across the river, arrives, and many of the passengers head for a tea shop famed for its samosas. The local bus is called the *bhook hartal*, the 'hunger-strike' bus.

'How did it get that name?' I ask one of the samosa-eaters.

'Well, it's an interesting story. For a long time we had been asking the authorities to provide a bus service for the local people and for the villagers who live off the roads. All the buses came from Srinagar or Rishikesh, and were taken up by pilgrims. The locals couldn't find room in them. But our pleas went unheard until the whole town, or most of it, decided to go on hunger-strike.'

'They nearly put me out of business too,' says the tea shop owner cheerfully. 'Nobody ate any samosas for two days!'

There is no cinema or public place of entertainment at Guptakashi, and the town goes to sleep early. And wakes early.

At six, the hillside, green from recent rain, sparkles in the morning sunshine. Snowcapped Chaukhamba (7,140 metres) is dazzling. The air is clear; no smoke or dust up here. The climate, I am told, is mild all the year round judging by the scent and shape of the flowers, and the boys call them champs, Hindi for champa blossom. Ukhimath, on the other side of the river, lies in the shadow. It gets the sun at nine. In winter, it must wait till afternoon.

Guptakashi has not yet been rendered ugly by the barrack-type architecture that has come up in some growing hill towns. The old double storeyed houses are built of stone, with gray slate roofs. They blend well with the hillside. Cobbled paths meander through the old bazaar.

One of these takes up to the famed Guptakashi temple, tucked away above the old part of the town. Here, as in Benaras, Shiva is worshipped as Vishwanath, and two underground streams representing the sacred Jamuna and Bhagirathi rivers feed the pool sacred to the God. This temple gives the town its name, Gupta-Kashi, the 'Invisible Benaras', just as Uttarkashi on the Bhagirathi is 'Upper Benaras'.

Guptakashi and its environs have so many lingams that the saying *'June kanhar utne shanhar'*—'As many stones, so many Shivas'—has become a proverb to describe its holiness.

From Guptakashi, pilgrims proceed north to Kedarnath, and the last stage of their journey—about a day's march—must be covered on foot or horseback. The temple of Kedarnath, situated at a height of 11,753 feet, is encircled by snowcapped peaks, and Atkinson has conjectured that 'the symbol of the *linga* may have arisen front the pointed peaks around his (God Shiva's) original home.'

The temple is dedicated to Sadashiva, the subterranean form of the God, who, according to Atkinson 'fleeing from the Pandavas took refuge here in the form of a he-buffalo and finding himself hard-pressed, dived into the ground leaving the hinder parts on the surface, which continue to be the subject of adoration.'

The other portions of the God are worshipped as follows: the arms at Tungnath, at a height of 13,000 feet, the face at Rudranath (12,000 feet), the belly at Madmaheshwar, eighteen miles northeast of Guptakashi; and the hair and head at Kalpeshwar, near Joshimath. These five sacred shrines form the Punch Kedar (five Kedars).

We leave the Mandakini to visit Tungnath on the Chandrashila range. But I will return to this river. It has captured my mind and heart.

A WALK THROUGH GARHWAL

I wake to what sounds like the din of a factory buzzer, but is in fact the music of a single vociferous cicada in the lime tree near my window.

Through the open window, I focus on a pattern of small, glossy lime leaves; then through them I see the mountains, the Himalayas, striding away into an immensity of sky.

'In a thousand ages of the gods I could not tell thee of the glories of Himachal.' So confessed a Sanskrit poet at the dawn of Indian history and he came closer than anyone else to capturing the spell of the Himalayas. The sea has had Conrad and Stevenson and Masefield, but the mountains continue to defy the written word. We have climbed their highest peaks and crossed their most difficult passes, but still they keep their secrets and their reserve; they remain remote, mysterious, spirit-haunted.

No wonder then, that the people who live on the mountain slopes in the mist-filled valleys of Garhwal have long since learned humility, patience and a quiet resignation. Deep in the crouching mist lie their villages, while climbing the mountain slopes are forests of rhododendron, spruce and deodar, soughing in the wind from the ice-bound passes. Pale women plough, they laugh at the thunder as their men go down to the plains for work; for little grows on the beautiful mountains in the north wind.

When I think of Manjari village in Garhwal, I see a small river, a tributary of the Ganga, rushing along the bottom of a steep, rocky valley. On the banks of the river and on the terraced hills above, there are small fields of corn, barley, mustard, potatoes and onions. A few fruit trees grow near the village. Some hillsides are rugged and bare, just masses of quartz or granite. On hills exposed to wind, only grass and small shrubs are able to obtain a foothold.

This landscape is typical of Garhwal, one of India's most northerly regions with its massive snow ranges bordering on Tibet. Although thinly populated, it does not provide much of a living for its people. Most Garliwali cultivators are poor, some are very poor. 'You have beautiful scenery,' I observed after crossing the first range of hills.

'Yes,' said my friend, 'but we cannot eat the scenery.'

And yet these are cheerful people, sturdy and with wonderful powers of endurance. Somehow they manage to wrest a precarious living from the unhelpful, calcinated soil. I am their guest for a few days.

My friend Gajadhar has brought me to his home, to his village above the little Nayar river. We took a train into the foothills and then we took a bus and finally, made dizzy by the hairpin bends devised in the last century by a brilliantly diabolical road-engineer, we alighted at the small hill station of Lansdowne, chief recruiting centre for the Garhwal Regiment.

Lansdowne is just over six thousand feet high. From there we walked, covering twenty-five miles between sunrise and sunset, until we came to Manjari village, clinging to the terraced slopes of a very proud, very permanent mountain.

And this is my fourth morning in the village.

Other mornings I was woken by the throaty chuckles of the red-billed blue magpies, as they glided between oak trees and medlars; but today the cicada has drowned all bird song. It is a little out of season for cicadas but perhaps this sudden warm spell in late September has deceived him into thinking it is mating season again.

Early though it is, I am the last to get up. Gajadhar is exercising in the courtyard, going through an odd combination of Swedish exercises and yoga. He has a fine physique with the sturdy legs that most Garhwalis possess. I am sure he will realize his ambition of joining the Indian Army as a cadet. His younger brother Chakradhar, who is slim and fair with high cheek-bones, is milking the family's buffalo. Normally, he would be on his long walk to school, five miles distant; but this is a holiday, so he can stay at home and help with the household chores.

His mother is lighting a fire. She is a handsome woman even though her ears, weighed down by heavy silver earrings, have lost their natural shape. Garhwali women usually invest their savings in silver ornaments. And at the time of marriage it is the boy's parents who make a gift of land to the parents of an attractive girl; a dowry system in reverse. There are fewer women than men in the hills and their good looks and sturdy physique give them considerable status among the men-folk.

Chakradhar's father is a corporal in the Indian Army and is away for most of the year.

When Gajadhar marries, his wife will stay in the village to help his mother and younger brother look after the fields, house, goats and buffalo. Gajadhar will see her only when he comes home on leave. He prefers it that way; he does not think a simple hill girl should be exposed to the sophisticated temptations of the plains.

The village is far above the river and most of the fields depend on rainfall. But water must be fetched for cooking, washing and drinking. And so, after a breakfast of hot sweet milk and thick *chajmaues* stuffed with minced radish, the brothers and I set off down the rough track to the river.

The still has climbed the mountains but it has yet to reach the narrow valley. We bathe in the river, Gajadhar and Chakradhar dive off a massive rock, but I wade in circumspectly, unfamiliar with the river's depths and currents. The water, a milky blue, has come from the melting snows; it is very cold. I bathe quickly and then dash for a strip of sand where a little sunshine has split down the mountainside in warm, golden pools of light. At the same time, the song of the whistling-thrush emerges like a dark secret from the wooded shadows. A little later, buckets filled, we toil up the steep mountain. We must go by a better path this time if we are not to come tumbling down with our buckets of water. As we climb we are mocked by a barbet that sits high up in a spruce calling feverishly in its monotonous mournful way.

'We call it the mewli bird,' says Gajadhar, 'there is a story about it. People say that the souls of men who have suffered injuries in the law courts of the plains and who have died of their disappointments, transmigrate into the mewli birds. That is why the birds are always crying *un, raee-oru, un nee ow*, which means "injustice, injustice!"'

The path leads us past a primary school, a small temple, and a single shop in which it is possible to buy salt, soap and a few other necessities. It is also the post office. And today it is serving as a lock-up.

The villagers have apprehended a local thief, who specializes in stealing jewellery from women while they are working in the fields. He is awaiting escort to the Lansdowne police station, and the shop-keeper-cum-postmaster-cum-constable brings him out for us to inspect. He is a mild-looking fellow, clearly shy of the small crowd that has gathered round him. I wonder how he manages to deprive the strong hill-women of their jewellery; it could not be by force! Any cases of crimes and violence are rare in Garhwal; and robbery, too, is uncommon for the simple reason that there is very little to rob.

The thief is rather glad of my presence, as it distracts attention from him. Strangers seldom come to Manjari. The crowd leaves him, turns to me, eager to catch a glimpse of the stranger in its midst. The children exclaim, point at me with delight, chatter among themselves. I might be a visitor from another planet instead of just an itinerant writer from the plains.

The postman has yet to arrive. The mail is brought in relays from Lansdowne. The Manjari postman who has to cover eight miles and delivers letters at several small villages on his route, should arrive around noon. He also serves as a newspaper, bringing the villagers news of the outside world. Over the years he has acquired a reputation for being highly inventive, sometimes creating his own news; so much so that when he told the villagers that men had landed on the moon, no one believed him. There are still a few sceptics.

Gajadhar has been walking out of the village every day, anxious to meet the postman. He is expecting a letter giving the results of his army entrance examination. If he is successful he will be called for an interview. And then, if he is accepted, he will be trained as an officer-cadet. After two years he will become a second lieutenant. His father, after twelve years in the army, is still only a corporal. But his father never went to school. There were no schools in the hills during his father's youth.

The Manjari school is only up to class five and it has about forty pupils. If these children (most of them boys) want to study any further, then, like Chakradhar, they must walk the five miles to the high school at the next big village.

'Don't you get tired walking ten miles every day?' I ask Chakradhar.

'I am used to it,' he says. 'I like walking.'

I know that he only has two meals a day—one at seven in the morning when he leaves home and the other at six or seven in the evening when he returns from school—and I ask him if he does not get hungry on the way.

'There is always the wild fruit,' he replies.

It appears that he is an expert on wild fruit: the purple berries of the thorny bilberry bushes ripening in May and June; wild strawberries like drops of blood on the dark green monsoon grass; small sour cherries and tough medlars in the winter months. Chakradhar's strong teeth and probing tongue extract whatever tang or sweetness lies hidden in them. And in March there are the rhododendron flowers. His mother makes them into jam. But Chakradhar likes them as they are: he places the petals on his tongue and chews till the sweet juice trickles down his throat.

He has never been ill.

'But what happens when someone is ill?' I ask knowing that in Manjari there are no medicines, no dispensary or hospital.

'He goes to bed until he is better,' says Gajadhar. 'We have a few home remedies. But if someone is very sick, we carry the person to the hospital at Lansdowne.' He pauses as though wondering how much he should say, then shrugs and says: 'Last year my uncle was very ill. He had a terrible pain in his stomach. For two days he cried out with the pain. So we made a litter and started out for Lansdowne. We had already carried him fifteen miles when he died. And then we had to carry him back again.'

Some of the villages have dispensaries managed by compounders but the remoter areas of Garhwal are completely without medical aid. To the outsider, life in the Garhwal hills may seem idyllic and the people simple. But the Garhwali is far from being simple and his life is one long struggle, especially if he happens to be living in a high altitude village snowbound for four months in the year, with cultivation coming to a standstill and people having to manage with the food gathered and stored during the summer months.

Fortunately, the clear mountain air and the simple diet keep the Garhwalis free from most diseases, and help them recover from the more common ailments. The greatest dangers come from unexpected disasters, such as an accident with an axe or scythe, or an attack by a wild animal. A few years back, several Manjari children and old women were killed by a man-eating leopard. The leopard was finally killed by the villagers who hunted it down with spears and axes. But the leopard that sometimes prowls round the village at night looking for a stray dog or goat, slinks away at the approach of a human.

I do not see the leopard but at night I am woken by a rumbling and thumping on the roof. I wake Gajadhar and ask him what is happening.

'It is only a bear,' he says.

'Is it trying to get in?'

'No, it's been in the cornfield and now it's after the pumpkins on the roof.'

A little later, when we look out of the small window, we see a black bear making off like a thief in the night, a large pumpkin held securely to his chest.

At the approach of winter when snow covers the higher mountains, the brown and black Himalayan bears descend to lower altitudes in search of food. Because they are short-sighted and suspicious of anything that moves, they can be dangerous; but, like most wild animals, they will avoid men if they can and are aggressive only when accompanied by their cubs.

Gajadhar advises me to run downhill if chased by a bear. He says that bears find it easier to run uphill than downhill.

I am not interested in being chased by a bear, but the following night Gajadhar and I stay up to try and prevent the bear from depleting his cornfield. We take up our position on a highway promontory of rock, which gives us a clear view of the moonlit field.

A little after midnight, the bear comes down to the edge of the field but he is suspicious and has probably smelt us. He is, however, hungry; and so, after standing up as high as possible on his hind legs and peering about to see if the field is empty, he comes cautiously out of the forest and makes his way towards the corn.

When about halfway, his attention is suddenly attracted by some Buddhist prayer-flags which have been strung up recently between two small trees by a band of wandering Tibetans. On spotting the flags, the bear gives a little grunt of disapproval and begins to move back into the forest; but the fluttering of the little flags is a puzzle that he feels he must make out (for a bear is one of the most inquisitive animals); so after a few backward steps, he again stops and watches them.

Not satisfied with this, he stands on his hind legs looking at the flags, first at one side and then at the other. Then seeing that they do not attack him and so not appear dangerous, he makes his way right up to the flags taking only two or three steps at a time and having a good look before each advance. Eventually, he moves confidently up to the flags and pulls them all down. Then, after careful examination of the flags, he moves into the field of corn.

But Gajadhar has decided that he is not going to lose any more corn, so he starts shouting, and the rest of the village wakes up and people come out of their houses beating drums and empty kerosene tins.

Deprived of his dinner, the bear makes off in a bad temper. He runs downhill and at a good speed too; and I am glad that I am not in his path just then. Uphill or downhill, an angry bear is best given a very wide berth.

For Gajadhar, impatient to know the result of his array entrance examination, the following day is a trial of his patience.

First, we hear that there has been a landslide and that the postman cannot reach us. Then, we hear that although there has been a landslide, the postman has already passed the spot in safety. Another alarming rumour has it that the postman disappeared with the landslide. This is soon denied. The postman is safe. It was only the mail-bag that disappeared.

And then, at two in the afternoon, the postman turns up. He tells us that there was indeed a landslide but that it took place on someone else's route. Apparently, a mischievous urchin who passed him on the way was responsible for all the rumours. But we suspect the postman of having something to do with them...

Gajadhar had passed his examination and will leave with me in the morning. We have to be up early in order to reach Lansdowne before dark. But Gajadhar's mother insists on celebrating her son's success by feasting her friends and neighbours. There is a partridge (a present from a neighbour who had decided that Gajadhar will make a fine husband for his daughter) and two chickens: rich fare for folk whose normal diet consists mostly of lentils, potatoes and onions.

After dinner, there are songs, and Gajadhar's mother sings of the homesickness of those who are separated from their loved ones and their home in the hills. It is an old Garhwali folk-song:

Oh, mountain-swift, you are from my father's home;
Speak, oh speak, in the courtyard of my parents,
My mother will hear you; She will send my brother to fetch me.
A grain of rice alone in the cooking pot
Cries, 'I wish I could get out!'
Likewise I wonder:
'Will I ever reach my father's house?'

The hookah is passed round and stories are told. Tales of ghosts and demons mingle with legends of ancient kings and heroes. It is almost midnight by the time the last guest has gone. Chakradhar approaches me as I am about to retire for the night.

'Will you come again?' he asks.

'Yes, I'll come again,' I reply. 'If not next year, then the year after. How many years are left before you finish school?'

'Four.'

'Four years. If you walk ten miles a day for four years, how many miles will that make?'

'Four thousand and six hundred miles,' says Chakradhar after a moment's thought, 'but we have two months' holiday each year. That means I'll walk about twelve thousand miles in four years.'

The moon has not yet risen. Lanterns swing in the dark.

The lanterns flit silently over the hillside and go out one by one. This Garhwali day, which is just like any other day in the hills, slips quietly into the silence of the mountains.

I stretch myself out on my cot. Outside the small window the sky is brilliant with stars. As I close my eyes, someone brushes against the lime tree, brushing its leaves; and the fresh fragrance of limes comes to me on the night air, making the moment memorable for all time.

OUR GREAT ESCAPE

It had been a lonely winter for a fourteen-year-old. I had spent the first few weeks of the vacation with my mother and stepfather in Dehra. Then they left for Delhi, and I was pretty much on my own. Of course, the servants were there to take care of my needs, but there was no one to keep me company. I would wander off in the mornings, taking some path up the hills, come back home for lunch, read a bit, and then stroll off again till it was time for dinner. Sometimes I walked up to my grandparents' house, but it seemed so different now, with people I didn't know occupying the house.

The three-month winter break over, I was almost eager to return to my boarding school in Shimla.

It wasn't as though I had many friends at school. I needed a friend but it was not easy to find one among a horde of rowdy, pea-shooting eighth formers, who carved their names on desks and stuck chewing gum on the class teacher's chair. Had I grown up with other children, I might have developed a taste for schoolboy anarchy; but in sharing my father's loneliness after his separation from my mother, and in being bereft of any close family ties, I had turned into a premature adult.

After a month in the eighth form, I began to notice a new boy, Omar, and then only because he was a quiet, almost taciturn person who took no part in the form's feverish attempt to imitate the Marx Brothers at the circus. He showed no resentment at the prevailing anarchy, nor did he make a move to participate in it. Once he caught me looking at him, and he smiled ruefully, tolerantly. Did I sense another adult in the class? Someone who was a little older than his years?

Even before we began talking to each other, Omar and I developed an understanding of sorts, and we'd nod almost respectfully to each other when we met in the classroom corridors or the environs of the dining hall or the dormitory. We were not in the same house. The house system practised its own form of apartheid, whereby a member of one house was not expected to fraternize with someone belonging to another. Those public schools certainly knew how to clamp you into compartments. However, these barriers vanished when Omar and I found ourselves selected for the School Colts' hockey team, Omar as a full-back, I as the goalkeeper.

The taciturn Omar now spoke to me occasionally, and we combined well on the field of play. A good understanding is needed between a goalkeeper and a full-back. We were on the same wavelength. I anticipated his moves; he was familiar with mine. Years later, when I read Conrad's *The Secret Sharer*, I thought of Omar.

It wasn't until we were away from the confines of school, classroom and dining hall that our friendship flourished. The hockey team travelled to Sanawar on the next mountain range, where we were to play a couple of matches against our old rivals, the Lawrence Memorial Royal Military School. This had been my father's old school, so I was keen to explore its grounds and peep into its classrooms.

Omar and I were thrown together a good deal during the visit to Sanawar, and in our more leisurely moments, strolling undisturbed around a school where we were guests and not pupils, we exchanged life histories and other confidences. Omar, too, had lost his father—had I sensed that before?—shot in some tribal encounter on the Frontier, for he hailed from the lawless lands beyond Peshawar. A wealthy uncle was seeing to Omar's education.

We wandered into the school chapel, and there I found my father's name—A. A. Bond—on the school's roll of honour board: old boys who had lost their lives while serving during the two World Wars.

'What did his initials stand for?' asked Omar.

'Aubrey Alexander.'

'Unusual names, like yours. Why did your parents call you Rusty?'

'I am not sure.' I told him about the book I was writing. It was my first one and was called *Nine Months* (the length of the school term, not a pregnancy), and it described some of the happenings at school and lampooned a few of our teachers. I had filled three slim exercise books with this premature literary project, and I allowed Omar to go through them. He must have been my first reader and critic.

'They're very interesting,' he said, 'but you'll get into trouble if someone finds them, especially Mr Fisher.'

I have to admit it wasn't great literature. I was better at hockey and football. I made some spectacular saves, and we won our matches against Sanawar. When we returned to Shimla, we were school heroes for a couple of days and lost some of our reticence; we were even a little more forthcoming with other boys. And then Mr Fisher, my housemaster, discovered my literary opus, *Nine Months*, under my mattress, and took it away and read it (as he told me later) from cover to cover. Corporal punishment then being in vogue, I was given six of the best with a springy Malacca cane, and my manuscript was torn up and deposited in Mr Fisher's wastepaper basket. All I had to show for my efforts were some purple welts on my bottom. These were proudly displayed to all who were interested, and I was a hero for another two days.

'Will you go away too when the British leave India?' Omar asked me one day.

'I don't think so,' I said. 'I don't have anyone to go back to in England, and my guardian, Mr Harrison, too seems to have no intention of going back.'

'Everyone is saying that our leaders and the British are going to divide the country. Shimla will be in India, Peshawar in Pakistan!'

'Oh, it won't happen,' I said glibly. 'How can they cut up such a big country?' But even as we chatted about the possibility, Nehru, Jinnah and Mountbatten, and all those who mattered, were preparing their instruments for major surgery.

Before their decision impinged on our lives and everyone else's, we found a little freedom of our own, in an underground tunnel that we discovered below the third flat.

It was really part of an old, disused drainage system, and when Omar and I began exploring it, we had no idea just how far it extended. After crawling along on our bellies for some twenty feet, we found ourselves in complete darkness. Omar had brought along a small pencil torch, and with its help we continued writhing forward (moving backwards would have been quite impossible) until we saw a glimmer of light at the end of the tunnel. Dusty, musty, very scruffy, we emerged at last onto a grassy knoll, a little way outside the school boundary.

It's always a great thrill to escape beyond the boundaries that adults have devised. Here we were in unknown territory. To travel without passports—that would be the ultimate in freedom!

But more passports were on their way—and more boundaries.

Lord Mountbatten, viceroy and governor-general-to-be,

came for our Founder's Day and gave away the prizes. I had won a prize for something or the other, and mounted the rostrum to receive my book from this towering, handsome man in his pinstripe suit. Bishop Cotton's was then the premier school of India, often referred to as the 'Eton of the East'. Viceroys and governors had graced its functions. Many of its boys had gone on to eminence in the civil services and armed forces. There was one 'old boy' about whom they maintained a stolid silence—General Dyer, who had ordered the massacre at Amritsar and destroyed the trust that had been building up between Britain and India.

Now Mountbatten spoke of the momentous events that were happening all around us—the War had just come to an end, the United Nations held out the promise of a world living in peace and harmony, and India, an equal partner with Britain, would be among the great nations...

A few weeks later, Bengal and the Punjab provinces were bisected. Riots flared up across northern India, and there was a great exodus of people crossing the newly-drawn frontiers of Pakistan and India. Homes were destroyed, thousands lost their lives.

The common room radio and the occasional newspaper kept us abreast of events, but in our tunnel, Omar and I felt immune from all that was happening, worlds away from all the pillage, murder and revenge. And outside the tunnel, on the pine knoll below the school, there was fresh untrodden grass, sprinkled with clover and daisies; the only sounds we heard were the hammering of a woodpecker and the distant insistent call of the Himalayan Barbet. Who could touch us there?

'And when all the wars are done,' I said, 'a butterfly will still be beautiful.'

'Did you read that somewhere?'

'No, it just came into my head.'

'Already you're a writer.'

'No, I want to play hockey for India or football for Arsenal. Only winning teams!'

'You can't win forever. Better to be a writer.'

When the monsoon arrived, the tunnel was flooded, the drain choked with rubble. We were allowed out to the cinema to see Laurence Olivier's *Hamlet*, a film that did nothing to raise our spirits on a wet and gloomy afternoon; but it was our last picture that year, because communal riots suddenly broke out in Shimla's Lower Bazaar, an area that was still much as Kipling had described it—'a man who knows his way there can defy all the police of India's summer capital'—and we were confined to school indefinitely.

One morning after prayers in the chapel, the headmaster announced that the Muslim boys—those who had their homes in what was now Pakistan—would have to be evacuated, sent to their homes across the border with an armed convoy.

The tunnel no longer provided an escape for us. The bazaar was out of bounds. The flooded playing field was deserted. Omar and I sat on a damp wooden bench and talked about the future in vaguely hopeful terms, but we didn't solve any problems. Mountbatten and Nehru and Jinnah were doing all the solving.

It was soon time for Omar to leave—he left along with some fifty other boys from Lahore, Pindi and Peshawar. The rest of us—Hindus, Christians, Parsis—helped them load their luggage into the waiting trucks. A couple of boys broke down and wept. So did our departing school captain, a Pathan who had been known for his stoic and unemotional demeanour. Omar waved cheerfully to me and I waved back. We had vowed to meet again some day.

The convoy got through safely enough. There was only one casualty—the school cook, who had strayed into an off-limits area in the foothill town of Kalika and been set upon by a mob. He wasn't seen again.

Towards the end of the school year, just as we were all getting ready to leave for the school holidays, I received a letter from Omar. He told me something about his new school and how he missed my company and our games and our tunnel to freedom. I replied and gave him my home address, but I did not hear from him again.

Some seventeen or eighteen years later, I did get news of Omar, but in an entirely different context. India and Pakistan were at war, and in a bombing raid over Ambala, not far from Shimla, a Pakistani plane was shot down. Its crew died in the crash. One of them, I learnt later, was Omar.

Did he, I wonder, get a glimpse of the playing fields we knew so well as boys? Perhaps memories of his schooldays flooded back as he flew over the foothills. Perhaps he remembered the tunnel through which we were able to make our little escape to freedom.

But there are no tunnels in the sky.

STREET OF THE RED WELL

The sun beats down on the sweltering city of Old Delhi. Not a breath of air stirs in the narrow, winding streets. This old Walled City, now over three hundred years old, has no open spaces, no sidewalks, no shady avenues. During the reign of Emperor Shah Jahan, a canal ran down the centre of the main thoroughfare, Chandni Chowk (street of the silversmiths), but the canal has long since been covered over, and the Yamuna river, from which water has been channelled, lies beyond the emperor's fort, the Red Fort of Delhi, where the Prime Minister speaks to the multitude every year on Independence Day.

It is not water that I seek most, but shelter from the heat and glare of the overhead sun. I have chosen what is quite possibly the hottest day in May, the temperature over 105 degrees Fahrenheit, to go walking in search of—what? A story, perhaps, and adventure. Or that is what I set out to do. The heat of the day has willed otherwise. I may be ready for an adventure, but no one else is interested. I am the only one walking the streets from choice.

Shopkeepers nod drowsily beneath whirring ceiling-fans. The pavement barber has taken his customer into the shelter of an awning. A fortune-teller has decided that there is nothing to predict and has fallen asleep under the same awning. A vegetable seller sprinkles water on his vegetables in a dispirited fashion. Those cauliflowers were fresh an hour ago: they look old already. Even the flies are drowsy. Instead of buzzing feverishly from place to place, they stagger about on tired legs.

It is the pigeons who have found all the coolest places. These birds have made the old city their own. New Delhi is for the crows who like to have a tree to sleep in, even if they take their meals from out of kitchens and verandahs. But the pigeons prefer buildings, and the older the buildings the better. They are familiar with every cool alcove or shady recess in the crumbling walls of neglected mosques and mansions.

A fat, supercilious pigeon watches me from the window ledge above a jeweller's shop. The pigeon's forebears settled here long before the British thought of taking Delhi. Conquerors have come and gone, Nadir Shah the Persian, Madhav Rao the Maratha, Gulam Kadir the Rohilla and generations of goldsmiths and silversmiths. Hindus and Muslims have made and lost fortunes in the city, but nothing has disturbed the tranquil life of these pigeons. Their gentle cooing can always be heard when there is a lull in the jagged symphony of traffic noise. How do they manage to sound so cool?

But here's welcome relief for humans: a shady corner in Lal Kuan bazaar (street of the Red Well), where an old man provides drinking water to thirsty wayfarers such as myself. His water is stored in a *surahi*, an earthenware jug that keeps the water sweet and cool. I bend down, cup my hands, and receive the sparkling liquid as my benefactor tilts the surahi towards me.

Lal Kuan. The Red Well. Of course it is no longer here, but the street still bears its name. And I like to think that here, in the middle of the street, where a bullock has gone to sleep, forcing the cyclists to make a detour, there was once a well, made of dark red brick, where the water bubbled forth all day. Imprisoned beneath the soil, held down by the crowded commercial houses of this old quarter, the water must still be there; it gives nourishment to an old peepul tree that grows beside a temple. It is the only tree in the street. It juts out from the temple wall growing straight and tall, dwarfing the two-storeyed houses. One of its roots, breaking throughout the ground, has curled up to provide a smooth, well-worn seat. And it is cool here, beneath the peepul.

On the other side of the road, a tall iron doorway is set in a high wall. Doors like this were only built in the previous century, when a wealthy merchant's house had to be a miniature fortress as well as a residence. I cannot see over the wall and I would like to know what lies behind the door. Perhaps a side street, perhaps a market, perhaps a garden, perhaps....

The door opens, not easily, because it had been left closed for a long time, but slowly and with much complaint. And beyond the door there is only an empty courtyard, covered with rubble, the ruins of the old house. I am about to turn away when I hear a deep tremendous murmur.

It is the cooing of many pigeons. But where are they?

I advance further into the ruin, and there, opening out in front of me, ready to receive me as the rabbit-hole was ready to receive Alice, is an old, disused well. I peer down into its murky depths. It is dark, very dark down there; but that is where the pigeons live, in the walls of this lost, long-forgotten well shut away from the rest of the city. I cannot see any water, so I drop a pebble over the side. It strikes the wall, and then, with a soft plop, touches water. At that instant there is a rush of air and a tremendous beating of wings, and a flock of pigeons. Thirty or forty of them fly out of the well, streak upwards, circle the building and then, falling into formation, wheel overhead, the sun gleaming white on their underwings.

I have discovered their secret. Now I know why they look so cool, so refreshed, while we who walk the streets of Old Delhi do so with parched mouths and drooping limbs. The pigeons are the only ones who still know about the Red Well.

FOOTLOOSE IN AGRA

I went to Agra in 1965, to see the Taj. But what interested me about the city had little to do with Emperor Shah Jahan's grand monument to his love.

The cycle rickshaw is the best way of getting about Agra. Its smooth gliding motion and leisurely rate of progress are in keeping with the pace of life in this old-world city. The rickshaw boy makes his way through the crowded bazaars, exchanging insults with tonga drivers, pedestrians and other cyclists; but once on the broad Mall or Taj Road, his curses change to carefree song and he freewheels along the tree-lined avenues. Old colonial-style bungalows still stand in large compounds shaded by peepul, banyan, neem and jamun trees.

Looking up, I notice a number of bright paper kites that flutter, dip and swerve in the cloudless sky. I cannot recall seeing so many kites before.

'Is it a festival today?' I ask,

'No, sahib,' says the rickshaw boy. 'Not even a holiday.'

'Then why so many kites?'

He does not even bother to look up. 'You can see kites every day, sahib.'

'I don't see them in Delhi.'

'Ah, but Delhi is a busy place. In Agra, people still fly kites.

There are kite-flying competitions every Sunday, and heavy bets are sometimes placed on the outcome.'

As we near the city, I notice kites stuck in trees or dangling from electric wires; but there are always others soaring up to take their place. I ask the rickshaw boy to tell me something about the kite-fliers and the kitemakers, but the subject bores him.

'You had better see the Taj today, sahib.'

'All right take me to it. I can lunch afterwards.'

It is difficult to view the Taj at noon. The sun strikes the white marble, and there is a great dazzle of reflected light. I stand there with averted eyes, looking at everything—the formal gardens, the surrounding walls of red sandstone, the winding river—everything except the monument I have come to see.

It is there, of course, very solid and real, perfectly preserved, with every jade, jasper or lapis lazuli playing its part in the overall design; and after a while, I can shade my eyes and take in a vision of shimmering white marble. The light rises in waves from the paving-stones, and the squares of black and white marble create an effect of running water. Inside the chamber it is cool and dark but rather musty, and I waste no time in hurrying out again into the sunlight.

I walk the length of a gallery and turn with some relief to the river scene. The sluggish Yamuna winds past Agra on its way to its union with the Ganga. I know the Yamuna well. I know it where it emerges from the foothills near Kalsi, cold and blue from the melting snows; I know it as it winds through fields of wheat and sugarcane and mustard, across the flat plains of Uttar Pradesh, sometimes placid, sometimes in flood. I know the river at Delhi, where its muddy banks are a patchwork of clothes spread out by the hundreds of washermen who serve the city and I know it at Mathura, where it is alive with huge turtles; Mathura, sacred city, whose beginnings are lost in antiquity.

And then the river winds its way to Agra, to this spot by the Taj, where parrots flash in the sunshine, kingfishers swoop low over the water, and a proud peacock struts across the lawns surrounding the monument.

I follow the peacock into a shady grove. It is quite tame and does not fly away. It leads me to a small boy who is sitting in the shade of a tree, feasting on a handful of small green fruit.

I have not seen the fruit before, and I ask the boy to tell me what it is. He offers me what looks like a hard green plum.

'It is the fruit from the Ashok tree,' says the boy. 'There are many such trees in the garden.'

'Are you allowed to take the fruit?'

'I am allowed,' he says, grinning. 'My father is the head gardener.' I bite into the fruit. It is hard and sour but not unpleasant.

'Do you live here?' I ask.

'Over the wall,' he says. 'But I come here everyday, to help my father and to eat the fruit.'

'So you see the Taj Mahal every day?'

I have seen it every day for as long as I can remember.'

'And I am seeing it for the first time…you're very lucky.'

He shrugs. 'If you see it once, or a hundred times, it is the same. It doesn't change.'

'Don't you like looking at it, then?'

'I like looking at the people who come here. They are always different. In the evening there will be many people.'

'You must have seen people from almost every country in the world.'

'That is so. They all come here to look at the Taj. Kings and Queens and Presidents and Prime Ministers and film stars and poor people too. And I look at them. In that way it isn't boring.'

'Well, you have the Taj to thank for that.'

He gazes thoughtfully at the shimmering monument.

His eyes are accustomed to the sharp sunlight. He sees the Taj every day, but at this moment he is really looking at it, thinking about it, wondering what magic it must possess to attract people from all corners of the earth, to bring them here walking through his father's well-kept garden so that he can have something new and fresh to look at each day.

A cloud—a very small cloud—passes across the face of the sun; and in the softened light I too am able to look at the Taj without screwing up my eyes.

As the boy said, it does not change. Therein lies beauty. For the effect on the traveller is the same today as it was three hundred years ago when Bernier wrote: 'Nothing offends the eye... No part can be found that is not skilfully wrought, or that has not its peculiar beauty.'

And so, for a few moments, this poem in marble is on view to two unimportant people—the itinerant writer and the gardener's boy.

We say nothing; there is really nothing to be said. (But now, a few months later, when I try to recapture the essence of that day, it is not the monument that I remember most vividly. The Taj is there of course; I still see it as a mirror for the sun. But what remain with me, more than anything else, are the passage of the river and the sharp flavour of the Ashok fruit.)

In the afternoon I walk through the old bazaars that lie to the west of Akbar's great red sandstone fort, and I am not surprised to find a small street that is almost entirely taken up by kite-shops. Most of them sell the smaller, cheaper kites, but one small dark shop has in it a variety of odd and fantastic creations. Stepping inside, I find myself face to face with the doyen of Agra's kite-makers, Hosain Ali, a feeble old man whose long beard is dyed red with the juice of mehendi leaves. He has just finished making a new kite from bamboo, paper and thin silk, and it lies outside in the sun, firming up. It is a pale pink kite, with a small green tail.

The old man is soon talking to me, for he likes to talk and is not very busy. He complains that few people buy kites these days (I find this hard to believe), and tells me that I should have visited Agra twenty-five years ago, when kite-flying was the sport of kings and even grown men found time to spend an hour or two every day with these dancing strips of paper. Now, he says, everyone hurries, hurries in a heat of hope, and delicate things like kites and daydreams are trampled underfoot. 'Once I made a wonderful kite,' says Hosain Ali nostalgically. 'It was unlike any kite seen in Agra. It had a number of small, very light paper discs trailing on a thin bamboo frame. At the end of each disc I fixed a sprig of grass, forming a balance on both sides. On the first and largest disc I painted a face and gave it eyes made of two small mirrors. The discs, which grew smaller from head to tail, gave the kite the appearance of a crawling serpent. It was very difficult to get this great kite off the ground. Only I could manage it.

'Of course, everyone heard of the Dragon Kite I had made, and word went about that there was some magic in its making. A large crowd arrived on the maidan to watch me fly the kite.

'At first the kite would not leave the ground. The discs made a sharp wailing sound, the sun was trapped in the little mirrors. My kite had eyes and tongue and a trailing silver tail. I felt it come alive in my hands. It rose from the ground, rose steeply into the sky, moving farther and farther away, with the sun still glinting in its dragon eyes. And when it went very high, it pulled fiercely on the twine, and my son had to help me with the reel.

'But still the kite pulled, determined to be free—yes, it had become a living thing—and at last the twine snapped, and the wind took the kite, took it over the rooftops and the waving trees and the river and the far hills for ever. No one ever saw where it fell. Sahib, are you listening? The Dragon Kite is lost, but for you I'll make a bright new poem to fly.'

'Make me one,' I say, moved by his tale, or rather by the manner of its telling. 'I will collect it tomorrow, before I leave Agra. Let it be a beautiful kite. I won't fly it. I'll hang it on my wall, and will not give it a chance to get away.'

It is evening, and the winter sun comes slanting through the intricate branches of a banyan tree, as a cycle rickshaw—a different one this time—brings me to a forgotten corner of Agra that I have always wanted to visit. This is the old Roman Catholic cemetery where so many early European travellers and adventurers lie buried.

Although it is quite probably the oldest Christian cemetery in northern India, it has none of that overgrown, crumbling look that is common to old cemeteries in monsoon lands. It is a bright, even cheerful place, and the jingle of tonga-bells and other street noises can be heard from any part of the grounds. The grass is cut, the gravestones are kept clean and most of the inscriptions are still readable.

The caretaker takes me straight to the oldest grave—this is the oldest known European grave in northern India—and it happens to be that of an Englishman, John Mildenhall. The lettering stands out clearly:

Here lies John Mildenhall, Englishman, who left London in 1599 and travelling to India through Persia, reached Agra in 1605 and spoke with the Emperor Akbar. On a second visit in 1614 he fell ill at Lahore, died at Ajmere, and was buried here through the good offices of Thomas Kerridge, Merchant.

During the seventeenth and eighteenth centuries, the Agra cemetery was considered blessed ground by Christians, and the dead were brought here from distant places. Thomas Kerridge must have put himself to considerable expense to bury his friend in Agra. Mildenhall was a romantic, who styled himself an envoy of Queen Elizabeth. Unfortunately he left no account of his travels, although a couple of his letters are quoted in the writings of Purchas, another English merchant, who lies buried in the Protestant cemetery a couple of furlongs away.

Nearby is the grave of the Venetian, Jerome Veronio, who died at Lahore. According to some old records, he had a hand in designing the Taj, modelling it on Humayun's tomb in Delhi. There had for long been a belief that this 'architect' of the Taj lay buried in the cemetery but no one knew where. Then in 1945, Father Hyacinth, Superior Regular of Agra, scraped the moss off a tombstone, revealing the simple epitaph: 'Here lies Jerome Veronio, who died at Lahore.'

Actually, there is no evidence that Veronio designed the Taj, and even if he had something to do with it, he was only one of a number of artists and architects who worked on its construction. The chief architect was Muhammed Sharif of Samarkand. Each drew a salary of one thousand rupees per month. Ismail Khan of Turkey was the dome-maker. A number of inlay workers, sculptors and masons were Hindus, including Manohar Singh of Lahore and Mohan Lal of Kanauj, both famous inlay workers.

A man of more authentic accomplishments was the Italian lapidary, Horten Bronzoni, whose grave lies at a short distance from Veronio's. He died on 11 August 1677. According to Tavernier, it was Bronzoni who cut the Koh-i-noor diamond; and, says Tavernier, he cut the stone very badly.

Bronzoni is again mentioned as having manufactured a model ship of war for Aurangzeb, who had been annoyed by the depredations of Portuguese pirates and was anxious to create a navy. The ship was floated in a huge tank and manoeuvred by a number of European artillerymen. It made a ridiculous sight and convinced the Emperor that a navy was out of the question.

There are over eighty old Armenian graves in the cemetery, but the only one that interests me is the tomb of Shah Azar Khan, an expert in the art of moulding a heavy cannon. One of these, 'Zamzamah', earned a measure of immortality in Kipling's *Kim*—'who holds *Zam-Zammah*, that "fire-breathing dragon", holds the Punjab, for the great green-bronze piece is always first of the conqueror's loot.' The gun was 14.6 feet long, and is still at Lahore.

Other historic tombs lie scattered about the cemetery, but the most striking and curious of them is the grave of Colonel Jon Hessing, who died in 1803. It is a miniature Taj Mahal, built of red sandstone. Although small compared to a Mughal tomb, it is large for a Christian grave, and could easily accommodate a living family of moderate proportions. Hessing came to India from Holland, and was one of a colourful band of freelance soldiers (most of them deserters) who served in Sindhia's Maratha army. Hessing, we are told, was a good, benevolent man and a great soldier. The tomb was built by his wife Alice, who it must be supposed, felt as tenderly towards the Colonel as Shah Jahan felt towards his queen. She could not afford marble. Even so, her 'Taj' cost a lakh of rupees.

Outside, in the street, people move about with casual unconcern.

Street-vendors occupy the pavement, unwilling that their rivals should take advantage of a brief absence. In the banyan tree, the sparrows and bulbuls are settling down for the night. A kite lies entangled in the upper branches.

THE GREAT TRAIN JOURNEY

Suraj waved to a passing train, and kept waving until only the spiralling smoke remained. He liked waving to trains. He wondered about the people in them, and about where they were going and what it would be like there. And when the train had passed, leaving behind only the hot, empty track, Suraj was lonely.

He was a little lonely now. His hands in his pockets, he wandered along the railway track, kicking at loose pebbles and sending them down the bank. Soon there were other tracks, a railway-siding, a stationary goods train.

Suraj walked the length of the goods train. The carriage doors were closed and, as there were no windows, he couldn't see inside. He looked around to see if he was observed, and then, satisfied that he was alone, began trying the doors. He was almost at the end of the train when a carriage door gave way to his thrust.

It was dark inside the carriage. Suraj stood outside in the bright sunlight, peering into the darkness, trying to recognize bulky, shapeless objects. He stepped into the carriage and felt around. The objects were crates, and through the cross-section of woodwork he felt straw. He opened the other door and the sun streamed into the compartment, driving out the musty darkness.

Suraj sat down on a packing-case, his chin cupped in his hands. The school was closed for the summer holidays, and he had been wandering about all day and still did not know what to do with himself. The carriage was bare of any sort of glamour. Passing trains fascinated him—moving trains, crowded trains, shrieking, panting trains all fascinated him—but this smelly, dark compartment filled him only with gloom and more loneliness.

He did not really look gloomy or lonely. He looked fierce at times, when he glared out at people from under his dark eyebrows, but otherwise he usually wore a contented look—and no one could guess just how deep his thoughts were!

Perhaps, if he had company, some fun could be had in the carriage. If there had been a friend with him, someone like Ranji…

He looked at the crates. He was always curious about things that were bolted or nailed down or in some way concealed from him—things like parcels and locked rooms—and carriage doors and crates!

He went from one crate to another, and soon his perseverance was rewarded. The cover of one hadn't been properly nailed down. Suraj got his fingers under the edge and prised up the lid. Absorbed in this operation, he did not notice the slight shudder that passed through the train.

He plunged his hands into the straw and pulled out an apple.

It was a dark, ruby-red apple, and it lay in the dusty palm of Suraj's hand like some gigantic precious stone, smooth and round and glowing in the sunlight. Suraj looked up, out of the doorway, and thought he saw a tree walking past the train.

He dropped the apple and stared.

There was another tree, and another, all walking past the door with increasing rapidity. Suraj stepped forward but lost his balance and fell on his hands and knees. The floor beneath him was vibrating, the wheels were clattering on the rails, the carriage was swaying. The trees were running now, swooping past the train, and the telegraph poles joined them in the crazy race.

Crouching on his hands and knees, Suraj stared out of the open door and realized that the train was moving, moving fast, moving away from his home and puffing into the unknown. He crept cautiously to the door and looked out. The ground seemed to rush away from the wheels. He couldn't jump. Was there, he wondered, any way of stopping the train? He looked around the compartment again: only crates of apples. He wouldn't starve, that was one consolation.

He picked up the apple he had dropped and pulled a crate nearer to the doorway. Sitting down, he took a bite from the apple and stared out of the open door.

'Greetings, friend,' said a voice from behind, and Suraj spun round guiltily, his mouth full of apple.

A dirty, bearded face was looking out at him from behind a pile of crates. The mouth was open in a wide, paan-stained grin.

'Er—namaste,' said Suraj apprehensively. 'Who are you?'

The man stepped out from behind the crates and confronted the boy.

'I'll have one of those, too,' he said, pointing to the apple.

Suraj gave the man an apple, and stood his ground while the carriage rocked on the rails. The man took a step forward, lost his balance, and sat down on the floor.

'And where are you going, friend?' he asked. 'Have you a ticket?'

'No,' said Suraj. 'Have you?'

The man pulled at his beard and mused upon the question but did not answer it. He took a bite from the apple and said, 'No, I don't have a ticket. But I usually reserve this compartment for myself. This is the first time I've had company. Where are you going? Are you a hippy like me?'

'I don't know,' said Suraj. 'Where does this train go?'

The scruffy ticketless traveller looked concerned for a moment, then smiled and said, 'Where do you want to go?'

'I want to go everywhere,' said Suraj. 'I want to go to England and China and Africa and Greenland. I want to go all over the world!'

'Then you're on the right train,' said the man. 'This train goes everywhere. First it will take you to the sea, and there you will have to get on a ship if you want to go to China.'

'How do I get on a ship?' asked Suraj.

The man, who had been fumbling about in the folds and pockets of his shabby clothes, produced a packet of bidis and a box of matches, and began smoking the aromatic leaf.

'Can you cook?' he asked.

'Yes,' said Suraj untruthfully.

'Can you scrub a deck?'

'Why not?'

'Can you sail a ship?'

'I can sail anything.'

'Then you'll get to China,' said the man.

He leant back against a crate, stuck his dirty feet up on another crate, and puffed contentedly at his bidi.

Suraj finished his apple, took another from the crate, and dug his teeth into it. He took aim with the core of the old apple and tried to hit a telegraph pole, but missed it by metres; it wasn't the same as throwing a cricket ball. Then, to make the apple more interesting, he began to take big bites to see if he could devour it in three mouthfuls. But it took him four bites to finish the apple, so he started on another.

Suraj had always wanted to be in a train, a train that would take him to strange new places, over hundreds and hundreds of kilometres. And here was a train doing just that, and he wasn't quite sure if it was what he really wanted…

The train was coming to a station. The engine whistled, slowed down. The number of railway lines increased, crossed, spread out in different directions. Before the train could come to a stop, Suraj's companion came to the door and jumped to the ground.

'You'd better keep out of sight if you don't want to be caught!' he called. And waving his hand, he disappeared into the jungle across the railway tracks.

The train was at a siding. Suraj couldn't see any signs of life, but he heard voices and the sound of carriage doors being opened and closed. He suspected that the apples wouldn't stay in the compartment much longer, so he stuffed one into each pocket, and climbed onto a wooden rack in a corner.

Presently men's voices were heard in the doorway. Two labourers stepped into the compartment and began moving the crates towards the door, where they were taken over by others. Soon the compartment was empty.

Suraj waited until the men had gone away before coming down from the rack. After about five minutes the train started again. It shunted up and down, then gathered speed and went rushing across the plain.

Suraj felt a thrill of anticipation. Where would they be going now? He wondered what his parents would do when he failed to come home that night; they would think he had run away, or been kidnapped, or been involved in an accident. They would have the police out and there would be search parties. Suraj would be famous: the boy who disappeared!

The train came out of the jungle and passed fields of sugarcane and villages of mud huts. Children shouted and waved to the train, though there was no one in it except Suraj, the guard and the engine-driver. Suraj waved back. Usually he was in a field, waving; today, he was actually on the train.

He was beginning to enjoy the ride. The train would take him to the sea. There would be ships with funnels and ships with sails, and there might even be one to take him across the ocean to some distant land. He felt a bit sorry for his mother and father—they *would* miss him... They would believe he had been lost for ever...! But one day, a fortune made, he would return home and then nobody would care any more about school reports and what he ate and why he came home late... Ranji would be waiting for him at the station, and Suraj would bring him back a present—an African lion, perhaps, or a transistor-radio... But he wished Ranji was with him now; he wished the ragged hippy was still with him. An adventure was always more fun when one had company.

He had finished both apples by the time the train showed signs of reaching another station. This time it seemed to be moving into the station itself, not just a siding. It passed a lot of signals and buildings and advertisement-boards before slowing to a halt beside a wide, familiar platform.

Suraj looked out of the door and caught sight of the board bearing the station's name. He was so astonished that he almost fell out of the compartment. He was back in his home town! After travelling forty or fifty kilometres, here he was, home again.

He couldn't understand it. The train hadn't turned, of that he was certain; and it hadn't been moving backwards, he was certain of that, too. He climbed out of the compartment and looked up and down the platform. Yes, the engine had changed ends! It was only the local apple train.

Suraj glowered angrily at everyone on the platform. It was as though the rest of the world had played a trick on him.

He made his way to the waiting-room and slipped into the street through the back door. He did not want a ticket-collector asking him awkward questions. It had been a free ride, and with that he comforted himself. Shrugging his shoulders, Suraj sauntered down the road to the bazaar. Some day, he thought, he'd take a train and really go somewhere; and he'd buy a ticket, just to make sure of getting there.

'I'm going everywhere,' he said fiercely. 'I'm going everywhere, and no one can stop me!'

THE INDIA I CARRIED WITH ME

I am now going back in time, to a period when I was caught between East and West, and had to make up my mind just where I belonged. I had been away from India for barely a month before I was longing to return. The insularity of the place where I found myself (Jersey, in the Channel Islands) had something to do with it, I suppose. There was little there to remind me of India or the East, not one brown face to be seen in the streets or on the beaches. I'm sure it's a different sort of place now; but fifty years ago it had nothing to offer by way of companionship or good cheer to a lonely, sensitive boy who had left home and friends in search of a 'better future'.

I had come to England with a dream of sorts, and I was to return to India with another kind of dream; but in between there were to be four years of dreary office work, lonely bed-sitting rooms, shabby lodging houses, cheap snack bars, hospital wards, and the struggle to write my first book and find a publisher for it.

I started work in a large departmental store called *Le Riche*. At eight in the morning, when I walked to the store, it was dark. At six in the evening, when I walked home, it was dark again. Where were all those sunny beaches Jersey was famous for? I would have to wait for summer to see them, and a Saturday afternoon to take a dip in the sea.

Occasionally, after an early supper, I would walk along the deserted seafront. If the tide was in and the wind was approaching gale-force, the waves would climb the sea wall and drench me with their cold salt spray. My aunt, with whom I was staying, thought I was quite mad to take this solitary walk; but I have always been at one with nature, even in its wilder moments, and the wind and the crashing waves gave me a sense of freedom, strengthened my determination to escape from the island and go my own way.

When I wasn't walking along the seafront, I would sit at the portable typewriter in my small attic room, and hammer out the rough chapters of the book that was to become my first novel. These were characters and incidents based on the journal I had kept during my last year in India. It was 1951, recalled in late 1952. An eighteen-year-old looking back on incidents in the life of a seventeen-year-old! Nostalgia and longing suffused those pages. How I longed to be back with my friends in the small town of Dehradun—a leafy place, sunny, fruit-laden, easy-going, every familiar corner etched clearly in my memory. Somehow, it had been that last year in Dehra that had brought me closer to the India that I had so far only taken for granted. An India of close and sometimes sentimental friendships. Of striking contrasts: a small cinema showing English pictures (a George Formby comedy or an American musical) and only a couple of hours away thousands taking a dip in the sacred water of the Ganga. Or outside the station, hundreds of pony-drawn tongas waiting to pick up passengers, while the more affluent climbed into their Ford Convertibles, Morris Minors, Baby Austins or flashy Packards and Daimlers.

But of course Dehra in the 1950s was a town of bicycles. Students, shopkeepers, Army cadets, office workers, all used them. The scooter (or Lambretta) had only just been invented, and it would be several years before it took over from the bicycle. It was still unaffordable for the great majority.

I was awkward on a bicycle and frequently fell off, breaking my arm on one occasion. But this did not prevent me from joining my friends on cycle rides to the sulphur springs, or to Premnagar (where the Military Academy was situated) or along the Haridwar road and down to the riverbed at Lachhiwala.

In Jersey, I found an old cycle belonging to my cousin, and I rode from St Helier, where we lived, to St Brelade's Bay, at the other end of the island. But returning after dark, I was hauled up for riding without lights. I had no idea that cycles had also to be equipped with lights. Back in Dehra, we never used them!

The attic room had no view, so one of my favourite occupations, gazing out of windows, came to a stop. But perhaps this was helpful in that it made me concentrate on the sheet of paper in my typewriter. After about six months, I had a book of sorts ready for submission to any publisher who was prepared to look at it. Meanwhile, I had been through at least three jobs and had even been offered a post in the Jersey Civil Service, having successfully taken the local civil service exam—something I had done out of sheer boredom, as I had no intention of settling permanently on the island.

I had been keeping a diary of sorts and in some of the entries I had expressed my desire to get back to India, and my discontent at having to stay with relatives who were unsympathetic, not only to my feelings for India but also to my ambitions to become a writer. The diary fell into my uncle's hands. He read it, and was naturally upset. We had a row. I was contrite; but a few days later I packed my suitcases (all two of them) and stepped on to the ferry that was to take me to Southampton and then to London. Lesson one: don't leave your personal diaries lying around!

But perhaps it was all for the best, otherwise I might have hung around in Jersey for another year or two, to the detriment of my personal happiness and my writing ambitions.

I arrived in London in the middle of a thick yellow November fog—those were the days of the killer London fogs—and after a search found the Students' Hostel where I was given a cubicle to myself. But I did not stay there very long; the available food was awful. As soon as I got an office job—not too difficult in the 1950s—I rented an attic room in Belsize Park, the first of many bed-sitters that I was to live in during my three-year sojourn in London.

From Belsize Park I was to move to Haverstock Hill (close to Hampstead Heath), then to South London for a short time, and finally to Swiss Cottage. Most of my landladies were Jewish—refugees from persecution in pre-War Europe—and I too was a refugee of sorts, still very unsure of where I belonged. Was it England, the land of my father, or India, the land of my birth? But my father had also been born in India, had grown up and made a living there, visiting *his* father's land, England, only a couple of times during his life.

The link with Britain was tenuous, based on heredity rather than upbringing. It was more in the mind. It was a literary England I had been drawn to, not a physical England. And in fact, I took several exploratory walks around 'literary' London, visiting houses or streets where famous writers had once lived; in particular the East End and Dockland, for I had grown up on the novels and stories of Dickens, Smollett, Captain Marryat, and W.W. Jacobs. But I did not make many English friends. If they were a reserved race, I was even more reserved. Always shy, I waited for others to take the initiative. In India, people will take the initiative, they lose no time in getting to know you. Not so in England. They were too polite to look at you. And in that respect, I was more English than the English.

The gentleman who lived on the floor below me occasionally went so far as to greet me with the observation, 'Beastly weather, isn't it?'

And I would respond by saying, 'Oh, perfectly beastly,' and pass on.

How different it was when I bumped into a Gujarati boy, Praveen, who lived on the basement floor. He gave me a winning smile, and I remember saying, 'Oh, to be in Bombay now that winter's here,' and immediately we were friends.

He was only seventeen, a year or two younger than me, and he was studying at one of the polytechnics with a view to getting into the London School of Economics. At that time, most of the Indians in London were students, the great immigration rush was still a long way off, and racial antagonisms were directed more at the recently arrived West Indians than at Asians.

Praveen took me on the rounds of the coffee bars, then proliferating all over London, and introduced me to other students, among them a Vietnamese called Thanh, who cultivated my friendship because, as he said, 'I want to speak English.' When he discovered that my accent was very un-English (you could have called it Welsh with an Anglo-Indian interaction), he dropped me like a hot brick. He was very frank; he was not interested in friendship, he said, only in improving his accent. I heard later that he'd attached himself to a young journalist from up north, who spoke Broad Yorkshire.

Most evenings I remained in my room and worked on my novel. From being a journal it had become a first person narrative, and now I was turning it into fiction in the third person. The title had also undergone a few changes, but finally I settled on *The Room on the Roof*.

Into it, I put all the love and affection I felt for the friends I had left behind in Dehra. It was more than nostalgia, it was a recreation of the people, places and incidents of that last year in India. I did not want it to fade away. The riverbanks at Haridwar, the mango-groves of the Doon, the poinsettias and bougainvillaea, the games on the parade ground, the chaat shops near the Clock Tower, the summer heat, the monsoon downpours, romping naked in the rain, sitting on railway platforms, gnawing at a stick of sugar cane, listening to street cries... All this and more came crowding upon me as I sat writing before the gas fire in my little room.

When it grew very cold, I used an old overcoat given to me by Diana Athill, the junior partner at Andre Deutsch, who had promised to publish *The Room* if I rewrote it as a novel. Another who encouraged me was a BBC producer, Prudence Smith, who got me to give a couple of talks on Radio's Third Programme. I felt I was getting somewhere; and when I found myself confined to the Hampstead General Hospital for almost a month, with a mysterious disease that had affected the vision in my right eye, I used the left to catch up on my reading and to write a couple of short stories.

A nurse brought a tray of books around the ward every afternoon, and thanks to this courtesy, I was able to discover the delightful stories of William Saroyan and Denton Welch's sensitive first novel *Maiden Voyage*. Saroyan, a Pulitzer Prize winner for his play *The Time of Your Life*, was then very successful and popular. Denton's promising career had been cut short by a terrible accident. Out cycling on a country road, he had been knocked down by a speeding motorist. He had lived for several years, struggling against crippling injuries and almost completing his sensitive autobiography *A Voice in the Clouds*. He was thirty-one when he died. Towards the end, he could only work for three or four minutes at a time. Complications set in, and the left side of his heart started failing. Even then he made a terrific effort to finish his book. His friend Eric wrote—'Denton was upheld by the high courage which seemed somehow the fruit of his rare intelligence.'

The work of these writers, together with the bottle of Guinness I was given every day as a tonic (they had found me somewhat undernourished), meant that I walked out of the hospital with a spring in my step and a determination to succeed.

But Andre Deutsch was still dithering over my book. The firm was doing well, but he didn't like taking risks. No publisher likes losing money. And he wasn't going to make much out of my novel, a subjective and unsensational work.

But I resented his indecision. So I returned the small amount he'd paid me by way of an option, and demanded the return of my manuscript. Back came an apologetic letter and an advance (then £50) against publication.

Today, almost fifty years later, the firm of Andre Deutsch has gone, but *The Room on the Roof* is still in print, still making friends. This is not something that I gloat over, it only goes to show that books are unpredictable commodities, and that the most successful authors and publishers often fall by the wayside. Publishers go out of business, writers fade from the public mind. Even Saroyan is forgotten now. I'll be forgotten too, someday.

There were to be further delays before *The Room* was published, and I was back in India when it did come out. By then I'd almost forgotten about the book! But it picked up the John Llewellyn Rhys Prize, an award that also went to V.S. Naipaul a year later, for his first book. It was then worth only £50. There were no big sponsors in those days. It is now sponsored by a British newspaper and is worth £5,000. This was turned down last year by another Indian writer, who disagreed with the paper's policies.

Meanwhile, in London, there were other distractions. I loved stage musicals, and if I had a little money to spare I went to the theatre, taking in such productions as *Porgy and Bess*, *Paint Your Wagon*, *Pal Joey*, *Teahouse of the August Moon*, and the occasional review. And of course the annual presentation of *Peter Pan* at the Scala Theatre, not far from where I worked. I had grown up on Peter Pan, first read to me by my father in distant Jamnagar, and at school I had read Barrie's other plays and been charmed by them; but, like operetta, they had gone out of fashion and only the ageless Peter remained. 'Do you believe in fairies?' he asks in the play. And to save Tinker Bell from extinction, I clapped with the rest of the audience. But did I really believe in fairies? I looked for them in Kensington Gardens, where Peter Pan's statue stood, and found a few mothers pushing their perambulators, but no fairies. And I looked in Hyde Park, but found only courting couples. And I looked all over Leicester Square, but instead of fairies I found prostitutes soliciting business. As I was still looking for romance, I crept back to my room and my portable typewriter—I would have to create my own romance.

The small portable had been in the windows of a Jersey department store, and every time I passed the store I glanced at the window to see if the typewriter was still there. It seemed to be waiting for me to come in and take it away. I longed to buy it, partly because I had to type out the final drafts of my book, and also because it looked very dainty and attractive. It was definitely out to seduce me. Finally, with the help of a loan from Mr Bromley, a kindly senior clerk, I bought the machine. It cost only £12, but that was three month's wages at the time. It accompanied me to London, and then a couple of years later to India, giving me good service in Dehradun, New

Delhi, and then Mussoorie where it finally succumbed to the damp monsoon climate.

My worldly possessions had increased, not only by the typewriter, but also by a record player that I had bought second-hand from a Thai student. I had become an ardent fan of the Black singer Eartha Kitt and had bought all her records; but they were no good without a player until the Thai boy came to my rescue. Then the sensual, throaty voice of Eartha reverberated through the lodging house, bringing complaints from the landlady and the gentleman downstairs. I had to keep the volume low, which wasn't much fun.

I was also fond of the clarinet (turj) playing of an Indian musician, Master Ibrahim, and I had some of his recordings, which transported me back to the streets and bazaars of small-town India. Light, lilting and tuneful, I preferred this sort of flute music to the warblings of the more popular songsters.

Praveen liked gangster films and wanted me to accompany him to anything which featured Humphrey Bogart, James Cagney, George Raft and other tough guys. Praveen wanted to be a tough guy himself and often struck a Bogart-like pose, cigarette dangling from the side of his mouth. There was nothing tough about Praveen, who was really rather delicate, but his affectations were charming and risible.

One day he announced that he was returning to India for a few months, as his ailing mother was anxious to see him. He asked me to come along too, to give him company during the three week voyage. To do so, I would have to throw up my job, but I had already thrown up several jobs. They were simply stop-gaps until I could establish myself as a writer. I hadn't the slightest intention or ambition of being a senior clerk or even an executive for the firm in which I was working. The only problem in leaving England then was that I would have to leave my book in limbo, as there was still no guarantee that Deutsch would publish it. But it was time I went on to write other things; time to strike out on my own, to take a chance with India. The ships were full of British and Anglo-Indian families coming to England, to make a 'better future' for themselves. I would do the opposite, go into reverse, and make my future, for good or ill, in the land of my birth.

My passport was in order, and I had only to give a week's notice to my employers. I had saved up about £200, and of this £50 went on the cost of my passage, London to Bombay. Praveen and I boarded the *S.S. Balory*, a Polish liner with a reputation for running into trouble. We had no difficulty in securing berths in tourist class. Praveen had every intention of returning to England to complete his studies. My own intentions were very vague. I knew there would be no job for me in India, but I was quietly confident that I could make a living from writing, and that too in the English language.

The *Balory* lived up to its reputation. Some of the crew went missing at Gibraltar. A passenger fell overboard in the Red Sea. Lifeboats were lowered, but he could not be found.

Praveen fell in love with an Egyptian girl who disembarked at Aden. He followed her ashore, and I had to run after him and get him back to the ship. As we docked at Ballard Pier, a fire broke out in one of the holds, but by then we were safely ashore. Praveen was swamped by relatives who carried him off to the suburbs of Bombay. I made my way to Victoria Terminus and boarded the Dehradun Express. It was a slow passenger train, which went chugging through several states in the general direction of northern India. Two days and two nights later we crawled through the eastern Doon. It was early March. The mango trees were in blossom, the peacocks were calling, and Belsize Park was far away.

A LONG WALK FOR BINA

I

A leopard, lithe and sinewy, drank at the mountain stream, and then lay down on the grass to bask in the late February sunshine. Its tail twitched occasionally and the animal appeared to be sleeping. At the sound of distant voices, it raised its head to listen, then stood up and leapt lightly over the boulders in the stream, disappearing among the trees on the opposite bank.

A minute or two later, three children came walking down the forest path. They were a girl and two boys, and they were singing in their local dialect an old song they had learnt from their grandparents.

Five more miles to go!
We climb through rain and snow.
A river to cross...
A mountain to pass...
Now we've four more miles to go!

Their school satchels looked new, their clothes had been washed and pressed. Their loud and cheerful singing startled a spotted forktail. The bird left its favourite rock in the stream and flew down the dark ravine.

'Well, we have only three more miles to go,' said the bigger boy, Prakash, who had been this way hundreds of times. 'But first we have to cross the stream.'

He was a sturdy twelve-year-old with eyes like black currants and a mop of bushy hair that refused to settle down on his head. The girl and her small brother were taking this path for the first time.

'I'm feeling tired, Bina,' said the little boy.

Bina smiled at him, and Prakash said, 'Don't worry, Sonu, you'll get used to the walk. There's plenty of time.' He glanced at the old watch he'd been given by his grandfather. It needed constant winding. 'We can rest here for five or six minutes.'

They sat down on a smooth boulder and watched the clear water of the shallow stream tumbling downhill. Bina examined the old watch on Prakash's wrist. The glass was badly scratched and she could barely make out the figures on the dial. 'Are you sure it still gives the right time?' she asked.

'Well, it loses five minutes every day, so I put it ten minutes ahead at night. That means by morning it's quite accurate! Even our teacher, Mr Mani, asks me for the time. If he doesn't ask, I tell him! The clock in our classroom keeps stopping.'

They removed their shoes and let the cold mountain water run over their feet. Bina was the same age as Prakash. She had pink cheeks, soft brown eyes and hair that was just beginning to lose its natural curls. Hers was a gentle face, but a determined little chin showed that she could be a strong person. Sonu, her younger brother, was ten. He was a thin boy who had been sickly as a child but was now beginning to fill out. Although he did not look very athletic, he could run like the wind.

II

Bina had been going to school in her own village of Koli, on the other side of the mountain. But it had been a primary school, finishing at Class 5. Now, in order to study in Class 6, she would have to walk several miles every day to Nauti, where there was a high school going up to Class 8. It had been decided that Sonu would also shift to the new school, to give Bina company. Prakash, their neighbour in Koli, was already a pupil at the Nauti school. His mischievous nature, which sometimes got him into trouble, had resulted in his having to repeat a year.

But this didn't seem to bother him. 'What's the hurry?' he had told his indignant parents. 'You're not sending me to a foreign land when I finish school. And our cows aren't running away, are they?'

'You would prefer to look after the cows, wouldn't you?' asked Bina, as they got up to continue their walk.

'Oh, school's all right. Wait till you see old Mr Mani. He always gets our names mixed up, as well as the subjects he's supposed to be teaching. At our last lesson, instead of maths, he gave us a geography lesson!'

'More fun than maths,' said Bina.

'Yes, but there's a new teacher this year. She's very young they say, just out of college. I wonder what she'll be like.'

Bina walked faster, and Sonu had some trouble keeping up with them. She was excited about the new school and the prospect of different surroundings. She had seldom been outside her own village, with its small school and single ration shop. The day's routine never varied—helping her mother in the fields or with household tasks like fetching water from the spring or cutting grass and fodder for the cattle. Her father, who was a soldier, was away for nine months in the year, and Sonu was still too small for the heavier tasks.

As they neared Nauti Village, they were joined by other children coming from different directions. Even where there were no major roads, the mountains were full of little lanes and shortcuts. Like a game of snakes and ladders, these narrow paths zigzagged around the hills and villages, cutting through fields and crossing narrow ravines until they came together to form a fairly busy road along which mules, cattle and goats joined the throng.

Nauti was a fairly large village, and from here a broader but dustier road started for Tehri. There was a small bus, several trucks and (for part of the way) a road roller. The road hadn't been completed because the heavy diesel roller couldn't take the steep climb to Nauti. It stood on the roadside halfway up the road from Tehri.

Prakash knew almost everyone in the area, and exchanged greetings and gossip with other children as well as with muleteers, bus drivers, milkmen and labourers working on the road. He loved telling everyone the time, even if they weren't interested.

'It's nine o'clock,' he would announce, glancing at his wrist. 'Isn't your bus leaving today?'

'Off with you!' the bus driver would respond, 'I'll leave when I'm ready.'

As the children approached Nauti, the small flat school buildings came into view on the outskirts of the village, fringed by a line of long-leaved pines. A small crowd had assembled on the one playing field. Something unusual seemed to have happened. Prakash ran forward to see what it was all about. Bina and Sonu stood aside, waiting in a patch of sunlight near the boundary wall.

Prakash soon came running back to them. He was bubbling over with excitement.

'It's Mr Mani!' he gasped. 'He's disappeared! People are saying a leopard must have carried him off!'

III

Mr Mani wasn't really old. He was about fifty-five and was expected to retire soon. But for the children, most adults over forty seemed ancient! And Mr Mani had always been a bit absent-minded, even as a young man.

He had gone out for his early morning walk, saying he'd be back by eight o'clock, in time to have his breakfast and be ready for class. He wasn't married, but his sister and her husband stayed with him. When it was past nine o'clock his sister presumed he'd stopped at a neighbour's house for breakfast (he loved tucking into other people's breakfast) and that he had gone on to school from there. But when the school bell rang at ten o'clock, and everyone but Mr Mani was present, questions were asked and guesses were made.

No one had seen him return from his walk, and enquiries made in the village showed that he had not stopped at anyone's house. For Mr Mani to disappear was puzzling; for him to disappear without his breakfast was extraordinary.

Then a milkman returning from the next village said he had seen a leopard sitting on a rock on the outskirts of the pine forest. There had been talk of a cattle-killer in the valley, of leopards and other animals being displaced by the construction of a dam. But as yet no one had heard of a leopard attacking a man. Could Mr Mani have been its first victim? Someone found a strip of red cloth entangled in a blackberry bush and went running through the village showing it to everyone. Mr Mani had been known to wear red pyjamas. Surely he had been seized and eaten! But where were his remains? And why had he been in his pyjamas?

Meanwhile, Bina and Sonu and the rest of the children had followed their teachers into the school playground. Feeling a little lost, Bina looked around for Prakash. She found herself facing a dark, slender young woman wearing spectacles, who must have been in her early twenties—just a little too old to be another student. She had a kind, expressive face and she seemed a little concerned by all that had been happening.

Bina noticed that she had lovely hands; it was obvious that the new teacher hadn't milked cows or worked in the fields!

'You must be new here,' said the teacher, smiling at Bina. 'And is this your little brother?'

'Yes, we've come from Koli Village. We were at school there.'

'It's a long walk from Koli. You didn't see any leopards, did you? Well, I'm new too. Are you in the Class 6?'

'Sonu is in the third. I'm in the sixth.'

'Then I'm your new teacher. My name is Tania Ramola. Come along, let's see if we can settle down in our classroom.'

◆

Mr Mani turned up at twelve o'clock, wondering what all the fuss was about. No, he snapped, he had not been attacked by a leopard; and yes, he had lost his pyjamas, and would someone kindly return them to him?

'How did you lose your pyjamas, sir?' asked Prakash.

'They were blown off the washing line!' snapped Mr Mani.

After much questioning, Mr Mani admitted that he had gone further than he had intended, and that he had lost his way coming back. He had been a bit upset because the new teacher, a slip of a girl, had been given charge of the sixth, while he was still with the fifth, along with that troublesome boy Prakash, who kept on reminding him of the time! The headmaster had explained that as Mr Mani was due to retire at the end of the year, the school did not wish to burden him with a senior class. But Mr Mani looked upon the whole thing as a plot to get rid of him. He glowered at Miss Ramola whenever he passed her. And when she smiled back at him, he looked the other way!

Mr Mani had been getting even more absent-minded of late—putting on his shoes without his socks, wearing his homespun waistcoat inside out, mixing up people's names and of course, eating other people's lunches and dinners. His sister had made a mutton broth for the postmaster, who was down with 'flu', and had asked Mr Mani to take it over in a thermos. When the postmaster opened the thermos, he found only a few drops of broth at the bottom—Mr Mani had drunk the rest somewhere along the way.

When sometimes Mr Mani spoke of his coming retirement, it was to describe his plans for the small field he owned just behind the house. Right now, it was full of potatoes, which did not require much looking after; but he had plans for growing dahlias, roses, French beans, and other fruits and flowers.

The next time he visited Tehri, he promised himself, he would buy some dahlia bulbs and rose cuttings. The monsoon season would be a good time to put them down. And meanwhile, his potatoes were still flourishing.

IV

Bina enjoyed her first day at the new school. She felt at ease with Miss Ramola, as did most of the boys and girls in her class. Tania Ramola had been to distant towns such as Delhi and Lucknow—places they had only heard about—and it was said that she had a brother who was a pilot and flew planes all over the world. Perhaps he'd fly over Nauti some day!

Most of the children had of course seen planes flying

overhead, but none of them had seen a ship, and only a few had been on a train. Tehri mountain was far from the railway and hundreds of miles from the sea. But they all knew about the big dam that was being built at Tehri, just forty miles away.

Bina, Sonu and Prakash had company for part of the way home, but gradually the other children went off in different directions. Once they had crossed the stream, they were on their own again.

It was a steep climb all the way back to their village. Prakash had a supply of peanuts that he shared with Bina and Sonu, and at a small spring they quenched their thirst.

When they were less than a mile from home, they met a postman who had finished his round of the villages in the area and was now returning to Nauti.

'Don't waste time along the way,' he told them. 'Try to get home before dark.'

'What's the hurry?' asked Prakash, glancing at his watch. 'It's only five o'clock.'

'There's a leopard around. I saw it this morning, not far from the stream. No one is sure how it got here. So don't take any chances. Get home early.'

'So, there really is a leopard,' said Sonu.

They took his advice and walked faster, and Sonu forgot to complain about his aching feet.

They were home well before sunset.

There was a smell of cooking in the air and they were hungry.

'Cabbage and roti,' said Prakash gloomily. 'But I could eat anything today.' He stopped outside his small slate-roofed house, and Bina and Sonu waved goodbye and carried on across a couple of ploughed fields until they reached their small stone house.

'Stuffed tomatoes,' said Sonu, sniffing just outside the front door.

'And lemon pickle,' said Bina, who had helped cut, sun and salt the lemons a month previously.

Their mother was lighting the kitchen stove. They greeted her with great hugs and demands for an immediate dinner. She was a good cook who could make even the simplest of dishes taste delicious. Her favourite saying was 'Home-made bread is better than roast meat abroad,' and Bina and Sonu had to agree.

Electricity had yet to reach their village, and they took their meal by the light of a kerosene lamp. After the meal, Sonu settled down to do a little homework, while Bina stepped outside to look at the stars.

Across the fields, someone was playing a flute. 'It must be Prakash,' thought Bina. 'He always breaks off on the high notes.' But the flute music was simple and appealing, and she began singing softly to herself in the dark.

V

Mr Mani was having trouble with the porcupines. They had been getting into his garden at night and digging up and eating his potatoes. From his bedroom window—left open now that the mild April weather had arrived—he could listen to them enjoying the vegetables he had worked hard to grow. Scrunch, scrunch! *Katar, katar*, as their sharp teeth sliced through the largest and juiciest of potatoes. For Mr Mani it was as though they were biting through his own flesh. And the sound of them digging industriously as they rooted up those healthy, leafy plants made him tremble with rage and indignation. The unfairness of it all!

Yes, Mr Mani hated porcupines. He prayed for their destruction, their removal from the face of the earth. But, as his friends were quick to point out, 'The creator made porcupines too,' and in any case you could never see the creatures or catch them, they were completely nocturnal.

Mr Mani got out of bed every night, torch in one hand, a stout stick in the other but, as soon as he stepped into the garden, the crunching and digging stopped and he was greeted by the most infuriating of silences. He would grope around in the dark, swinging wildly with the stick, but not a single porcupine was to be seen or heard. As soon as he was back in bed, the sounds would start all over again—scrunch, scrunch, katar, katar...

Mr Mani came to his class tired and dishevelled, with rings under his eyes and a permanent frown on his face. It took some time for his pupils to discover the reason for his misery, but when they did, they felt sorry for their teacher and took to discussing ways and means of saving his potatoes from the porcupines.

It was Prakash who came up with the idea of a moat or water ditch. 'Porcupines don't like water,' he said knowledgeably.

'How do you know?' asked one of his friends.

'Throw water on one and see how it runs! They don't like getting their quills wet.'

There was no one who could disprove Prakash's theory, and the class fell in with the idea of building a moat, especially as it meant getting most of the day off.

'Anything to make Mr Mani happy,' said the headmaster, and the rest of the school watched with envy as the pupils of Class 5, armed with spades and shovels collected from all parts of the village, took up their positions around Mr Mani's potato field and began digging a ditch.

By evening, the moat was ready, but it was still dry and the porcupines got in again that night and had a great feast.

'At this rate,' said Mr Mani gloomily, 'there won't be any potatoes left to save.'

But the next day, Prakash and the other boys and girls managed to divert the water from a stream that flowed past the village.

They had the satisfaction of watching it flow gently into the ditch. Everyone went home in a good mood. By nightfall, the ditch had overflowed, the potato field was flooded, and Mr Mani found himself trapped inside his house. But Prakash and his friends had won the day. The porcupines stayed away that night!

◆

A month had passed, and wild violets, daisies and buttercups now sprinkled the hill slopes and, on her way to school, Bina gathered enough to make a little posy. The bunch of flowers fitted easily into an old ink well. Miss Ramola was delighted to find this little display in the middle of her desk.

'Who put these here?' she asked in surprise.

Bina kept quiet, and the rest of the class smiled secretively. After that, they took turns bringing flowers for the classroom.

On her long walks to school and home again, Bina became aware that April was the month of new leaves. The oak leaves were bright green above and silver beneath, and when they rippled in the breeze they were clouds of silvery green. The path was strewn with old leaves, dry and crackly. Sonu loved kicking them around.

Clouds of white butterflies floated across the stream. Sonu was chasing a butterfly when he stumbled over something dark and repulsive. He went sprawling on the grass. When he got to his feet, he looked down at the remains of a small animal.

'Bina! Prakash! Come quickly!' he shouted.

It was part of a sheep, killed some days earlier by a much larger animal.

'Only a leopard could have done this,' said Prakash.

'Let's get away, then,' said Sonu. 'It might still be around!'

'No, there's nothing left to eat. The leopard will be hunting elsewhere by now. Perhaps it's moved on to the next valley.'

'Still, I'm frightened,' said Sonu. 'There may be more leopards!'

Bina took him by the hand. 'Leopards don't attack humans!' she said.

'They will, if they get a taste for people!' insisted Prakash.

'Well, this one hasn't attacked any people as yet,' said Bina, although she couldn't be sure. Hadn't there been rumours of a leopard attacking some workers near the dam? But she did not want Sonu to feel afraid, so she did not mention the story. All she said was, 'It has probably come here because of all the activity near the dam.'

All the same, they hurried home. And for a few days, whenever they reached the stream, they crossed over very quickly, unwilling to linger too long at that lovely spot.

VI

A few days later, a school party was on its way to Tehri to see the new dam that was being built.

Miss Ramola had arranged to take her class, and Mr Mani, not wishing to be left out, insisted on taking his class as well. That meant there were about fifty boys and girls taking part in the outing. The little bus could only take thirty. A friendly truck driver agreed to take some children if they were prepared to sit on sacks of potatoes. And Prakash persuaded the owner of the diesel roller to turn it around and head it back to Tehri—with him and a couple of friends up on the driving seat.

Prakash's small group set off at sunrise, as they had to walk some distance in order to reach the stranded road roller. The bus left at 9.00 a.m. with Miss Ramola and her class, and Mr Mani and some of his pupils. The truck was to follow later.

It was Bina's first visit to a large town, and her first bus ride.

The sharp curves along the winding, downhill road made several children feel sick. The bus driver seemed to be in a tearing hurry. He took them along at a rolling, rollicking speed, which made Bina feel quite giddy. She rested her head on her arms and refused to look out of the window. Hairpin bends and cliff edges, pine forests and snow-capped peaks, all swept past her, but she felt too ill to want to look at anything. It was just as well—those sudden drops, hundreds of feet to the valley below, were quite frightening. Bina began to wish that she hadn't come—or that she had joined Prakash on the road roller instead!

Miss Ramola and Mr Mani didn't seem to notice the lurching and groaning of the old bus. They had made this journey many times. They were busy arguing about the advantages and disadvantages of large dams—an argument that was to continue on and off for much of the day.

Meanwhile, Prakash and his friends had reached the roller. The driver hadn't turned up, but they managed to reverse it and get it going in the direction of Tehri. They were soon overtaken by both bus and truck but kept moving along at a steady chug. Prakash spotted Bina at the window of the bus and waved cheerfully. She responded feebly.

Bina felt better when the road levelled out near Tehri. As they crossed an old bridge over the wide river, they were startled by a loud bang that made the bus shudder. A cloud of dust rose above the town.

'They're blasting the mountain,' said Miss Ramola.

'End of a mountain,' said Mr Mani, mournfully.

While they were drinking cups of tea at the bus stop, waiting for the potato truck and the road roller, Miss Ramola and Mr Mani continued their argument about the dam. Miss Ramola maintained that it would bring electric power and water for irrigation to large areas of the country, including the surrounding area. Mr Mani declared that it was a menace, as it was situated in an earthquake zone. There would be a terrible disaster if the dam burst! Bina found it all very confusing. And what about the animals in the area, she wondered, what would happen to them?

The argument was becoming quite heated when the potato truck arrived. There was no sign of the road roller, so it was decided that Mr Mani should wait for Prakash and his friends while Miss Ramola's group went ahead.

◆

Some eight or nine miles before Tehri, the road roller had broken down, and Prakash and his friends were forced to walk. They had not gone far, however, when a mule train came along—five or six mules that had been delivering sacks of grain in Nauti. A boy rode on the first mule, but the others had no load.

'Can you give us a ride to Tehri?' called Prakash.

'Make yourselves comfortable,' said the boy.

There were no saddles, only gunny sacks strapped on to the mules with rope. They had a rough but jolly ride down to the Tehri bus stop. None of them had ever ridden mules; but they had saved at least an hour on the road.

Looking around the bus stop for the rest of the party, they could find no one from their school. And Mr Mani, who should have been waiting for them, had vanished.

VII

Tania Ramola and her group had taken the steep road to the hill above Tehri. Half an hour's climbing brought them to a little plateau which overlooked the town, the river and the dam site.

The earthworks for the dam were only just coming up, but a wide tunnel had been bored through the mountain to divert the river into another channel. Down below, the old town was still spread out across the valley, and from a distance, it looked quite charming and picturesque.

'Will the whole town be swallowed up by the waters of the dam?' asked Bina.

'Yes, all of it,' said Miss Ramola. 'The clock tower and the old palace. The long bazaar, and the temples, the schools and the jail and hundreds of houses, for many miles up the valley. All those people will have to go—thousands of them! Of course, they'll be resettled elsewhere.'

'But the town's been here for hundreds of years,' said Bina. 'They were quite happy without the dam, weren't they?'

'I suppose they were. But the dam isn't just for them—it's for the millions who live further downstream, across the plains.'

'And it doesn't matter what happens to this place?'

'The local people will be given new homes somewhere else.' Miss Ramola found herself on the defensive and decided to change the subject. 'Everyone must be hungry. It's time we had our lunch.'

Bina kept quiet. She didn't think the local people would want to go away. And it was a good thing, she mused, that there was only a small stream and not a big river running past her village. To be uprooted like this—a town and hundreds of villages—and put down somewhere on the hot, dusty plains—seemed to her unbearable.

'Well, I'm glad I don't live in Tehri,' she said.

She did not know it, but all the animals and most of the birds had already left the area. The leopard had been among them.

◆

They walked through the colourful, crowded bazaar, where fruit sellers did business beside silversmiths, and pavement vendors sold everything from umbrellas to glass bangles. Sparrows attacked sacks of grain, monkeys made off with bananas, and stray cows and dogs rummaged in refuse bins, but nobody took any notice. Music blared from radios. Buses blew their horns. Sonu bought a whistle to add to the general din, but Miss Ramola told him to put it away. Bina had kept five rupees aside, and now she used it to buy a cotton headscarf for her mother.

As they were about to enter a small restaurant for a meal, they were joined by Prakash and his companions; but of Mr Mani there was still no sign.

'He must have met one of his relatives,' said Prakash. 'He has relatives everywhere.'

After a simple meal of rice and lentils, they walked the length of the bazaar without finding Mr Mani. At last, when they were about to give up the search, they saw him emerge from a by-lane, a large sack slung over his shoulder.

'Sir, where have you been?' asked Prakash. 'We have been looking for you everywhere.'

On Mr Mani's face was a look of triumph.

'Help me with this bag,' he said breathlessly.

'You've bought more potatoes, sir,' said Prakash.

'Not potatoes, boy. Dahlia bulbs!'

VIII

It was dark by the time they were all back in Nauti. Mr Mani had refused to be separated from his sack of dahlia bulbs, and had been forced to sit in the back of the truck with Prakash and most of the boys.

Bina did not feel so ill on the return journey. Going uphill was definitely better than going downhill! But by the time the bus reached Nauti it was too late for most of the children to walk back to the more distant villages. The boys were put up in different homes, while the girls were given beds in the school verandah.

The night was warm and still. Large moths fluttered around the single bulb that lit the verandah. Counting moths, Sonu soon fell asleep. But Bina stayed awake for some time, listening to the sounds of the night. A nightjar went tonk-tonk in the bushes, and somewhere in the forest an owl hooted softly. The sharp call of a barking deer travelled up the valley from the direction of the stream. Jackals kept howling. It seemed that there were more of them than ever before.

Bina was not the only one to hear the barking deer. The leopard, stretched full length on a rocky ledge, heard it too. The leopard raised its head and then got up slowly. The deer was its natural prey. But there weren't many left, and that was why the leopard, robbed of its forest by the dam, had taken to attacking dogs and cattle near the villages.

As the cry of the barking deer sounded nearer, the leopard left its lookout point and moved swiftly through the shadows towards the stream.

IX

In early June, the hills were dry and dusty, and forest fires broke out, destroying shrubs and trees, killing birds and small animals. The resin in the pines made these trees burn more fiercely, and the wind would take sparks from the trees and carry them into the dry grass and leaves, so that new fires would spring up before the old ones had died out. Fortunately, Bina's village was not in the pine belt; the fires did not reach it. But Nauti was surrounded by a fire that raged for three days, and the children had to stay away from school.

And then, towards the end of June, the monsoon rains arrived and there was an end to forest fires. The monsoon lasts three months and the lower Himalayas would be drenched in rain, mist and cloud for the next three months.

The first rain arrived while Bina, Prakash and Sonu were returning home from school. Those first few drops on the dusty path made them cry out with excitement. Then the rain grew heavier and a wonderful aroma rose from the earth.

'The best smell in the world!' exclaimed Bina.

Everything suddenly came to life. The grass, the crops, the trees, the birds. Even the leaves of the trees glistened and looked new.

That first wet weekend, Bina and Sonu helped their mother plant beans, maize and cucumbers. Sometimes, when the rain was very heavy, they had to run indoors. Otherwise they worked in the rain, the soft mud clinging to their bare legs.

Prakash now owned a dog, a black dog with one ear up and one ear down. The dog ran around getting in everyone's way, barking at cows, goats, hens and humans, without frightening any of them. Prakash said it was a very clever dog, but no one else seemed to think so. Prakash also said it would protect the village from the leopard, but others said the dog would be the first to be taken—he'd run straight into the jaws of Mr Spots!

In Nauti, Tania Ramola was trying to find a dry spot in the quarters she'd been given. It was an old building and the roof was leaking in several places. Mugs and buckets were scattered about the floor in order to catch the drips.

Mr Mani had dug up all his potatoes and presented them to the friends and neighbours who had given him lunches and dinners. He was having the time of his life, planting dahlia bulbs all over his garden.

'I'll have a field of many-coloured dahlias!' he announced. 'Just wait till the end of August!'

'Watch out for those porcupines,' warned his sister. 'They eat dahlia bulbs too!'

Mr Mani made an inspection tour of his moat, no longer

in flood, and found everything in good order. Prakash had done his job well.

◆

Now, when the children crossed the stream, they found that the water level had risen by about a foot. Small cascades had turned into waterfalls. Ferns had sprung up on the banks. Frogs chanted.

Prakash and his dog dashed across the stream. Bina and Sonu followed more cautiously. The current was much stronger now and the water was almost up to their knees. Once they had crossed the stream, they hurried along the path, anxious not to be caught in a sudden downpour.

By the time they reached school, each of them had two or three leeches clinging to their legs. They had to use salt to remove them. The leeches were the most troublesome part of the rainy season. Even the leopard did not like them. It could not lie in the long grass without getting leeches on its paws and face.

One day, when Bina, Prakash and Sonu were about to cross the stream they heard a low rumble, which grew louder every second. Looking up at the opposite hill, they saw several trees shudder, tilt outwards and begin to fall. Earth and rocks bulged out from the mountain, then came crashing down into the ravine.

'Landslide!' shouted Sonu.

'It's carried away the path,' said Bina. 'Don't go any further.'

There was a tremendous roar as more rocks, trees and bushes fell away and crashed down the hillside.

Prakash's dog, who had gone ahead, came running back, tail between his legs.

They remained rooted to the spot until the rocks had stopped falling and the dust had settled. Birds circled the area, calling wildly. A frightened barking deer ran past them.

'We can't go to school now,' said Prakash. 'There's no way around.'

They turned and trudged home through the gathering mist.

In Koli, Prakash's parents had heard the roar of the landslide. They were setting out in search of the children when they saw them emerge from the mist, waving cheerfully.

X

They had to miss school for another three days, and Bina was afraid they might not be able to take their final exams. Although Prakash was not really troubled at the thought of missing exams, he did not like feeling helpless just because their path had been swept away. So he explored the hillside until he found a goat-track going around the mountain. It joined up with another path near Nauti. This made their walk longer by a mile, but Bina did not mind. It was much cooler now that the rains were in full swing.

The only trouble with the new route was that it passed close to the leopard's lair. The animal had made this area its own since being forced to leave the dam area.

One day, Prakash's dog ran ahead of them barking furiously. Then he ran back whimpering.

'He's always running away from something,' observed Sonu. But a minute later he understood the reason for the dog's fear.

They rounded a bend and Sonu saw the leopard standing in their way. They were struck dumb—too terrified to run. It was a strong, sinewy creature. A low growl rose from its throat. It seemed ready to spring.

They stood perfectly still, afraid to move or say a word. And the leopard must have been equally surprised. It stared at them for a few seconds, then bounded across the path and into the oak forest.

Sonu was shaking. Bina could hear her heart hammering.

Prakash could only stammer: 'Did you see the way he sprang? Wasn't he beautiful?'

He forgot to look at his watch for the rest of the day.

A few days later, Sonu stopped and pointed to a large outcrop of rock on the next hill.

The leopard stood far above them, outlined against the sky. It looked strong, majestic. Standing beside it were two young cubs.

'Look at those little ones!' exclaimed Sonu.

'So it's a female, not a male,' said Prakash.

'That's why she was killing so often,' said Bina. 'She had to feed her cubs too.'

They remained still for several minutes, gazing up at the leopard and her cubs. The leopard family took no notice of them.

'She knows we are here,' said Prakash, 'but she doesn't care. She knows we won't harm them.'

'We are cubs too!' said Sonu.

'Yes,' said Bina. 'And there's still plenty of space for all of us. Even when the dam is ready there will still be room for leopards and humans.'

XI

The school exams were over. The rains were nearly over too. The landslide had been cleared, and Bina, Prakash and Sonu were once again crossing the stream.

There was a chill in the air, for it was the end of September.

Prakash had learnt to play the flute quite well, and he played on the way to school and then again on the way home. As a result, he did not look at his watch so often. One morning they found a small crowd in front of Mr Mani's house.

'What could have happened?' wondered Bina. 'I hope he hasn't got lost again.'

'Maybe he's sick,' said Sonu.

'Maybe it's the porcupines,' said Prakash.

But it was none of these things.

Mr Mani's first dahlia was in bloom, and half the village had turned up to look at it! It was a huge red double dahlia, so heavy that it had to be supported with sticks. No one had ever seen such a magnificent flower!

Mr Mani was a happy man. And his mood only improved over the coming week, as more and more dahlias flowered—crimson, yellow, purple, mauve, white—button dahlias, pom-pom dahlias, spotted dahlias, striped dahlias... Mr Mani had them all! A dahlia even turned up on Tania Ramola's desk—he got along quite well with her now—and another brightened up the headmaster's study.

A week later, on their way home—it was almost the last day of the school term—Bina, Prakash and Sonu talked about what they might do when they grew up.

'I think I'll become a teacher,' said Bina. 'I'll teach children about animals and birds, and trees and flowers.'

'Better than maths!' said Prakash.

'I'll be a pilot,' said Sonu. 'I want to fly a plane like Miss Ramola's brother.'

'And what about you, Prakash?' asked Bina.

Prakash just smiled and said, 'Maybe I'll be a flute player,' and he put the flute to his lips and played a sweet melody.

'Well, the world needs flute players too,' said Bina, as they fell into step beside him.

The leopard had been stalking a barking deer. She paused when she heard the flute and the voices of the children. Her own young ones were growing quickly, but the girl and the two boys did not look much older.

They had started singing their favourite song again.

Five more miles to go!
We climb through rain and snow,
A river to cross...
A mountain to pass...
Now we've four more miles to go!

The leopard waited until they had passed, before returning to the trail of the barking deer.

THE LAST TONGA RIDE

It was a warm spring day in Dehra, and the walls of the bungalow were aflame with flowering bougainvillaea. The papayas were ripening. The scent of sweetpeas drifted across the garden. Grandmother sat in an easy chair in a shady corner of the verandah, her knitting needles clicking away, her head nodding now and then. She was knitting a pullover for my father. 'Delhi has cold winters,' she had said; and although the winter was still eight months away, she had set to work on getting our woollens ready.

In the Kathiawar states, touched by the warm waters of the Arabian Sea, it had never been cold but Dehra lies at the foot of the first range of the Himalayas.

Grandmother's hair was white; her eyes were not very strong but her fingers moved quickly with the needles and the needles kept clicking all morning.

When Grandmother wasn't looking, I picked geranium leaves, crushed them between my fingers and pressed them to my nose.

I had been in Dehra with my grandmother for almost a month and I had not seen my father during this time. We had never before been separated for so long. He wrote to me every week, and sent me books and picture postcards; and I would walk to the end of the road to meet the postman as early as possible, to see if there was any mail for us.

We heard the jingle of tonga-bells at the gate, and a familiar horse-buggy came rattling up the drive.

'I'll see who's come,' I said, and ran down the verandah steps and across the garden.

It was Bansi Lal in his tonga. There were many tongas and tonga-drivers in Dehra but Bansi was my favourite driver. He was young and handsome and he always wore a clean white shirt and pyjamas. His pony, too, was bigger and faster than the other tonga ponies. Bansi didn't have a passenger, so I asked him, 'What have you come for, Bansi?'

'Your grandmother sent for me, *dost*.' He did not call me 'chota sahib' or 'baba', but 'dost' and this made me feel much more important. Not every small boy could boast of a tonga-driver for his friend!

'Where are you going, Granny?' I asked, after I had run back to the verandah.

'I'm going to the bank.'

'Can I come too?'

'Whatever for? What will you do in the bank?'

'Oh, I won't come inside, I'll sit in the tonga with Bansi.'

'Come along, then.'

We helped Grandmother into the back seat of the tonga, and then I joined Bansi in the driver's seat. He said something to his pony, and the pony set off at a brisk trot, out of the gate and down the road.

'Now, not too fast, Bansi,' said Grandmother, who didn't like anything that went too fast—tonga, motor car, train or bullock-cart.

'Fast?' said Bansi. 'Have no fear, Memsahib. This pony has never gone fast in its life. Even if a bomb went off behind us, we could go no faster. I have another pony, which I use for racing when customers are in a hurry. This pony is reserved for you, Memsahib.'

There was no other pony, but Grandmother did not know this, and was mollified by the assurance that she was riding in the slowest tonga in Dehra.

A ten-minute ride brought us to the bazaar. Grandmother's bank, the Allahabad Bank, stood near the clock tower. She was gone for about half an hour and during this period Bansi and I sauntered about in front of the shops. The pony had been left with some green stuff to munch.

'Do you have any money on you?' asked Bansi.

'Four annas,' I said.

'Just enough for two cups of tea,' said Bansi, putting his arm round my shoulders and guiding me towards a tea stall. The money passed from my palm to his.

'You can have tea, if you like,' I said. 'I'll have a lemonade.'

'So be it, friend. A tea and a lemonade, and be quick about it,' said Bansi to the boy in the stall, and presently the drinks were set before us and Bansi was making a sound rather like his pony when he drank, while I burped my way through some green, gaseous stuff that tasted more like soap than lemonade.

When Grandmother came out of the bank, she looked pensive, and did not talk much during the ride back to the house except to tell me to behave myself when I leaned over to pat the pony on its rump. After paying off Bansi, she marched straight indoors.

'When will you come again?' I asked Bansi.

'When my services are required, dost. I have to make a living, you know. But I tell you what, since we are friends, the next time I am passing this way after leaving a fare, I will jingle my bells at the gate and if you are free and would like a ride—a fast ride—you can join me. It won't cost you anything.

Just bring some money for a cup of tea.'

'All right—since we are friends,' I said.

'Since we are friends.'

And touching the pony very lightly with the handle of his whip, he sent the tonga rattling up the drive and out of the gate. I could hear Bansi singing as the pony cantered down the road.

Ayah was waiting for me in the bedroom, her hands resting on her broad hips—sure sign of an approaching storm.

'So you went off to the bazaar without telling me,' she said. (It wasn't enough that I had Grandmother's permission!) 'And all this time I've been waiting to give you your bath.'

'It's too late now, isn't it?' I asked hopefully.

'No, it isn't. There's still an hour left for lunch. Off with your clothes!'

While I undressed, Ayah berated me for keeping the company of tonga-drivers like Bansi. I think she was a little jealous.

'He is a rogue, that man. He drinks, gambles and smokes opium. He has TB and other terrible diseases. So don't you be too friendly with him, understand, baba?'

I nodded my head sagely but said nothing. I thought Ayah was exaggerating, as she always did about people, and besides, I had no intention of giving up free tonga rides.

As my father had told me, Dehra was a good place for trees, and Grandmother's house was surrounded by several kinds— peepul, seem, mango, jackfruit, papaya and an ancient banyan tree. Some of the trees had been planted by my father and grandfather.

'How old is the jackfruit tree?' I asked Grandmother.

'Now let me see,' said Grandmother, looking very thoughtful. 'I should remember the jackfruit tree. Oh yes, your grandfather put it down in 1927. It was during the rainy season. I remember, because it was your father's birthday and we celebrated it by planting a tree. 14 July 1927. Long before you were born!'

The banyan tree grew behind the house. Its spreading branches, which hung to the ground and took root again, formed a number of twisting passageways in which I liked to wander. The tree was older than the house, older than my grandparents, as old as Dehra. I could hide myself in its branches behind thick, green leaves and spy on the world below.

It was an enormous tree, about sixty feet high, and the first time I saw it I trembled with excitement because I had never seen such a marvellous tree before. I approached it slowly, even cautiously, as I wasn't sure the tree wanted my friendship. It looked as though it had many secrets. There were sounds and movement in the branches but I couldn't see who or what made the sounds.

The tree made the first move, the first overture of friendship. It allowed a leaf to fall.

The leaf brushed against my face as it floated down, but before it could reach the ground I caught and held it. I studied the leaf, running my fingers over its smooth, glossy texture. Then I put out my hand and touched the rough bark of the tree and this felt good to me. So I removed my shoes and socks as people do when they enter a holy place; and finding first a foothold and then a handhold on that broad trunk, I pulled myself up with the help of the tree's aerial roots.

As I climbed, it seemed as though someone was helping me; invisible hands, the hands of the spirit in the tree, touched me and helped me climb.

But although the tree wanted me, there were others who were disturbed and alarmed by my arrival. A pair of parrots suddenly shot out of a hole in the trunk and, with shrill cries, flew across the garden—flashes of green and red and gold. A squirrel looked out from behind a branch, saw me, and went scurrying away to inform his friends and relatives.

I climbed higher, looked up, and saw a red beak poised above my head. I shrank away, but the hornbill made no attempt to attack me. He was relaxing in his home, which was a great hole in the tree trunk. Only the bird's head and great beak were showing. He looked at me in a rather bored way, drowsily opening and shutting his eyes.

'So many creatures live here,' I said to myself. 'I hope none of them are dangerous!'

At that moment, the hornbill lunged at a passing cricket. Bill and tree trunk met with a loud and resonant 'Tonk!'

I was so startled that I nearly fell out of the tree. But it was a difficult tree to fall out of! It was full of places where one could sit or even lie down. So I moved away from the hornbill, crawled along a branch that had sent out supports, and so moved quite a distance from the main body of the tree. I left its cold, dark depths for an area penetrated by shafts of sunlight.

No one could see me. I lay flat on the broad branch hidden by a screen of leaves. People passed by on the road below. A sahib in a sun-helmet. His memsahib twirling a coloured silk sun-umbrella. Obviously she did not want to get too brown and be mistaken for a country-born person. Behind them, a pram wheeled along by a nanny.

Then there were a number of Indians; some in white dhotis, some in western clothes, some in loincloths. Some with baskets on their heads. Others with coolies to carry their baskets for them.

A cloud of dust, the blare of a horn, and down the road, like an out-of-condition dragon, came the latest Morris touring car. Then cyclists. Then a man with a basket of papayas balanced on his head. Following him, a man with a performing monkey.

This man rattled a little hand drum, and children followed the man and the monkey along the road. They stopped in the shade of a mango tree on the other side of the road. The little red monkey wore a frilled dress and a baby's bonnet. It danced for the children, while the man sang and played his drum.

The clip-clop of a tonga pony, and Bansi's tonga came rattling down the road. I called down to him and he reined in with a shout of surprise, and looked up into the branches of the banyan tree.

'What are you doing up there?' he cried.

'Hiding from Grandmother,' I said.

'And when are you coming for that ride?'

'On Tuesday afternoon,' I said.

'Why not today?'

'Ayah won't let me. But she has Tuesdays off.'

Bansi spat red paan juice across the road. 'Your ayah is jealous,' he said.

'I know,' I said. 'Women are always jealous, aren't they? I suppose it's because she doesn't have a tonga.'

'It's because she doesn't have a tonga-driver,' said Bansi, grinning up at me. 'Never mind. I'll come on Tuesday—that's the day after tomorrow, isn't it?'

I nodded down to him, and then started backing along my branch, because I could hear Ayah calling in the distance. Bansi leant forward and smacked his pony across the rump, and the tonga shot forward.

'What were you doing up there?' asked Ayah a little later.

'I was watching a snake cross the road,' I said. I knew she couldn't resist talking about snakes. There weren't as many in Dehra as there had been in Kathiawar and she was thrilled that I had seen one.

'Was it moving towards you or away from you?' she asked.

'It was going away.'

Ayah's face clouded over. 'That means poverty for the beholder,' she said gloomily.

Later, while scrubbing me down in the bathroom, she began to air all her prejudices, which included drunkards ('they die quickly anyway'), misers ('they get murdered sooner or later') and tonga-drivers ('they have all the vices').

'You are a very lucky boy,' she said suddenly, peering closely at my tummy.

'Why?' I asked. 'You just said I would be poor because I saw a snake going the wrong way.'

'Well, you won't be poor for long. You have a mole on your tummy, and that's very lucky. And there is one under your armpit, which means you will be famous. Do you have one on the neck? No, thank God! A mole on the neck is the sign of a murderer!'

'Do you have any moles?' I asked.

Ayah nodded seriously, and pulling her sleeve up to her shoulder, showed me a large mole high on her arm.

'What does that mean?' I asked.

'It means a life of great sadness,' said Ayah gloomily.

'Can I touch it?' I asked.

'Yes, touch it,' she said, and taking my hand, she placed it against the mole.

'It's a nice mole,' I said, wanting to make Ayah happy. 'Can I kiss it?'

'You can kiss it,' said Ayah.

I kissed her on the mole.

'That's nice,' she said.

Tuesday afternoon came at last, and as soon as Grandmother was asleep and Ayah had gone to the bazaar, I was at the gate, looking up and down the road for Bansi and his tonga. He was not long in coming. Before the tonga turned into the road, I could hear his voice, singing to the accompaniment of the carriage bells. He reached down, took my hand, and hoisted me on to the seat beside him. Then we went off down the road at a steady jogtrot. It was only when we reached the outskirts of the town that Bansi encouraged his pony to greater efforts. He rose in his seat, leaned forward and slapped the pony across the haunches. From a brisk trot we changed to a carefree canter. The tonga swayed from side to side. I clung to Bansi's free arm, while he grinned at me, his mouth red with paan juice.

'Where shall we go, dost?' he asked.

'Nowhere,' I said. 'Anywhere.'

'We'll go to the river,' said Bansi.

The 'river' was really a swift mountain stream that ran through the forests outside Dehra, joining the Ganga about fifteen miles away. It was almost dry during the winter and early summer; in flood during the monsoon.

The road out of Dehra was a gentle decline and soon we were rushing headlong through the tea gardens and eucalyptus forests, the pony's hoofs striking sparks off the metalled road, the carriage wheels groaning and creaking so loudly that I feared one of them would come off and that we would all be thrown into a ditch or into the small canal that ran beside the road. We swept through mango groves, through guava and litchi orchards, past broad-leaved sal and shisham trees. Once in the sal forest, Bansi turned the tonga on to a rough cart track, and we continued along it for about a furlong, until the road dipped down to the stream bed.

'Let us go straight into the water,' said Bansi. 'You and I and the pony!' And he drove the tonga straight into the middle of the stream, where the water came up to the pony's knees.

'I am not a great one for baths,' said Bansi, 'but the

pony needs one, and why should a horse smell sweeter than its owner?' Saying which, he flung off his clothes and jumped into the water.

'Better than bathing under a tap!' he cried, slapping himself on the chest and thighs. 'Come down, dost, and join me!'

After some hesitation I joined him, but had some difficulty in keeping on my feet in the fast current. I grabbed at the pony's tail, and hung on to it, while Bansi began sloshing water over the patient animal's back.

After this, Bansi led both me and the pony out of the stream and together we gave the carriage a good washing down. I'd had a free ride and Bansi got the services of a free helper for the long overdue spring cleaning of his tonga. After we had finished the job, he presented me with a packet of aam papad—a sticky toffee made from mango pulp—and for some time I tore at it as a dog tears at a hit of old leather. Then I felt drowsy and lay down on the brown, sun-warmed grass. Crickets and grasshoppers were telephoning each other from tree and bush and a pair of bluejays rolled, dived and swooped acrobatically overhead.

Bansi had no watch. He looked at the sun and said, 'It is past three. When will that ayah of yours be home? She is more frightening than your grandmother!'

'She comes at four.'

'Then we must hurry back. And don't tell her where we've been, or I'll never be able to come to your house again. Your grandmother's one of my best customers.'

'That means you'd be sorry if she died.'

'I would indeed, my friend.'

Bansi raced the tonga back to town. There was very little motor traffic in those days, and tongas and bullock-carts were far more numerous than they are today.

We were back five minutes before Ayah returned. Before Bansi left, he promised to take me for another ride the following week.

◆

The house in Dehra had to be sold. My father had not left any money; he had never realized that his health would deteriorate so rapidly from the malarial fevers that had grown in frequency; he was still planning for the future when he died. Now that my father had gone, Grandmother saw no point in staying on in India; there was nothing left in the bank and she needed money for our passages to England, so the house had to go. Dr Ghose, who had a thriving medical practice in Dehra, made her a reasonable offer, which she accepted.

Then things happened very quickly. Grandmother sold most of our belongings, because as she said, we wouldn't be able to cope with a lot of luggage. The *kabari*s came in droves, buying our crockery, furniture, carpets and clocks at throwaway prices. Grandmother hated parting with some of her possessions, such as the carved giltwood mirror, her walnut-wood armchair and her rosewood writing desk, but it was impossible to take them with us. They were carried away in a bullock-cart.

Ayah was very unhappy at first but cheered up when Grandmother got her a job with a tea-planter's family in Assam. It was arranged that she could stay with us until we left Dehra.

We left at the end of September, just as the monsoon clouds broke up, scattered, and were driven away by soft breezes from the Himalayas. There was no time to revisit the island where my father and I had planted our trees. And in the urgency and excitement of the preparations for our departure, I forgot to recover my small treasures from the hole in the banyan tree. It was only when we were in Bansi's tonga, on the way to the station, that I remembered my top, catapult and Iron Cross. Too late! To go back for them would mean missing the train.

'Hurry!' urged Grandmother nervously. 'We mustn't be late for the train, Bansi.'

Bansi flicked the reins and shouted to his pony, and for once in her life Grandmother submitted to being carried along the road at a brisk trot.

'It's five to nine,' she said, 'and the train leaves at nine.'

'Do not worry, Memsahib. I have been taking you to the station for fifteen years, and you have never missed a train!'

'No,' said Grandmother. 'And I don't suppose you'll ever take me to the station again, Bansi.'

'Times are changing, Memsahib. Do you know that there is now a taxi—a *motor car*—competing with the tongas of Dehra? You are lucky to be leaving. If you stay, you will see me starve to death!'

'We will all starve to death if we don't catch that train,' said Grandmother.

'Do not worry about the train, it never leaves on time, and no one expects it to. If it left at nine o' clock, everyone would miss it.'

Bansi was right. We arrived at the station at five minutes past nine, and rushed on to the platform, only to find that the train had not yet arrived.

The platform was crowded with people waiting to catch the same train or to meet people arriving on it. Ayah was there already, standing guard over a pile of miscellaneous luggage. We sat down on our boxes and became part of the platform life at an Indian railway station.

Moving among piles of bedding and luggage were sweating, cursing coolies; vendors of magazines, sweetmeats, tea and betel-leaf preparations; also stray dogs, stray people and sometimes a stray stationmaster. The cries of the vendors mixed with the general clamour of the station and the shunting of a steam engine in the yards. 'Tea, hot tea!' Sweets, papads, hot stuff, cold drinks, toothpowder, pictures of film stars, bananas, balloons, wooden toys, clay images of the gods. The platform had become a bazaar.

Ayah was giving me all sorts of warnings.

'Remember, baba, don't lean out of the window when the train is moving. There was that American boy who lost his head last year! And don't eat rubbish at every station between here and Bombay. And see that no strangers enter the compartment. Mr Wilkins was murdered *and* robbed last year!'

The station bell clanged, and in the distance there appeared a big, puffing steam engine, painted green and gold and black. A stray dog, with a lifetime's experience of trains, darted away across the railway lines. As the train came alongside the platform, doors opened, window shutters fell, faces appeared in the openings, and even before the train had come to a stop, people were trying to get in or out.

For a few moments there was chaos. The crowd surged backward and forward. No one could get out. No one could get in. A hundred people were leaving the train, two hundred were getting into it. No one wanted to give way.

The problem was solved by a man climbing out of a window. Others followed his example and the pressure at the doors eased and people started squeezing into their compartments.

Grandmother had taken the precaution of reserving berths in a first-class compartment, and assisted by Bansi and half a dozen coolies, we were soon inside with all our luggage. A whistle blasted and we were off! Bansi had to jump from the running train.

As the engine gathered speed, I ignored Ayah's advice and put my head out of the window to look back at the receding platform. Ayah and Bansi were standing on the platform, waving to me and I kept waving to them until the train rushed into the darkness and the bright lights of Dehra were swallowed up in the night. New lights, dim and flickering, came into existence as we passed small villages. The stars too were visible and I saw a shooting star streaking through the heavens.

I remembered something that Ayah had once told me, that stars are the spirits of good men, and I wondered if that shooting star was a sign from my father that he was aware of our departure and would be with us on our journey. And I remembered something else that Ayah had said—that if one wished on a shooting star, one's wish would be granted, provided of course that one thrust all five fingers into the mouth at the same time!

'What on earth are you doing?' asked Grandmother staring at me as I thrust my hand into my mouth.

'Making a wish,' I said.

'Oh,' said Grandmother.

She was preoccupied, and didn't ask me what I was wishing for; nor did I tell her.

OF RIVERS AND PILGRIMS

It's a funny thing, but long before I arrive at a place I can usually tell whether I am going to like it or not. Thus, while I was still some twenty miles from the district town of Pauri, I felt it was not going to be my sort of place, and sure enough it wasn't. A seedy, overgrown place, with too many government offices. On the other hand, while Nandprayag was still out of sight, I knew I was going to like it. And I did.

Perhaps it's something in the wind—emanations of an atmosphere—that carry to me well before I arrive at my destination. I can't really explain it, and of course it's silly to make judgements in advance. But it does happen.

Anyway, I felt I was nearing home as soon as the bus brought me into the cheerful roadside hamlet, a little way above the Nandakini River's confluence with the Alaknanda. A prayag is a meeting place of two rivers, hence Nandprayag, the place where these two mountain rivers meet. As there are many rivers in the Garhwal Himalayas, all linking up to join either the Ganga or the Yamuna, it follows that there are numerous prayags, in themselves places of pilgrimage as well as wayside halts en route to the higher Hindu shrines at Kedarnath and Badrinath. Nowhere else in these mountains are there so many temples, sacred streams, holy places, and holy men.

Some little way above Nandprayag's sleepy little bazaar is

a tourist rest house. It has a well-kept garden surrounded by fruit trees and is a little distance from the general hubbub of the main road.

Above it is the old pilgrim path. Just over twenty years ago, if you were a pilgrim intent on seeking salvation at the abode of the gods, you travelled on foot all the way from the plains, climbing about 200 miles in a couple of months. Those pilgrims had the time, the faith, and the endurance. Illness and misadventure often dogged their footsteps, but what was a little suffering if at the end of the day they arrived at the very portals of heaven?

Today's pilgrims may not be lacking in devotion, but most of them do expect to come home again.

Along the old pilgrim path are several handsome houses, set among mango trees and the fronds of the papaya and banana. Higher up the hill the pine forests commence, but down here it is almost subtropical. Nandprayag is only about 3,000 feet above sea level—a height at which the vegetation is usually lush, provided there is protection from the wind.

In one of these double-storeyed houses lives Devki Nandan, a scholar and recluse. He welcomes me into his home and plies me with food till I am close to bursting. He has a great love for this little corner of Garhwal and proudly shows me his collection of cuttings of articles about the area. One is from a travelogue by Sister Nivedita—an Englishwoman, Margaret Noble, who became an interpreter of Hinduism to the West. Visiting Nandprayag in 1928, she wrote:

> Nandprayag is a place that ought to be famous for its beauty and order. For a mile or two before reaching it we had noticed the superior character of the agriculture and even some careful gardening of fruits and vegetables. The peasantry also suddenly grew handsome, not unlike

> the Kashmiris. The town itself is new, rebuilt since the Gohna flood, and its temple stands far out across the fields on the shore of the Prayag. But in this short time a wonderful energy has been at work on architectural carvings and the little place is full of gem-like beauties. As the road crosses the river, I noticed two or three old Pathan tombs, the only traces of Mohammedanism that we had seen north of Srinagar in Garhwal.

Little has changed since Sister Nivedita's visit. There is still a small and thriving Pathan population in Nandprayag. In fact, when I called on Mr Nandan, he was in the act of sending out Eid greetings to his Muslim friends. Some of the old graves have disappeared in the debris from new road cuttings. As for the beautiful temple described by Sister Nivedita, I learned that it had been swept away by a mighty flood in 1970 when a cloudburst and subsequent landslide up-river resulted in great destruction downstream.

◆

Mr Nandan remembers the time when he walked to the small hill station of Pauri to join the old Messmore Christian Mission School, where so many famous sons of Garhwal received their early education. It took him four days marching to get to Pauri. Now it is just four hours by bus. It was only after the Chinese invasion of 1962 that there was a sudden spurt in road building in the northern hill districts. Before that, everyone walked and thought nothing of it.

Sitting on my own that same evening in the little garden of the rest house, I heard innumerable birds break into song. I did not see them, because the light was fading and the trees were dark; but I heard the rather melancholy call of the hill dove, the ascending trill of the koel, and much shrieking, whistling, and twittering that I could not assign to any particular species.

Now, once again, while I sit on the lawn surrounded by zinnias in full bloom, I am teased by that feeling of having been here before, on this lush hillside, among the pomegranates and oleanders. Is it some childhood memory asserting itself? As far as I know, I never travelled in these parts.

It's true that Nandprayag resembles some parts of the Doon Valley (where I grew up) before the Doon was submerged by a tidal wave of humanity. But in the Doon there is no great river running past your garden. Here there are two, and they are also part of this feeling of belonging.

◆

Presently, the room boy joins me for a chat on the lawn. He is in fact running the rest house in the absence of the manager. Wherever I go in India, the manager is usually absent; it seems to make no difference. A coach-load of pilgrims is due at any moment, but until they arrive the place is empty and only the birds can be heard.

The room boy's name is Janakpal and he tells me something about his village on the next mountain, where a marauding leopard has been carrying off goats and cattle. He doesn't think much of the laws protecting leopards—nothing can be done unless the animal becomes a man-eater.

A shower of rain descends on us, and so do the pilgrims. Janakpal leaves me to attend to his duties. But I am not left alone for long. A youngster with a cup of tea is the next to interview me. He wants me to take him to Mussoorie or New Delhi. He is fed up, he says, with washing dishes here.

'You are better off here,' I tell him sincerely. 'In Mussoorie you will have twice as many dishes to wash. In Delhi, ten times as many.'

'Yes, but there are cinemas and video and TV there,' he says, leaving me without an argument. Bird song may have charms for me, but not for the restless dishwasher in tranquil Nandprayag.

The rain stops and I go for a walk. The pilgrims keep to themselves, but the locals are always ready to talk. I remember a saying (and it may have originated in these hills), which goes: 'All men are my friends. I have only to meet them.' In Nandprayag, where life still moves at a leisurely and civilized pace, one is constantly meeting them.

A WAYSIDE TEA SHOP

The Jaunpur range in Garhwal is dry, brown and rocky. Water is hard to find, and green fields are to be seen only far down in the valley, near the Aglar or some smaller stream. Elsewhere only monsoon crops are grown.

I have walked five miles without finding a spring or even a shady spot along the sun-blistered path, and I am beginning to wonder if the only living creatures in the area are the big lizards, who slither about on the hot surface of the rocks and stare at me with unblinking eyes. Just as I am asking myself if it is better to be a lizard than a thirsty trekker, I round a bend and discover a small mountain oasis: a crooked little shack tucked away in a cleft of the hillside. Growing beside the shack is a single pine tree, humming softly in the faint breeze that drifts across the mountains.

When one tree suddenly appears in this way, lonely and dignified in the midst of a vast treeless silence, it can be more beautiful than a forest.

There is no glamour about the shack, a loose stone structure with a tin roof held down by stones. But it is a tea shop, one of those little pockets of pioneering mankind that spring up in the mountain wilderness to serve the weary traveller. Go where you will in Garhwal, you will always find a tea shop to sustain you just when you feel you have reached the end of your tether.

The shopkeeper, Megh Chand, a man of indeterminate

age—the cold dry winds from the snows have crinkled his face like a walnut but his teeth are sound and his eyes are clear—greets me as a long-lost friend, although we are meeting for the first time.

'Do you live here alone?' I ask.

'Sometimes I am alone,' he says. 'My family is down in the village, looking after the fields. It is quite far—six miles. So I go home once a week, and then my son comes up to look after the shop.'

Megh Chand tells me that he has been starved of good conversation. 'Next year,' he says, sitting down on the steps of his shop, 'the government will be widening the road, and then the buses will be able to stop here. For many years, I have depended on the mule drivers, but they do not have much money to spend. Once the buses come, I will have many customers. Then, perhaps I will be able to afford to go to Delhi for my operation.'

'What operation?'

'Oh, a *rasoli*—a growth—in my stomach. Sometimes, the pain is very bad. I went to the hospital in Mussoorie, but they told me I would have to go to Delhi for an operation. Whenever someone is seriously ill, they say, "Go to Delhi!" Does the whole world go to Delhi to get treated? My uncle was told to go to Delhi for an operation. He went from one hospital to another until his money was finished, and then he came back to the village and died within a week. So maybe, I won't go for the operation. The money is needed here. Once the buses come, I will have to keep sweets and biscuits and other things, and a boy to help me cook a few meals. All I can offer you today is a bun. It was made in Delhi, I am told.'

'I'd rather have your lassi than a Delhi bun,' I protest. 'But where do you get your water?' I ask.

'Come, I will show you,' he says, and takes me round to the back of the shack and through an unexpected gap in the hillside.

It gives me a breathtaking glimpse of snow-clad mountains striding into the sky. It is cool and shady on the northern face of the hill, and here, issuing from a rock, is a trickle of water. Yellow primulas grow in clusters along the edges of a damp, dripping rock face. The water collects in a small stone trough.

'There is no other *cheshma* (spring) along this road,' he says, 'and the buses can't go down into the ravine, unless they fall into it. So, they have to stop here!' He is triumphant.

We return to the shopfront, where a milkman has just arrived with a container of milk. He too sits down for rest, refreshment and conversation. Next year, if the road is ready (and it is a big if, because with hill roads, you can never be sure), and if he can afford the fare (an even bigger if), the milkman will be able to use the bus. But there are some who will walk anyway, because they have always been walking. Or ride mules because they have been doing it all their lives.

Still, when the road comes, time will take on new dimensions for Megh Chand. Even in remote mountain areas, buses must keep to some sort of schedule, and Megh Chand will have to be sure that his pot is on the boil and be on the lookout for arrivals and departures. He will be better off than he is today but he is aware that prosperity has its pitfalls. He remembers a cousin, who opened a small grocery shop on a new bus route near Devprayag. One day, some young hooligans got off the bus, looted his shop and left him battered and bruised. It was the sort of thing that had never happened before...

It is time for me to be on my way. 'I hope the road will soon be ready,' I say in parting. 'I hope you will make lots of money. I hope you will be able to go to Delhi for your operation. And I hope I can come this way again.'

Hill-man or plains-man, we have only our hopes to keep us going.

FLOWERS ON THE GANGA

Flowers floating down the river: yellow and scarlet cannas, roses, jasmine, hibiscus. They are placed in boats made of broad leaves; then consigned to the waters with a prayer. The strong current carries them swiftly downstream, and they bob about on the water for fifty, sometimes a hundred yards, before being submerged in the river. Do the prayers sink too, or do they reach the hearts of the many gods who have favoured Haridwar—'Door of Hari or Vishnu'—these several hundred years?

The river issues through a gorge in the mountains with a low booming sound. It does not break its banks until it levels out over the flat plains of Uttar Pradesh and Bihar. It is fast and muddy; but this does not deter thousands from descending the steps of the bathing ghats and plunging into the cold, snow-fed waters, for the Ganga washes away all sin.

Says the Mahabharata: 'To repeat her name brings purity, to see her secures prosperity, to bathe in or drink her waters saves seven generations of our race... There is no place of pilgrimage like the Ganga, no god like Vishnu...'

Almost every child knows the story of how the Ganga descended from heaven. For 1,000 years, King Sagara's great-grandson stood with his hands upraised, praying for water to enable him to make the funeral oblations for the ashes of his 60,000 grand-uncles. Almost all the gods were involved in the affair. Finally, when the waters of the Ganga were released from heaven and the river reached the earth, the prince mounted his chariot and drove towards the spot where the ashes of his kinsmen lay. Wherever he went, the Ganga meekly followed. Gods, nymphs, demons, giants, sages and great snakes, all joined in the procession, and as the river followed in the footsteps of the prince, the whole multitude of created beings bathed in her sacred waters and washed away their sins.

♦

The multitude that followed the prince could be the same multitude that throngs the riverfront today. I see no one who is not delighted at the prospect of entering the water. '*Ganga-Mai ki jai*!' The cry goes up mostly from the older people who have come here, many for the last time, to make their peace with the gods. Only their ashes will make the trip again.

It is a big crowd, although this is just an ordinary day of the week and not an occasion of special religious significance. Every day is a good day for bathing in the Ganga. But at the time of major festivals, such as Baisakhi, elaborate arrangements have to be made, including special trains and police reinforcements, to take care of the great influx of pilgrims. The number of pilgrims at the Baisakhi festival usually exceeds one lakh. During the Kumbh Mela, held every twelve years, there may be as many as five lakh present on the great bathing-day. This is ten times the normal population of Haridwar. And when one realizes that the town is bounded by the steep Siwalik Hills on one side and the river on the other, and has one main street leading to the riverfront, it is not surprising that in the past, large numbers of people were crushed to death in stampedes at the narrow entrance to the ghats.

Fortunately the main street is a broad and pleasant thoroughfare. Although Haridwar is ancient (the Chinese traveller, Hsuen Tsang, records a visit made in the seventh century), little remains of earlier settlements. There are only two or three old temples. But the present buildings—tall, balconied structures put up in the 1920s and 1930s—have a certain old-world charm. Even new houses follow the same pattern. This isn't conscious planning; it is simply that Haridwar is a conservative town and clings to its traditions.

Most of the buildings along the road are *dharamshala*s. The road is shaded by tall old peepul and banyan trees. In some places the trees reach right across the street to touch the roofs of the three-storey buildings on the other side. At several places, I find small peepul saplings growing out of the walls of buildings. One young peepul has sprung up in the fork of an adult kadam tree and will probably throttle it in time. No one fells the sacred peepul. It is better that walls should crumble or kadam trees wither. At least this guarantees the survival of one species of tree in a world where forests are rapidly disappearing.

Peepuls live for hundreds of years, and Haridwar's oldest trees must have been here before the present town reached maturity. Some will be as old as the eleventh-century Maya-devi temple, which is probably the oldest temple in Haridwar. On a sultry day, there can be no pleasanter spot than the shade of a peepul tree; the leaves are perpetually in motion, even when there is no breeze, and spin around in currents of their own making. It is no wonder that the man who plants a peepul is blessed by generations of Hindus to come.

While I stand beneath one of these giant trees, a devout and elderly man approaches with a watering-can and, circling the tree, waters the soil around the base of the trunk. I move out of the way of his sprinkler watching the ritual in some surprise. It has been raining steadily for some days, and the tree should have no need of water.

'Why are you watering it?' I ask.

'Why does one water anything?' asks the old man. 'So that it may grow and flourish, of course.'

'But it's been raining almost every day.'

'Rain is something else,' he says. 'I am not responsible for the rain; this is water from the Ganga, and I have fetched it myself. That makes a lot of difference.'

I cannot argue. He waters the tree with love; and his love for the tree, as much as rainwater or river water, is what makes it flourish.

Leaving the main street, I enter the bazaar.

The Haridwar Bazaar is a long, narrow, winding street, probably the oldest part of the town, and free of all vehicular traffic. The road is no more than four yards wide. The small shops are spilling over with sweets, pickles, bead-necklaces, sacred texts, ritual designs, festival images and pictures of the gods in vibrant technicolour. There is something in these naive, gaudy prints that acts as a transformer, making the more abstract Hindu philosophies comprehensible to anxious farmer or acquisitive taxi driver.

The bazaar winds and turns back upon itself, and eventually I find myself back at the riverfront, gazing out across the river at the forested foothills. Few of the pilgrims on the bathing-steps can realize that sometimes at night a tiger stands on the opposite bank watching the bright illuminations of the temples, or that elephants listen to the rumbling of the trains bringing pilgrims to Haridwar from all parts of India.

It is evening now, and there are fewer people at the ghats. Most of the bathers are family people—farmers and small shopkeepers with their women, children and aged parents. One does not see many students or young people in Western clothes.

Haridwar is old-fashioned and so are most of the people who come here.

◆

Charity, too, is old-fashioned, and Haridwar thrives on charity: donations to the temples and alms to the beggars, mendicants and itinerant ash-smeared sadhus. The beggars do not follow one about as in the larger cities. They are confident of receiving coins from the pilgrims who pass by on the steps to the river. They simply sit there, occasionally calling out, but preferring to listen to the music of small coins dropping into brass begging-bowls.

Close by are the money changers, squatting before baskets which are brimming over with small change. In the rest of the country there is a shortage of small coins, and shopkeepers often decline to provide change; but in Haridwar, you can change any number of notes for small coins. You are going to leave all the coins here anyway, when you distribute them along the riverfront.

As the pilgrims leave the ghats, the joy of having accomplished their mission bursts forth in songs of praise: 'Henceforth no more pain, no more sickness; all will be well in future; Ganga-mai ki jai.'

More flowers are being sold; and now the leaf-boats are lit by diyas. The little boats are swept away, sometimes travelling a considerable distance before being upset by submerged rocks or inquisitive fish.

I, too, send an offering downstream, but my boat sails beneath the legs of a late bather, and disappears beneath the pilgrim. My boat is lost; but my rose petals still float on the Ganga.

It has been said that if the Ganga ran dry, all life in India would cease. There is no likelihood of that happening. The Ganga is overgenerous, as the annual floods will testify. So long as the Himalayas stand, this river will flow to the sea and millions will come to immerse their bodies, their sins and their prayers in its sacred waters.

THE GIRL ON THE TRAIN

I had the train compartment to myself up to Rohana, then a girl got in. The couple who saw her off were probably her parents; they seemed very anxious about her comfort, and the woman gave the girl detailed instructions as to where to keep her things, when not to lean out of windows, and how to avoid speaking to strangers.

They called their goodbyes and the train pulled out of the station. As I was going blind at the time, my eyes sensitive only to light and darkness, I was unable to tell what the girl looked like; but I knew she wore slippers from the way they slapped against her heels.

It would take me some time to discover something about her looks, and perhaps I never would. But I liked the sound of her voice, and even the sound of her slippers.

'Are you going all the way to Dehra?' I asked.

I must have been sitting in a dark corner, because my voice startled her. She gave a little exclamation and said, 'I didn't know anyone else was here.'

Well, it often happens that people with good eyesight fail to see what is right in front of them. They have too much to take in, I suppose. Whereas people who cannot see (or see very little) have to take in only the essentials, whatever registers most tellingly on their remaining senses.

'I didn't see you either,' I said. 'But I heard you come in.'

I wondered if I would be able to prevent her from discovering that I was blind. Provided I keep to my seat, I thought, it shouldn't be too difficult.

The girl said, 'I'm getting off at Saharanpur. My aunt is meeting me there.'

'Then I had better not get too familiar,' I replied. 'Aunts are usually formidable creatures.'

'Where are you going?' she asked.

'To Dehra, and then to Mussoorie.'

'Oh, how lucky you are. I wish I were going to Mussoorie. I love the hills. Especially in October.'

'Yes, this is the best time,' I said, calling on my memories. 'The hills are covered with wild dahlias, the sun is delicious, and at night you can sit in front of a logfire and drink a little brandy. Most of the tourists have gone, and the roads are quiet and almost deserted. Yes, October is the best time.'

She was silent. I wondered if my words had touched her, or whether she thought me a romantic fool. Then I made a mistake.

'What is it like outside?' I asked.

She seemed to find nothing strange in the question. Had she noticed already that I could not see? But her next question removed my doubts.

'Why don't you look out of the window?' she asked.

I moved easily along the berth and felt for the window ledge. The window was open, and I faced it, making a pretence of studying the landscape. I heard the panting of the engine, the rumble of the wheels, and, in my mind's eye, I could see telegraph posts flashing by.

'Have you noticed,' I ventured, 'that the trees seem to be moving while we seem to be standing still?'

'That always happens,' she said. 'Do you see any animals?'

'No,' I answered quite confidently. I knew that there were hardly any animals left in the forests near Dehra.

I turned from the window and faced the girl, and for a while we sat in silence.

'You have an interesting face,' I remarked. I was becoming quite daring, but it was a safe remark. Few girls can resist flattery. She laughed pleasantly—a clear ringing laugh.

'It's nice to be told I have an interesting face. I'm tired of people telling me I have a pretty face.'

Oh, so you do have a pretty face, thought I; and aloud I said, 'Well, an interesting face can also be pretty.'

'You are a very gallant young man,' she said, 'but why are you so serious?'

I thought, then, I would try to laugh for her, but the thought of laughter only made me feel troubled and lonely.

'We'll soon be at your station,' I said.

'Thank goodness it's a short journey. I can't bear to sit in a train for more than two or three hours.'

Yet I was prepared to sit there for almost any length of time, just to listen to her talking. Her voice had the sparkle of a mountain stream. As soon as she left the train, she would forget our brief encounter; but it would stay with me for the rest of the journey, and for some time after.

The engine's whistle shrieked, the carriage wheels changed their sound and rhythm, the girl got up and began to collect her things. I wondered if she wore her hair in a bun, or if it was plaited; perhaps it was hanging loose over her shoulders, or was it cut very short?

The train drew slowly into the station. Outside, there was the shouting of porters and vendors and a high-pitched female voice near the carriage door; that voice must have belonged to the girl's aunt.

'Goodbye,' the girl said.

She was standing very close to me, so close that the perfume from her hair was tantalizing. I wanted to raise my hand and touch her hair, but she moved away. Only the scent of perfume still lingered where she had stood.

There was some confusion in the doorway. A man, getting into the compartment, stammered an apology. Then the door banged, and the world was shut out again. I returned to my berth. The guard blew his whistle and we moved off. Once again, I had a game to play and a new fellow traveller.

The train gathered speed, the wheels took up their song, the carriage groaned and shook. I found the window and sat in front of it, staring into the daylight that was darkness for me.

So many things were happening outside the window: it could be a fascinating game, guessing what went on out there.

The man who had entered the compartment broke into my reverie.

'You must be disappointed,' he said. 'I'm not nearly as attractive a travelling companion as the one who just left.'

'She was an interesting girl,' I said. 'Can you tell me—did she keep her hair long or short?'

'I don't remember,' he said, sounding puzzled. 'It was her eyes I noticed, not her hair. She had beautiful eyes—but they were of no use to her. She was completely blind. Didn't you notice?'

THE WOMAN ON PLATFORM NO. 8

It was my second year at boarding school, and I was sitting on platform no. 8 at Ambala station, waiting for the northern-bound train. I think I was about twelve at the time. My parents considered me old enough to travel alone, and I had arrived by bus at Ambala early in the evening; now there was a wait till midnight before my train arrived. Most of the time I had been pacing up and down the platform, browsing through the bookstall, or feeding broken biscuits to stray dogs; trains came and went, the platform would be quiet for a while and then, when a train arrived, it would be an inferno of heaving, shouting, agitated human bodies. As the carriage doors opened, a tide of people would sweep down upon the nervous little ticket collector at the gate; and every time this happened I would be caught in the rush and swept outside the station. Now tired of this game and of ambling about the platform, I sat down on my suitcase and gazed dismally across the railway tracks.

Trolleys rolled past me, and I was conscious of the cries of the various vendors—the men who sold curds and lemon, the sweetmeat seller, the newspaper boy—but I had lost interest in all that was going on along the busy platform, and continued to stare across the railway tracks, feeling bored and a little lonely.

'Are you all alone, my son?' asked a soft voice close behind me.

I looked up and saw a woman standing near me. She was leaning over, and I saw a pale face and dark, kind eyes. She wore no jewels, and was dressed very simply in a white sari.

'Yes, I am going to school,' I said, and stood up respectfully. She seemed poor, but there was a dignity about her that commanded respect.

'I have been watching you for some time,' she said. 'Didn't your parents come to see you off?'

'I don't live here,' I said. 'I had to change trains. Anyway, I can travel alone.'

'I am sure you can,' she said, and I liked her for saying that, and I also liked her for the simplicity of her dress, and for her deep, soft voice and the serenity of her face.

'Tell me, what is your name?' she asked.

'Arun,' I said.

'And how long do you have to wait for your train?'

'About an hour, I think. It comes at twelve o'clock.'

'Then come with me and have something to eat.'

I was going to refuse, out of shyness and suspicion, but she took me by the hand, and then I felt it would be silly to pull my hand away. She told a coolie to look after my suitcase, and then she led me away down the platform. Her hand was gentle, and she held mine neither too firmly nor too lightly. I looked up at her again. She was not young. And she was not old. She must have been over thirty, but had she been fifty, I think she would have looked much the same.

She took me into the station dining room, ordered tea and samosas and jalebis, and at once I began to thaw and take a new interest in this kind woman. The strange encounter had little effect on my appetite. I was a hungry schoolboy, and I ate as much as I could in as polite a manner as possible. She took obvious pleasure in watching me eat, and I think it was the food that strengthened the bond between us and cemented our friendship, for under the influence of the tea and sweets I began to talk quite freely, and told her about my school, my friends, my likes and dislikes. She questioned me quietly from time to time, but preferred listening; she drew me out very well, and I had soon forgotten that we were strangers. But she did not ask me about my family or where I lived, and I did not ask her where she lived. I accepted her for what she had been to me—a quiet, kind and gentle woman who gave sweets to a lonely boy on a railway platform...

After about half an hour we left the dining room and began walking back along the platform. An engine was shunting up and down beside platform no. 8, and as it approached, a boy leapt off the platform and ran across the rails, taking a shortcut to the next platform. He was at a safe distance from the engine, but as he leapt across the rails, the woman clutched my arm. Her fingers dug into my flesh, and I winced with pain. I caught her fingers and looked up at her, and I saw a spasm of pain and fear and sadness pass across her face. She watched the boy as he climbed the platform, and it was not until he had disappeared in the crowd that she relaxed her hold on my arm. She smiled at me reassuringly and took my hand again, but her fingers trembled against mine.

'He was all right,' I said, feeling that it was she who needed reassurance.

She smiled gratefully at me and pressed my hand. We walked together in silence until we reached the place where I had left my suitcase. One of my school fellows, Satish, a boy of about my age, had turned up with his mother.

'Hello, Arun!' he called. 'The train's coming in late, as usual. Did you know we have a new headmaster this year?'

We shook hands, and then he turned to his mother and

said: 'This is Arun, Mother. He is one of my friends, and the best bowler in the class.'

'I am glad to know that,' said his mother, a large imposing woman who wore spectacles. She looked at the woman who held my hand and said: 'And I suppose you're Arun's mother?'

I opened my mouth to make some explanation, but before I could say anything the woman replied: 'Yes, I am Arun's mother.'

I was unable to speak a word. I looked quickly up at the woman, but she did not appear to be at all embarrassed, and was smiling at Satish's mother.

Satish's mother said, 'It's such a nuisance having to wait for the train right in the middle of the night. But one can't let the child wait here alone. Anything can happen to a boy at a big station like this—there are so many suspicious characters hanging about. These days one has to be very careful of strangers.'

'Arun can travel alone, though,' said the woman beside me, and somehow I felt grateful to her for saying that. I had already forgiven her for lying; and besides, I had taken an instinctive dislike to Satish's mother.

'Well, be very careful, Arun,' said Satish's mother looking sternly at me through her spectacles. 'Be very careful when your mother is not with you. And never talk to strangers!'

I looked from Satish's mother to the woman who had given me tea and sweets, and back at Satish's mother.

'I like strangers,' I said.

Satish's mother definitely staggered a little, as obviously she was not used to being contradicted by small boys. 'There you are, you see! If you don't watch over them all the time, they'll walk straight into trouble. Always listen to what your mother tells you,' she said, wagging a fat little finger at me. 'And never, never talk to strangers.'

I glared resentfully at her, and moved closer to the woman who had befriended me. Satish was standing behind his mother, grinning at me, and delighting in my clash with his mother. Apparently he was on my side.

The station bell clanged, and the people who had till now been squatting resignedly on the platform began bustling about.

'Here it comes!' shouted Satish, as the engine whistle shrieked and the front lights played over the rails.

The train moved slowly into the station, the engine hissing and sending out waves of steam. As it came to a stop, Satish jumped on the footboard of a lighted compartment and shouted, 'Come on, Arun, this one's empty!' and I picked up my suitcase and made a dash for the open door.

We placed ourselves at the open windows, and the two women stood outside on the platform, talking up to us. Satish's mother did most of the talking.

'Now don't jump on and off moving trains as you did just now,' she said. 'And don't stick your heads out of the windows, and don't eat any rubbish on the way.' She allowed me to share the benefit of her advice, as she probably didn't think my 'mother' a very capable person. She handed Satish a bag of fruit, a cricket bat and a big box of chocolates, and told him to share the food with me. Then she stood back from the window to watch how my 'mother' behaved.

I was smarting under the patronizing tone of Satish's mother, who obviously thought mine a very poor family; and I did not intend giving the other woman away. I let her take my hand in hers, but I could think of nothing to say. I was conscious of Satish's mother staring at us with hard, beady eyes, and I found myself hating her with a firm, unreasoning hate. The guard walked up the platform, blowing his whistle for the train to leave. I looked straight into the eyes of the woman who held my hand, and she smiled in a gentle, understanding way. I leaned out of the window then, and put my lips to her cheek and kissed her.

The carriage jolted forward, and she drew her hand away.

'Goodbye, Mother!' said Satish, as the train began to move slowly out of the station. Satish and his mother waved to each other.

'Goodbye,' I said to the other woman, 'goodbye—Mother…' I didn't wave or shout, but sat still in front of the window, gazing at the woman on the platform. Satish's mother was talking to her, but she didn't appear to be listening; she was looking at me as the train took me away. She stood there on the busy platform, a pale sweet woman in white, and I watched her until she was lost in the milling crowd.

THE NIGHT TRAIN AT DEOLI

When I was at college I used to spend my summer vacations in Dehra, at my grandmother's place. I would leave the plains early in May and return late in July. Deoli was a small station about thirty miles from Dehra. It marked the beginning of the heavy jungles of the Indian terai.

The train would reach Deoli at about five in the morning when the station would be dimly lit with electric bulbs and oil lamps, and the jungle across the railway tracks would just be visible in the faint light of dawn. Deoli had only one platform, an office for the stationmaster and a waiting room. The platform boasted a tea stall, a fruit vendor and a few stray dogs; not much else, because the train stopped there for only ten minutes before rushing on into the forests.

Why it stopped at Deoli, I don't know. Nothing ever happened there. Nobody got off the train and nobody got on. There were never any coolies on the platform. But the train would halt there a full ten minutes and then a bell would sound, the guard would blow his whistle, and presently Deoli would be left behind and forgotten.

I used to wonder what happened in Deoli behind the station walls. I always felt sorry for that lonely little platform and for the place that nobody wanted to visit. I decided that one day I would get off the train at Deoli and spend the day there just to please the town.

The Night Train at Deoli

I was eighteen, visiting my grandmother, and the night train stopped at Deoli. A girl came down the platform selling baskets.

It was a cold morning and the girl had a shawl thrown across her shoulders. Her feet were bare and her clothes were old but she was a young girl, walking gracefully and with dignity.

When she came to my window, she stopped. She saw that I was looking at her intently, but at first she pretended not to notice. She had pale skin, set off by shiny black hair and dark, troubled eyes. And then those eyes, searching and eloquent, met mine.

She stood by my window for some time and neither of us said anything. But when she moved on, I found myself leaving my seat and going to the carriage door. I stood waiting on the platform looking the other way. I walked across to the tea stall. A kettle was boiling over a small fire, but the owner of the stall was busy serving tea somewhere on the train. The girl followed me behind the stall.

'Do you want to buy a basket?' she asked. 'They are very strong, made of the finest cane…'

'No,' I said, 'I don't want a basket.'

We stood looking at each other for what seemed a very long time, and she said, 'Are you sure you don't want a basket?'

'All right, give me one,' I said, and took the one on top and gave her a rupee, hardly daring to touch her fingers.

As she was about to speak, the guard blew his whistle. She said something, but it was lost in the clanging of the bell and the hissing of the engine. I had to run back to my compartment. The carriage shuddered and jolted forward.

I watched her as the platform slipped away. She was alone on the platform and she did not move, but she was looking at me and smiling. I watched her until the signal box came in the way and then the jungle hid the station. But I could still see her standing there alone…

I stayed awake for the rest of the journey. I could not rid my mind of the picture of the girl's face and her dark, smouldering eyes.

But when I reached Dehra the incident became blurred and distant, for there were other things to occupy my mind. It was only when I was making the return journey, two months later, that I remembered the girl.

I was looking out for her as the train drew into the station, and I felt an unexpected thrill when I saw her walking up the platform. I sprang off the footboard and waved to her.

When she saw me, she smiled. She was pleased that I remembered her. I was pleased that she remembered me. We were both pleased and it was almost like a meeting of old friends.

She did not go down the length of the train selling baskets but came straight to the tea stall. Her dark eyes were suddenly filled with light. We said nothing for some time but we couldn't have been more eloquent.

I felt the impulse to put her on the train there and then, and take her away with me. I could not bear the thought of having to watch her recede into the distance of Deoli station. I took the baskets from her hand and put them down on the ground. She put out her hand for one of them, but I caught her hand and held it.

'I have to go to Delhi,' I said.

She nodded. 'I do not have to go anywhere.'

The guard blew his whistle for the train to leave, and how I hated the guard for doing that.

'I will come again,' I said. 'Will you be here?'

She nodded again and, as she nodded, the bell clanged and the train slid forward. I had to wrench my hand away from the girl and run for the moving train.

This time I did not forget her. She was with me for the

remainder of the journey and for long after. All that year she was a bright, living thing. And when the college term finished, I packed in haste and left for Dehra earlier than usual. My grandmother would be pleased at my eagerness to see her.

I was nervous and anxious as the train drew into Deoli, because I was wondering what I should say to the girl and what I should do. I was determined that I wouldn't stand helplessly before her, hardly able to speak or do anything about my feelings.

The train came to Deoli, and I looked up and down the platform but I could not see the girl anywhere.

I opened the door and stepped off the footboard. I was deeply disappointed and overcome by a sense of foreboding. I felt I had to do something and so I ran up to the stationmaster and said, 'Do you know the girl who used to sell baskets here?'

'No, I don't,' said the stationmaster. 'And you'd better get on the train if you don't want to be left behind.'

But I paced up and down the platform and stared over the railings at the station yard. All I saw was a mango tree and a dusty road leading into the jungle. Where did the road go? The train was moving out of the station and I had to run up the platform and jump for the door of my compartment. Then, as the train gathered speed and rushed through the forests, I sat brooding in front of the window.

What could I do about finding a girl I had seen only twice, who had hardly spoken to me, and about whom I knew nothing—absolutely nothing—but for whom I felt a tenderness and responsibility that I had never felt before?

My grandmother was not pleased with my visit after all, because I didn't stay at her place more than a couple of weeks. I felt restless and ill at ease. So I took the train back to the plains, meaning to ask further questions of the stationmaster at Deoli.

But at Deoli there was a new stationmaster. The previous man had been transferred to another post within the past week. The new man didn't know anything about the girl who sold baskets. I found the owner of the tea stall, a small, shrivelled-up man, wearing greasy clothes, and asked him if he knew anything about the girl with the baskets.

'Yes, there was such a girl here. I remember quite well,' he said. 'But she has stopped coming now.'

'Why?' I asked. 'What happened to her?'

'How should I know?' said the man. 'She was nothing to me.'

And once again I had to run for the train.

As Deoli platform receded, I decided that one day I would have to break journey there, spend a day in the town, make enquiries, and find the girl who had stolen my heart with nothing but a look from her dark, impatient eyes.

With this thought I consoled myself throughout my last term in college. I went to Dehra again in the summer and when, in the early hours of the morning, the night train drew into Deoli station, I looked up and down the platform for signs of the girl, knowing I wouldn't find her but hoping just the same.

Somehow, I couldn't bring myself to break journey at Deoli and spend a day there. (If it was all fiction or a film, I reflected, I would have got down and cleared up the mystery and reached a suitable ending to the whole thing.) I think I was afraid to do this.

I was afraid of discovering what really happened to the girl. Perhaps she was no longer in Deoli, perhaps she was married, perhaps she had fallen ill...

In the past few years I have passed through Deoli many times, and I always look out of the carriage window half expecting to see the same unchanged face smiling up at me. I wonder what happens in Deoli, behind the station walls. But I will never break my journey there. I prefer to keep hoping and dreaming and looking out of the window up and down that lonely platform, waiting for the girl with the baskets.

I never break my journey at Deoli but I pass through as often as I can.

RUNNING AWAY

Once, during my schooldays, my friend Daljit and I decided to run away. The main reason for running away was not to get back to the bazaars of Dehra, which we both missed, but to reach my uncle's ship in Jamnagar, Gujarat.

Uncle Jim was one of my father's cousins. He used to write to me off and on throughout the years. His letters came in envelopes that bore colourful stamps of different countries. They came from Valparaiso, San Diego, San Francisco, Buenos Aires, Dar-es-Salaam, Mombasa, Freetown, Singapore, Bombay, Marseilles, London…these were some of the places where Uncle Jim's ship called. He was seldom on the same route, and seemed to move leisurely across the oceans of the earth, calling at ports that had only the most romantic associations for me, for I had already read Stevenson, Captain Marryat, some Conrad and W.W. Jacobs.

In his letters, Uncle Jim often spoke of my joining him at sea—'When you are a little older, Ruskin.'

But I felt I was old enough then. I was sick of school and sick of my guardian. But that was not all. I was in love with the world. I wanted to see the world, every corner of it, the places I had read about in books—the junks and sampans of Hong Kong, the palm-fringed lagoons of the Indies, the streets of London, the beautiful ebony-skinned people of Africa, the bright birds and exotic plants of the Amazon...

When Uncle Jim's last letter had arrived, telling me that his ship would call at Jamnagar towards the end of the month, I felt a deep thrill of anticipation. Here was my chance at last! True, Uncle Jim had said nothing about my joining him, but he was not to know that I was seriously considering it.

It was not simply a question of walking out of school and taking a quick ride down to the docks. Jamnagar, on the west coast, was at least eight hundred miles from my school. I doubt if I would have made the attempt if Daljit had not agreed to come too. It isn't much fun running away on your own. It is even worse if you have a companion who is full of enthusiasm at the beginning and then backs out at the last moment. This leaves one feeling defeated and crushed. Daljit was not that kind of companion. He meant the things he said. About a month earlier, when I had told him of my uncle's ship and my wish to get to it, he had said, without a moment's hesitation: 'I'm coming too!' Daljit lived impulsively. Sometimes, he made mistakes. But he never went halfway and stopped. Someone had to stop him; otherwise he did whatever it was he set out to do.

Running away from school! It is not to be recommended to everyone. Parents and teachers would disapprove. Or would they, deep down in their hearts? Everyone has wanted to run away at some time in his life: if not from a bad school or an unhappy home then from something equally unpleasant. Running away seems to be in the best of traditions. Huck Finn did it. So did Master Copperfield and Oliver Twist. So did Kim. Various enterprising young men have run away to sea. Most great men have run away from school at some stage in their lives; and if they haven't, then perhaps it is something they should have done.

Anyway, Daljit and I ran away from school, and we did it quite successfully too, up to a point. But then, all this happened in India, which, though it forms only two per cent of the world's land mass, has fifteen per cent of its population, and so it is an easy place to hide in, or be lost in, or disappear in, and never be seen or heard of again!

Not that we intended to disappear. We were headed for a particular place, and as soon as I took my first step into the unknown, that first step on the slippery pine needles below the school, I knew quite definitely that I wasn't running away from anything, but that I was running *towards* something. Call it a dream, if you like. I was running towards a dream.

A narrow path ran downhill from the school to the road to Dehra, and we followed it until it levelled out, running parallel with the small stream that rumbled down the mountainside. We followed the stream for a mile, walking swiftly and silently, until we met the bridle path which was little more than a mule track going steeply down the last hills to the valley.

The going was easy. We knew the road well. And by the time we reached the last foothills, it was beginning to rain, not heavily, but as a light, thin drizzle.

We took shelter in a small dhaba on the outskirts of a village. The *dhabawallah* was sleeping, and his dog, a mangy pariah with only one ear, sniffed at us in a friendly way instead of chasing us off the premises. We sat down on an old bench and watched the sun rising over the distant mountains.

This is something I have always remembered. Not because it was a more beautiful sunrise than on any other day, but because the special importance of that morning made me look at everything in a new way, hence the details still stand out in my memory.

As the sky grew lighter, the pines and deodars stood out

clearly, and the birds came to life. A black bird started it all with a low, mellow call, and then the thrushes began chattering in the bushes. A barbet shrieked monotonously at the top of a spruce tree, and, as the sky grew lighter still, a flock of bright green parrots flew low over the trees.

The drizzle continued and there was a bright crimson glow in the east. And then, quite suddenly, the sun shot through a gap in the clouds, and the lush green monsoon grass sprang into relief. Both Daljit and I were wonderstruck. Never before had we been up so early. Hundreds of spiderwebs—which were spun in trees and bushes and on the grass, where they would not normally have been noticed—were now clearly visible, spangled with gold and silver raindrops. The strong silk threads of the webs held the light rain and the sun, making each drop of water look like a tiny jewel.

A great wild dahlia, its scarlet flowers drenched and heavy, sprawled over the hillside and an emerald-green grasshopper reclined on a petal, stretching its legs in the sunshine.

The dhabawallah was now up. His dog, emboldened by his master's presence, began to bark at us. The man lit a charcoal fire in a *choolah*, and put on it a kettle of water to boil.

'Would you like to eat something?' he asked conversationally in Hindi.

'No, just tea for us,' I said.

He placed two brass tumblers on a table.

'The milk hasn't yet been delivered,' he said. 'You're very early.'

'We'll take the tea without milk,' said Daljit. 'But give us lots of sugar.'

'Sugar is costly these days. But because you are schoolboys and need more, you can help yourselves.'

'Oh, we are not schoolboys,' I said hurriedly.

'Not at all,' added Daljit.

'We are just tourists,' I lied unconvincingly.

'We have to catch the early train at Dehra,' offered Daljit.

'But there's no train before ten o'clock,' said the puzzled dhabawallah.

'It is the ten o'clock train we are catching!' said Daljit smartly. 'Do you think we will be down in time?'

'Oh yes, there's plenty of time…'

The dhabawallah poured out steaming hot tea into the tumblers and placed the sugar bowl in front of us. 'At first I thought you were schoolboys,' he said with a laugh. 'I thought you were running away.'

Daljit almost gave us away by laughing nervously.

'What made you think that?' he asked.

'Oh, I've been here many years,' the dhabawallah replied, gesturing towards the small clearing in which his little wooden stall stood, almost like a trading outpost in a wild country. 'Schoolboys always pass this way when they're running away!'

'Do many run away?' I asked. I felt a little downcast at the thought that Daljit and I were not the first to embark on such an adventure.

'Not many. Just two or three every year. They get as far as the railway station in Dehra and there they're caught!'

'It is silly of them to get caught,' said Daljit disgustedly.

'Are they always caught?' I asked.

'Always! I give them a glass of tea on their way down, and I give them a glass of tea on their way up, when they are returning with their teachers.'

'Well, you won't be seeing *us* again,' said Daljit, ignoring the warning look that I gave him.

'Ah, but you aren't schoolboys!' said the shopkeeper, beaming at us. 'And you aren't running away!'

We paid for our tea and hurried on down the path. The parrots flew over again, screeching loudly, and settled in a litchi tree. The sun was warmer now, and, as the altitude decreased, the temperature and humidity rose and we could almost smell the heat of the plains rising to meet us.

The hills levelled out into the rolling countryside, patterned with fields. Rice had been planted out, and the sugarcane was waist-high.

The path had become quite slushy. Removing our shoes and wrapping them in newspaper, we walked barefoot in the soft mud. All these little out-of-routine acts simply added to our excitement and thrill, making everything quite unforgettable for life.

'It's about three miles into Dehra,' I said. 'We must go round the town. By now, everyone in school will be up and they'll have found out we've gone!'

'We must avoid the Dehra station then,' said Daljit.

'We'll walk to the next station, Raiwala. Then we'll hop onto the first train that comes along.'

'How far must we walk?'

'About ten miles.'

'Ten miles!' Daljit looked dismayed. 'It'll take us all day!'

'Well, we can't stop here nor can we wander about in Dehra, neither can we enter the station. We have to keep on walking.'

'Alright, we'll keep on walking. I suppose the beginning of an adventure is always the most difficult part.'

Soon, the fields were giving way to jungle. But there were still some fields of sugarcane stretching away from the railway lines.

'How much further do we have to walk?' asked Daljit impatiently. 'Is Raiwala in the middle of the jungle?'

'Yes, I think it is. We've covered about four miles I suppose. Six to go! It's funny how some miles seem longer than others.

It depends on what one is thinking about, I suppose. If our thoughts are pleasant, the miles are not so long.'

'Then let's keep thinking pleasant thoughts. Isn't there a short cut anywhere? You've been in these forests before.'

'We'll take the fire-path through the jungle. It'll save us three or four miles. But we'll have to swim or wade across a small river. The rains have only just started, so the water shouldn't be too swift or deep.'

Heavy forests have paths cut through them at various places to prevent forest fires from spreading easily. These paths are not used much by people, since they don't lead anywhere in particular, but they are frequently used by the larger animals.

We had gone about a mile along the path when we heard the sound of rushing water. The path emerged from the forest of sal trees and stopped on the banks of the small river I had mentioned earlier. The main bridge across the river stood on the main road, about three miles downstream.

'It isn't more than waist-deep anywhere,' I said. 'But the water is swift and the stones are slippery.'

We removed our clothes and tied everything into two bundles which we carried on our heads. Daljit was a well-built boy, strong in the arms and thighs. I was slimmer. But I had quick reflexes.

The stones were quite slippery underfoot, and we stumbled, hindering rather than helping each other. We stopped midstream, waist-deep, hesitating about going any further for fear of being swept off our feet.

'I can hardly stand,' said Daljit.

'It shouldn't get worse,' I said hopefully. But the current was strong, and I felt very wobbly at the knees.

Daljit tried to move forward, but slipped and went over backwards into the water, bringing me down too. He began kicking and thrashing about in fear, but eventually, using me as a support, he came up spouting water like a whale.

When we found we were not being swept away, we stopped struggling and cautiously made our way to the opposite bank, but we had been thrust about twenty yards downstream.

We rested on warm sand while a hot sun beat down on us. Daljit sucked at a cut in his hand. But we were soon up and walking again, hungry now, and munching biscuits.

'We haven't far to go,' I said.

'I don't want to think about it,' said Daljit.

We shuffled along the forest path, tired but not discouraged.

Soon we were on the main road again, and there were fields and villages on either side. A cool breeze came in across the open plain, blowing down from the hills. In the fields, there was a gentle swaying movement as the wind stirred the sugarcane. Then, the breeze came down the road, and dust began to swirl and eddy around us. Out of the dust, behind us, came the rumble of cart wheels.

'Ho! Heeyah! Heeyah!' shouted the driver of the cart. The bullocks snorted and came lumbering through the dust. We moved to the side of the road.

'Are you going to Raiwala?' called Daljit. 'Can you take us with you?'

'Climb up!' said the man, and we ran through the dust and clambered on to the back of the moving cart.

The cart lurched forward and rattled and bumped so much that we had to cling to its sides to avoid falling off. It smelt of grass and mint and cow-dung cakes. The driver had a red cloth tied round his head, and wore a tight vest and a dhoti. He was smoking a *beedi* and yelling at his bullocks, and he seemed to have forgotten our presence. We were too busy clinging to the sides of the cart to bother about making conversation. Before long we were involved in the traffic of Raiwala—a small but busy market town. We jumped off the bullock cart and walked beside it.

'Should we offer him any money?' I asked.

'No. He will be offended. He is not a taxi driver.'

'Alright, we'll just say thank you.'

We called out our thanks to the cart driver, but he didn't look back. He appeared to be talking to his bullocks.

'I'm hungry,' declared Daljit. 'We haven't had a proper meal since last night.'

'Then let's eat,' I said. 'Come on, Daljit.'

We walked through the small Raiwala bazaar, looking in at the tea and sweet shops until we found the cheapest-looking dhaba. A servant-boy brought us rice and dal and Daljit ordered an ounce of ghee, which he poured over the curry. The meal cost us two rupees but we could have as much dal as we wanted, and between us we finished four bowls of it.

'We'll rest at the station,' I said as we emerged from the dhaba. 'We'll buy second-class tickets, and rest in the first-class waiting room. No one will check on us. We look first class, don't we?'

'Not after that walk through the jungle,' replied Daljit.

But we did occupy the best waiting room and Daljit made himself comfortable in an armchair. A train eventually came chugging in, and we were soon on our way to Delhi.

It didn't take us long to find a hotel once we got off at the Old Delhi Railway Station. It was called the Great Oriental Hotel, and was just behind the police station in Chandni Chowk. It didn't pretend to be even a third-class hotel, and for five rupees we were given a small back room that had a window overlooking the godown of an Afghan spice merchant. The powerful smell of asafoetida came up from the courtyard below.

We were tired and hot, so we tossed our belongings down on the floor and took turns at the bathroom tap. Then we stretched out on the only cot in the room and slept through the afternoon, oblivious to the noises from the street, the attentions of the insect population in the hotel mattress, and the creaking of the old fan overhead.

It was late evening when we woke up, and we were hungry again. Daljit opened the door and shouted. Presently, a servant-boy appeared.

'Bring us tea, toast, two big omelettes and a bottle of tomato sauce,' ordered Daljit with a confidence that I wished I had.

The omelettes, when they arrived twenty minutes later, were tiny. Both had obviously been made from one egg. The sauce had been diluted with water, and the toasts were burnt. The salt was damp, and we had to prise open the salt-cellar to get to it. The pepper, however, came out in a generous rush and made up the major portion of the meal. As our hunger had not been satisfied by this poor fare, we ordered eggs again, boiled eggs this time. No matter how tiny, they would have to be whole.

'Let's go out,' said Daljit after we had eaten the eggs. 'It's stuffy in here.'

'I'm still sleepy,' I said.

'Then I'll go out for a little while. I may go to the gurdwara.'

'Alright, but don't get lost.'

Drowsy, I closed my eyes, but the sounds of the city's unceasing traffic came through the window. Ships and distant ports seemed very far away but so did hills and mountain streams.

I fell asleep and woke up only when Daljit returned.

'I've solved our problem!' he said, beaming. 'We won't bother with the train. I met a truck driver, and he has offered to take us as far as Jaipur. That's more than a hundred miles. It will be quite safe to take a train from Jaipur.'

'When can your friend take us?'

'The truck leaves at four o'clock in the morning.'

'There's no rest for the wicked,' I said. 'Still, the less time we lose the better. It's Wednesday, and my uncle's ship might sail on Saturday. What will we have to pay?'

'Nothing. It's a free ride. The driver is a Sikh, and I persuaded him that we are related to each other through the marriage of my brother-in-law to his sister-in-law's niece!'

◆

At four the next morning, we made our way towards the Red Fort, its ramparts dark against the starry sky. The streets that had been teeming with so much life the previous evening were now deserted. The street lamps shed lonely pools of light on the pavements. The occasional car glided silently past, but it belonged to another kind of world altogether.

Near the Fort, we found a couple of dhabas that were still open. They did business with the truck drivers who slept by day and drove by night.

Our driver, a tall, bearded Sikh, loomed over us out of the darkness. He had a companion with him, also a Sikh, who was still in his underwear.

'You can get in at the back,' said the driver in his thick Punjabi, which I could follow sufficiently well. 'We'll be off in a few minutes.'

The truck was parked beneath a peepul tree. We pulled ourselves up into the back of the open truck, only to find our way barred by what seemed at first to be a prehistoric monster.

The monster snorted once, stamped heavily on the boards, and sent us tumbling backwards.

'Bhaiyyaji!' cried Daljit to the driver. 'There's some kind of animal in here!'

'Don't worry, it's only Mumta,' said our friend.

'But what is it doing in here?'

'She is going with us. I am taking her to the market in Jaipur. So get in with her boys, and make yourselves comfortable.'

There was now enough light to enable us to take a closer look at our travelling companion. She was a full-grown buffalo from the Punjab.

'An excellent buffalo,' said Daljit, who appeared to be familiar with the finer points of these animals. 'Notice her blue eyes!'

'I didn't know buffaloes had blue eyes,' I said dryly.

'Only the best buffaloes have them,' said Daljit. 'Blue-eyed buffaloes give more milk than brown-eyed ones.'

Fortunately for us, the Sardarji started the truck and an early morning breeze, blowing across the river, swept away some of the stench so typical of buffaloes.

We were soon out of Delhi and bowling along at a fair speed on the road to Jaipur. The recent rain had waterlogged low-lying areas, and the herons, cranes and snipe were numerous. Fields and trees were alive with strange, beautiful birds: the long-tailed king crow, blue jays and weaver birds, and occasionally the great white-headed kite, which is said to be Garuda, Lord Vishnu's famous steed.

As we travelled further into Rajasthan, the peacocks became more numerous; so did the camels loping along the side of the road in straight, orderly lines. And, as the vegetation grew less and the desert took over, the people themselves grew more colourful, as though to make up for the absence of colour in the landscape. The women wore wide red skirts, and gold and silver ornaments. They were handsome, tall, fair and strong. The men were tall too and the older among them had flowing white beards.

As the day grew older, and the sun rose higher in the sky, the traffic on the road increased; but our truck driver, instead of slowing down, drove faster. Perhaps he was in a hurry to dispose of the buffalo. Soon he was trying to overtake another truck.

The truck in front was moving fast too, and its driver had no intention of giving up the middle of the road. It was piled high with stacks of sugarcane.

'It's going to be a race!' cried Daljit excitedly, standing up against the buffalo, in order to get a better view.

The road was not wide enough to take two large vehicles at once, and as the other truck wouldn't make way, ours had to fall in behind it, almost suffocating us with the exhaust fumes. We were thrown to the floorboards as the truck lurched over the ruts in the rough road, and Mumta, getting nervous, almost trampled us. Then there was a tremendous bump, a grinding of brakes, and we came to a stop.

As the dust cleared, we made out our driver's bearded face gazing anxiously down at us.

'Are you alright?' he asked gruffly.

'I think so,' I said.

'Did you overtake the other truck?' asked Daljit.

'No,' grunted our friend. 'He would not give way. You had better come in front.'

We agreed without any hesitation and his assistant rather grudgingly joined the buffalo.

After a few miles, the driver became friendly and told us that his name was Gurnam Singh.

It was getting dark by the time we reached Jaipur, so we were not able to see much of the city. We spent the night in the truck, sleeping in the back with Gurnam Singh. Mumta had been disposed of on the way. Jaipur nights can be chilly, even in summer, so Gurnam Singh considerately shared his bedding with us. Because he was accustomed to sleeping in the body of the truck, he was soon asleep, snoring loudly and rhythmically.

Daljit and I tossed and turned restlessly. He kicked me several times in the night. The floor of the truck was hard, and retained various buffalo smells.

We had hardly fallen asleep (or so it seemed), when Gurnam Singh woke us up, saying that it was almost four o'clock and that he had to start on his return journey, this time with a load of red sandstone.

'What a life!' exclaimed Daljit, sleepily rubbing his eyes with one hand. 'I'd hate to be a truck driver.'

'One has to live somehow,' philosophized Gurnam Singh. 'I like driving. I knew how to drive when I was merely six or seven. The money is not so bad either. Now, when I get back to Delhi, I will have two days off, which I will spend with my wife and children. Goodbye friends, and if you pass through Delhi again, you will find me near the walls of the Red Fort.'

We waved to him as he shot off in his truck, throwing up huge clouds of dust, making a great noise and probably waking the local inhabitants. Dogs barked, and a cock began to crow.

We were on the outskirts of the city, facing a large lake. On the other side was open country, bare hills and desert. We could also make out the ruins of a building—probably a palace or a hunting lodge—among some thorn bushes and babul trees.

'Let's go out there,' suggested Daljit. 'We can bathe in the lake and rest. Then later in the morning we can come into the city and find out about trains.'

We set out along the shores of the lake, and it was a good half-hour before we reached the opposite bank.

There was no one in the fields, but a camel was going round and round a well, drawing up water in small trays. Smoke rose from houses in a nearby village, and the notes of a flute floated over to us on the still morning air.

It took us about twenty minutes to reach the ruin, which

seemed like an old hunting lodge put up by some Rajput prince when game must have been plentiful.

The gate of the lodge was blocked with rubble, but part of the wall had crumbled apart and we climbed through the gap and found ourselves in a stone-paved courtyard in the centre of which stood a dry, disused stone fountain. A small peepul tree was growing from the crack in the floor of the fountain. Finding nothing to do there, we made our way to the railway tracks again.

Daljit and I snuck on to a goods train. It was a hard night's journey. The train was agonizingly slow and stopped at many places. At one small station, a number of sacks filled with what must have been cattle-fodder were tossed into the wagon, almost burying us in our fitful sleep. But we found they were comfortable to rest on and lay stretched out on top of them until the first light of morning.

As the sky cleared, we knew we were not far from our journey's end. The landscape had undergone a complete change. We had left the desert for the coastal plain.

The tall waving palms parted, and then I spotted the sea.

It was the sea as I had always dreamt of it ever since my days in Kathiawar with my father. It was vast, lonely and blue, blue as the sky was blue, and the first ship I saw was a sailing-ship, an Arab dhow, listing slightly in the mild breeze that blew onto the shore.

The train stopped at a small bridge spanning a stream that wound its way across the plain down to the sea. We got down there and trudged the rest of the way to our destination.

Two hours later, we were at Jamnagar.

We stopped near a small tea shop and watched other people eating laddoos and *bhelpuri*. We couldn't even afford a coconut.

'Where is the harbour?' I asked the shopkeeper.

'Two miles from here,' he replied.

'Are there any ships in the port?' I asked, relieved yet anxious.

'What do you want with a ship?'

'What does anyone want with a ship?'

'Well there's only one and it sails today, so you had better hurry if you want to go away on it.'

'Let's go,' said Daljit.

'Wait!' said a young man who was lounging against the counter. 'It will take you almost an hour to get there if you walk. I will take you in my cart.' He pointed to a shabby pony cart close by. The pony did not look as though it wanted to go anywhere.

'My pony is fast!' said the young man, following our glances. 'Never go by appearances. She may look tired but she runs like a champion! Get in friends, I will charge you only one rupee.'

'We don't have any money,' I said. 'We'll walk.'

'Fifty paisa, then,' he said. 'Fifty paisa and a glass of tea. Jump in my friends!'

'All right,' agreed Daljit. 'There's no time to lose. Fifty paisa and buy your own tea.'

We climbed into the cart, and the youth jumped up in front and cracked his whip. The pony lurched forward, the wheels rattled and shook, and we set off down the bazaar road at a tremendous trot.

'I didn't know you had fifty paisa left,' I said.

'I don't,' Daljit replied. 'But we'll worry about that later. Your uncle can pay!'

As soon as we were out of the town and on the open road to the sea, the pony went faster. She couldn't help doing so, as the road was downhill. The wind blew my hair across my eyes, and the salty tang of the sea was in the air.

Daljit shook me in his excitement.

'We will soon be at the harbour,' he yelled joyfully. 'And then away at last!'

The driver called out endearments to his pony, and, exhilarated by the sea breeze and the comparative speed of his carriage, he burst into song. As we turned a bend in the road, the sea-front came into view. There were several small dhows close to the shore, and fishing-boats were beached on the sand. The fishermen were drying their nets while their children ran naked in the surf. A steamer stood out on the sea and though I could not make out its name from that distance, I was sure it was the *Iris*.

The cart stopped at the beginning of the pier, and we tumbled out and began running along the pier. But even as we ran, it became clear to me that the ship was moving away from us, moving out to the sea. Its propeller sent small waves rippling back to the pier.

'Captain!' I shouted. 'Uncle Jim! Wait for us!'

A lascar standing in the stern waved to us; but that was all. I stood at the end of the pier, waving my hands and shouting into the wind.

'Captain! Uncle Jim! Wait for us!'

Nobody answered. The seagulls, wheeling in the wake of the steamer, seemed to take up the cry—'Captain, Captain...'

The ship drew further away, gaining speed. And still I called to it in a hoarse, pleading voice. Yokohama, San Diego, Valparaiso, London, all slipped away forever...

TIME STOPS AT SHAMLI

The Dehra Express usually drew into Shamli at about five o'clock in the morning, at which time the station would be dimly lit and the jungle across the tracks would just be visible in the faint light of dawn. Shamli is a small station at the foot of the Siwalik hills, and the Siwaliks lie at the foot of the Himalayas, which in turn lie at the feet of God.

The station, I remember, had only one platform, an office for the stationmaster, and a waiting room. The platform boasted a tea-stall, a fruit vendor and a few stray dogs; not much else was required, because the train stopped at Shamli for only five minutes before rushing on into the forests.

Why it stopped at Shamli, I never could tell. Nobody got off the train and nobody got in. There were never any coolies on the platform. But the train would stand there a full five minutes, and the guard would blow his whistle, and presently Shamli would be left behind and forgotten…until I passed that way again…

I was paying my relations in Saharanpur an annual visit, when the night train stopped at Shamli. I was thirty-six at the time, and still single.

On this particular journey, the train came into Shamli just as I awoke from a restless sleep. The third class compartment was crowded beyond capacity, and I had been sleeping in an upright position, with my back to the lavatory door. Now someone was trying to get into the lavatory. He was obviously hardpressed for time.

'I'm sorry, brother,' I said, moving as much as I could do to one side.

He stumbled into the closet without bothering to close the door.

'Where are we now?' I asked the man sitting beside me. He was smoking a strong aromatic bidi.

'Shamli station,' he said, rubbing the palm of a large calloused hand over the frosted glass of the window.

I let the window down and stuck my head out. There was a cool breeze blowing down the platform, a breeze that whispered of autumn in the hills. As usual there was no activity, except for the fruit-vendor walking up and down the length of the train with his basket of mangoes balanced on his head. At the tea-stall, a kettle was steaming, but there was no one to mind it. I rested my forehead on the window-ledge, and let the breeze play on my temples. I had been feeling sick and giddy but there was a wild sweetness in the wind that I found soothing.

'Yes,' I said to myself, 'I wonder what happens in Shamli, behind the station walls.'

My fellow passenger offered me a bidi. He was a farmer, I think, on his way to Dehra. He had a long, untidy, sad moustache.

We had been more than five minutes at the station. I looked up and down the platform, but nobody was getting on or off the train. Presently, the guard came walking past our compartment.

'What's the delay?' I asked him.

'Some obstruction further down the line,' he said.

'Will we be here long?'

'I don't know what the trouble is. About half an hour, at the least.'

My neighbour shrugged and, throwing the remains of his bidi out of the window, closed his eyes and immediately fell asleep. I moved restlessly in my seat, and then the man came out of the lavatory, not so urgently now, and with obvious peace of mind. I closed the door for him.

I stood up and stretched; and this stretching of my limbs seemed to set in motion a stretching of the mind, and I found myself thinking: 'I am in no hurry to get to Saharanpur, and I have always wanted to see Shamli, behind the station walls. If I get down now, I can spend the day here, it will be better than sitting in this train for another hour. Then in the evening I can catch the next train home.'

In those days, I never had the patience to wait for second thoughts, and so I began pulling my small suitcase out from under the seat.

The farmer woke up and asked, 'What are you doing, brother?'

'I'm getting out,' I said.

He went to sleep again.

It would have taken at least fifteen minutes to reach the door, as people and their belongings cluttered up the passage; so I let my suitcase down from the window and followed it on to the platform.

There was no one to collect my ticket at the barrier, because there was obviously no point in keeping a man there to collect tickets from passengers who never came; and anyway, I had a through-ticket to my destination, which I would need in the evening.

I went out of the station and came to Shamli.

◆

Outside the station there was a neem tree, and under it stood a tonga. The tonga-pony was nibbling at the grass at the foot of the tree. The youth in the front seat was the only human in sight; there were no signs of inhabitants or habitation. I approached the tonga, and the youth stared at me as though he couldn't believe his eyes.

'Where is Shamli?' I asked.

'Why, friend, this is Shamli,' he said.

I looked around again, but couldn't see any signs of life. A dusty road led past the station and disappeared in the forest.

'Does anyone live here?' I asked.

'I live here,' he said, with an engaging smile. He looked an amiable, happy-go-lucky fellow. He wore a cotton tunic and dirty white pyjamas.

'Where?' I asked.

'In my tonga, of course,' he said. 'I have had this pony five years now. I carry supplies to the hotel. But today the manager has not come to collect them. You are going to the hotel? I will take you.'

'Oh, so there's a hotel?'

'Well, friend, it is called that. And there are a few houses too, and some shops, but they are all about a mile from the station. If they were not a mile from here, I would be out of business.'

I felt relieved, but I still had the feeling of having walked into a town consisting of one station, one pony and one man.

'You can take me,' I said. 'I'm staying till this evening.'

He heaved my suitcase into the seat beside him, and I climbed in at the back. He flicked the reins and slapped his pony on the buttocks; and, with a roll and a lurch, the buggy moved off down the dusty forest road.

'What brings you here?' asked the youth.

'Nothing,' I said. 'The train was delayed, I was feeling bored, and so I got off.'

He did not believe that; but he didn't question me further. The sun was reaching up over the forest, but the road lay in the shadow of tall trees, eucalyptus, mango and neem.

'Not many people stay in the hotel,' he said. 'So it is cheap. You will get a room for five rupees.'

'Who is the manager?'

'Mr Satish Dayal. It is his father's property. Satish Dayal could not pass his exams or get a job, so his father sent him here to look after the hotel.'

The jungle thinned out, and we passed a temple, a mosque, a few small shops. There was a strong smell of burnt sugar in the air, and in the distance I saw a factory chimney: that, then, was the reason for Shamli's existence. We passed a bullock-cart laden with sugarcane. The road went through fields of cane and maize and then, just as we were about to re-enter the jungle, the youth pulled his horse to a side road and the hotel came in sight.

It was a small white bungalow, with a garden in the front, banana trees at the sides and an orchard of guava trees at the back. We came jingling up to the front verandah. Nobody appeared, nor was there any sign of life on the premises.

'They are all asleep,' said the youth.

I said, 'I'll sit in the verandah and wait.' I got down from the tonga, and the youth dropped my case on the verandah steps. Then he stood in front of me, smiling amiably, waiting to be paid.

'Well, how much?' I asked.

'As a friend, only one rupee.'

'That's too much,' I complained. 'This is not Delhi.'

'This is Shamli,' he said. 'I am the only tonga-driver in Shamli. You may not pay me anything, if that is your wish.

But then, I will not take you back to the station this evening, you will have to walk.'

I gave him the rupee. He had both charm and cunning, an effective combination.

'Come in the evening at about six,' I said.

'I will come,' he said, with an infectious smile, 'Don't worry.'

I waited till the tonga had gone round the bend in the road before walking up the verandah steps.

The doors of the house were closed, and there were no bells to ring. I didn't have a watch, but I judged the time to be a little past six o'clock. The hotel didn't look very impressive; the whitewash was coming off the walls, and the cane-chairs on the verandah were old and crooked. A stag's head was mounted over the front door, but one of its glass eyes had fallen out. I had often heard hunters speak of how beautiful an animal looked before it died, but how could anyone with a true love of the beautiful care for the stuffed head of an animal, grotesquely mounted, with no resemblance to its living aspect?

I felt too restless to take any of the chairs. I began pacing up and down the verandah, wondering if I should start banging on the doors. Perhaps the hotel was deserted; perhaps the tonga-driver had played a trick on me. I began to regret my impulsiveness in leaving the train. When I saw the manager I would have to invent a reason for coming to his hotel. I was good at inventing reasons. I would tell him that a friend of mine had stayed here some years ago, and that I was trying to trace him. I decided that my friend would have to be a little eccentric (having chosen Shamli to live in), that he had become a recluse, shutting himself off from the world; his parents—no, his sister—for his parents would be dead—had asked me to find him if I could; and, as he had last been heard of in Shamli, I had taken the opportunity to enquire after him. His name would be Major Roberts, retired.

I heard a tap running at the side of the building, and walking around, found a young man bathing at the tap. He was strong and well-built, and slapped himself on the body with great enthusiasm. He had not seen me approaching, and I waited until he had finished bathing and had began to dry himself.

'Hullo,' I said.

He turned at the sound of my voice, and looked at me for a few moments with a puzzled expression; he had a round, cheerful face and crisp black hair. He smiled slowly, but it was a more genuine smile than the tonga-driver's. So far I had met two people in Shamli, and they were both smilers; that should have cheered me, but it didn't. 'You have come to stay?' he asked, in a slow easy-going voice.

'Just for the day,' I said. 'You work here?'

'Yes, my name is Daya Ram. The manager is asleep just now, but I will find a room for you.'

He pulled on his vest and pyjamas, and accompanied me back to the verandah. Here he picked up my suitcase and, unlocking a side door, led me into the house. We went down a passageway; then Daya Ram stopped at the door on the right, pushed it open, and took me into a small, sunny room that had a window looking out on the orchard. There was a bed, a desk, a couple of cane-chairs, and a frayed and faded red carpet.

'Is it alright?' asked Daya Ram.

'Perfectly alright.'

'They have breakfast at eight o'clock. But if you are hungry, I will make something for you now.'

'No, it's alright. Are you the cook too?'

'I do everything here.'

'Do you like it?'

'No,' he said, and then added, in a sudden burst of confidence, 'There are no women for a man like me.'

'Why don't you leave, then?'

'I will,' he said, with a doubtful look on his face. 'I will leave...'

After he had gone I shut the door and went into the bathroom to bathe. The cold water refreshed me and made me feel one with the world. After I had dried myself, I sat on the bed, in front of the open window. A cool breeze, smelling of rain, came through the window and played over my body. I thought I saw a movement among the trees.

And getting closer to the window, I saw a girl on a swing. She was a small girl, all by herself, and she was swinging to and fro and singing, and her song carried faintly on the breeze.

I dressed quickly, and left my room. The girl's dress was billowing in the breeze, her pigtails flying about. When she saw me approaching, she stopped swinging, and stared at me. I stopped a little distance away.

'Who are you?' she asked.

'A ghost,' I replied.

'You look like one,' she said.

I decided to take this as a compliment, as I was determined to make friends. I did not smile at her, because some children dislike adults who smile at them all the time.

'What's your name?' I asked.

'Kiran,' she said, 'I'm ten.'

'You are getting old.'

'Well, we all have to grow old one day. Aren't you coming any closer?'

'May I?' I asked.

'You may. You can push the swing.'

One pigtail lay across the girl's chest; the other behind her shoulder. She had a serious face, and obviously felt she had responsibilities; she seemed to be in a hurry to grow up, and I suppose she had no time for anyone who treated her as a child. I pushed the swing, until it went higher and higher, and then I stopped pushing, so that she came lower each time and we could talk.

'Tell me about the people who live here,' I said.

'There is Heera,' she said. 'He's the gardener. He's nearly a hundred. You can see him behind the hedges in the garden. You can't see him unless you look hard. He tells me stories—a new story every day. He's much better than the people in the hotel, and so is Daya Ram.'

'Yes, I met Daya Ram.'

'He's my bodyguard. He brings me nice things from the kitchen when no one is looking.'

'You don't stay here?'

'No, I live in another house; you can't see it from here. My father is the manager of the factory.'

'Aren't there any other children to play with?' I asked.

'I don't know any,' she said.

'And the people staying here?'

'Oh, they.' Apparently Kiran didn't think much of the hotel guests. 'Miss Deeds is funny when she's drunk. And Mr Lin is the strangest.'

'And what about the manager, Mr Dayal?'

'He's mean. And he gets frightened of slightest things. But Mrs Dayal is nice; she lets me take flowers home. But she doesn't talk much.'

I was fascinated by Kiran's ruthless summing up of the guests. I brought the swing to a standstill and asked, 'And what do you think of me?'

'I don't know as yet,' said Kiran quite seriously. 'I'll think about you.'

◆

As I came back to the hotel, I heard the sound of a piano in one of the front rooms. I didn't know enough about music to be able to recognize the piece, but it had sweetness and melody, though it was played with some hesitancy. As I came nearer, the sweetness deserted the music, probably because the piano was out of tune.

The person at the piano had distinctive Mongolian features, and so I presumed he was Mr Lin. He hadn't seen me enter the room, and I stood beside the curtains of the door, watching him play. He had full round lips and high, slanting cheekbones. His eyes were large and round and full of melancholy. His long, slender fingers hardly touched the keys.

I came nearer; and then he looked up at me, without any show of surprise or displeasure, and kept on playing.

'What are you playing?' I asked.

'Chopin,' he said.

'Oh, yes. It's nice, but the piano is fighting it.'

'I know. This piano belonged to one of Kipling's aunts. It hasn't been tuned since the last century.'

'Do you live here?'

'No, I come from Calcutta,' he answered readily. 'I have some business here with the sugarcane people actually, though I am not a businessman.' He was playing softly all the time, so that our conversation was not lost in the music. 'I don't know anything about business. But I have to do something.'

'Where did you learn to play the piano?'

'In Singapore. A French lady taught me. She had great hopes of my becoming a concert pianist when I grew up. I would have toured Europe and America.'

'Why didn't you?'

'We left during the war, and I had to give up my lessons.'

'And why did you go to Calcutta?'

'My father is a Calcutta businessman. What do you do, and why do you come here?' he asked. 'If I am not being too inquisitive.'

Before I could answer, a bell rang, loud and continuously, drowning the music and conversation.

'Breakfast,' said Mr Lin.

A thin dark man, wearing glasses, stepped nervously into the room and peered at me in an anxious manner.

'You arrived last night?'

'That's right,' I said, 'I just want to stay the day. I think you're the manager?'

'Yes. Would you like to sign the register?'

I went with him past the bar and into the office. I wrote my name and Mussoorie address in the register, and the duration of my stay. I paused at the column marked 'Profession', thought it would be best to fill it with something and wrote 'Author'.

'You are here on business?' asked Mr Dayal.

'No, not exactly. You see, I'm looking for a friend of mine who was heard of in Shamli, about three years ago. I thought I'd make a few enquiries in case he's still here.'

'What was his name? Perhaps he stayed here.'

'Major Roberts,' I said. 'An Anglo-Indian.'

'Well, you can look through the old registers after breakfast.'

He accompanied me into the dining-room. The establishment was really more of a boarding house than a hotel, because Mr Dayal ate with his guests. There was a round mahogany dining-table in the centre of the room, and Mr Lin was the only one seated at it. Daya Ram hovered about with plates and trays. I took my seat next to Lin, and, as I did so, a door opened from the passage, and a woman of about thirty-five came in.

She had on a skirt and blouse, which accentuated a firm,

well-rounded figure, and she walked on high-heels, with a rhythmical swaying of the hips. She had an uninteresting face, camouflaged with lipstick, rouge and powder—the powder so thick that is had become embedded in the natural lines of her face—but her figure compelled admiration.

'Miss Deeds,' whispered Lin.

There was a false note to her greeting.

'Hallo, everyone,' she said heartily, straining for effect. 'Why are you all so quiet? Has Mr Lin been playing the Funeral March again?' She sat down and continued talking. 'Really, we must have a dance or something to liven things up. You must know some good numbers Lin, after your experience in Singapore night-clubs. What's for breakfast? Boiled eggs. Daya Ram, can't you make an omelette for a change? I know you're not a professional cook, but you don't have to give us the same thing every day, and there's absolutely no reason why you should burn the toast. You'll have to do something about a cook, Mr Dayal.' Then she noticed me sitting opposite her. 'Oh, hallo,' she said, genuinely surprised. She gave me a long appraising look.

'This gentleman,' said Mr Dayal introducing me, 'is an author.'

'That's nice,' said Miss Deeds. 'Are you married?'

'No,' I said. 'Are you?'

'Funny, isn't it,' she said, without taking offence, 'No one in this house seems to be married.'

'I'm married,' said Mr Dayal.

'Oh, yes, of course,' said Miss Deeds. 'And what brings you to Shamli?' she asked, turning to me.

'I'm looking for a friend called Major Roberts.'

Lin gave an exclamation of surprise. I thought he had seen through my deception.

But another game had begun.

'I knew him,' said Lin. 'A great friend of mine.'

◆

'Yes,' continued Lin. 'I knew him. A good chap, Major Roberts.'

Well, there I was, inventing people to suit my convenience, and people like Mr Lin started inventing relationships with them. I was too intrigued to try and discourage him. I wanted to see how far he would go.

'When did you meet him?' asked Lin, taking the initiative.

'Oh, only about three years back. Just before he disappeared. He was last heard of in Shamli.'

'Yes, I heard he was here,' said Lin. 'But he went away, when he thought his relatives had traced him. He went into the mountains near Tibet.'

'Did he?' I said, unwilling to be instructed further. 'What part of the country? I come from the hills myself. I know the Mana and Niti passes quite well. If you have any idea of exactly where he went. I think I could find him.' I had the advantage in this exchange, because I was the one who had originally invented Roberts. Yet I couldn't bring myself to end his deception, probably because I felt sorry for him. A happy man wouldn't take the trouble of inventing friendships with people who didn't exist; he'd be too busy with friends who did.

'You've had a lonely life, Mr Lin?' I asked.

'Lonely?' said Mr Lin, with forced incredulousness. 'I'd never been lonely till I came here a month ago. When I was in Singapore—'

'You never get any letters though, do you?' asked Miss Deeds suddenly.

Lin was silent for a moment. Then he said, 'Do you?'

Miss Deeds lifted her head a little, as a horse does when it is annoyed, and I thought her pride had been hurt; but then she laughed unobstrusively and tossed her head.

'I never write letters,' she said. 'My friends gave me up as hopeless years ago. They know it's no use writing to me, because they rarely get a reply. They call me the Jungle Princess.'

Mr Dayal tittered, and I found it hard to suppress a smile. To cover up my smile I asked, 'You teach here?'

'Yes, I teach at the girl's school,' she said with a frown. 'But don't talk to me about teaching. I have enough of it all day.'

'You don't like teaching?'

She gave an aggressive look. 'Should I?' she asked.

'Shouldn't you?' I said.

She paused, and then said, 'Who are you, anyway, the Inspector of Schools?'

'No,' said Mr Dayal who wasn't following very well. 'He's a journalist.'

'I've heard they are nosey,' said Miss Deeds.

Once again Lin interrupted to steer the conversation away from a delicate issue.

'Where's Mrs Dayal this morning?' asked Lin.

'She spent the night with our neighbours,' said Mr Dayal. 'She should be here after lunch.'

It was the first time Mrs Dayal had been mentioned. Nobody spoke either well or ill of her; I suspected that she kept her distance from the others, avoiding familiarity. I began to wonder about Mrs Dayal.

◆

Daya Ram came in from the verandah, looking worried.

'Heera's dog has disappeared,' he said. 'He thinks a leopard took it.'

Heera, the gardener, was standing respectfully outside on

the verandah steps. We all hurried out to him, firing questions which he didn't try to answer.

'Yes. It's a leopard,' said Kiran, appearing from behind Heera. 'It's going to come into the hotel,' she added cheerfully.

'Be quiet,' said Satish Dayal crossly.

'There are pug marks under the trees,' said Daya Ram.

Mr Dayal, who seemed to know little about leopards or pug marks, said, 'I will take a look,' and led the way to the orchard, the rest of us trailing behind in an ill-assorted procession.

There were marks on the soft earth in the orchard (they could have been a leopard's), which went in the direction of the riverbed. Mr Dayal paled a little and went hurrying back to the hotel. Heera returned to the front garden, the least excited, the most sorrowful. Everyone else was thinking of a leopard, but he was thinking of the dog.

I followed him, and watched him weeding the sunflower beds. His face wrinkled like a walnut, but his eyes were clear and bright. His hands were thin and bony, but there was a deftness and power in the wrist and fingers, and the weeds flew fast from his spade. He had cracked, parchment-like skin. I could not help thinking of the gloss and glow of Daya Ram's limbs, as I had seen them when he was bathing, and wondered if Heera's had once been like that and if Daya Ram's would ever be like this, and both possibilities—or were they probabilities?—saddened me. Our skin, I thought, is like the leaf of a tree, young and green and shiny; then it gets darker and heavier, sometimes spotted with disease, sometimes eaten away; then fading, yellow and red, then falling, crumbling into dust or feeding the flames of fire. I looked at my own skin, still smooth, not coarsened by labour; I thought of Kiran's fresh rose-tinted complexion; Miss Deed's skin, hard and dry; Lin's pale taut skin, stretched tightly across his prominent cheeks and forehead; and Mr Dayal's grey skin, growing thick hair. And I wondered about Mrs Dayal and the kind of skin she would have.

'Did you have the dog for long?' I asked Heera.

He looked up with surprise, for he had been unaware of my presence.

'Six years, sahib,' he said. 'He was not a clever dog, but he was very friendly. He followed me home one day, when I was coming back from the bazaar. I kept telling him to go away, but he wouldn't. It was a long walk and so I began talking to him. I liked talking to him, and I have always talked with him, and we have understood each other. That first night, when I came home, I shut the gate between us. But he stood on the other side, looking at me with trusting eyes. Why did he have to look at me like that?'

'So, you kept him?'

'Yes, I could never forget the way he looked at me. I shall feel lonely now, because he was my only companion. My wife and son died long ago. It seems I am to stay here forever, until everyone has gone, until there are only ghosts in Shamli. Already the ghosts are here...'

I heard a light footfall behind me and turned to find Kiran. The bare-footed girl stood beside the gardener, and with her toes, began to pull at the weeds.

'You are a lazy one,' said the old man. 'If you want to help me, sit down and use your hands.'

I looked at the girl's fair round face, and in her bright eyes I saw something old and wise; and I looked into the old man's wise eyes, and saw something forever bright and young. The skin cannot change the eyes; the eyes are the true reflection of a man's age and sensibilities; even a blind man has hidden eyes.

'I hope we shall find the dog,' said Kiran. 'But I would like a leopard. Nothing ever happens here.'

'Not now,' sighed Heera. 'Not now... Why, once there was a band and people danced till morning, but now...'

'I have always been here,' said Heera. 'I was here before Shamli.'

'Before the station?'

'Before there was a station, or a factory, or a bazaar. It was a village then, and the only way to get here was by bullock-cart. Then a bus service was started, then the railway lines were laid and a station built, then they started the sugar factory, and for a few years Shamli was a town. But the jungle was bigger than the town. The rains were heavy and malaria was everywhere. People didn't stay long in Shamli. Gradually, they went back into the hills. Sometimes I too want to go back to the hills, but what is the use when you are old and have no one left in the world except a few flowers in a troublesome garden. I had to choose between the flowers and the hills, and I chose the flowers. I am tired now, and old, but I am not tired of flowers.'

I could see that his real world was the garden; there was more variety in his flower-beds than there was in the town of Shamli. Every month, every day, there were new flowers in the garden, but there were always the same people in Shamli.

I left Kiran with the old man, and returned to my room. It must have been about eleven o'clock.

◆

I was facing the window when I heard my door being opened. Turning, I perceived the barrel of a gun moving slowly round the edge of the door. Behind the gun was Satish Dayal, looking hot and sweaty. I didn't know what his intentions were; so, deciding it would be better to act first and reason later, I grabbed a pillow from the bed and flung it in his face. I then threw myself at his legs and brought him crashing down to the ground.

When we got up, I was holding the gun. It was an old Enfield rifle, probably dating back to the Afghan wars; the kind that goes off at the least encouragment.

'But—but—why?' stammered the dishevelled and alarmed Mr Dayal.

'I don't know,' I said menacingly. 'Why did you come in here pointing this at me?'

'I wasn't pointing it at you. It's for the leopard.'

'Oh, so you came into my room looking for a leopard? You have, I presume, been stalking one about the hotel?' (By now I was convinced that Mr Dayal had taken leave of his senses and was hunting imaginary leopards.)

'No, no,' cried the distraught man, becoming more confused, 'I was looking for you. I wanted to ask you if you could use a gun. I was thinking we should go looking for the leopard that took Heera's dog. Neither Mr Lin nor I can shoot.'

'Your gun is not up-to-date.' I said. 'It's not at all suitable for hunting leopards. A stout stick would be more effective. Why don't we arm ourselves with lathis and make a general assault?'

I said this banteringly, but Mr Dayal took the idea quite seriously. 'Yes, yes,' he said with alacrity, 'Daya Ram has got one or two lathis in the godown. The three of us could make an expedition. I have asked Mr Lin but he says he doesn't want to have anything to do with leopards.'

'What about our Jungle Princess?' I said. 'Miss Deeds should be pretty good with a lathi.'

'Yes, yes,' said Mr Dayal humourlessly, 'but we'd better not ask her.'

Collecting Daya Ram and two lathis, we set off for the orchard and began following the pug marks through the trees. It took us ten minutes to reach the riverbed, a dry hot rocky place; then we went into the jungle, Mr Dayal keeping well to the rear. The atmosphere was heavy and humid, and there was not a breath of air amongst the trees. When a parrot squawked suddenly, shattering the silence, Mr Dayal let out a startled exclamation and started for home.

'What was that?' he asked nervously.

'A bird,' I explained.

'I think we should go back now,' he said, 'I don't think the leopard's here.'

'You never know with leopards,' I said, 'They could be anywhere.'

Mr Dayal stepped away from the bushes. 'I'll have to go,' he said. 'I have a lot of work. You keep a lathi with you, and I'll send Daya Ram back later.'

'That's very thoughtful of you,' I said.

Daya Ram scratched his head and reluctantly followed his employer back through the trees. I moved on slowly down the little-used path, wondering if I should also return. I saw two monkeys playing on the branch of a tree, and decided that there could be no danger in the immediate vicinity.

Presently, I came to a clearing where there was a pool of fresh clear water. It was fed by a small stream that came suddenly, like a snake, out of the long grass. The water looked cool and inviting; laying down the lathi and taking off my clothes, I ran down the bank until I was waist-deep in the middle of the pool. I splashed about for some time, before emerging; then I lay on the soft grass and allowed the sun to dry my body. I closed my eyes and gave myself up to beautiful thoughts. I had forgotten all about leopards.

I must have slept for about half an hour because when I awoke, I found that Daya Ram had come back and was vigorously thrashing about in the narrow confines of the pool. I sat up and asked him the time.

'Twelve o'clock,' he shouted, coming out of water, his dripping body all gold and silver in sunlight. 'They will be waiting for dinner.'

'Let them wait,' I said.

It was a relief to talk to Daya Ram, after the uneasy conversations in the lounge and dining-room.

'Dayal sahib will be angry with me.'

'I'll tell him we found the trail of the leopard, and that we went so far into the jungle that we lost our way. As Miss Deeds is so critical of the food, let her cook the meal.'

'Oh, she only talks like that,' said Daya Ram. 'Inside she is very soft. She is too soft in some ways.'

'She should be married.'

'Well, she would like to be. Only there is no one to marry her. When she came here she was engaged to be married to an English army captain; I think she loved him, but she is the sort of person who cannot help loving many men all at once, and the captain could not understand that—it is just the way she is made, I suppose. She is always ready to fall in love.'

'You seem to know,' I said.

'Oh, yes.'

We dressed and walked back to the hotel. In a few hours, I thought, the tonga will come for me and I will be back at the station; the mysterious charm of Shamli will be no more, but whenever I pass this way I will wonder about these people, about Miss Deeds and Lin and Mrs Dayal.

Mrs Dayal... She was the one person I was yet to meet; it was with some excitement and curiosity that I looked forward to meeting her; she was about the only mystery left to Shamli, now, and perhaps she would be no mystery when I met her. And yet... I felt that perhaps she would justify the impulse that made me get down from the train.

I could have asked Daya Ram about Mrs Dayal, and so satisfied my curiosity; but I wanted to discover her for myself. Half the day was left to me, and I didn't want my game to finish too early.

I walked towards the verandah, and the sound of the piano came through the open door.

'I wish Mr Lin would play something cheerful,' said Miss Deeds. 'He's obsessed with the Funeral March. Do you dance?'

'Oh no,' I said.

She looked disappointed. But when Lin left the piano, she went into the lounge and sat down on the stool. I stood at the door watching her, wondering what she would do.

Lin left the room, somewhat resentfully.

She began to play an old song, which I remembered having heard in a film or on a gramophone record. She sang while she played, in a slightly harsh but pleasant voice:

Rolling round the world
Looking for the sunshine
I know I'm going to find some day...

Then she played *Am I blue?* and *Darling, Je Vous Aime Beaucoup*. She sat there singing in a deep husky voice, her eyes a little misty, her hard face suddenly kind and sloppy. When the gong rang, she broke off playing, and shook off her sentimental mood, and laughed derisively at herself.

I don't remember that lunch. I hadn't slept much since the previous night and I was beginning to feel the strain of my journey. The swim had refreshed me, but it had also made me drowsy. I ate quite well, though, of rice and kofta curry, and then, feeling sleepy, made for the garden to find a shady tree.

There were some books on the shelf in the lounge, and I ran my eye over them in search of one that might condition sleep. But they were too dull to do even that. So I went into the garden, and there was Kiran on the swing, and I went to her tree and sat down on the grass.

'Did you find the leopard?' she asked.

'No,' I said, with a yawn.

'Tell me a story.'

'You tell me one,' I said.

'Alright. Once there was a lazy man with long legs, who was always yawning and wanting to fall asleep...'

I watched the swaying motions of the swing and the movements of the girl's bare legs, and a tiny insect kept buzzing about in front of my nose... 'and fall asleep, and the reason for this was that he liked to dream.' I blew the insect away, and the swing became hazy and distant, and Kiran was a blurred figure in the trees...

'...liked to dream, and what do you think he dreamt about...?' Dreamt about, dreamt about...

♦

When I awoke there was that cool rain-scented breeze blowing across the garden. I remember lying on the grass with my eyes closed, listening to the swishing of the swing. Either I had not slept long, or Kiran had been a long time on the swing; it was moving slowly now, in a more leisurely fashion, without much sound. I opened my eyes and saw that my arm was stained with the juice of the grass beneath me. Looking up, I expected to see Kiran's legs waving above me. But instead I saw dark slim feet, and above them the folds of a sari. I straightened up against the trunk of the tree to look closer at Kiran, but Kiran wasn't there, it was someone else on the swing, a young woman in a pink sari and with a red rose in her hair.

She had stopped the swing with her foot on the ground, and she was smiling at me.

It wasn't a smile you could see, it was a tender fleeting movement that came suddenly and was gone at the same time, and its going was sad. I thought of the others' smiles, just as I had thought of their skins: the tonga-driver's friendly, deceptive grin; Daya Ram's wide sincere smile; Miss Deed's cynical, derisive smile. And looking at Sushila, I knew a smile could never change. She had always smiled that way.

'You haven't changed,' she said.

I was standing up now, though still leaning against the tree for support. Though I had never thought much about the *sound* of her voice, it seemed as familiar as the sounds of yesterday.

'You haven't changed either,' I said. 'But where did you come from?' I wasn't sure yet if I was awake or dreaming.

She laughed, as she had always laughed at me.

'I came from behind the tree. The little girl has gone.'

'Yes, I'm dreaming,' I said helplessly.

'But what brings you here?'

'I don't know. At least I didn't know when I came. But it must have been you. The train stopped at Shamli, and I don't know why, but I decided I would spend the day here, behind the station walls. You must be married now, Sushila.'

'Yes, I am married to Mr Dayal, the manager of the hotel. And what has been happening with you?'

'I am still a writer, still poor, and still living in Mussoorie.'

'When were you last in Delhi?' she asked. 'I don't mean Delhi, I mean at home.'

'I have not been to your home since you were there.'

'Oh, my friend,' she said, getting up suddenly and coming to me, 'I want to talk to you. I want to talk about our home and Sunil and our friends and all those things that are so far away now. I have been here two years, and I am already feeling old. I keep remembering our home, how young I was, how happy, and I am all alone with memories. But now *you* are here! It was a bit of magic, I came through the trees after Kiran had gone, and there you were, fast asleep under the tree. I didn't wake you then, because I wanted to see you wake up.'

'As I used to watch you wake up...'

She was near me and I could look at her more closely. Her cheeks did not have the same freshness; they were a little pale, and she was thinned now, but her eyes were the same, smiling the same way. Her voice was the same. Her fingers, when she took my hand, were the same warm delicate fingers.

'Talk to me,' she said. 'Tell me about yourself.'

'You tell me,' I said.

'I am here,' she said. 'That is all there is about myself.'

'Then let us sit down and I'll talk.'

'Not here.' She took my hand and led me through the trees. 'Come with me.'

I heard the jingle of a tonga-bell and a faint shout; I stopped and laughed.

'My tonga,' I said. 'It has come to take me back to the station.'

'But you are not going,' said Sushila, immediately downcast.

'I will tell him to come in the morning,' I said. 'I will spend the night in your Shamli.'

I walked to the front of the hotel where the tonga was waiting. I was glad no one else was in sight. The youth was smiling at me in his most appealing manner.

'I'm not going today,' I said. 'Will you come tomorrow morning?'

'I can come whenever you like, friend. But you will have to pay for every trip, because it is a long way from the station even if my tonga is empty.'

'Alright, how much?'

'Usual fare, friend, one rupee.'

I didn't try to argue but resignedly gave him the rupee. He cracked his whip and pulled on the reins, and the carriage moved off.

'If you don't leave tomorrow,' the youth called out after me, 'you'll never leave Shamli!'

I walked back to the trees, but I couldn't find Sushila.

'Sushila, where are you?' I called, but I might have been speaking to the trees, for I had no reply. There was a small path going through the orchard, and on the path I saw a rose petal. I walked a little further and saw another petal. They were from Sushila's red rose. I walked on down the path until I had skirted the orchard, and then the path went along the fringe of the jungle, past a clump of bamboos, and here the grass was a lush green as though it had been constantly watered. I was still finding rose petals. I heard the chatter of seven sisters, and the call of hoopoe. The path bent to meet a stream; there was a willow coming down to the water's edge, and Sushila was waiting there.

'Why didn't you wait?' I said.

'I wanted to see if you were as good at following me as you used to be.'

'Well, I am,' I said, sitting down beside her on the grassy bank of the stream. 'Even if I'm out of practice.'

'Yes, I remember the time you climbed onto an apple tree to pick some fruit for me. You got up alright but then you couldn't come down again. I had to climb up myself and help you.'

'I don't remember that,' I said.

'Of course you do.'

'It must have been your other friend, Pramod.'

'I never climbed trees with Pramod.'

'Well, I don't remember.'

I looked at the little stream that ran past us. The water was no more than ankle-deep, cold and clear and sparkling, like the mountain-stream near my home. I took off my shoes, rolled up my trousers and put my feet in water. Sushila's feet joined mine.

At first I had wanted to ask her about her marriage, whether she was happy or not, what she thought of her husband; but now I couldn't ask her these things, they seemed far away and of little importance. I could think of nothing she had in common with Mr Dayal; I felt that her charm and attractiveness and warmth could not have been appreciated, or even noticed, by that curiously distracted man. He was much older than her, of course; probably older than me; he was obviously not her choice but her parents'; and so far they were childless. Had there been children, I don't think Sushila would have minded Mr Dayal as her husband. Children would have made up for the absence of passion—or was there passion in Satish Dayal? I remembered having heard that Sushila had been married to a man she didn't like; I remembered having shrugged off the news, because it meant she would never come my way again, and I have never yearned after something that has been irredeemably lost. But she had come my way again. And was she still lost? That was what I wanted to know…

'What do you do with yourself all day?' I asked.

'Oh, I visit the school and help with the classes. It is the only interest I have in this place. The hotel is terrible. I try to keep away from it as much as I can.'

'And what about the guests?'

'Oh, don't let us talk about them. Let us talk about ourselves. Do you have to go tomorrow?'

'Yes, I suppose so. Will you always be in this place?'

'I suppose so.'

That made me silent. I took her hand, and my feet churned up the mud at the bottom of the stream. As the mud subsided, I saw Sushila's face reflected in the water; and looking up at her again, into her dark eyes, the old yearning returned and I wanted to care for her and protect her, I wanted to take her away from that place, from sorrowful Shamli; I wanted her to live again. Of course, I had forgotten all about my poor finances, Sushila's family, and the shoes I wore, which were my last pair. The uplift I was experiencing in this meeting with Sushila, who had always, throughout her childhood and youth, bewitched me as no other had ever bewitched me, made me reckless and impulsive.

I lifted her hand to my lips and kissed her in the soft of the palm.

'Can I kiss you?' I said.

'You have just done so.'

'Can I kiss you?' I repeated.

'It is not necessary.'

I leaned over and kissed her slender neck. I knew she would like this, because that was where I had kissed her often before. I kissed her in the soft of the throat, where it tickled.

'It is not necessary,' she said, but she ran her fingers through my hair and let them rest there. I kissed her behind the ear then, and kept my mouth to her ear and whispered, 'Can I kiss you?'

She turned her face to me so that we were deep in each other's eyes, and I kissed her again, and we put our arms around each other and lay together on the grass, with the water running over our feet; and we said nothing at all, simply lay there for what seemed like several years, or until the first drop of rain.

It was a big wet drop, and it splashed on Sushila's cheek,

just next to mine, and ran down to her lips, so that I had to kiss her again. The next big drop splattered on the tip of my nose, and Sushila laughed and sat up. Little ringlets were forming on the stream where the raindrops hit the water, and above us there was a pattering on the banana leaves.

'We must go,' said Sushila.

We started homewards, but had not gone far before it was raining steadily, and Sushila's hair came loose and streamed down her body. The rain fell harder, and we had to hop over pools and avoid the soft mud. Sushila's sari was plastered to her body, accentuating her ripe, thrusting breasts, and I was excited to passion, and pulled her beneath a big tree and crushed her in my arms and kissed her rain-kissed mouth. And then I thought she was crying, but I wasn't sure, because it might have been the raindrops on her cheeks.

'Come away with me,' I said. 'Leave this place. Come away with me tomorrow morning. We will go somewhere where nobody will know us or come between us.'

She smiled at me and said, 'You are still a dreamer, aren't you?'

'Why can't you come?'

'I am married; it is as simple as that.'

'If it is that simple, you can come.'

'I have to think of my parents, too. It would break my father's heart if I were to do what you are proposing. And you are proposing it without a thought for the consequences.'

'You are too practical,' I said.

'If women were not practical, most marriages would be failures.'

'So, your marriage is a success?'

'Of course it is, as a marriage. I am not happy and I do not love him, but neither am I so unhappy that I should hate him. Sometimes, for our own sakes, we have to think of the happiness of others. What happiness would we have living in hiding from everyone we once knew and cared for? Don't be a fool. I am always here and you can come to see me, and nobody will be made unhappy by it. But take me away and we will only have regrets.'

'You don't love me,' I said foolishly.

'That sad word, love,' she said, and became pensive and silent.

I could say no more. I was angry again, and rebellious, and there was no one and nothing to rebel against. I could not understand someone who was afraid to break away from an unhappy existence lest that existence should become unhappier; I had always considered it an admirable thing to break away from security and respectability. Of course it is easier for a man to do this, a man can look after himself, he can do without neighbours and the approval of the local society. A woman, I reasoned, would do anything for love, provided it was not at the price of security; for a woman loves security as much as a man loves independence.

'I must go back now,' said Sushila. 'You follow a little later.'

'All you wanted to do was talk,' I complained.

She laughed at that, and pulled me playfully by the hair; then she ran out from under the tree, springing across the grass, and the wet mud flew up and flecked her legs. I watched her through the thin curtain of rain, until she reached the verandah. She turned to wave to me, and then skipped into the hotel. She was still young; but I was no younger.

◆

The rain had lessened, but I didn't know what to do with myself. The hotel was uninviting, and it was too late to leave Shamli. If the grass hadn't been wet I would have preferred to sleep under a tree rather than return to the hotel to sit at that alarming dining-table.

I came out from under the trees and crossed the garden. But instead of making for the verandah I went round to the back of the hotel. Smoke issuing from the barred window of a back room told me I had probably found the kitchen. Daya Ram was inside, squatting in front of a stove, stirring a pot of stew. The stew smelt appetizing. Daya Ram looked up and smiled at me.

'I thought you must have gone,' he said.

'I'll go in the morning,' I said, pulling myself upon an empty table. Then I had one of my sudden ideas and said, 'Why don't you come with me? I can find you a good job in Mussoorie. How much do you get paid here?'

'Fifty rupees a month. But I haven't been paid for three months.'

'Could you get your pay before tomorrow morning?'

'No, I won't get anything until one of the guests pays a bill. Miss Deeds owes about fifty rupees on whisky alone. She will pay up, she says, when the school pays her salary. And the school can't pay her until they collect the children's fees. That is how bankrupt everyone is in Shamli.'

'I see,' I said, though I didn't see. 'But Mr Dayal can't hold back your pay just because his guests haven't paid their bills.'

'He can, if he hasn't got any money.'

'I see,' I said, 'Anyway, I will give you my address. You can come when you are free.'

'I will take it from the register,' he said.

I edged over to the stove and, leaning over, sniffed at the stew. 'I'll eat mine now,' I said; and without giving Daya Ram a chance to object, I lifted a plate off the shelf, took hold of the stirring-spoon and helped myself from the pot.

'There's rice too,' said Daya Ram.

I filled another plate with rice and then got busy with my fingers. After ten minutes, I had finished. I sat back comfortably in the hotel, in ruminative mood. With my stomach full, I could take a more tolerant view of life and people. I could understand Sushila's apprehensions, Lin's delicate lying and Miss Deed's aggressiveness. Daya Ram went out to sound the dinner-gong, and I trailed back to my room.

From the window of my room I saw Kiran running across the lawn, and I called to her, but she didn't hear me. She ran down the path and out of the gate, her pigtails beating against the wind.

The clouds were breaking and coming together again, twisting and spiralling their way across a violet sky. The sun was going down behind the Siwaliks. The sky there was blood-shot. The tall slim trunks of the eucalyptus tree were tinged with an orange glow; the rain had stopped, and the wind was a soft, sullen puff, drifting sadly through the trees. There was a steady drip of water from the eaves of the roof on to the window-sill. Then the sun went down behind the old, old hills, and I remembered my own hills, far beyond these.

The room was dark but I did not turn on the light. I stood near the window, listening to the garden. There was a frog warbling somewhere, and there was a sudden flap of wings overhead. Tomorrow morning I would go, and perhaps I would come back to Shamli one day, and perhaps not; I could always come here looking for Major Roberts, and, who knows, one day I might find him. What should he be like, this lost man? A romantic, a man with a dream, a man with brown skin and blue eyes, living in a hut on a snowy mountain-top, chopping wood and catching fish and swimming in cold mountain streams; a rough, free man with a kind heart and a shaggy beard, a man who owed allegiance to no one, who gave a damn for money and politics and cities and civilizations, who was his own master, who lived at one with nature knowing no fear. But that was not Major Roberts—that was the man I wanted to be. He was not a Frenchman or an Englishman, he was me, a dream of myself. If only I could find Major Roberts.

When Daya Ram knocked on the door and told me the others had finished dinner, I left my room and made for the lounge. It was quite lively in the lounge. Satish Dayal was at the bar, Lin at the piano, and Miss Deeds in the centre of the room, executing a tango on her own. It was obvious she had been drinking heavily.

'All on credit,' complained Mr Dayal to me. 'I don't know when I'll be paid, but I don't dare to refuse her anything for fear she starts breaking up the hotel.'

'She could do that, too,' I said. 'It comes down without much encouragement.'

Lin began to play a waltz (I think it was waltz), and then I found Miss Deeds in front of me, saying 'Wouldn't you like to dance, old boy?'

'Thank you,' I said, somewhat alarmed. 'I hardly know how to.'

'Oh, come on, be a sport,' she said, pulling me away from the bar. I was glad Sushila wasn't present; she wouldn't have minded, but she'd have laughed as she always laughed when I made a fool of myself.

We went round the floor in what I suppose was waltz-time, though all I did was mark time to Miss Deeds' motions; we were not very steady—this was because I was trying to keep her at arm's length, whilst she was determined to have me crushed to her bosom. At length, Lin finished the waltz. Giving him a grateful look, I pulled myself free. Miss Deeds went over to the piano, leant right across it, and said, 'Play something lively, dear Mr Lin, play some hot stuff.'

To my surprise, Mr Lin, without so much as an expression of distaste or amusement, began to execute what I suppose was the frug or the jitterbug. I was glad she hadn't asked me to dance that one with her.

It all appeared very incongruous to me: Miss Deeds letting herself go in crazy abandonment, Lin playing the piano with great seriousness and Mr Dayal watching from the bar with an anxious frown. I wondered what Sushila would have thought of them now.

Eventually, Miss Deeds collapsed on the couch breathing heavily. 'Give me a drink,' she cried.

With the noblest of intentions I took her a glass of water. Miss Deeds took a sip and made a face. 'What's this stuff?' she asked. 'It is different.'

'Water,' I said.

'No,' she said, 'now don't joke, tell me what it is.'

'It's water, I assure you,' I said.

When she saw that I was serious, her face coloured up, and I thought she would throw the water at me; but she was too tired to do this, and contented herself by throwing the glass over her shoulder. Mr Dayal made a dive for the flying glass, but he wasn't in time to rescue it, and it hit the wall and fell to pieces on the floor.

Mr Dayal wrung his hands. 'You'd better take her to her room,' he said, as though I were personally responsible for her behaviour just because I'd danced with her.

'I can't carry her alone,' I said, making an unsuccessful attempt at helping Miss Deeds up from the couch.

Mr Dayal called for Daya Ram, and the big amiable youth came lumbering into the lounge. We took an arm each and helped Miss Deeds, feet dragging, across the room. We got her to her room and on to her bed. When we were about to withdraw she said, 'Don't go, my dear, stay with me a little while.'

Daya Ram had discreetly slipped outside. With my hand on the doorknob I said, 'Which of us?'

'Oh, are there two of you?' said Miss Deeds, without a trace of disappointment.

'Yes, Daya Ram helped me carry you here.'

'Oh, and who are you?'

'I'm the writer. You danced with me, remember?'

'Of course. You dance divinely, Mr Writer. Do stay with me. Daya Ram can stay too if he likes.'

I hesitated, my hand on the doorknob. She hadn't opened her eyes all the time I'd been in the room, her arms hung loose, and one bare leg hung over the side of the bed. She was fascinating somehow, and desirable, but I was afraid of her. I went out of the room and quietly closed the door.

◆

As I lay awake in bed I heard the jackal's 'pheau', the cry of fear, which it communicates to all the jungle when there is danger about, a leopard or a tiger. It was a weird howl, and between each note there was a kind of low gurgling. I switched off the light and peered through the closed window. I saw the jackal at the edge of the lawn. It sat almost vertically on its haunches, holding its head straight up to the sky, making the neighbourhood vibrate with the eerie violence of its cries. Then suddenly it started up and ran off into the trees.

Before getting back into bed I made sure the window was fast. The bull-frog was singing again, 'ing-ong; ing-ong', in some foreign language. I wondered if Sushila was awake too, thinking about me. It must have been almost eleven o'clock. I thought of Miss Deeds, with her leg hanging over the edge of the bed. I tossed restlessly, and then sat up. I hadn't slept for two nights but I was not sleepy. I got out of bed without turning on the light and, slowly opening my door, crept down the passageway. I stopped at the door of Miss Deed's room. I stood there listening, but I heard only the ticking of the big clock that might have been in the room or somewhere in the passage. I put my hand on the doorknob, but the door was bolted. That settled the matter.

I would definitely leave Shamli the next morning. Another day in the company of these people and I would be behaving like them. Perhaps I was already doing so! I remembered the tonga-driver's words, 'Don't stay too long in Shamli or you will never leave!'

When the rain came, it was not with a preliminary patter or shower, but all at once, sweeping across the forest like a massive wall, and I could hear it in the trees long before it reached the house. Then it came crashing down on the corrugated roofing, and the hailstones hit the window panes with a hard metallic sound, so that I thought the glass would break. The sound of thunder was like the booming of big guns, and the lightning kept playing over the garden. At every flash of lightning I sighted the swing under the tree, rocking and leaping in the air as though some invisible, agitated being was sitting on it. I wondered about Kiran. Was she sleeping through all this, blissfully unconcerned, or was she lying awake in bed, starting at every clash of thunder, as I was; or was she up and about, exulting in the storm? I half expected to see her come running through the trees, through the rain, to stand on the swing with her hair blowing wild in the wind, laughing at the thunder and the angry skies. Perhaps I did see her, perhaps she was there.

I wouldn't have been surprised if she were some forest nymph, living in the hole of a tree, coming out sometimes to play in the garden.

A crash, nearer and louder than any thunder so far, made me sit up in the bed with a start. Perhaps lightning had struck the house. I turned on the switch, but the light didn't come on. A tree must have fallen across the line.

I heard voices in the passage, the voices of several people. I stepped outside to find out what had happened, and started at the appearance of a ghostly apparition right in front of me; it was Mr Dayal standing on the threshold in an oversized pyjama suit, a candle in his hand.

'I came to wake you,' he said. 'This storm.'

He had the irritating habit of stating the obvious.

'Yes, the storm,' I said. 'Why is everybody up?'

'The back wall has collapsed and part of the roof has fallen in. We'd better spend the night in the lounge, it is the safest room. This is a very old building,' he added apologetically.

'Alright,' I said. 'I am coming.'

The lounge was lit by two candles; one stood over the piano, the other on a small table near the couch. Miss Deeds was on the couch, Lin was at the piano-stool, looking as though he would start playing Stravinsky any moment, and Mr Dayal was fussing about the room. Sushila was standing at a window, looking out at the stormy night. I went to the window and touched her, She didn't look round or say anything. The lightning flashed and her dark eyes were pools of smouldering fire.

'What time will you be leaving?' she said.

'The tonga will come for me at seven.'

'If I come,' she said. 'If I come with you, I will be at the station before the train leaves.'

'How will you get there?' I asked, and hope and excitement rushed over me again.

'I will get there,' she said. 'I will get there before you. But if I am not there, then do not wait, do not come back for me. Go on your way. It will mean I do not want to come. Or I will be there.'

'But are you sure?'

'Don't stand near me now. Don't speak to me unless you have to.' She squeezed my fingers, then drew her hand away. I sauntered over to the next window, then back into the centre of the room. A gust of wind blew through a cracked window-pane and put out the candle near the couch.

'Damn the wind,' said Miss Deeds.

◆

The window in my room had burst open during the night, and there were leaves and branches strewn about the floor. I sat down on the damp bed, and smelt eucalyptus. The earth was red, as though the storm had bled it all night.

After a little while, I went into the verandah with my suitcase, to wait for the tonga. It was then that I saw Kiran under the trees. Kiran's long black pigtails were tied up in a red ribbon, and she looked fresh and clean like the rain and the red earth. She stood looking seriously at me.

'Did you like the storm?' she asked.

'Some of the time,' I said. 'I'm going soon. Can I do anything for you?'

'Where are you going?'

'I'm going to the end of the world. I'm looking for Major Roberts, have you seen him anywhere?'

'There is no Major Roberts,' she said perceptively. 'Can I come with you to the end of the world?'

'What about your parents?'

'Oh, we won't take them.'

'They might be annoyed if you go off on your own.'

'I can stay on my own. I can go anywhere.'

'Well, one day I'll come back here and I'll take you everywhere and no one will stop us. Now is there anything else I can do for you?'

'I want some flowers, but I can't reach them,' she pointed to a hibiscus tree that grew against the wall. It meant climbing the wall to reach the flowers. Some of the red flowers had fallen during the night and were floating in a pool of water.

'Alright,' I said and pulled myself up on the wall. I smiled down into Kiran's serious upturned face. 'I'll throw them to you and you can catch them.'

I bent a branch, but the wood was young and green, and I had to twist it several times before it snapped.

'I hope nobody minds,' I said, as I dropped the flowering branch to Kiran.

'It's nobody's tree,' she said.

'Sure?'

She nodded vigorously. 'Sure, don't worry.'

I was working for her and she felt immensely capable of protecting me. Talking and being with Kiran, I felt a nostalgic longing for the childhood: emotions that had been beautiful because they were never completely understood.

'Who is your best friend?' I said.

'Daya Ram,' she replied. 'I told you so before.'

She was certainly faithful to her friends.

'And who is the second best?'

She put her finger in her mouth to consider the question; her head dropped sideways in concentration.

'I'll make you the second best,' she said.

I dropped the flowers over her head. 'That is so kind of you. I'm proud to be your second best.'

I heard the tonga bell, and from my perch on the wall saw the carriage coming down the driveway. 'That's for me,' I said. 'I must go now.'

I jumped down the wall. And the sole of my shoe came off at last.

'I knew that would happen,' I said.

'Who cares for shoes,' said Kiran.

'Who cares,' I said.

I walked back to the verandah, and Kiran walked beside me, and stood in front of the hotel while I put my suitcase in the tonga.

'You nearly stayed one day too late,' said the tonga-driver. 'Half the hotel has come down, and tonight the other half will come down.'

I climbed into the back seat. Kiran stood on the path, gazing intently at me.

'I'll see you again,' I said.

'I'll see you in Iceland or Japan,' she said. 'I'm going everywhere.'

'Maybe,' I said, 'maybe you will.'

We smiled, knowing and understanding each other's importance. In her bright eyes I saw something old and wise. The tonga-driver cracked his whip, the wheels cracked, the carriage rattled down the path. We kept waving to each other. In Kiran's hand was a spring of hibiscus. As she waved, the blossoms fell apart and danced a little in the breeze.

◆

Shamli station looked the same as it had the day before. The same train stood at the same platform, and the same dogs prowled beside the fence. I waited on the platform until the bell clanged for the train to leave, but Sushila did not come.

Somehow, I was not disappointed. I had never really expected her to come. Unattainable, Sushila would always be more bewitching and beautiful than if she were mine.

Shamli would always be there. And I could always come back, looking for Major Roberts.

FROM THE POOL TO THE GLACIER

My Boyhood Pool

It was going to rain. I could see the rain moving across the foothills, and I could smell it on the breeze. But instead of turning homewards I pushed my way through the leaves and brambles that grew across the forest path. I had heard the sound of running water at the bottom of the hill, and I was determined to find this hidden stream.

I had to slide down a rock-face into a small ravine and there I found the stream running over a bed of shingle; I removed my shoes and started walking upstream. A large, glossy black bird with a curved red beak hooted at me as I passed; and a paradise flycatcher—this one I couldn't fail to recognize, with its long fan-tail beating the air—swooped across the stream. Water trickled down from the hillside, from amongst ferns and grasses and wild flowers; and the hills, rising steeply on either side, kept the ravine in shadow. The rocks were smooth, almost soft, and some of them were grey and some yellow. A small waterfall came down the rocks and formed a deep, round pool of apple-green water.

When I saw the pool, I turned and ran home. I wanted to tell Anil and Kamal about it. It began to rain, but I didn't stop to take shelter, I ran all the way home—through the sal forest, across the dry riverbed through the outskirts of the town.

Though Anil usually chose the adventures we were to have, the pool was my own discovery, and I was proud of it. 'We'll call it Rusty's Pool,' said Kamal. 'And remember, it's a secret pool. No one else must know of it.'

I think it was the pool that brought us together more than anything else.

Kamal was the best swimmer. He dived off rocks and went gliding about under the water like a long golden fish. Anil had strong legs and arms, and he threshed about with much vigour but little skill. I could dive off a rock too, but I usually landed on my stomach.

There were slim silver fish in the stream. At first we tried catching them with a line, but they soon learnt the art of taking the bait without being caught on the hook. Next we tried a bedsheet (Anil had removed it from his mother's laundry) which we stretched across one end of the stream; but the fish wouldn't come anywhere near it. Eventually, Anil, without telling us, procured a stick of gunpowder. And Kamal and I were startled out of an afternoon siesta by a flash across the water and a deafening explosion. Half the hillside tumbled into the pool, and Anil along with it. We got him out, along with a large supply of stunned fish which were too small for eating. Anil, however, didn't want all his work to go to waste; so he roasted the fish over a fire and ate them himself.

The effects of the explosion gave Anil another idea, which was to enlarge our pool by building a dam across one end. This he accomplished with our combined labour. But he had chosen a week when there had been heavy rain in the hills, and we had barely finished the dam when a torrent of water came rushing down the bed of the stream and burst our earthworks, flooding the ravine. Our clothes were carried away by the current, and we had to wait until it was night before creeping into town through the darkest alleyways. Anil was spotted at a street corner, but he posed as a naked sadhu and began calling for alms, and finally slipped in through the back door of his house without being recognized. I had to lend Kamal some of my clothes, and these, being on the small side, made him look odd and gangly. Our other activities at the pool included wrestling and buffalo-riding.

We wrestled on a strip of sand that ran beside the stream. Anil had often attended wrestling akharas and was something of an expert. Kamal and I usually combined against him, and after five or ten minutes of furious, unscientific struggle, we usually succeeded in flattening Anil into the sand. Kamal would sit on his head, and I would sit on his legs, until he admitted defeat. There was no fun in taking him on singly, because he knew too many tricks for us.

We rode on a couple of buffaloes that sometimes came to drink and wallow in the more muddy parts of the stream. Buffaloes are fine, sluggish creatures, always in search of a soft, slushy resting place. We would climb on their backs, and kick and yell and urge them forward; but on no occasion did we succeed in getting them to carry us anywhere. If they tired of our antics, they would merely roll over on their backs, taking us with them into a bed of muddy water.

Not that it mattered how muddy we got, because we had only to dive into the pool to get rid of it all. The buffaloes couldn't get to the pool because of its narrow outlet and the slippery rocks.

If it was possible for Anil and me to leave our homes at night, we would come to the pool for a swim by moonlight. We would often find Kamal there before us. He wasn't afraid of the dark or the surrounding forest, where there were panthers and jungle cats. We bathed silently at nights, because the stillness of the surrounding jungle seemed to discourage high spirits; but sometimes Kamal would sing—he had a clear, ringing voice—and we would float the red, long-fingered poinsettias downstream.

The pool was to be our principal meeting place during the coming months. It was not that we couldn't meet in town. But the pool was secret, known only to us, and it gave us a feeling of conspiracy and adventure to meet there after school. It was at the pool that we made our plans: it was at the pool that we first spoke of the glacier; but several weeks and a few other exploits were to pass before the particular dream materialized.

Ghosts on the Verandah

Anil's mother's memory was stored with an incredible amount of folklore, and she would sometimes astonish us with her stories of spirits and mischievous ghosts.

One evening, when Anil's father was out of town, and Kamal and I had been invited to stay the night at Anil's upper-storey flat in the bazaar, his mother began to tell us about the various types of ghosts she had known. Mulia, a servant-girl, having just taken a bath, came out on the verandah with her hair loose.

'My girl, you ought not to leave your hair loose like that,' said Anil's mother. 'It is better to tie a knot in it.'

'But I have not oiled it yet,' said Mulia.

'Never mind, but you should not leave your hair loose towards sunset. There are spirits called jinns who are attracted to long hair and pretty black eyes like yours. They may be tempted to carry you away!'

'How dreadful!' exclaimed Mulia, hurriedly tying a knot

in her hair, and going indoors to be on the safe side. Kamal, Anil and I sat on a string cot, facing Anil's mother, who sat on another cot. She was not much older than thirty-two, and had often been mistaken for Anil's elder sister; she came from a village near Mathura, a part of the country famous for its gods and spirits, and demons.

'Can you see jinns, aunty-ji?' I asked.

'Sometimes,' she said. 'There was an Urdu teacher in Mathura, whose pupils were about the same age as you. One of the boys was very good at his lessons. One day, while he sat at his desk in a corner of the classroom, the teacher asked him to fetch a book from the cupboard that stood at the far end of the room. The boy, who felt lazy that morning, didn't move from his seat. He merely stretched out his hand, took the book from the cupboard, and handed it to the teacher. Everyone was astonished, because the boy's arm had stretched about four yards before touching the book! They realized that he was a jinn; that was the reason for his being so good at games and exercises that required great agility.'

'Well, I wish I was a jinn,' said Anil. 'Especially for volleyball matches.'

Anil's mother then told us about *munjia*, a mischievous ghost who lives in lonely peepul trees. When a munjia is annoyed, he rushes out from his tree and upsets tongas, bullock-carts and cycles. Even a bus is known to have been upset by a munjia.

'If you are passing beneath a peepul tree at night,' warned Anil's mother, 'be careful not to yawn without covering your mouth or snapping your fingers in front of it. If you don't remember to do that, the munjia will jump down your throat and completely ruin your digestion!'

In an attempt to change the subject, Kamal mentioned that a friend of his had found a snake in his bed one morning.

'Did he kill it?' asked Anil's mother anxiously.

'No, it slipped away,' said Kamal.

'Good,' she said. 'It is lucky if you see a snake early in the morning.'

'It won't bite you if you let it alone,' she said.

By eleven o'clock, after we had finished our dinner and heard a few more ghost stories—including one about Anil's grandmother, whose spirit paid the family a visit—Kamal and I were most reluctant to leave the company on the verandah and retire to the room that had been set apart for us. It did not make us feel any better to be told by Anil's mother that we should recite certain magical verses to keep away the more mischievous spirits. We tried one, which went—

Bhoot, pret, pisach, dana
Chhoo mantar, sab nikal jana,
Mano, mano, Shiv ka kahna...

which, roughly translated, means—

Ghosts, spirits, goblins, sprites,
Away you fly, don't come tonight,
Or with great Shiva you'll have to fight!

Shiva, the Destroyer, is one of the three major Hindu deities.

But the more we repeated the verse, the more uneasy we became, and when I got into bed (after carefully examining it for snakes), I couldn't lie still, but kept twisting and turning and looking at the walls for moving shadows. Kamal attempted to raise our spirits by singing softly, but this only made the atmosphere more eerie. After a while, we heard someone knocking at the door, and the voices of Anil and the maidservant. Getting up and opening the door, I found them looking pale and anxious. They, too, had succeeded in frightening themselves as a result of Anil's mother's stories.

'Are you all right?' asked Anil. 'Wouldn't you like to sleep in our part of the house? It might be safer. Mulia will help us carry the beds across!'

'We're quite all right,' protested Kamal and I, refusing to admit we were nervous; but we were hustled along to the other side of the flat as though a band of ghosts was conspiring against us. Anil's mother had been absent during all this activity but suddenly we heard her screaming from the direction of the room we had just left.

'Rusty and Kamal have disappeared!' she cried. 'Their beds have gone, too!'

And then, when she came out on the verandah and saw us dashing about in our pyjamas, she gave another scream and collapsed on a cot.

After that, we didn't allow Anil's mother to tell us ghost stories at night.

To the Hills

At the end of August, when the rains were nearly over, we met at the pool to make plans for the autumn holidays. We had bathed, and were stretched out in the shade of the fresh, rain-washed sal trees, when Kamal, pointing vaguely to the distant mountains, said: 'Why don't we go to the Pindari Glacier?'

'The glacier!' exclaimed Anil. 'But that's all snow and ice!'

'Of course it is,' said Kamal. 'But there's a path through the mountains that goes all the way to the foot of the glacier. It's only fifty-four miles!'

'Do you mean we must—*walk* fifty-four miles?'

'Well, there's no other way,' said Kamal. 'Unless you prefer to sit on a mule. But your legs are too long, they'll be trailing along the ground. No, we'll have to walk. It will take us about ten days to get to the glacier and back, but if we take enough food there'll be no problem. There are dak bungalows to stay in at night.'

'Kamal gets all the best ideas,' I said. 'But I suppose Anil and I will have to get our parents' permission. And some money.'

'My mother won't let me go,' said Anil. 'She says the mountains are full of ghosts. And she thinks I'll get up to some mischief. How can one get up to mischief on a lonely mountain?'

'I'm sure it won't be dangerous, people are always going to the glacier. Can you see that peak above the others on the right?' Kamal pointed to the distant snow-range, barely visible against the soft blue sky. 'The Pindari Glacier is below it. It's at 12,000 feet, I think, but we won't need any special equipment. There'll be snow only for the final two or three miles. Do you know that it's the beginning of the river Sarayu?'

'You mean our river?' asked Anil, thinking of the little river that wandered along the outskirts of the town, joining the Ganga further downstream.

'Yes. But it's only a trickle where it starts.'

'How much money will we need?' I asked, determined to be practical.

'Well, I've saved twenty rupees,' said Kamal.

'But won't you need that for your books?' I asked.

'No, this is extra. If each of us brings twenty rupees, we should have enough. There's nothing to spend money on, once we are up on the mountains. There are only one or two villages on the way, and food is scarce, so we'll have to take plenty of food with us. I learnt all this from the Tourist Office.'

'Kamal's been planning this without our knowledge,' complained Anil.

'He always plans in advance,' I said. 'But it's a good idea, and it should be a fine adventure.'

'All right,' said Anil. 'But Rusty will have to be with me when I ask my mother. She thinks Rusty is very sensible, and might let me go if he says it's quite safe.' And he ended the discussion by jumping into the pool, where we soon joined him.

Though my mother hesitated about letting me go, my father said it was a wonderful idea, and was only sorry because he couldn't accompany us himself (which was a relief, as we didn't want our parents along); and though Anil's father hesitated—or rather, because he hesitated—his mother said, yes, of course Anil must go, the mountain air would be good for his health. A puzzling remark, because Anil's health had never been better. The bazaar people, when they heard that Anil might be away for a couple of weeks, were overjoyed at the prospect of a quiet spell, and pressed his father to let him go.

On a cloudy day promising rain, we bundled ourselves into the bus that was to take us to Kapkote (where people lose their caps and coats, punned Anil), the starting point of our trek. Each of us carried a haversack, and we had also brought along a good-sized bedding roll which, apart from blankets, also contained rice and flour thoughtfully provided by Anil's mother. We had no idea how we would carry the bedding roll once we started walking; but an astrologer had told Anil's mother it was a good day for travelling, so we didn't worry much over minor details.

We were soon in the hills, on a winding road that took us up and up, until we saw the valley and our town spread out beneath us, the river a silver ribbon across the plain. Kamal pointed to a patch of dense sal forest and said, 'Our pool must be there!' We took a sharp bend, and the valley disappeared, and the mountains towered above us.

We had dull headaches by the time we reached Kapkote;

but when we got down from the bus, a cool breeze freshened us. At the wayside shop, we drank glasses of hot, sweet tea, and the shopkeeper told us we could spend the night in one of his rooms. It was pleasant at Kapkote, the hills wooded with deodar trees, the lower slopes planted with fresh green paddy. At night, there was a wind moaning in the trees, and it found its way through the cracks in the windows and eventually through our blankets. Then, right outside the door, a dog began howling at the moon. It had been a good day for travelling, but the astrologer hadn't warned us that it would be a bad night for sleep.

Next morning, we washed our faces at a small stream about a hundred yards from the shop, and filled our water-bottles for the day's march. A boy from the nearby village sat on a rock, studying our movements.

'Where are you going?' he asked, unable to suppress his curiosity.

'To the glacier,' said Kamal.

'Let me come with you,' said the boy. 'I know the way.'

'You're too small,' said Anil. 'We need someone who can carry our bedding roll.'

'I'm small,' said the boy, 'but I'm strong. I'm not a weakling like the boys in the plains.' Though he was shorter than any of us, he certainly looked sturdy, and had a muscular, well-knit body and pink cheeks. 'See!' he said; and picking up a rock the size of a football, he heaved it across the stream.

'I think he can come with us,' I said.

And the boy, whose name was Bisnu, dashed off to inform his people of his employment—we had agreed to pay him a rupee a day for acting as our guide and 'sherpa'.

And then we were walking—at first, above the little Sarayu River, then climbing higher along the rough mule-track, always within sound of the water. Kamal wanted to bathe in the river.

I said it was too far, and Anil said we wouldn't reach the dak bungalow before dark if we went for a swim. Regretfully, we left the river behind, and marched on through a forest of oaks, over wet, rotting leaves that made a soft carpet for our feet. We ate at noon, under an oak. As we didn't want to waste any time making a fire—not on this first crucial day—we ate beans from a tin and drank most of our water.

In the afternoon, we came to the river again. The water was swifter now, green and bubbling, still far below us. We saw two boys in the water, swimming in an inlet that reminded us of our own secret pool. They waved, and invited us to join them. We returned their greeting; but it would have taken us an hour to get down to the river and up again; so we continued on our way.

We walked fifteen miles on the first day—our speed was to decrease after this—and we were at the dak bungalow by six o'clock. Bisnu busied himself collecting sticks for a fire. Anil found the bungalow's watchman asleep in a patch of fading sunlight, and roused him. The watchman, who hadn't been bothered by visitors for weeks, grumbled at our intrusion, and opened a room for us. He also produced some potatoes from his quarters, and these were roasted for dinner.

It became cold after the sun had gone down, and we remained close to Bisnu's fire. The damp sticks burnt fitfully. But Bisnu had justified his inclusion in our party. He had balanced the bedding roll on his shoulders as though it were full of cotton wool instead of blankets. Now he was helping with the cooking. And we were glad to have him sharing our hot potatoes and strong tea.

There were only two beds in the room, and we pushed these together, apportioning out the blankets as fairly as possible. Then the four of us leapt into bed, shivering in the cold. We were already over 5,000 feet. Bisnu, in his own peculiar way, had wrapped a scarf around his neck, though a cotton singlet and shorts were all that he wore for the night.

'Tell us a story, Rusty,' said Anil. 'It will help us fall asleep.'

I told them one of his mother's stories, about a boy and a girl who had been changed into a pair of buffaloes; and then Bisnu told us about the ghost of a sadhu, who was to be seen sitting in the snow by moonlight, not far from the glacier. Far from putting us to sleep, this story kept us awake for hours.

'Aren't you asleep yet?' I asked Anil in the middle of the night.

'No, you keep kicking me,' he lied.

'We don't have enough blankets,' complained Kamal, 'it's too cold to sleep.'

'I never sleep till it's very late,' mumbled Bisnu from the bottom of the bed.

No one was prepared to admit that our imaginations were keeping us awake.

After a little while we heard a thud on the corrugated tin sheeting, and then the sound of someone—or something—scrambling about on the roof. Anil, Kamal and I sat up in bed, startled out of our wits. Bisnu, who had been winning the race to be fast asleep, merely turned over on his side and grunted.

'It's only a bear,' he said. 'Didn't you notice the pumpkins on the roof? Bears love pumpkins.'

For half an hour, we had to listen to the bear as it clambered about on the roof, feasting on the watchman's ripening pumpkins. Finally, there was silence. Kamal and I crawled out of our blankets and went to the window. And through the frosted glass we saw a Himalayan black bear ambling across the slope in front of the bungalow, a fat pumpkin held between its paws.

To the River

It was raining when we woke, and the mountains were obscured by a heavy mist. We delayed our departure, playing football on the verandah with one of the pumpkins that had fallen off the roof. At noon, the rain stopped, and the sun shone through the clouds. As the mist lifted, we saw the snow range, the great peaks of Nanda Kot and Trisul stepping into the sky.

'It's different up here,' said Kamal. 'I feel like a different person.'

'That's the altitude,' I said. 'As we go higher, we'll get lighter in the head.'

'Anil is light in the head already,' said Kamal. 'I hope the altitude isn't too much for him.'

'If you two are going to be witty,' said Anil, 'I shall go off with Bisnu, and you'll have to find the way yourselves.'

Bisnu grinned at each of us in turn to show us that he wasn't taking sides; and after a breakfast of boiled eggs, we set off on our trek to the next bungalow.

Rain had made the ground slippery, and we were soon ankle-deep in slush. Our next bungalow lay in a narrow valley, on the banks of the rushing Pindar River, which twisted its way through the mountains. We were not sure how far we had to go, but nobody seemed in a hurry. On an impulse, I decided to hurry on ahead of the others. I wanted to be waiting for them at the river.

The path dropped steeply, then rose and went round a big mountain. I met a woodcutter and asked him how far it was to the river. He was a short, stocky man, with gnarled hands and a weathered face.

'Seven miles,' he said. 'Are you alone?'

'No, the others are following, but I cannot wait for them.

If you meet them, tell them I'll be waiting at the river.'

The path descended steeply now, and I had to run a little. It was a dizzy, winding path. The hillside was covered with lush green ferns and, in the trees, unseen birds sang loudly. Soon, I was in the valley, and the path straightened out. A girl was coming from the opposite direction. She held a long, curved knife, with which she had been cutting grass and fodder. There were rings in her nose and ears, and her arms were covered with heavy bangles. The bangles made music when she moved her hands—it was as though her hands spoke a language of their own.

'How far is it to the river?' I asked.

The girl had probably never been near the river, or she may have been thinking of another one, because she replied, 'Twenty miles,' without any hesitation.

I laughed, and ran down the path. A parrot screeched suddenly, flew low over my head—a flash of blue and green—and took the course of the path, while I followed its dipping flight, until the path rose and the bird disappeared into the trees.

A trickle of water came from the hillside, and I stopped to drink. The water was cold and sharp and very refreshing. I had walked alone for nearly an hour. Presently I saw a boy ahead of me, driving a few goats along the path.

'How far is it to the river?' I asked, when I caught up with him.

The boy said, 'Oh, not far, just around the next hill.'

As I was hungry, I produced some dry bread from my pocket and, breaking it in two, offered half to the boy. We sat on the grassy hillside and ate in silence. Then we walked on together and began talking; and I did not notice the smarting of my feet and the distance I had covered. But after some time the boy had to diverge along another path, and I was once more on my own.

I missed the village boy. I looked up and down the path, but I could see no one, no sign of Anil and Kamal and Bisnu, and the river was not in sight either. I began to feel discouraged. But I couldn't turn back; I was determined to be at the river before the others.

And so I walked on, along the muddy path, past terraced fields and small stone houses, until there were no more fields and houses, only forest and sun and silence.

The silence was oppressive and a little frightening. It was different from the silence of a room or an empty street. Nor was there any movement, except for the bending of grass beneath my feet, and the circling of a hawk high above the fir trees.

And then, as I rounded a sharp bend, the silence broke into sound.

The sound of the river.

Far down in the valley, the river tumbled over itself in its impatience to reach the plains. I began to run, slipped and stumbled, but continued running.

And the water was blue and white and wonderful.

When Anil, Kamal and Bisnu arrived, the four of us bravely decided to bathe in the little river. The late afternoon sun was still warm, but the water—so clear and inviting—proved to be ice-cold. Only twenty miles upstream the river emerged as a little trickle from the glacier, and in its swift descent down the mountain slopes it did not give the sun a chance to penetrate its waters. But we were determined to bathe, to wash away the dust and sweat of our two days' trudging, and we leapt about in the shallows like startled porpoises, slapping water on each other, and gasping with the shock of each immersion. Bisnu, more accustomed to mountain streams than ourselves, ventured across in an attempt to catch an otter but wasn't fast enough. Then we were on the springy grass, wrestling each other in order to get warm.

The bungalow stood on a ledge just above the river, and the sound of the water rushing down the mountain defile could be heard at all times. The sound of the birds, which we had grown used to, was drowned by the sound of the water; but the birds themselves could be seen, many-coloured, standing out splendidly against the dark green forest foliage: the red-crowned jay, the paradise flycatcher, the purple whistling-thrush, others we could not recognize.

Higher up the mountain, above some terraced land where oats and barley were grown, stood a small cluster of huts. This, we were told by the watchman, was the last village on the way to the glacier. It was, in fact, one of the last villages in India, because if we crossed the difficult passes beyond the glacier, we would find ourselves in Tibet. We told the watchman we would be quite satisfied if we reached the glacier.

Then Anil made the mistake of mentioning the Abominable Snowman, of whom we had been reading in the papers. The people of Nepal believe in the existence of the Snowman, and our watchman was a Nepali.

'Yes, I have seen the Yeti,' he told us. 'A great shaggy flat-footed creature. In the winter, when it snows heavily, he passes by the bungalow at night. I have seen his tracks the next morning.'

'Does he come this way in the summer?' I asked anxiously. We were sitting before another of Bisnu's fires, drinking tea with condensed milk, and trying to get through a black, sticky sweet which the watchman had produced from his tin trunk.

'The Yeti doesn't come here in the summer,' said the old man. 'But I have seen the Lidini sometimes. You have to be careful of her.'

'What is a Lidini?' asked Kamal.

'Ah!' said the watchman mysteriously. 'You have heard of the Abominable Snowman, no doubt, but there are few who have heard of the Abominable Snowwoman! And yet she is by far the more dangerous of the two!'

'What is she like?' asked Anil, and we all craned forward.

'She is of the same height as the Yeti—about seven feet when her back is straight—and her hair is much longer. She has very long teeth and nails. Her feet face inwards, but she can run very fast, especially downhill. If you see a Lidini, and she chases you, always run away in an uphill direction. She tires quickly because of her feet. But when running downhill she has no trouble at all, and you have to be very fast to escape her!'

'Well, we're all good runners,' said Anil with a nervous laugh, 'but it's just a fairy story, I don't believe a word of it.'

'But you *must* believe fairy stories,' I said, remembering a performance of Peter Pan in London, when those in the audience who believed in fairies were asked to clap their hands in order to save Tinker Bell's life. 'Even if they aren't true,' I added, deciding there was a world of difference between Tinker Bell and the Abominable Snowwoman.

'Well, I don't believe there's a Snowman or a Snowwoman!' declared Anil.

The watchman was most offended and refused to tell us anything about the Sagpa and Sagpani; but Bisnu knew about them, and later, when we were in bed, he told us that they were similar to Snowmen but much smaller. Their favourite pastime was sleeping, and they became very annoyed if anyone woke them, and became ferocious, and did not give one much time to start running uphill. The Sagpa and Sagpani sometimes kidnapped small children and, taking them to their cave, would look after the children very carefully, feeding them on fruits, honey, rice, and earthworms.

'When the Sagpa isn't looking,' he said, 'you can throw the earthworms over your shoulder.'

The Glacier

It was a fine sunny morning when we set out to cover the last seven miles to the glacier. We had expected this to be a stiff climb, but the last dak bungalow was situated at well over 10,000 feet above sea level, and the ascent was to be fairly gradual.

And suddenly, abruptly, there were no more trees. As the bungalow dropped out of sight, the trees and bushes gave way to short grass and little blue and pink alpine flowers. The snow peaks were close now, ringing us in on every side. We passed waterfalls, cascading hundreds of feet down precipitous rock faces, thundering into the little river. A great golden eagle hovered over us for some time.

'I feel different again,' said Kamal.

'We're very high now,' I said. 'I hope we won't get headaches.'

'I've got one already,' complained Anil. 'Let's have some tea.'

We had left our cooking utensils at the bungalow, expecting to return there for the night, and had brought with us only a few biscuits, chocolate and a thermos of tea. We finished the tea, and Bisnu scrambled about on the grassy slopes, collecting wild strawberries. They were tiny strawberries, very sweet, and they did nothing to satisfy our appetites. There was no sign of habitation or human life.

The only creatures to be found at that height were the gorals—sure-footed mountain goats—and an occasional snow leopard, or a bear.

We found and explored a small cave, and then, turning a bend, came unexpectedly upon the glacier.

The hill fell away, and there, confronting us, was a great white field of snow and ice, cradled between two peaks that could only have been the abode of the gods. We were speechless for several minutes. Kamal took my hand and held on to it for reassurance; perhaps he was not sure that what he saw was real. Anil's mouth hung open. Bisnu's eyes glittered with excitement.

We proceeded cautiously on the snow, supporting each other on the slippery surface; but we could not go far, because we were quite unequipped for any high-altitude climbing. It was pleasant to feel that we were the only boys in our town who had climbed so high. A few black rocks jutted out from the snow, and we sat down on them, to feast our eyes on the view. The sun reflected sharply from the snow, and we felt surprisingly warm.

'Let's sunbathe!' said Anil, on a sudden impulse.

'Yes, let's do that!' I said.

In a few minutes, we had taken off our clothes and, sitting on the rocks, were exposing ourselves to the elements. It was delicious to feel the sun crawling over my skin. Within half an hour I was post-box red, and so was Bisnu, and the two of us decided to get into our clothes before the sun scorched the skin off our backs. Kamal and Anil appeared to be more resilient to sunlight, and laughed at our discomfiture. Bisnu and I avenged ourselves by gathering up handfuls of snow and rubbing it on their backs. We dressed quickly enough after that, Anil leaping about like a performing monkey.

Meanwhile, almost imperceptibly, clouds had covered some of the peaks, and white mist drifted down the mountain slopes. It was time to get back to the bungalow; we would barely make it before dark.

We had not gone far when lightning began to sizzle about the mountaintops followed by waves of thunder.

'Let's run!' shouted Anil. 'We can get shelter in the cave!'

The clouds could hold themselves in no longer, and the rain came down suddenly, stinging our faces as it was whipped up by an icy wind. Half-blinded, we ran as fast as we could along the slippery path, and stumbled, drenched and exhausted, into the little cave.

The cave was mercifully dry, and not very dark. We remained at the entrance, watching the rain sweep past us, listening to the wind whistling down the long gorge.

'It will take some time to stop,' said Kamal.

'No, it will pass soon,' said Bisnu. 'These storms are short and fierce.'

Anil produced his pocketknife, and to pass the time we carved our names in the smooth rock of the cave.

'We will come here again, when we are older,' said Kamal, 'and perhaps our names will still be here.'

It had grown dark by the time the rain stopped. A full moon helped us find our way, we went slowly and carefully. The rain had loosened the earth, and stones kept rolling down the hillside. I was afraid of starting a landslide.

'I hope we don't meet the Lidini now,' said Anil fervently.

'I thought you didn't believe in her,' I said.

'I don't,' replied Anil. 'But what if I'm wrong?'

We saw only a mountain goat, the goral, poised on the brow of a precipice, silhouetted against the sky.

And then the path vanished.

Had it not been for the bright moonlight, we might have walked straight into an empty void. The rain had caused a landslide, and where there had been a narrow path there was now only a precipice of loose, slippery shale.

'We'll have to go back,' said Bisnu. 'It will be too dangerous to try and cross in the dark.'

'We'll sleep in the cave,' I suggested.

'We've nothing to sleep in,' said Anil. 'Not a single blanket between us and nothing to eat!'

'We'll just have to rough it till morning,' said Kamal. 'It will be better than breaking our necks here.'

We returned to the cave, which did at least have the virtue of being dry. Bisnu had matches, and he made a fire with some dry sticks which had been left in the cave by a previous party. We ate what was left of a loaf of bread.

There was no sleep for any of us that night. We lay close to each other for comfort, but the ground was hard and uneven. And every noise we heard outside the cave made us think of leopards and bears and even the Abominable Snowmen.

We got up as soon as there was a faint glow in the sky. The snow peaks were bright pink, but we were too tired and hungry and worried to care for the beauty of the sunrise. We took the path to the landslide, and once again looked for a way across. Kamal ventured to take a few steps on the loose pebbles, but the ground gave way immediately, and we had to grab him by the arms and shoulders to prevent him from sliding a hundred feet down the gorge.

'Now what are we going to do?' I asked.

'Look for another way,' said Bisnu.

'But do you know of any?'

And we all turned to look at Bisnu, expecting him to provide the solution to our problem.

'I have heard of a way,' said Bisnu, 'but I have never used it. It will be a little dangerous, I think. The path has not been used for several years—not since the traders stopped coming in from Tibet.'

'Never mind, we'll try it,' said Anil.

'We will have to cross the glacier first,' said Bisnu. 'That's the main problem.'

We looked at each other in silence. The glacier didn't look difficult to cross, but we know that it would not be easy for novices. For almost two furlongs it consisted of hard, slippery ice.

Anil was the first to arrive at a decision.

'Come on,' he said. 'There's no time to waste.'

We were soon on the glacier. And we remained on it for a long time. For every two steps forward, we slid one step backward. Our progress was slow and awkward. Sometimes, after advancing several yards across the ice at a steep incline, one of us would slip back and the others would have to slither down to help him up. At one particularly difficult spot, I dropped our water bottle and, grabbing at it, lost my footing, fell full-length and went sliding some twenty feet down the ice slope.

I had sprained my wrist and hurt my knee, and was to prove a liability for the rest of the trek.

Kamal tied his handkerchief around my hand, and Anil took charge of the water bottle, which we had filled with ice. Using my good hand to grab Bisnu's legs whenever I slipped, I struggled on behind the others.

It was almost noon, and we were quite famished, when we put our feet on grass again. And then we had another steep climb, clutching at roots and grasses, before we reached the path that Bisnu had spoken about. It was little more than a goat-track, but it took us around the mountain and brought us within sight of the dak bungalow.

'I could eat a whole chicken,' said Kamal.

'I could eat two,' I said.

'I could eat a Snowman,' said Bisnu.

'And I could eat the chowkidar,' said Anil.

Fortunately for the chowkidar, he had anticipated our hunger; and when we staggered into the bungalow late in the afternoon, we found a meal waiting for us. True, there was no chicken—but, so ravenous did we feel, that even the lowly onion tasted delicious!

We had Bisnu to thank for getting us back successfully. He had brought us over mountain and glacier with all the skill and confidence of a boy who had the Himalaya in his blood.

We took our time getting back to Kapkote; fished in the Sarayu River; bathed with the village boys we had seen on our way up; collected strawberries and ferns and wild flowers; and finally said goodbye to Bisnu.

Anil wanted to take Bisnu along with us, but the boy's parents refused to let him go, saying that he was too young for the life of a city; but we were of the opinion that Bisnu could have taught the city boys a few things.

'Never mind,' said Kamal. 'We'll go on another trip next year, and we'll take you with us, Bisnu. We'll write and let you know our plans.'

This promise made Bisnu happy, and he saw us off at the bus stop, shouldering our bedding to the end. Then he skimmed up the trunk of a fir tree to have a better view of us leaving, and we saw him waving to us from the tree as our bus went round the bend from Kapkote, and the hills were left behind and the plains stretched out below.

COLD BEER AT CHUTMALPUR

Just outside the small market town of Chutmalpur (on the way back from Delhi) one is greeted by a large signboard with just two words on it: Cold Beer. The signboard is almost as large as the shop from which the cold beer is dispensed; but after a gruelling five-hour drive from Delhi, in the heat and dust of May, a glass of chilled beer is welcome—except, of course, to teetotallers who will find other fizzy ways to satiate their thirst.

Chutmalpur is not the sort of place you'd choose to retire in. But it has its charms, not the least of which is its Sunday Market, when the varied produce of the rural interior finds its way on to the dusty pavements, and the air vibrates with noise, colour and odours. Carpets of red chillies, seasonal fruits, stacks of grain and vegetables, cheap toys for the children, bangles of lac, wooden artifacts, colourful underwear, sweets of every description, *churan* to go with them...

'*Lakar hajam, gather hajam!*' cries the churan-seller. Translated: digest wood, digest stones! That is, if you partake of this particular digestive pill which, when I tried it, appeared to be one part hing (asafoetida) and one part gunpowder. Things are seldom what they seem to be. Passing through the small town of Purkazi, I noticed a signboard which announced the availability of 'Books'—just that. Intrigued, I stopped to find out more about this bookshop in the wilderness. Perhaps I'd find a rare tome to add to my library. Peeping in, I discovered that the dark interior was stacked from floor to ceiling with exercise books! Apparently the shop owner was the supplier for the district.

Rare books can be seen in Roorkee, in the university's old library. Here, not many years ago, a First Folio Shakespeare turned up and was celebrated in the Indian press as a priceless discovery. Perhaps it's still there.

Also in the library is a bust of Sir Proby Cautley, who conceived and built the Ganga Canal, which starts at Haridwar and passes through Roorkee on its way across the Doab. Hardly anyone today has heard of Cautley, and yet surely his achievement outstrips that of many Englishmen in India—soldiers and statesmen who became famous for doing all the wrong things.

Cautley's Canal

Cautley came to India at the age of seventeen and joined the Bengal Artillery. In 1825, he assisted Captain Robert Smith, the engineer in charge of constructing the Eastern Yamuna Canal. By 1836 he was Superintendent-General of Canals. From the start, he worked towards his dream of building a Ganga Canal, and spent six months walking and riding through the jungles and countryside, taking each level and measurement himself, sitting up all night to transfer them to his maps. He was confident that a 500-kilometre canal was feasible. There were many objections and obstacles to his project, most of them financial, but Cautley persevered and eventually persuaded the East India Company to back him.

Digging for the canal began in 1839. Cautley had to make his own bricks—millions of them—his own brick kiln, and his own mortar. A hundred thousand tonnes of lime went into the mortar, the other main ingredient of which was *surkhi*, made by grinding over-burnt bricks to a powder. To reinforce the mortar, *ghur*, ground lentils and jute fibres were added to it.

Initially, opposition came from the priests in Haridwar, who felt that the waters of the holy Ganga would be imprisoned. Cautley pacified them by agreeing to leave a narrow gap in the dam through which the river water could flow unchecked. He won over the priests when he inaugurated his project with *aarti*, and the worship of Ganesh, the god of good beginnings. He also undertook the repair of the sacred bathing ghats along the river. The canal banks were also to have their own ghats with steps leading down to the water.

The headworks of the canal are at Haridwar, where the Ganga enters the plains after completing its majestic journey through the Himalayas. Below Haridwar, Cautley had to dig new courses for some of the mountain torrents that threatened the canal. He collected them into four steams and took them over the canal by means of four passages. Near Roorkee, the land fell away sharply and there Cautley had to build an aqueduct, a masonry bridge that carries the canal for half a kilometre across the Solani torrent—a unique engineering feat. At Roorkee, the canal is twenty-five metres higher than the parent river, which flows almost parallel to it.

Most of the excavation work on the canal was done mainly by the Oads, a gypsy tribe who were professional diggers for most of northwest India. They took great pride in their work. Though extremely poor, Cautley found them a happy and carefree lot who worked in a very organized manner.

When the canal was formally opened on the 8 April 1854, its main channel was 348 miles long, its branches 306 and the distributaries over 3,000. Over 7,67,000 acres in 5,000 villages were irrigated. One of its main branches re-entered the Ganga at Kanpur; it also had branches to Fatehgarh, Bulandshahr and Aligarh.

Cautley's achievements did not end there. He was also actively involved in Dr Falconer's fossil expedition in the Siwaliks. He presented to the British Museum an extensive collection of fossil mammalia—including hippopotamus and crocodile fossils, evidence that the region was once swamp land or an inland sea. Other animal remains found there included the sabre-toothed tiger; Elephis ganesa, an elephant with a trunk ten-and-a-half feet long; a three-toed ancestor of the horse; the bones of a fossil ostrich; and the remains of giant cranes and tortoises. Exciting times, exciting finds.

Nor did Cautley's interests and activities end in fossil excavation. My copy of Surgeon General Balfour's *Cyclopaedia of India* (1873) lists a number of fascinating reports and papers by Cautley. He wrote on a submerged city, twenty feet underground, near Behut in the Doab; on the coal and lignite in the Himalayas; on gold washings in the Siwalik Hills, between the Yamuna and Sutlej rivers; on a new species of snake; on the m astodons of the Siwaliks; on the manufacture of tar; and on *Panchukkis* or corn mills.

How did he find time for all this, I wonder. Most of his life was spent in tents, overseeing the canal work or digging up fossils. He had a house in Mussoorie (one of the first), but he could not have spent much time in it. It is today part of the Manav Bharti School, and there is still a plaque in the office stating that Cautley lived there. Perhaps he wrote some of his reports and expositions during brief sojourns in the hills. It is said that his wife left him, unable to compete against the rival attractions of canals and fossils remains.

I wonder, too, if there was any follow up on his reports of the submerged city—is it still there, waiting to be re-discovered—or his findings on gold washings in the Siwaliks. Should my royalties ever dry up, I might just wonder off into the Siwaliks, looking for 'gold in them that hills'. Meanwhile, whenever I travel by road from Delhi to Haridwar, and pass over that placid canal at various places en route, I think of the man who spent more than twenty years of his life in executing this magnificent project, and others equally demanding. And then, his work done, walking away from it all without thought of fame or fortune.

A Jungle Princess

From Roorkee, separate roads lead to Haridwar, Saharanpur and Dehradun. And from the Saharanpur road, you can branch off to Paonta Sahib, with its famous gurudwara glistening above the blue waters of the Yamuna. Still blue up here, but not so blue by the time it enters Delhi. Industrial affluents and human waste soon muddy the purest of rivers.

From Paonta you can turn right to Herbertpur, a small township originally settled by an Anglo-Indian family early in the nineteenth century. As may be inferred by its name, Herbert was the scion of the family, but I have been unable to discover much about him. When I was a boy, the Carberry family owned much of the land around here, but by the time Independence came, only one member of the family remained—Doreen, a sultry, dusky beauty who become known in Dehra as the 'Jungle Princess'. Her husband had deserted her, but she had a small daughter who grew up on the land. Doreen's income came from her mango and guava orchards, and she seemed quite happy living in this isolated rural area near the river. Occasionally, she came into Dehradun, a bus ride of a couple of hours, and she would visit my mother, a childhood friend, and occasionally stay overnight.

On one occasion we went to Doreen's jungle home for a couple of days. I was just seven or eight years old. I remember Doreen's daughter (about my age) teaching me to climb trees. I managed the guava tree quite well, but some of the others were too difficult for me.

How did this Jungle Princess manage to live by herself in this remote area, where her house, orchard and fields were bordered by forest on one side and the river on the other?

Well, she had her servants, of course, and they were loyal to her. She also possessed several guns and could handle them very well. I saw her bring down a couple of pheasants with her twelve-bore spread shot. She had also killed a cattle-lifting tiger that had been troubling a nearby village, and a marauding leopard that had taken one of her dogs. So she was quite capable of taking care of herself. When I last saw her, some twenty-five years ago, she was in her seventies. I believe she sold her land and went to live elsewhere with her daughter, who, by then, had a family of her own.

THE KIPLING ROAD

Remember the old road,
The steep stony path
That took us up from Rajpur,
Toiling and sweating
And grumbling at the climb,
But enjoying it all the same.
At first the hills were hot and bare,
But then there were trees near Jharipani
And we stopped at the Halfway House
And swallowed lungfuls of diamond-cut air.
Then onwards, upwards, to the town,
Our appetites to repair!

Well, no one uses the old road any more.
Walking is out of fashion now.
And if you have a car to take you
Swiftly up the motor road
Why bother to toil up a disused path?
You'd have to be an old romantic like me
To want to take that route again.
But I did it last year,
Pausing and plodding and gasping for air—
Both road and I being a little worse for wear!

But I made it to the top and stopped to rest
And looked down to the valley and the silver stream
Winding its way towards the plains.
And the land stretched out before me, and the years fell
   away,
And I was a boy again,
And the friends of my youth were there beside me,
And nothing had changed.

—'Remember the Old Road'

As boys we would often trudge up from Rajpur to Mussoorie by the old bridle-path, the road that used to serve the hill-station in the days before the motor road was built. Before 1900, the traveller to Mussoorie took a tonga from Saharanpur to Dehradun, spent the night at a Rajpur hotel, and the following day came up the steep seven-mile path on horseback, or on foot, or in a dandy (a crude palanquin) held aloft by two, sometimes four, sweating coolies.

The railway came to Dehradun in 1904, and a few years later the first motor car made it to Mussoorie, the motor road following the winding contours and hairpin bends of the old bullock cart road. Rajpur went out of business; no one stopped there any more, the hotels became redundant, and the bridle-path was seldom used except by those of us who thought it would be fun to come up on foot.

For the first two or three miles you walked in the hot sun, along a treeless path. It was only at Jharipani (at approximately 4,000 ft) that the oak forests began, providing shade and shelter. Situated on a spur of its own was the Railways school, Oakgrove, still there today, providing a boarding-school education to the children of Railway personnel. My mother and her sisters came from a Railway family, and all of them studied at Oakgrove in the 1920s. So did a male cousin, who succumbed to cerebral malaria during the school term. In spite of the salubrious climate, mortality was high among schoolchildren.

There were no cures then for typhoid, cholera, malaria, dysentery and other infectious diseases.

Above Oakgrove was Fairlawn, the palace of the Nepali royal family. There was a sentry box outside the main gate, but there was never any sentry in it, and on more than one occasion I took shelter there from the rain. Today it's a series of cottages, one of which belongs to *Outlook*'s editor, [the late] Vinod Mehta, who seeks shelter there from the heat and dust of Delhi.

From Jharipani we climbed to Barlowganj, where another venerable institution, St George's College, crowns the hilltop. Then on to Bala Hissar, once the home-in-exile of an Afghan king, and now the grounds of Wynberg Allen, another school. In later years I was to live near this school, and it was its then Principal, Rev. W. Biggs, who told me that the bridle-path was once known as the Kipling Road.

Why was that, I asked. Had Kipling ever come up that way? Rev. Biggs wasn't sure, but he referred me to *Kim,* and the chapter in which Kim and the Lama leave the plains for the hills. It begins thus:

> They had crossed the Siwaliks and the half-tropical Doon, left Mussoorie behind them, and headed north along the narrow hill-roads. Day after day they struck deeper into the huddled mountains, and day after day Kim watched the lama return to a man's strength. Among the terraces of the Doon he had leaned on the boy's shoulder, ready to profit by wayside halts. Under the great ramp to Mussoorie he drew himself together as an old hunter faces a well-remembered bank, and where he should have sunk

exhausted swung his long draperies about him, drew a deep double lungful of the diamond air, and walked as only a hillman can.

This description is accurate enough, but it is not evidence that Kipling actually came this way, and his geography becomes quite confusing in the subsequent pages—as Peter Hopkirk discovered when he visited Mussoorie a few years ago, retracing Kim's journeys for his book *Quest for Kim*. Hopkirk spent some time with me in this little room where I am now writing, but we were unable to establish the exact route that Kim and the Lama took after traversing Mussoorie. Presumably they had come up the bridle-path. But then? After that, Kipling becomes rather vague.

Mussoorie does not really figure in Rudyard Kipling's prose or poetry. The Simla Hills were his beat. As a journalist he was a regular visitor to Simla, then the summer seat of the British Raj.

But last year my Swiss friend, Anilees Goel, brought me proof that Kipling had indeed visited Mussoorie. Among his unpublished papers and other effects in the Library of Congress, there exists an album of photographs, which includes two of the Charleville Hotel, Mussoorie, where he had spent the summer of 1888. On a photograph of the office he had inscribed these words:

> And there were men with a thousand wants
> And women with babes galore
> But the dear little angels in Heaven know
> That Wutzler *never* swore.

Wutzler was the patient, long-suffering manager of this famous hotel, now the premises of the Lal Bahadur Shastri National Academy of Administration.

A second photograph is inscribed with the caption 'Quarters at the Charleville, April-July 88', and carries this verse:

A burning sun in cloudless skies
    and April dies,
A dusty Mall—three sunsets splendid
    and May is ended,
Grey mud beneath—grey cloud o'erhead
    and June is dead.
A little bill in late July
    And then we fly.

Pleasant enough, but hardly great verse, and I'm not surprised that Kipling did not publish these lines.

However, we now know that he came to Mussoorie and spent some time here, and that he would have come up by the old bridle-path (there was no other way except by bullock cart on the long and tortuous cast road), and Rev. Biggs and the others were right in calling it the Kipling Road, although officially that was never its name.

As you climb up from Barlowganj, you pass a number of pretty cottages—May Cottage, Wakefield, Ralston Manor, Wayside Hall—and these old houses all have stories to tell, for they have stood mute witness to the comings and goings of all manner of people.

Take Ralston Manor. It was witness to an impromptu cremation, probably Mussoorie's first European cremation, in the late 1890s. There is a small chapel in the grounds of Ralston, and the story goes that a Mr and Mrs Smallman had been living in the house, and Mr Smallman had expressed a wish to be cremated at his death. When he died, his widow decided to observe his wishes and had her servants build a funeral pyre in the garden. The cremation was well underway when someone rode by and looked in to see what was happening. The unauthorized cremation was reported to the authorities and Mrs Smallman had to answer some awkward questions. However, she was let off with a warning (a warning not to cremate any future husbands?) and later she built the little chapel on the site of the funeral pyre—in gratitude or as penance, or as a memorial, we are not told. But the chapel is still there, and this little tale is recorded in *Chowkidar* (Autumn 1995), the journal of the British Association for Cemeteries in South Asia (BACSA).

As we move further up the road, keeping to the right, we come to Wayside Hall and Wayside Cottage, which have the advantage of an open sunny hillside and views to the north and east. I lived in the cottage for a couple of years, back in 1966–67, as a tenant of the Powell sisters who lived in the Hall.

There were three sisters, all in their seventies; they had survived their husbands. Annie, the eldest, had a son who lived abroad; Martha, the second, did not have children; Dr Simmonds, the third sister, had various adopted children who came to see her from time to time. They were God-fearing, religious folk, but not bigots; never chided me for not going to church. Annie's teas were marvellous; snacks and savouries in abundance.

They kept a beautiful garden.

'Why go to church?' I said. 'Your garden is a church.'

In spring and summer it was awash with poppies, petunia, phlox, larkspur, calendula, snapdragons and other English flowers. During the monsoon, the gladioli took over, while magnificent dahlias reared up from the rich foliage. During the autumn came zinnias and marigolds and cosmos. And even during the winter months there would be geraniums and primulae blooming in the verandah.

Honeysuckle climbed the wall outside my window, filling my bedroom with its heady scent. And wisteria grew over the main gate. There was perfume in the air.

Annie herself smelt of freshly baked bread. Dr Simmonds smelt of Pears' baby soap. Martha smelt of apples. All good smells, emanating from good people.

Although they lived on their own, without any men on the premises, they never felt threatened or insecure. Mussoorie was a safe place to live in then, and still is to a great extent—much safer than towns in the plains, where the crime rate keeps pace with the population growth.

Annie's son, Gerald, then in his sixties, did come out to see them occasionally. He had been something of a shikari in his youth—or so he claimed—and told me he could call up a panther from the valley without any difficulty. To do this, he made a contraption out of an old packing case, with a hole bored in the middle, then he passed a length of thick wire through the hole, and by moving the wire backwards and forward produced a sound not dissimilar to the sawing, coughing sound made by a panther during the mating season.

Gerry invited me to join him on a steep promontory overlooking a little stream. I did so with some trepidation. Hunting had never been my forte, and normally I preferred to go along with Ogden Nash's dictum, 'If you meet a panther, don't anther!'

However, Gerry's gun looked powerful enough, and I believed him when he told me he was a crack shot. I have always taken people at their word. One of my failings I suppose.

Anyway, we positioned ourselves on this ledge, and Gerry started producing panther noises with his box. His Master's Voice (HMV) would have been proud of it. Nothing happened for about twenty minutes, and I was beginning to lose patience when we were answered by the cough and grunt of what could only have been a panther. But we couldn't see it! Gerry produced a pair of binoculars and trained them on some distant object below, which turned out to be a goat. The growling continued—and then it was just above us! The panther had made a detour and was now standing on a rock and staring down, no doubt wondering which of us was making such attractive mating calls. Gerry swung round, raised his gun and fired. He missed by a couple of feet, and the panther bounded away, no doubt disgusted with the proceedings.

We returned to Wayside Hall, and revived ourselves with brandy and soda.

'We'll get it next time, old chap,' said Gerry. But although we tried, the panther did not put in another appearance. Gerry's panther call sounded genuine enough, but neither he nor I nor his wired box looked anything like a female panther.

AT THE END OF THE ROAD

Choose your companions carefully when you are walking in the hills. If you are accompanied by the wrong person—by which I mean someone who is temperamentally very different to you—that long hike you've been dreaming of could well turn into a nightmare.

This has happened to me more than once. The first time, many years ago, when I accompanied a businessman-friend to the Pindari Glacier in Kumaon. He was in such a hurry to get back to his executive's desk in Delhi that he set off for the Glacier as though he had a train to catch, refusing to spend any time admiring the views, looking for birds or animals, or greeting the local inhabitants. By the time we had left the last dak bungalow at Phurkia, I was ready to push him over a cliff. He probably felt the same way about me.

On our way down, we met a party of Delhi University boys who were on the same trek. They were doing it in a leisurely, good-humoured fashion. They were very friendly and asked me to join them. On an impulse, I bid farewell to my previous companion—who was only too glad to dash off downhill to where his car was parked at Kapkote—while I made a second ascent to the Glacier, this time in better company.

Unfortunately, my previous companion had been the one with the funds. My new friends fed me on the way back, and in Nainital I pawned my watch so that I could have enough for the bus ride back to Delhi. Lesson Two: always carry enough money with you; don't depend on a wealthy friend!

Of course, it's hard to know who will be a 'good companion' until you have actually hit the road together. Sharing a meal or having a couple of drinks together is not the same as tramping along on a dusty road with the water bottle down to its last drop. You can't tell until you have spent a night in the rain, or lost the way in the mountains, or finished all the food, whether both of you have stout hearts and a readiness for the unknown.

I like walking alone, but a good companion is well worth finding. He will add to the experience. 'Give me a companion of my way, be it only to mention how the shadows lengthen as the sun declines,' wrote Hazlitt.

Pratap was one such companion. He had invited me to spend a fortnight with him in his village above the Nayar river in Pauri-Garhwal. In those days, there was no motor-road beyond Lansdowne and one had to walk some thirty miles to get to the village.

But first, one had to get to Lansdowne. This involved getting into a train at Dehra Dun, getting out at Luxor (across the Ganga), getting into another train, and then getting out again at Najibabad and waiting for a bus to take one through the Tarai to Kotdwara.

Najibabad must have been one of the least inspiring places on earth. Hot, dusty, apparently lifeless. We spent two hours at the bus-stand, in the company of several donkeys, also quartered there. We were told that the area had once been the favourite hunting ground of a notorious dacoit, Sultana Daku, whose fortress overlooked the barren plain. I could understand him taking up dacoity—what else was there to do in such a place—and presumed that he looked elsewhere for his loot, for in Nazibabad there was nothing worth taking. In due course he was betrayed and hanged by the British, when they should instead have given him an OBE for stirring up the sleepy countryside.

There was a short branch line from Nazibabad to Kotdwara, but the train wasn't leaving that day, as the engine driver was unaccountably missing. The bus driver seemed to be missing too, but he did eventually turn up, a little worse for some late night drinking. I could sympathize with him. If in 1940, Nazibabad drove you to dacoity, in 1960 it drove you to drink.

Kotdwara, a steamy little town in the foothills, was equally depressing. It seemed to lack any sort of character. Here we changed buses, and moved into higher regions, and the higher we went, the nicer the surroundings; by the time we reached Lansdowne, at 6,000 feet, we were in good spirits.

The small hill station was a recruiting centre for the Garhwal Rifles (and still is), and did not cater to tourists. There were no hotels, just a couple of tea-stalls where a meal of dal and rice could be obtained. I believe it is much the same forty years on. Pratap had a friend who was the caretaker of an old, little used church, and he bedded us down in the vestry. Early next morning we set out on our long walk to Pratap's village.

I have covered longer distances on foot, but not all in one day. Thirty miles of trudging up hill and down and up again, most of it along a footpath that traversed bare hillsides where the hot May sun beat down relentlessly. Here and there we found a little shade and a freshet of spring water, which kept us going; but we had neglected to bring food with us apart from a couple of rock-hard buns probably dating back to colonial times, which we had picked up in Lansdowne. We were lucky to meet a farmer who gave us some onions and accompanied us part of the way.

Onions for lunch? Nothing better when you're famished. In the West they say, 'Never talk to strangers.' In the East they say, 'Always talk to strangers.' It was this stranger who gave us sustenance on the road, just as strangers had given me company on the way to the Pindar Glacier. On the open road there are no strangers. You share the same sky, the same mountain, the same sunshine and shade. On the open road we are all brothers.

The stranger went his way, and we went ours. 'Just a few more bends,' according to Pratap, always encouraging to the novice plainsman. But I was to be a hillman by the time we returned to Dehra! Hundreds of 'just a few more bends', before we reached the village, and I kept myself going with my off-key rendering of the old Harry Lauder song—

Keep right on to the end of the road,
Keep right on to the end.
If your way be long, let your heart be strong,
So keep right on round the bend.

By the time we'd done the last bend, I had a good idea of how the expression 'going round the bend' had came into existence. A maddened climber, such as I, had to negotiate one bend too many...

But Pratap was the right sort of companion. He adjusted his pace to suit mine; never lost patience; kept telling me I was a great walker. We arrived at the village just as night fell, and there was his mother waiting for us with a tumbler of milk.

Milk! I'd always hated the stuff (and still do) but that day I was grateful for it and drank two glasses. Fortunately it was cold. There was plenty of milk for me to drink during my two-week stay in the village, as Pratap's family possessed at least three productive cows. The milk was supplemented by thick rotis, made from grounded maize, seasonal vegetables, rice and a species of lentil peculiar to the area and very difficult to digest. Health-food friends would have approved of this fare, but it did not agree with me, and I found myself constipated most of the time. Still, better to be constipated than to be in free flow.

The point I am making is that it is always wise to carry your own food on a long hike or treks in the hills. Not that I could have done so, as Pratap's guest; he would have taken it as an insult. By the time I got back to Dehra—after another exhausted trek, and more complicated bus and train journeys—I felt quite famished and out of sorts. I bought some eggs and bacon rashers from the grocery store across the road from Astley Hall, and made myself a scrumptious breakfast. I am not much of a cook, but I can fry an egg and get the bacon nice and crisp. My needs are simple really. To each his own!

On another trek, from Mussoorie to Chamba (before the motor-road came into existence) I put two tins of sardines into my knapsack but forgot to take along a can-opener. Three days later I was back in Dehra, looking very thin indeed, and with my sardine tins still intact. That night I ate the contents of both tins.

Reading an account of the same trek undertaken by John Lang about a hundred years earlier, I was awestruck by his description of the supplies that he and his friends took with them.

Here he is, writing in Charles Dickens' magazine, *Household Words*, in the issue of 30 January 1858:

> In front of the club-house our marching establishment had collected, and the one hundred and fifty coolies were laden with the baggage and stores. There were tents, camp tables, chairs, beds, bedding, boxes of every kind, dozens of cases of wine-port, sherry and claret-beer, ducks, fowls, geese, guns, umbrellas, great coats and the like.

He then goes on to talk of lobsters, oysters and preserved soups.

I doubt if I would have got very far on such fare. I took the same road in October 1958, a century later; on my own and without provisions except for the aforementioned sardine tins. By dusk I had reached the village of Kaddukhal, where the local shopkeeper put me up for the night.

I slept on the floor, on a sheepskin infested by fleas. They were all over me as soon as I lay down, and I found it impossible to sleep. I fled the shop before dawn.

'Don't go out before daylight,' warned my host. 'There are bears around.'

But I would sooner have faced a bear than that onslaught from the denizens of the sheepskin. And I reached Chamba in time for an early morning cup of tea.

♦

Most Himalayan villages lie in the valleys, where there are small streams, some farmland and protection from the biting winds that come through the mountain passes. The houses are usually made of large stones, and have sloping slate roofs so the heavy monsoon rain can run off easily. During the sunny autumn months, the roofs are often covered with pumpkins, left there to ripen in the sun.

One October night, when I was sleeping at a friend's house just off the Tehri road, I was awakened by a rumbling and thumping on the roof. I woke my friend Jai and asked him what was happening.

'It's only a bear,' he said.
'Is it trying to get in?'
'No. It's after the pumpkins.'

A little later, when we looked out of a window, we saw a black bear making off through a field, leaving a trail of half-eaten pumpkins.

In winter, when snow covers the higher ranges, the Himalayan bears descend to lower altitudes in search of food. Sometimes they forage in fields. And because they are shortsighted and suspicious of anything that moves, they can be dangerous. But, like most wild animals, they avoid humans as much as possible.

Village folk always advise me to run downhill if chased by a bear. They say bears find it easier to run uphill than down. I have yet to be chased by a bear, and will happily skip the experience. But I have seen a few of these mountain bears and they are always fascinating to watch.

Himalayan bears enjoy corn, pumpkins, plums and apricots. Once, while I was sitting in an oak tree on Pari Tibba, hoping to see a pair of pine-martens that lived nearby, I heard the whining grumble of a bear, and presently a small bear ambled into the clearing beneath the tree.

He was little more than a cub, and I was not alarmed. I sat very still, waiting to see what the bear would do.

He put his nose to the ground and sniffed his way along until he came to a large anthill. Here he began huffing and puffing, blowing rapidly in and out of his nostrils so that the dust from the anthill flew in all directions. But the anthill had been deserted, and so, grumbling, the bear made his way up a nearby plum tree. Soon he was perched high in the branches. It was then that he saw me.

The bear at once scrambled several feet higher up the tree and lay flat on a branch. Since it wasn't a very big branch, there was a lot of bear showing on either side. He tucked his head behind another branch. He could no longer see me, so he apparently was satisfied that he was hidden, although he couldn't help grumbling.

Like all bears, this one was full of curiosity. So, slowly, inch by inch, his black snout appeared over the edge of the branch. As soon as he saw me, he drew his head back and hid his face.

He did this several times. I waited until he wasn't looking, then moved some way down my tree. When the bear looked over and saw that I was missing, he was so pleased that he stretched right across to another branch and helped himself to a plum. At that, I couldn't help bursting into laughter.

The startled young bear tumbled out of the tree, dropped through the branches some fifteen feet, and landed with a thump in a pile of dried leaves. He was unhurt, but fled from the clearing, grunting and squealing all the way.

Another time, my friend Jai told me that a bear had been active in his cornfield. We took up a post at night in an old cattle shed, which gave a clear view of the moonlit field.

A little after midnight, the bear came down to the edge of the field. She seemed to sense that we had been about. She was hungry, however. So, after standing on her hind legs and peering around to make sure the field was empty, she came cautiously out of the forest.

The bear's attention was soon distracted by some Tibetan prayer flags, which had been strung between two trees. She gave a grunt of disapproval and began to back away, but the fluttering of the flags was a puzzle that she wanted to solve. So she stopped and watched them.

Soon the bear advanced to within a few feet of the flags, examining them from various angles. Then, seeing that they posed no danger, she went right up to the flags and pulled them down. Grunting with apparent satisfaction, she moved into the field of corn.

Jai had decided that he didn't want to lose any more of his crop, so he started shouting. His children woke up and soon came running from the house, banging on empty kerosene tins.

Deprived of her dinner, the bear made off in a bad temper. She ran downhill at a good speed, and I was glad that I was not in her way.

Uphill or downhill, an angry bear is best given a very wide path.

◆

Sleeping out, under the stars, is a very romantic conception. 'Stones thy pillow, earth thy bed,' goes an old hymn, but a rolled-up towel or shirt will make a more comfortable pillow. Do not settle down to sleep on sloping ground, as I did once when I was a Boy Scout during my prep school days. We had camped at Tara Devi, on the outskirts of Shimla, and as it was a warm night I decided to sleep outside our tent. In the middle of the night I began to roll. Once you start rolling on a steep hillside, you don't stop. Had it not been for a thorny dog-rose bush, which halted my descent, I might well have rolled over the edge of a precipice.

I had a wonderful night once, sleeping on the sand on the banks of the Ganga above Rishikesh. It was a balmy night, with just a faint breeze blowing across the river, and as I lay there looking up at the stars, the lines of a poem by R.L. Stevenson kept running through my head:

> *Give to me the life I love,*
> *Let the lave go by me,*
> *Give the jolly heaven above*
> *And the byway nigh me.*
> *Bed in the bush with stars to see,*
> *Bread I dip in the river—*
> *There's the life for a man like me,*
> *There's the life for ever.*

The following night I tried to repeat the experience, but the jolly heaven above opened up in the early hours, the rain came pelting down, and I had to run for shelter to the nearest Ashram. Never take Mother Nature for granted!

The best kind of walk, and this applies to the plains as well as to the hills, is the one in which you have no particular destination when you set out.

'Where are you off?' asked a friend of mine the other day, when he met me on the road.

'Honestly, I have no idea,' I said, and I was telling the truth.

I did end up in Happy Valley, where I met an old friend whom I hadn't seen for years. When we were boys, his mother used to tell us stories about the *bhoot*s that haunted her village near Mathura. We reminisced and then went our different ways. I took the road to Hathipaon and met a schoolgirl who covered ten miles every day on her way to and from her school. So there were still people who used their legs, though out of necessity rather than choice.

Anyway, she gave me a story to write and thus I ended the day with two stories, one a memoir and the other based on a fresh encounter. And all because I had set out without a plan. The adventure is not in getting somewhere, it's the on-the-way experience. It is not the expected; it's the surprise. Not the fulfilment of prophecy, but the providence of something better than that prophesied.

THE ROAD TO ANJANI SAIN

Fog, mist, cloud, rain and mildew—these were the things the British must have looked for when selecting suitable sites for the hill stations they set up in the Himalayan foothills 150 years ago: Simla, Mussoorie, Darjeeling, Dalhousie, Nainital, all soggy with monsoon or winter mist and dripping oaks and deodars. The climate must have reminded them of their homes on the English moors or the Scottish highlands.

I have survived all that through the forty or so mountain monsoons that have been thrown at me; and having gone through the annual ritual of wiping the mildew from my books and a certain green fungus from my one and only suit, I decided some years ago to leave cloud country behind for a few days and be the guest of Cyril Raphael, at the Bhuvneshwari Mahila Ashram (a social service organization), at Anjani Sain in Tehri-Garhwal.

Pine country this, dry and bracing, with the scent of pine resin in the air. I have always thought 5,000 to 6,000 feet a healthier altitude to live at, but perhaps I'm prejudiced, having been born in Kasauli, which is pine rather than deodar country. Anjani Sain is about the same height and gets the sun all day. Given adequate food and pure water, it's a healthy place to live. Contrary to what most people think, Garhwal is not a poverty-stricken area. Almost everyone has a bit of land and does at least have the traditional *do-roti* for sustenance, which is more than can be said for the urban unemployed in other parts of northern India. But medical facilities are certainly lacking.

This area has always been known as Khas-patti, probably because it was special in several ways—climate-wise and probably economy-wise too. Down in the flat valley, there are green fields and even mango trees, the descent to lower altitudes being quite sudden in these parts. The small Anjani Sain bazaar, with its single bank, post office, and chemist's shop, shimmers in the noon sun; it looks like a set for a gunfight like in old westerns. But this is, generally, a peaceful area.

At the ashram, I am in time for an early lunch—thick rotis made from *mandwa* (millets)—two of these are more than enough for me! Endless glasses of milky tea will see me through till supper time.

Towering over Anjani Sain, and blessing all those who live or pass beneath, is the Chanderbadni temple, dedicated to one of the incarnations of the goddess Parvati. As this is not one of the main pilgrim routes, the temple does not get as many visitors as some of the other sacred shrines in the hills. Below the Chanderbadni peak is a rest-house, for those who wish to break their journey here.

Anjani Sain lies midway between Tehri and Devprayag—a two-hour bus ride from either place. I came via Tehri, the road climbing steeply above the hot, dusty town that is destined to be submerged by the waters of the Tehri Dam. The dam should have been ready by now, but having been the subject of a great deal of controversy, work on it has progressed in fits and starts.

I am told that this entire region is 'eco-fragile', one of those words bandied around at seminars all, over the world. Well, I am not an expert in these matters, (and who is, I wonder?) but I should think most of our earth is 'eco-fragile', having had to put up with hundreds of thousands of years of human civilization.

Do we stop all development in the name of preserving the environment? Or do we move on regardless? *Proceed with caution* would be the rational person's answer. But are human beings really rational?

Old Tehri was no beauty spot, and New Tehri (growing rapidly above it), is even uglier; from a distance it looks like a giant cemetery.

When the architecture of suburban Delhi is brought to the hills, what is there to say? You just look the other way.

Fortunately the defaced mountain is soon left behind, and as it slips out of sight and we ascend into the pine regions, the eye is soothed by the pretty, slate-covered houses of the villages and their little gardens ablaze with marigolds and yellow and bronze chrysanthemums.

Chrysanthemums love this climate. Down in the fields there are patches of crimson *cholai* (amaranth) interspersed with the fresh green of young wheat.

And here be leopards! My companion tells me of one that strolls down the motor road every evening, forcing the local bus to go around him. His presence also accounts for the absence of stray dogs.

Suddenly in the distance I see what at first glance appears to be a cloud or a large white sailing ship. On approaching, it turns out to be the freshly white-washed buildings of the Bhuvneshwari Mahila Ashram, clinging to the steep slopes of the mountain.

Here, for two or three days, I find rest and sustenance. The manifold activities of the ashram, (directed mainly towards the welfare of widows and small children) are there for all to see, and I recall the relief work undertaken by its young field workers after the Uttarkashi earthquake last year—they had rushed to the area before the government agencies could swing into action.

However, as a social worker I am somewhat inept. I am just a frazzled old writer who now seeks a refuge from the all-pervasive clutter of tourism that makes ordinary life almost impossible in our hill stations.

I hope the land-grabbers and the real estate 'developers' never get this far. They are welcome to their malls and artificial lakes and concrete parks. Just so long as I am free to escape from it all, to sit here at Anjani Sain contemplating a large white rose in Cyril's garden, while the rest of the world watches video.

THE MAGIC OF TUNGNATH

The mountains and valleys of Garhwal never fail to spring surprises on the traveller in search of the picturesque. It is impossible to know every corner of the Himalayas, which means that there are always new corners to discover; forest or meadow, mountain stream or wayside shrine.

The temple of Tungnath, at a little over 12,000 ft, is the highest shrine on the inner Himalayan range. It lies just below the Chandrashila peak. Some way off the main pilgrim routes, it is less frequented than Kedarnath or Badrinath, although it forms a part of the Kedar temple establishment. The priest here is a local man, a Brahmin from the village of Maku; the other Kedar temples have South Indian priests, a tradition begun by Sankaracharya, the eighth-century Hindu reformer and revivalist.

Tungnath's lonely eminence gives it a magic of its own. To get there (or beyond it), one passes through some of the most delightful temperate forests in the Garhwal Himalayas. Pilgrim or trekker or just plain rambler, such as myself, one comes away a better man, forest-refreshed and more aware of what the earth was really like before mankind began to strip it bare.

Duiri Tal, a small lake, lies cradled on the hill above Ukhimath at a height of 8,000 ft. It was the favourite spot of one of Garhwal's earliest British Commissioners, J.H. Batten, whose administration continued for twenty years (1836–56). He wrote:

> The day I reached there it was snowing and young trees were laid prostrate under the weight of snow, the lake was frozen over to a depth of about two inches. There was no human habitation, and the place looked a veritable wilderness. The next morning when the sun appeared, the Chaukhamba and many other peaks extending as far as Kedarnath seemed covered with a new quilt of snow as if close at hand. The whole scene was so exquisite that one could not tire of gazing at it for hours. I think a person who has a subdued settled despair in his mind would all of a sudden feel a kind of bounding and exalting cheerfulness which will be imparted to his frame by the atmosphere of Duiri Tal.

This feeling of uplift can be experienced almost anywhere along the Tungnath range. Duiri Tal is still some way way off the beaten track, and anyone wishing to spend the night there should carry a tent; but further along this range, the road ascends to Dugalbeta (at about 9,000 ft) where a PWD rest house, gaily painted, has come up like some exotic orchid in the midst of a lush meadow topped by excelsia pines and pencil cedars. Many an official who has stayed here has rhapsodized on the charms of Dugalbeta; and if you are unofficial (and therefore not entitled to stay in the bungalow), you can move on to Chopta, lusher still, where there is accommodation of a sort for pilgrims and other hardy souls. Two or three little tea-shops provide mattresses and quilts. The Garhwal Mandal Vikas Nigam has put up a rest house. These tourist rest houses, scattered over the length and breadth of Garhwal, are a great boon to travellers; but during the pilgrims season (May/June), they are filled to overflowing, and if you turn up unexpectedly, you might have to take your pick of tea-shop or 'dharamsala', something of a lucky dip, since they vary a good deal in comfort and cleanliness.

The trek from Chopta to Tungnath is only three and a half miles, but in that distance one ascends about 3,000 ft and the pilgrim may be forgiven for feeling that at places he is on a perpendicular path. Like a ladder to heaven, I couldn't help thinking.

In spite of its steepness, my companion, the redoubtable climber Ganesh Saili, insisted that we take a short cut. After clawing our way up tufts of alpine grass, which formed the rungs of our ladder, we were stuck and had to inch our way down again, so that the ascent of Tungnath began to resemble a game of Snakes and Ladders.

A tiny guardian-temple dedicated to Lord Ganesh surprised on top. Nor was I really fatigued; for the cold fresher air and the verdant greenery surrounding us was like an intoxicant. Myriads of wild flowers grew on the open slopes—buttercups, anemones, wild strawberries, forget-me-nots, rock-cross, enough to rival Bhyunders' Valley of Flowers at this time of the year.

But before reaching these alpine meadows, we climb through a rhododendron forest, and here one finds at least three species of this flower: the red-flowering tree rhododendron (found throughout the Himalayas between 6,000 ft and 10,000 ft); a second variety, the Almatta, with flowers that are light red or rosy in colour; and the third, Chimul or white variety, found at heights ranging between 10,000 ft and 13,000 ft. The Chimul is a brushwood, seldom more than twelve feet high and growing slantingly due to the heavy burden of snow it has to carry for almost six months in a year.

The brushwood rhododendrons are the last trees on our ascent, for as we approach Tungnath, the treeline ends and

The Magic of Tungnath

there is nothing between the earth and the sky except grass and rock and tiny flowers. Above us, a couple of crows dive-bomb a hawk, who does his best to escape their attentions. Crows are the world's great survivors. They are capable of living at any height and in any climate; as much at home in the back streets of Delhi as on the heights of Tungnath.

Another survivor, up here at any rate, is the Pika, a sort of mouse-hare, who looks neither like a mouse nor a hare but rather like a tiny guinea-pig; small ears, no tail, grey-brown fur and chubby feet. They emerge from their holes under the rock to forage for grasses on which to feed. Their simple diet and thick fur enable them to live in extreme cold, and they have been found at 16,000 ft, which is higher than where any mammal lives. The Garhwalis call this little creature the *runda*—at any rate, that's what the temple priest called it, adding that it was not averse to entering houses and helping itself to grain and other delicacies. So perhaps there's more in it of mouse than of hare.

These little rundas were with us all the way from Chopta to Tungnath, peering out from their rocks or scampering about on the hillside, seemingly unconcerned by our presence. At Tungnath they live beneath the temple flagstones. The priest's grandchildren were having a game discovering their burrows; the rundas would go in at one hole and pop at another; they must have had a system of underground passages.

When we arrived, clouds had gathered over Tungnath, as they do almost every afternoon. The temple looked austere in the gathering gloom.

To some, the name 'tung' indicates 'lofty', from the position of the temple on the highest peak outside the main chain of the Himalayas; others derive it from the word 'tangna'—'to be suspended'—in allusion to the form under which the deity is worshipped here. The form is the Swayambhu Ling; and on

Shivratri or the night of Shiva, the true believer may, 'with the eye of faith', see the lingam increase in size; but 'to the evil-minded no such favour is granted'.

The temple, though not very large, is certainly impressive, mainly because of its setting and the solid slabs of grey granite from which it is built. The whole place somehow reminds me of Emily Bronte's *Wuthering Heights*—bleak, wind-swept, open to the skies. And as you look down from the temple at the little half-deserted hamlet that serves it in summer, the eye is met by grey slate roofs and piles of stones, with just a few hardy souls in residence, for the majority of pilgrims now prefer to spend the night down at Chopta.

Even the temple priest, attended by his son and grandsons, complains bitterly of cold. To spend every day barefoot on those cold flagstones must indeed be a hardship. I wince after five minutes of it, made worse by stepping into a puddle of icy water. I shall never make a good pilgrim; no reward for me in this world or the next. But the pandit's feet are literally thick-skinned, and the children seem oblivious to the cold. Still, in October they must be happy to descend to Maku, their home village on the slopes below Dugalbeta.

It begins to rain as we leave the temple. We pass herds of sheep huddled in the ruined dharamsala. The crows are still rushing about the grey weeping skies, although the hawk has very sensibly gone away. A runda sticks his nose out from his hole, probably to take a look at the weather. There is a clap of thunder and he disappears, like the white rabbit in *Alice in Wonderland*. We are halfway down the Tungnath 'ladder' when it begins to rain quite heavily. And now we pass our first genuine pilgrims, a group of intrepid Bengalis who are heading straight into the storm. They are without umbrellas or raincoats, but they are not to be deterred.

Oaks and rhododendrons flash past as we dash down the steep, winding path. Another short cut, and rock-climber Ganesh Saili takes a tumble, but is cushioned by moss and buttercups. My wristwatch strikes a rock and the glass is shattered. No matter. Time here is of little or no significance. Away with time! Is this, I wonder, the 'bounding and exciting cheerfulness' experienced by Batten and now manifesting itself in me?

The tea-shop beckons. How would one manage in the hills without these wayside tea-shops? Miniature inns, they provide food, shelter and even lodging to dozens at a time.

We sit on a bench between a Gujar herdsman and a pilgrim who is too feverish to make the climb to the temple. He accepts my offer of an aspirin to go with his tea. We tackle some buns—rock-hard, to match our environment—and wash the pellets down with hot sweet tea.

There is a small shrine here, too, right in front of the tea-shop. It is a slab or rock roughly shaped like a lingam, and it is daubed with vermilion and strewn with offerings of wild flowers. The mica in the rock gives it a beautiful sheen.

I suppose Hinduism comes closest to being a nature religion. Rivers, rocks, trees, plants, animals and birds, all play their part, both in mythology and in everyday worship. This harmony is most evident in these remote places, where god and mountains coexist. Tungnath, as yet unspoilt by a materialistic society, exerts its magic on all who come here with open mind and heart.

AWAY FROM HOME

Wars and upheavals destroy lives, but it is always worth remembering that life and humanity are bigger than them. We hear of heroic stands and superhuman perseverance, but fortitude and resilience are usually found in mundane things and are easily missed.

It was in Jersey, in UK's Channel Islands, that I first realized this. I was there for a year in the early 1950s. It was a quiet and very law-abiding island. Even through the German occupation during World War II, the islanders had gone about their business—mostly fishing and growing tomatoes—without paying much heed to the occupying power. And when the war ended in Europe, the Germans simply melted away and the islanders carried on growing their tomatoes. It was as though nothing had happened.

◆

There are memories that we fear and run away from all our lives. But we also find solace in memory, often in unexpected ways, as unbidden images return from our past.

When I was living in London as a young man in the 1950s, I was homesick and miserable, separated by a thousand miles of ocean, plain and desert from my beloved Himalayas. And then one morning the depressing London fog became a mountain mist, and the sound of traffic became the *hoo-hoo-hoo* of the wind in the branches of tall deodar trees.

I remembered a little mountain path from my boyhood which led my restless feet into a cool forest of oak and rhododendron, and then on to the windswept crest of a naked hilltop. The hill was called Cloud's End. It commanded a view of the plains on one side, and of the snow peaks on the other. Little silver rivers twisted across the valley below, where the rice fields formed a patchwork of emerald green.

During the rains, clouds enveloped the valley but left the hill alone, an island in the sky. Wild sorrel grew among the rocks, and there were many flowers—convolvulus, clover, wild begonia, dandelion—sprinkling the hillside. On the spur of the hill stood the ruins of an old brewery. The roof had long since disappeared and the rain had beaten the stone floors smooth and yellow. Some enterprising Englishman had spent a lifetime here making beer for his thirsty compatriots down in the plains. Now, moss and ferns grew from the walls. In a hollow beneath a flight of worn steps, a wildcat had made its home. It was a beautiful grey creature, black-striped, with pale green eyes. Sometimes it watched me from the steps or the wall, but it never came near.

No one lived on the hill, except occasionally a coal burner in a temporary grass-thatched hut. But villagers used the path, grazing their sheep and cattle on the grassy slopes. Each cow or sheep had a bell suspended from its neck, to let the shepherd boy know of its whereabouts. The boy could then lie in the sun and eat wild strawberries without fear of losing his animals.

I remembered some of the shepherd boys and girls.

There was a boy who played a flute. Its rough, sweet, straightforward notes travelled clearly across the mountain air. He would greet me with a nod of his head, without taking the flute from his lips. There was a girl who was nearly always cutting grass for fodder. She wore heavy bangles on her feet, and long silver earrings. She did not speak much either, but she always had a wide grin on her face when she met me on the path. She used to sing to herself, or to the sheep, or to the grass, or to the sickle in her hand.

◆

It was March 1955 and I was returning to India, to everything I had missed keenly during my three years in the UK. Although I was twenty-one, and had been earning my own living for over three years, in many ways I was still a boy, with a boy's thoughts and dreams—dreams of romance and high adventure and good companionship. And I was still a lonely boy, alone on that big ship—passengers and crew all strangers to me—still sailing to an uncertain future.

I had two books with me—Thoreau's *Walden* and Richard Jefferies's *The Story of My Heart*—both reflecting my burgeoning interest in the natural world—but during the day the cabin was hot and stuffy, and the decks too crowded, so I postponed most of my reading until the journey was over. But at night, when it was cool on deck, and most of the passengers were down below, watching a film or drinking Polish vodka (it was a Polish ship), I would sit out under the stars while the ship ploughed on through the Red Sea. There was no sound but the dull thunder of the ship's screws and the faint tinkle of music from an open porthole.

And as I sat there, pondering on my future, a line from Thoreau kept running through my head. 'Why should I feel lonely? Is not our planet in the Milky Way?'

Wherever I went, the stars were there to keep me company. And I knew that as long as I responded, in both a physical and mystical way, to the natural world—sea, sun, earth, moon and stars—I would never feel lonely upon this planet.

SOUNDS OF THE SEA

For years I had this large sea-shell, and by putting it to my ear I could hear the distant sob and hiss of the sea— or so I fancied, until this romantic notion was dispelled by twelve-year-old Mukesh, who told me that the same effect could be obtained by holding an empty cup to my ear. He was right, of course. In fact, the cup sounds better than the shell! And for years I'd gone on imagining that the sound of the sea was somehow trapped in my shell... But I still cling to it, for it takes me back to Jamnagar, on the west coast of India, and memories of sea and sand, small steamers and large Arab dhows plying across the Gulf of Kutch.

My small hand in my father's, I explored with him the little port's harbour and beach, bringing home shells of considerable variety, and even, on one occasion, a small crab, which lived in a spare bathtub for several days and was forgotten—until a visiting aunt, deciding on a tub-bath after a long train journey, found it keeping her company among the soap-suds. Amidst much clamour and consternation, it was evicted from the house and dropped into a nearby well. But my aunt was convinced that I had deliberately placed it in the tub, and refused to speak to me for the rest of her stay.

A small British steamer was often in port, and my father and I would visit the captain, a good-natured Welshman who gave me chocolates, a great treat in those days, for Jamnagar was too small a place for a Western confectionery shop. I was ready to go to sea with Captain Jenkins, convinced that chocolates were only to be found on tramp steamers.

We left Jamnagar when the Second World War broke out and my father joined the RAF. It was to be some ten years before I saw the sea again, for I went to boarding school in the hills. I was still in my teens, but now bereft of my father, when I set sail from Bombay in the *S. S. Strathnaver*, a beautiful P&O liner, one of a fleet, its sister ships being the *Strathaird* and *Stratheden*. Those were the days of the big passenger liners, before fast air travel put an end to leisurely ocean voyages. It took just over a fortnight to reach Southampton or London, but there was never a dull moment on the voyage. Apart from interesting shipboard acquaintances—the sort of mixed company that gave Somerset Maugham material for his stories—there were also colourful ports of call: Aden, Port Said, Marseilles, Gibraltar. At Marseilles, I decided to miss the coach-tour and instead walk into the town. After three hours of walking along miles and miles of dockland, I finally reached the outskirts of the city—just in time to catch the coach back to the ship!

But later, living in London, I never tired of walking among the docks and wharfs along the Thames, for many of those places were associated with the novels of Dickens, which had inspired me to become a writer. Limehouse, Wapping, Shadwell Stairs, the Mile End Road, the East India Docks, these were all places I knew from *Bleak House, Dombey and Son*, and *Our Mutual Friend*. And there was the fog, a thick peasouper, that seemed to have lingered on from the fog that had enveloped the characters and the action in *Bleak House*, setting the tone for that masterpiece. London, I am told, no longer has fogs—they are dispersed by modern and scientific means—and although the air no doubt is cleaner and healthier now, I feel sure some of the magic has gone—along with the East End of old.

From London's dockland to the Channel Islands was a short trip but a considerable change. I lived on the island of Jersey for two years. It had a number of bays and inlets of great charm and beauty, and it was here that I learnt to watch the tides advancing and retreating, and discovered that the tides make different sounds in different places.

Every tide has its own music, and those who live near lonely shores soon learn to recognize the familiar ripple, throb, sob or sigh. And sometimes the tide comes up from the deep against four steep sand-bank and roars defiance.

The tide-rip that pushes through the Channel Islands off the Norman coast has a smoother thud than most, though it comes from the same Atlantic as the harsher-sounding waters among the Orkneys. The difference may be that the channel tides move through purple waters that have drifted up from sunny Portugal, while the other has a shiver from the coast of Greenland.

The music of sea waters is wonderfully varied. Every bay and headland and strait has its note, which the local fisherfolk recognize even in time of dense fog; a note that guides them home or that helps them locate the place for their fishing.

For many years I have been living far from the sea. Sometimes I feel the urge to go down to the sea again, all the way from the Himalayas to Cape Comorin. And maybe I will one day.

Meanwhile, if I wish to listen to the sound of the sea, there's always my sea-shell—or Mukesh's tea-cup.

DELHI IS NOT FAR (EXTRACT)

We lay on our island, in the shade of a thorn bush, watching a pair of sarus cranes on the opposite bank prancing and capering around each other; tall, stork-like birds, with naked red heads and long red legs.

'We might be saruses in some future life,' I said.

'I hope so,' said Suraj. 'Even if it means being born on a lower level. I would like to be a beautiful white bird. I am tired of being a man, but I do not want to leave the world altogether. It is very lovely, sometimes.'

'I would like to be a sacred bird,' I said. 'I don't wish to be shot at.'

'Aren't saruses sacred? Look how they enjoy themselves.'

'They are making love. That is their principal occupation apart from feeding themselves. And they are so devoted to each other that if one bird is killed the other will haunt the scene for weeks, calling distractedly. They have even been known to pine away and die of grief. That's why they are held in such affection by people in villages.'

'So many birds are sacred.'

We saw a bluejay swoop down from a tree—a flash of blue—and carry off a grasshopper.

Both the bluejay and Lord Siva are called Nilkanth. Siva has a blue throat, like the bluejay, because out of compassion for the human race he swallowed a deadly poison which was meant to destroy the world. He kept the poison in his throat and would not let it go any further.

'Are squirrels sacred?' asked Suraj, curiously watching one fumbling with a piece of bread that we had thrown away.

'Krishna loved them. He would take them in his arms and stroke them with his long, gentle fingers. That is why they have four dark lines down their backs from head to tail. Krishna was very dark-skinned, and the lines are the marks of his fingers.'

'We should be gentle to animals... Why do we kill so many of them?'

'It is not so important that we do not kill them—it is important that we respect them. We must acknowledge their right to live on this earth. Everywhere, birds and animals are finding it more difficult to survive, because we are destroying their homes. They have to keep moving as the trees and the green grass keep disappearing.'

Flowers in Pipalnagar—do they exist?

I have known flowers in poetry, and as a child I knew a garden in Lucknow where there were fields of flowers, and another garden where only roses grew. In the fields round Pipalnagar I have seen dandelions that evaporate when you breathe on them, and sometimes a yellow buttercup nestling among thistles. But in our mohalla, there are no flowers except one. This is a marigold growing out of a crack in my balcony.

I have removed the plaster from the base of the plant, and filled in a little earth, which I water every morning. The plant is healthy, and sometimes it produces a little orange marigold, which I pluck and give away before it dies.

Sometimes Suraj keeps the flower in his tray, among the combs and scent bottles and buttons that he sells. Sometimes he offers the flower to a passing child—to a girl who runs away; or it might be a boy who tears the flower to shreds. Some children keep it; others give flowers to Suraj when he passes their houses.

Suraj has a flute which he plays whenever he is tired of going from house to house.

He will sit beneath a shady banyan or peepul, put his tray aside, and take out his flute. The haunting little notes travel down the road in the afternoon stillness, and children come to sit beside him and listen to the flute music. They are very quiet when he plays, because there is a little sadness about his music, and children especially can sense that sadness.

Suraj has made flutes out of pieces of bamboo; but he never sells them, he gives them away to the children he likes. He will sell anything, but not his flutes.

Sometimes Suraj plays his flutes at night, when I am lying awake on the cot, unable to sleep; and even when I fall asleep, the flute is playing in my dreams. Sometimes he brings it with him to the crooked tree, and plays it for the benefit of the birds; but the parrots only make harsh noises and fly away.

Once, when Suraj was playing his flute to a group of children, he had a fit. The flute fell from his hands, and he began to roll about in the dust on the roadside. The children were frightened and ran away.

But they did not stay away for long. The next time they heard the flute play, they came to listen as usual.

As Suraj and I walked over a hill near the limestone quarries, past the shacks of the Rajasthani labourers, we met a funeral procession on its way to the cremation ground. Suraj placed his hand on my arm and asked me to wait until the procession had passed. At the same time a cyclist dismounted and stood at the side of the road. Others hurried on, without glancing at the little procession.

'I was taught to respect the dead in this way,' said Suraj. 'Even if you do not respect a man in life, you should respect him in death. The body is unimportant, but we should honour it out of respect for the man's mind.'

'It is a good custom,' I said.

'It must be difficult to live on after one you have loved has died.'

'I don't know. It has not happened to me. If a love is strong, I cannot see its end... It cannot end in death, I feel... Even physically, you would exist for me somehow.'

He was asleep when I returned late at night from a card game in which I had lost fifty rupees. I was a little drunk, and when I tripped near the doorway, he woke up; and though he did not open his eyes, I felt he was looking at me.

I felt very guilty and ashamed, because he had been ill that day, and I had forgotten it. Now there was no point in saying I was sorry. Drunkenness is really a vice, because it degrades a man, and humiliates him.

Prostitution is degrading, but a prostitute can still keep her dignity; thieving is degrading according to the character of the theft; begging is degrading but it is not as undignified as drunkenness. In all our vices we are aware of our degradation; but in drunkenness we lose our pride, our heads, and, above all, our natural dignity. We become so obviously and helplessly 'human', that we lose our glorious animal identity.

I sat down at the side of the bed, and bending over Suraj, whispered, 'I got drunk and lost fifty rupees, what am I to do about it?'

He smiled, but still he didn't open his eyes, and I kicked

off my sandals and pulled off my shirt and lay down across the foot of the bed. He was still burning with fever, I could feel it radiating through the sheet.

We were silent for a long time, and I didn't know if he was awake or asleep; so I pressed his foot and said, 'I'm sorry,' but he was asleep now, and did not hear me.

Moonlight.

Pipalnagar looks clean in the moonlight, and my thoughts are different from my daytime thoughts.

The streets are empty, and the moon probes the alleyways, and there is a silver dustbin, and even the slush and the puddles near the bus stop shimmer and glisten.

Kisses in the moonlight. Hungry kisses. The shudder of bodies clinging to each other on the moonswept floor.

A drunken quarrel in the street. Voices rise and fall. The nightwatchman waits for the trouble to pass, and then patrols the street once more, banging the lathi on the pavement.

Kamla asleep. She sleeps like an angel. I go downstairs and walk in the moonlight. I met Suraj coming home, his books under his arm; he has been studying late with Aziz, who keeps a junk shop near the station. Their exams are only a month off. I am confident that Suraj will be successful; I am only afraid that he will work himself to a standstill; with his weak chest and the uncertainty of his fits, he should not walk all day and read all night.

When I wake in the early hours of the morning and Kamla stirs beside me in her sleep (her hair so laden with perfume that my own sleep has been fitful and disturbed), Suraj is still squatting on the floor, reading by the light of the kerosene lamp.

And even when he has finished reading he does not sleep, but asks me to walk with him before the sun rises, and, as women were not made to get up before the sun, we leave Kamla stretched out on the cot, relaxed and languid; small breasts and a boy's waist; her hair tumbling about the pillow; her mouth slightly apart, her lips still swollen and bruised with kisses.

I have been seeking through sex something beyond sex—a union with all mankind.

A NIGHT WALK HOME

No night is so dark as it seems.
Here in Landour, on the first range of the Himalayas, I have grown accustomed to the night's brightness—moonlight, starlight, lamplight, firelight! Even fireflies light up the darkness.

Over the years, the night has become my friend. On the one hand, it gives me privacy; on the other, it provides me with limitless freedom.

Not many people relish the dark. There are some who will even sleep with their lights burning all night. They feel safer that way. Safer from the phantoms conjured up by their imaginations. A primeval instinct, perhaps, going back to the time when primitive man hunted by day and was in turn hunted by night.

And yet, I have always felt safer by night, provided I do not deliberately wander about on clifftops or roads where danger is known to lurk. It's true that burglars and lawbreakers often work by night, their principal object being to get into other people's houses and make off with the silver or the family jewels. They are not into communing with the stars. Nor are late-night revellers, who are usually to be found in brightly lit places and are thus easily avoided. The odd drunk stumbling home is quite harmless and probably in need of guidance.

I feel safer by night, yes, but then I do have the advantage of living in the mountains, in a region where crime and random violence are comparatively rare. I know that if I were living in a big city in some other part of the world, I would think twice about walking home at midnight, no matter how pleasing the night sky would be.

Walking home at midnight in Landour can be quite eventful, but in a different sort of way. One is conscious all the time of the silent life in the surrounding trees and bushes. I have smelt a leopard without seeing it. I have seen jackals on the prowl. I have watched foxes dance in the moonlight. I have seen flying squirrels flit from one treetop to another. I have observed pine martens on their nocturnal journeys, and listened to the calls of nightjars and owls and other birds who live by night. Not all on the same night, of course. That would be a case of too many riches all at once. Some night walks can be uneventful. But usually there is something to see or hear or sense. Like those foxes dancing in the moonlight. One night, when I got home, I sat down and wrote these lines:

> *As I walked home last night,*
> *I saw a lone fox dancing*
> *In the bright moonlight.*
> *I stood and watched; then*
> *Took the low road, knowing*
> *The night was his by right.*
> *Sometimes, when words ring true,*
> *I'm like a lone fox dancing*
> *In the morning dew.*

Who else, apart from foxes, flying squirrels and night-loving writers are at home in the dark? Well, there are the nightjars, not much to look at, although their large, lustrous eyes gleam uncannily in the light of a lamp. But their sounds are distinctive. The breeding call of the Indian nightjar resembles the sound of a stone skimming over the surface of a frozen pond; it can be heard for a considerable distance. Another species utters a loud grating call, which, when close at hand, sounds exactly like a whiplash cutting the air. 'Horsfield's nightjar' (with which I am more familiar in Mussoorie) makes a noise similar to that made by striking a plank with a hammer.

I must not forget the owls, those most celebrated of night birds, much maligned by those who fear the night. Most owls have very pleasant calls. The little jungle owlet has a note which is both mellow and musical. One misguided writer has likened its call to a motorcycle starting up, but this is libel. If only motorcycles sounded like the jungle owl, the world would be a more peaceful place to live and sleep in.

Then there is the little scops owl, who speaks only in monosyllables, occasionally saying 'wow' softly but with great deliberation. He will continue to say 'wow' at intervals of about a minute, for several hours throughout the night.

Probably the most familiar of Indian owls is the spotted owlet, a noisy bird who pours forth a volley of chuckles and squeaks in the early evening and at intervals all night. Towards sunset, I watch the owlets emerge from their holes one after another. Before coming out, each puts out a queer little round head with staring eyes. After they have emerged they usually sit very quietly for a time as though only half awake. Then, all of a sudden, they begin to chuckle, finally breaking out in a torrent of chattering. Having in this way 'psyched' themselves into the right frame of mind, they spread their short, rounded wings and sail off for the night's hunting.

And I wend my way homewards. 'Night with her train of stars' is always enticing. The poet Henley found her so. But he also wrote of 'her great gift of sleep', and it is this gift that I am now about to accept with gratitude and humility.

ON FOOT WITH FAITH

All my life I've been a walking person. To this day, I have neither owned nor driven a car, bus, tractor, aeroplane, motor-boat, scooter, truck or steam-roller. Forced to make a choice, I would drive a steam-roller, because of its slow but solid progress and unhurried finality.

In my early teens, I did for a brief period ride a bicycle, until I rode into a bullock cart and broke my arm, the accident only serving to underline my unsuitability for wheeled conveyance or any conveyance that is likely to take my feet off the ground. Although dreamy and absent-minded, I have never walked into a bullock cart.

Perhaps there is something to be said for sun signs. Mine being Taurus, I have, like the bull, always stayed close to grass, and have lived my life at my own leisurely pace, only being stirred into furious activity when goaded beyond endurance. I have every sympathy for bulls and none for bull-fighters.

I was born in the Kasauli Military Hospital in 1934, and was baptized in the little Anglican church that still stands in this hill station. My father had done his schooling at the Lawrence Royal Military School, at Sanwar, a few miles away, but he had gone into 'tea' and then teaching, and at the time I was born, he was out of a job.

But my earliest memories are not of Kasauli, for we left

when I was two or three months old; they are of Jamnagar, a small state in coastal Kathiawar, where my father took a job as English tutor to several young princes and princesses. This was in the tradition of Forster and Ackerley, but my father did not have literary ambitions, although after his death I was to come across a notebook filled with love poems addressed to my mother, presumably while they were courting.

This was where the walking really began, because Jamnagar was full of palaces and spacious lawns and gardens. And by the time I was three, I was exploring much of this territory on my own, with the result that I encountered my first cobra who, instead of striking me dead as the best fictional cobras are supposed to do, allowed me to pass.

Living as he did so close to the ground, and sensitive to every footfall, that intelligent snake must have known instinctively that I presented no threat, that I was just a small human discovering the use of his legs. Envious of the snake's swift gliding movements, I went indoors and tried crawling about on my belly, but I wasn't much good at it. Legs were better.

Amongst my father's pupils in one of these small states were three beautiful princesses. One of them was about my age, but the other two were older, and they were the ones at whose feet I worshipped. I think I was four or five when I had this crush on two 'older' girls—eight and ten respectively. At first I wasn't sure that they were girls, because they always wore jackets and trousers and kept their hair quite short. But my father told me they were girls, and he never lied to me.

My father's schoolroom and our own living quarters were located in one of the older palaces, situated in the midst of a veritable jungle of a garden. Here I could roam to my heart's content, amongst marigolds and cosmos growing rampant in the long grass. An ayah or a bearer was often sent post-haste after me, to tell me to beware of snakes and scorpions.

One of the books read to me as a child was a work called *Little Henry and His Bearer*, in which little Henry converts his servant to Christianity. I'm afraid something rather different happened to me. My ayah, bless her soul, taught me to eat paan and other forbidden delights from the bazaar, while the bearer taught me to abuse in choice Hindustani—an attribute that has stood me in good stead over the years.

Neither of my parents was overly religious, and religious tracts came my way far less frequently than they do today (*Little Henry* was a gift from a distant aunt). Today everyone seems to feel I have a soul worth saving, whereas when I was a boy, I was left severely alone by both preachers and adults. In fact the only time I felt threatened by religion was a few years later when, visiting the aunt I have mentioned, I happened to fall down her steps and sprain my ankle. She gave me a triumphant look and said, 'See what happens when you don't go to church!'

My father was a good man. He taught me to read and write long before I started going to school, although it's true to say that I first learned to read upside down. This happened because I would sit on a stool in front of the three princesses watching them read and write, and so the view I had of their books was an upside-down one; I still read that way occasionally, especially when a book begins to get boring.

My mother was at least twelve years younger than my father, and liked going out to parties and dances. She was quite happy to leave me in the care of the ayah and bearer and other servants. I had no objection to the arrangement. The servants indulged me, and so did my father, bringing me books, toys, comics, chocolates, and of course stamps, when he returned from visits to Bombay.

Walking along the beach, collecting seashells, I got into the habit of staring hard at the ground, a habit that has stayed with me all my life. Apart from helping my thought processes, it also results in my picking up odd objects—coins, keys, broken bangles, marbles, pens, bits of crockery, pretty stones, ladybirds, feathers, snail-shells, seashells! Occasionally, of course, this habit results in my walking some way past my destination (if I happen to have one). And why not? It simply means discovering a new and different destination, sights and sounds that I might not have experienced had I concluded my walk exactly where it was supposed to end. And I am not looking at the ground all the time. Sensitive like the snake to approaching footfalls, I look up from time to time to examine the faces of passers-by just in case they have something they wish to say to me.

A bird singing in a bush or tree has my immediate attention; so does any unfamiliar flower or plant, particularly if it grows in an unusual place such as a crack in a wall or rooftop, or in a yard full of junk where I once found a rose bush blooming on the roof of an old Ford car.

There are other kinds of walks that I shall come to later but it wasn't until I came to Dehra and my grandmother's house that I really found my feet as a walker.

In 1939, when World War II broke out, my father joined the RAF, and my mother and I went to stay with her mother in Dehradun, while my father found himself in a tent on the outskirts of Delhi.

It took two or three days by train from Jamnagar to Dehradun, but trains were not quite as crowded then as they are today and, provided no one got sick, a long train journey was something of an extended picnic, with halts at quaint little stations, railway meals in abundance brought by waiters in smart uniforms, an ever-changing landscape, bridges over mighty rivers, forest, desert, farmland, everything sun-drenched, the air clear and unpolluted except when dust storms swept across the plains.

Bottled drinks were a rarity then, the occasional lemonade or 'Vimto' being the only aerated soft drink, apart from soda water, which was always available for whisky pegs. We made our own orange juice or lime juice, and took it with us.

By journey's end we were wilting and soot-covered, but Dehra's bracing winter climate soon brought us back to life.

Scarlet poinsettia leaves and trailing bougainvillaea adorned the garden walls, while in the compounds grew mangoes, lichis, papayas, guavas, and lemons large and small. It was a popular place for retiring Anglo-Indians, and my maternal grandfather, after retiring from the Railways, had built a neat, compact bungalow on Old Survey Road. There it stands today, unchanged except in ownership. Dehra was a small, quiet, garden town, only parts of which are still recognizable now, forty years after I first saw it.

I remember waking in the train early one morning, and looking out of the window at heavy forest trees of every description but mostly sal and shisharm; here and there a forest glade, or a stream of clear water—quite different from the muddied waters of the streams and rivers we had crossed the previous day. As we passed over a largish river (the Song) we saw a herd of elephants bathing; and leaving the forests of the Siwalik hills, we entered the Doon valley, where fields of rice and flowering mustard stretched away to the foothills.

Outside the station we climbed into a tonga, or pony trap, and rolled creakingly along quiet roads until we reached my grandmother's house. Grandfather had died a couple of years previously and Grandmother lived alone, except for occasional visits from her married daughters and their families, and from her unmarried but wandering son Ken, who was to turn up from time to time, especially when his funds were low. Granny also had a tenant, Miss Kellner, who occupied a portion of the bungalow.

Miss Kellner had been crippled in a carriage accident in Calcutta when she was a girl, and had been confined to a chair all her adult life. She had been left some money by her parents, and was able to afford an ayah and four stout palanquin-bearers, who carried her about when she wanted the chair moved, and took her for outings in a real sedan chair or sometimes a rickshaw—she had both. Her hands were deformed and she could scarcely hold a pen, but she managed to play cards quite dexterously and taught me a number of card games, which I have now forgotten. Miss Kellner was the only person with whom I could play cards: she allowed me to cheat.

Granny employed a full-time gardener, a wizened old character named Dhuki (Sad), and I don't remember that he ever laughed or smiled. I'm not sure what deep tragedy dwelt behind those dark eyes (he never spoke about himself, even when questioned) but he was tolerant of me, and talked to me about the flowers and their characteristics.

There were rows and rows of sweet peas, beds full of phlox and sweet-smelling snapdragons, geraniums on the verandah steps, hollyhocks along the garden wall. Behind the house were the fruit trees, somewhat neglected since my grandfather's death, and it was here that I liked to wander in the afternoons, for the old orchard was dark and private and full of possibilities. I made friends with an old jackfruit tree, in whose trunk was a large hole in which I stored marbles, coins, catapults, and other treasures, much as a crow stores the bright objects it picks up during its peregrinations.

I have never been a great tree-climber, having a tendency to fall off branches, but I liked climbing walls (and still do), and it was not long before I had climbed the wall behind the orchard, to drop into unknown territory and explore the bazaars and by-lanes of Dehra.